DESCENT INTO DUST

Also by Jacqueline Lepore

Coming Soon

THE CYPRIAN QUEEN

DESCENT INTO DUST

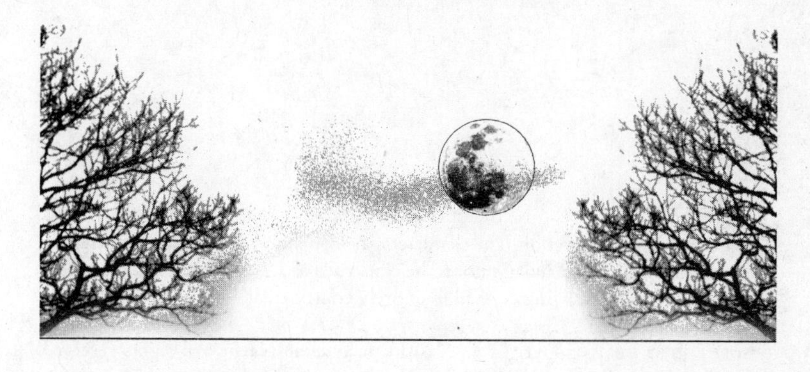

JACQUELINE LEPORE

AVON

An Imprint of HarperCollins*Publishers*

3/10 14

This book is a work of fiction. The characters, incidents, and dialogue are drawn from the author's imagination and are not to be construed as real. Any resemblance to actual events or persons, living or dead, is entirely coincidental.

HarperCollins books may be purchased for educational, business, or sales promotional use. For information please write: Special Markets Department, HarperCollins Publishers, 10 East 53rd Street, New York, NY 10022.

FIRST EDITION

Designed by Diahann Sturge

Library of Congress Cataloging-in-Publication Data
Lepore, Jacqueline.
Descent into dust / Jacqueline Lepore. — 1st ed.
p. cm.
ISBN 978-0-06-187812-1
1. Vampires—Fiction. 2. Great Britain—History—Victoria, 1837–1901—Fiction.
I. Title.
PS3612.E64D47 c2010
813'.6—dc22 2009029005

10 11 12 13 14 OV/RRD 10 9 8 7 6 5 4 3 2 1

Acknowledgments

Writing a novel is not as much of a solitary process as one might think. Like Emma, I have my band of compatriots, each of whom played a role in the writing of this book.

I want to thank Christina Hogrebe at Jane Rotrosen Agency for her suggestions and enthusiastic representation. Big thanks go to Kate Nintzel at HarperCollins. Her insightful additions and editorial expertise have been invaluable not only to the book but also to the series as a whole.

I owe a great debt to the people who helped me during the writing of the book, all of them excellent writers in their own right. They are Krisann McFarland, Kate Klemm, Lori Kaiser, and Kay Cochran. They contributed so much to my writing that I wonder where I would be without them. More than that, they are dear friends and I count myself lucky to have them. Much love to Donna Birdsell and Sally Stotter, both of whom made significant contributions.

Very special thanks to my family: Kelly (whose key suggestions got me on the right track early on), Lindsey (who introduced me to other vampires), and Luke (who played a lot of video games and left me alone to write). I saved the best for last: my husband did the most. He debated, discussed, and pondered with me the various points of development in this Emma Andrews idea. His input was instrumental in pounding out everything from the basic concept to the final read. For this and so many other things—thank you, Mick.

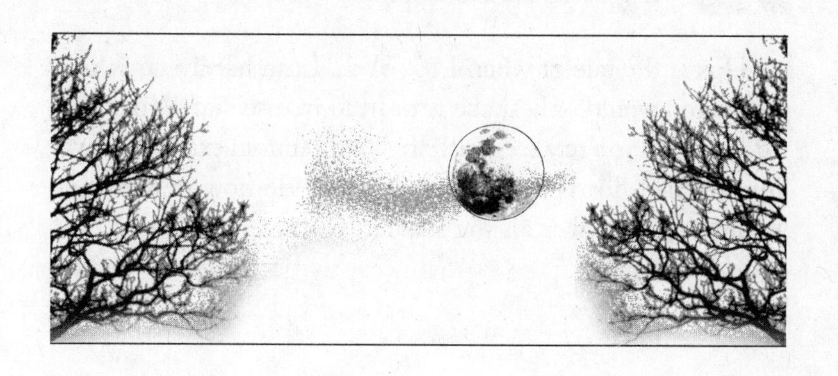

Come in under the shadow of this red rock,
And I will show you something different from either
Your shadow at morning striding behind you
Or your shadow at evening rising to meet you;
I will show you fear in a handful of dust.
T. S. Eliot, "The Waste Land" (1922)

Images of shadow and dust—how these words shattered me when I read them in this recently published poem, penned by one who could never know my story. Though the poet was a stranger, his verse took me in its fist and cast me on a rushing flood tide into the past, back to all which I have held in secret for this long time.

With these words beckoning, rattling around in my brain and giving me no peace (*I will show you fear in a handful of dust*), I cannot resist the pull of memory. And though it is many decades later, it all comes back to me; back even to those early days when the terror was new and I was dangerously untrained. When I was young and did not yet know I had a secret.

And I think it is time. I feel it is. Time to tell my story. A truly remarkable story.

This is the tale of when I . . . Well, I can hardly say it outright. You would only shake your head in disbelief. What I am about to tell you requires faith. It should unfold exactly the way it happened, for perhaps then you will see how it was—and know that every word is the absolute truth.

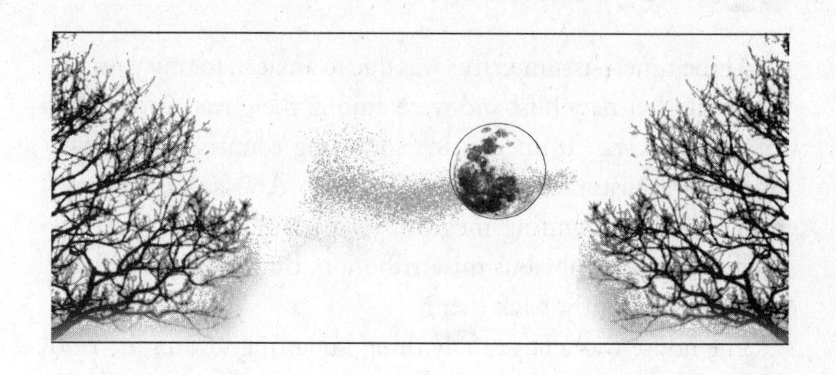

Chapter One

I was twenty-three years of age in March of 1862 when I traveled to my cousin's home in the countryside of Wiltshire. The fifth day of that wretched month found me huddled in my carriage, the drizzly gray gloom outside soaking a bone-deep chill into every aching part of my body, which had been roughly abused by the long confinement and ill-kept roads I'd traveled coming up from Dartmoor.

I did not know then that these would be the closing days of ordinary life. The only suggestion of the monumental changes about to occur was the headache that had come upon me after my crossing of the Dart River. The pain, as fine as tiny needles being pushed into my temples, increased as I traversed the chalk downs and approached Dulwich Manor.

At the time, I assumed this was due to anxiety, for my younger sister and her new husband were among the guests invited for an extended stay at my cousin's sprawling country house. As I was long accustomed to contending with Alyssa without anything like this haunting megrim, I suppose I should not have made this rather obvious misattribution. But how could I have thought differently, back then?

The house was a large, ugly thing, squatting low on the land like a spider on a softly rounded hilltop. Stones blacked with lichen and soot formed a plain rectangle of unadorned walls dotted liberally with cross-hatched windows, lying dormant under leaden skies. There was no sign of life about it or any of the outbuildings. Everyone had taken shelter from the rain.

I emerged into a light drizzle and drew the cowl of my cloak over my head. At the top of the impressive set of carved steps, a very correct-looking butler awaited. "Emma Andrews, Mrs. Dulwich's cousin," I told him.

He did not quite meet my gaze, as all good servants manage not to do, as he opened the door wider and ushered me inside to a vaulted hall. I was instantly struck by the feeling of being very, very small in a very, very large place. The gas jets on the wall leaked only a small puddle of light in which I stood; beyond that, I saw only shadowy hints of the rest of the room.

"I shall tell madam you have arrived," the butler intoned soberly.

Once alone, I quickly checked my appearance in a pier glass hung on the wall. I was decidedly damp. My hair was nearly a ruin. The expensive gown I had donned that morning, thinking it would lend me courage, had been a bad choice. There was nothing to be done about the crushed silk. A smart travel dress would have been better, had I owned one. But such things

required seamstress consultations and fittings, all amounting to too much time, time I never seemed to make room for in my ordinary routines. I did take comfort in the fine brushed wool of my cloak, which Simon, my husband, had given me for Christmas last year, a month before he died. It was of excellent quality.

A voice brought me up sharp. "I am most put out that the weather is foul," my cousin, Mary, said as she swept into the hall. "I wanted to show the house to its full advantage."

She posed regally in the hall of the Jacobean house, her pride radiating from her. She knew her surroundings elevated her, as wealth is apt to do. She had married well and that is always a woman's conceit.

And yet, it had not been mine. My late husband, Simon, had left me his wealth, something I found made my rather ordinary life a bit more convenient than it had previously been, but little else had changed because of it. I certainly took no pride in showing it off.

"The house is magnificent, Mary. I am anxious to see what you have done with its restoration. It seems very grand indeed."

That pleased her, thawed her a bit. She cocked her chin at me and turned slightly so that I might press a kiss upon her cheek, in a rather pretentious gesture for a woman only three years my senior. But I complied. I have no trouble indulging others' vanities, if they are harmless.

"Come then, Emma," she said, "the parlor is through here. Give Penwys your cloak. Alyssa and Alan have already arrived. I know she is anxious to see you. Penwys will see your things are delivered to your room and the servants will put everything to rights. You'll want to freshen up."

I did, but it would take too much time and I was feeling

impatient to join the others. "I can go upstairs after my things have been unpacked. And to tell you the truth, a cuppa right now would be lovely."

"Very well," she said primly.

She was showing off a bit, taking on the same airs Alyssa was so fond of. And just as with my sister, they had the tendency to prick my sore spot and make me wicked.

"But please direct your man to be very careful with my portmanteau," I said. "It is old, and I take extra care of it since it had been my mother's."

The mention of my beautiful, tragic mother changed her expression to one rife with thoughts best left unsaid. "Your belongings will be treated with the respect they deserve."

We proceeded together down a short corridor. Above, a series of large arches stretched across the high ceiling like ribs, giving me the unsettling feeling of traversing the interior of a vast corporeal chest. My eye was caught by some words carved at the apex of the last of these stone vaults, just above the heavy double doors beyond which I could hear the muffled sounds of conversation. An odd place for decoration, I mused. It would be easily overlooked as it was placed high overhead. But I could read the three words.

Corruptio optimi pessima.

I stopped. Something strange and unpleasant fluttered through me. The air went crisp, as if ionizing in preparation for an electrical strike.

Mary saw me staring. "Interesting, isn't it? Those carvings are all over the house. The man who built the original manor was a bishop, back before Henry, when the papists still had the run of the place." She laughed. "It's a curiously religious dwell-

ing, as a result, and I've kept it that way through the restoration. These ominous sayings carved here and there are terribly quaint, don't you agree?"

My voice was dry as dust. "Do you know what it means?"

She must have forgotten my unfortunate habit of overburdening my brain with reading, for she thought I didn't know. "I believe it means 'The best of men are incorruptible.'"

It did not. The fact that she didn't know made my unease grow. It felt to me—very strongly so—that it should be important for the owner of this house to understand what was written into its very bones. The correct translation was "Corruption of the best is worst."

The fingers of pain in my forehead dug deeper and my hand pressed at my temple as Mary flung open the doors to the drawing room. "Emma has finally arrived," she announced as she swept me inside.

My eyes sought and found the woman seated on the long divan. Alyssa, my sister, nearly five years my junior—luminously beautiful, newly married, and still very much annoyed with me for my intractable stubbornness in insisting on not being anything like her.

Roger, Mary's husband, a tall, lanky fellow with a crown of curls that never came close to appearing tame, hurried toward me. "Emma, you are absolutely glowing with good health." He embraced me, then bent to kiss my hand in the French manner. "I daresay your loveliness increases each time I see you. I trust you are faring well these days?"

He was thinking of Simon—of my loss, and his, for they had been friends. His sincere affection touched me as it had three years ago on the occasion of my father's death. Then, too, he had shown special solicitude toward me, even over my sister's delicate sobs.

"Roger, it is so very good to see you," I replied sincerely. "Your home is . . . quite unique. How are you liking living back here, lord of the manor in the house where you grew up?"

He made a face as he drew my arm through his. "The house is atrocious, it always was." Leaning closer, he lowered his tone conspiratorially. "Do not tell my wife I said so, but I find it depressing. We have been here but a fortnight and I am already longing for our lesser lodgings in Cheltenham. But Mary will have me play the country gentleman now that the house is ours."

"And Henrietta? It must be all a great adventure to her, a new house, woods to explore . . ."

"She is a quiet child," he said, not answering my question.

"She is an absolute angel, and if you have scruples about being a braggart over her, I do not."

He laughed. It was no secret that I absolutely doted on the child, had done from the day of her birth. She was what my uncle Peter, who was the wisest man I knew, called an "old soul": a calm, peaceful presence with a serene nature and penetrating mind. "Perhaps she and I shall do a bit of exploring tomorrow," I suggested. "We can have an adventure or two."

He hesitated, frowning slightly. "I'd prefer it if she kept close to the grounds. Henrietta is hardly familiar with the surroundings, and with you as her guide, someone who is equally unknowledgeable of the safe—well, that is to say, the better-traveled areas—I think it best if excursions out of doors are kept to a minimum for now."

"Why, certainly," I murmured, somewhat dismayed by his excessive caution.

"Oh, dear, I almost forgot," he added with a snap of his fingers. "We are going for rabbit in a day or two. You must join the shooting party; I will not take no for an answer from you, even at the risk of my wife's darkest scowl. Like those hearty ladies of the American West, you are an excellent shot and I require you with me."

That was why I liked Roger so well. He didn't seem to mind my being unconventional. Only Simon had liked me just as I was. "You must remember my paltry skills at riding, which may hold the party back. And as for my cousin's scowl, it will be substantial, I should think."

"But I do approve, and a husband must have his way every once in a while." He patted my hand resting in the crook of his arm. "Now, let me introduce you before Mary scolds me for neglecting my duties. I am to make a toast to the queen. Come let me get you a glass."

He steered me to the elderly curate, Mr. Bedford, and his pleasant wife. Mr. Bedford was a large man, with not a wisp of a hair on his head. His wife was a straight-shouldered matron whose beauty had not quite faded. Turning from them, Roger introduced me to a knot of men who were discussing the quality of local horse breeding, where I was presented to the local squire, Sir William Pentworth, and his son Ted. The former had little interest in me, and I likewise in him. The latter, however, a rather rakish-looking young man, perhaps a year or two my junior, gave me an utterly male look that bordered on impertinence, and immediately lifted my spirits.

Another was introduced as George Hess, a retired Oxford don. Sporting a wild mane of gunmetal-gray hair and a keen, intelligent face, Mr. Hess proved a friendly man with the air of an elder statesman. I felt an immediate affinity toward his gentle presence as we exchanged pleasantries, after which I fortified myself and at last approached Alyssa and Alan.

"You are late," she murmured, taking in my wrinkled skirts and then on upward to the softly curling hair at my temple. "I've been waiting for you all day. Alan and I arrived yesterday, you know."

I made the only response I could as I bent down to kiss her cheek. "Darling, you are absolutely lovely."

This was no faint praise. Alyssa was perfectly beautiful. Fair where I was dark, petite where I was tall, plump where I was lean, we looked nothing like sisters, a fact attributed to our having had different mothers.

Alan Spence, posted like a sentry behind his wife's chair, inclined his head in my direction. I nodded in reply. Alyssa's husband was a cold man, handsome in the extreme, and devoted to my sister nearly as deeply as he was to himself. He did not like me, nor I him, but neither one of us would dream of giving the other so much satisfaction as to ever demonstrate even a hint of anything less than cordiality.

We were all given glasses of sherry and Roger led the salute. "To Her Majesty Queen Victoria," he bellowed, raising his glass up high. We followed suit and chimed out agreement, after which we found seats. The curate's wife settled down by me. She was the chatty sort and immediately launched into a discussion of the area, the grand houses, which delighted Alyssa, and the old Roman road that cuts across the chalk downs close by.

"Did I not read about Avebury having a stone circle like Stonehenge near here?" I asked.

Mr. Hess joined us, taking an empty seat to my right. "Several of them, in fact, and an entire complex of avenues and barrows

as well. We are not nearly as famous, but known well enough."

"It is because many of the stones have been removed," Mrs. Bedford chimed in.

Mr. Hess's expression of distress was acute. "Oh, the pity of it. But there are still enough remains to keep me busy."

Mrs. Bedford smiled at him. "Mr. Hess has come to the area to study the ruins. He has several absolutely grisly theories as to the purpose of the monuments."

"I was persuaded once to go to Stonehenge," Alyssa said. "I found it unutterably boring. Nothing to see but large rocks, and not very pretty ones at that."

My sister could be charming, but never when she was in a snit, as she was now. We had yet to make our amends, she and I, and she would sulk until the proper ritual had been observed.

"I am not familiar with the term 'barrow,'" I said to Hess.

"It is, in effect, a mass tomb."

Alyssa gasped and gave an exaggerated shiver. "How dreadful."

Hess smiled at her. "Our barrow is part of an avenue of standing stones that stretches all the way to West Kennett. What we call The Sanctuary is the other end of the line, where stones once stood in a circle. The West Kennett stones are still present and quite majestic."

Mrs. Bedford poured a second cup of tea for herself. "Who was that who studied the stones, Mr. Hess, who wrote that book to which you are always referring?"

"It was William Stukely," Hess replied, his enthusiasm growing. "He called it *The Great Stone Serpent*. The combination of the structures create the shape of a snake as it lies on the countryside. The complex almost certainly had to do with funerary purposes. The ancients were quite devoted to the dead, you know. It is noteworthy that the serpent, by virtue of its cycle of renewal in shedding its skin, is considered a symbol of eternal life." He paused, and smiled sheepishly. "I am lecturing, am I not? I tend to do so. Forgive me."

"Not at all," I rushed, for I wished very much to hear more.

Alan sniffed and rolled his eyes. "I warn you from handing too much significance to the habits of these long-gone peoples. Weren't they the ones who worshipped trees?"

Alyssa joined him in a stifled snicker.

I sat back, adding a small amount of sugar before taking my first sip of the tea, darting a sharp look at my brother-in-law. It would not do if Alan continued to mock Mr. Hess, whom I had decided I liked very much.

"What a silly conversation," Mary declared. "Worshipping trees, indeed. That is a stunning shawl, Alyssa. Is it Chinese?"

The transition was expertly done. My sister grew more cheerful. "Oh, it was my grandmother's. You know how that generation loved all things Oriental. The prince regent's influence." She smiled, rearranging the silk, obviously feeling very proud that she, too, could speak a word or two on history. I had to credit her—no one knew the history of clothing better.

The conversation went the way of fashion plates and the merits of silk over taffeta for evening gowns. I sipped my tea, savoring the feeling of the heat on the back of my throat and closing my eyes against my returning headache. Placing two fingers against my temple, I rubbed gently.

"Emma?" Roger's tone was almost strident. "You are not unwell, are you?"

My eyelids flew open to find everyone looking at me.

"Roger, darling, that cannot affect us," Mary chided in a

strained voice that conveyed a meaning beyond her words. A tense silence fell.

"Is something the matter?" Alyssa inquired suddenly.

"No, dear. It is nothing. You mustn't worry," Mary said quickly.

"There is an illness in the village," Roger explained.

"But that is among the farmers, darling," Mary countered, her face growing florid.

"Illness?" Alan said, his eyebrows rising slightly. On Alan, this was an expression of great alarm.

"It is nothing to be concerned about." Mary spoke with authority. She picked up the pot and refilled all of our cups without asking permission. "A family lost several children recently. It was very sad, their deaths coming as they did one right after the other. We sent food and blankets to them, of course."

"The house had to be quarantined—"

"—which prevented the illness from spreading to the village," Mary was quick to add. "So, it was only the one family affected."

"And the man outside town," Roger added darkly. "He was found in the road, dead, apparently of the same wasting disease."

The band around my head constricted. Outside, the icy tap of a forceful rain began. It sounded like the light touch of sharpened nails on the old leaded glass windows. A maid moved quickly to draw the hangings, and the sound was muffled behind folds of green velvet.

"It is nothing contagious," Mary assured everyone.

"We do not know the nature of the illness." Roger was grave.

Mary put the pot down with a resounding thud. The lid clattered and the noise jerked all of our attention to her. "An unfortunate sickness of the local crofters is a sad story, to be sure, but it is of no consequence to any of us here. Illness occurs, Roger, we cannot become overset by it. Now, we are going to have a wonderful visit and put all thoughts of such unfortunate happenings out of our heads."

There was an awkward silence, ended when Mrs. Bedford said with pointed cheerfulness, "Well, I for one am looking forward to bowls tomorrow." She turned to her husband. "I do hope the weather holds, for I love a good match of bowls, isn't that right, dear?"

Mary was happy to have a change of subject introduced and launched into a discussion of the activities she had planned, but I could see Roger's brow remained furrowed. His disquiet sat heavy with me, for I felt a strange mood hovering over me as well, a sense of something not right. But I did not yet imagine what it was.

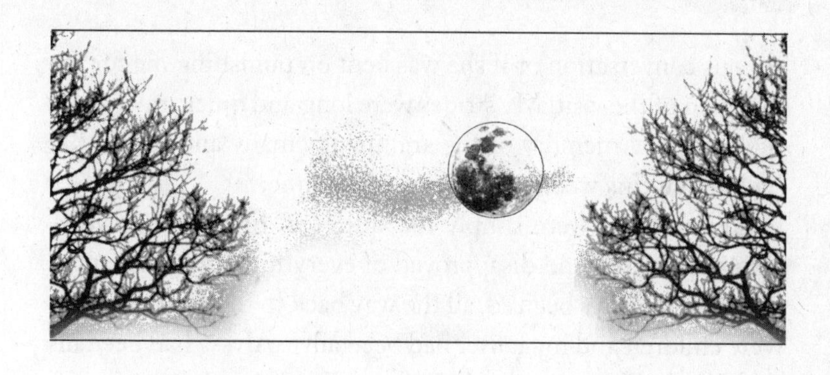

Chapter Two

I awoke early the following day, startled out of sleep by some unremembered dream. The skies had cleared during the night, parting the veil of mists which had shrouded Dulwich's grounds yesterday and splashing them with the lemony sunlight of morning. The cheerfulness of the day invited me outdoors.

I required no more than fifteen minutes to make a quick toilette and don sturdy boots. I slipped out of the house unseen, for no one was yet awake, and set off on a brisk walk toward Overton, my intention to travel the short distance to the ancient monument of standing stones described last night.

The headache was still with me, although sleep had done it good. I wondered if Alyssa would thaw enough for us to have a serious conversation or if she was bent on punishing me for the duration of the visit. My strides were long and quick, my energy fueled by the memory of the arguments, many and futile, that had driven this wedge between us over time.

Alyssa and I were simply too different. She adored everything I despised and disapproved of everything that enchanted me. It had always been so, all the way back to the time when we were children and my father had been alive. Alyssa had been his pet. She had but to enter the room and he'd break into a broad smile, beaming at her—prim and pretty in a ruffled dress, her blond hair shining like the sun. While he loved me—that was never in question—the specter of my mother always stood between us. Quite often I would notice how he looked at me: so quietly, so still, so wary.

When I was old enough to understand why he gazed at me thus, I wanted to shout: "I am well. I am not like her." I'd seen that careful scrutiny in the eyes of others; saw it still to this day. They look for the taint of my mother's madness. What a frustrating impossibility it is to try to prove one's self sane. No matter how I remained rational, calm, tractable, pleasant, there is always that small element of doubt that perhaps the demons which lived in my mother's fragile mind had been passed on to me. No, no one would ever completely trust my mind. Not even I.

I had not known her, my mother. I had no memory of her, for she died when I was a small child. Laura existed on as a mysterious figure whom I had heard spoken of only in whispers, more as a ghost than a parent.

It did not take me long to find the avenue that stretched across the downs. The stones leaned drunkenly in some instances but were solid and surprisingly beautiful against the green and blue of the plain. I followed them away from the village, up to the place on Overton Hill, which Mrs. Bedford and Mr. Hess had called The Sanctuary, to view where the circle of sarcen stones had stood long ago.

The name intrigued me. A sanctuary was, of course, a place of shelter, of safety. I had never really had such a thing, even in my childhood home. Certainly not living under the watchful, worried gaze of my father, and not in the sights of my stepmother Judith's stern eye.

But those days were long past, and I was free. Simon had given me that freedom, I reflected as I crossed the empty circle. As a widow of independent means, I had no one telling me what to do. No father, no husband.

And yet, without those ties—not a single person whose regard I would strive for—I was left with one enormous emptiness. It was possible my existence in this world would have come and gone and in the end amount to nothing of much consequence. I had never strived for greatness, but one wishes to matter. To someone.

I took note of a thorn tree as I passed it, a rather rangy mess of branches tangled around a slender trunk. Perhaps it was Alan's snide comment about worshipping trees that made me notice it. That, and the way it stood all alone. Other trees clustered back in the hedgerows, a row of courtiers keeping respectful distance. Although the hawthorn wasn't very large, the branches were dangerous arms laden with slender spikes, and that itself demanded respect.

As I drew closer, I noticed something on the trunk, words carved in the rough bark. *The Blood is the Life.*

I recognized the phrase from the Old Testament. It had to do with laws of keeping food clean. Or was it a New Testament reference to Holy Eucharist?

I cannot remember now why I reached out my hand. I don't suppose there was really any specific reason. I just wanted to touch those letters. I paused, my palm outstretched, not quite touching the bark, and suddenly I felt a tiny vibration where the lines creased my flesh.

Frozen, I stood and let the current wash over me, galvanizing me to the soles of my sensible boots. My headache flared like a torch set alight, and I cried out from the pain. Tiny points of light danced on the periphery of my vision as the world blurred, swayed.

Then I felt . . . something. Something inside me was tearing, like the parting of a veil. A flash, a dark memory illuminated for a moment in the manner of a match struck, flaring, then quickly snuffed. I heard the sound of someone crying. A woman. My heart seized in my chest as I thought: *It is my mother!*

I dropped my hand and stumbled backward, fumbling for my footing. The feeling vanished, leaving me tingling and dazed. I struggled for composure. What had happened to me? What was that energy I had felt?

Suddenly I was eager to be back to the house. I turned away from the hawthorn, my eyes searching for the manor. As I did so, my foot struck an object on the ground and I looked down. I saw shards of pottery underfoot, about five largish pieces.

Curious, I stooped to pick them up, noting the clean break lines. They fit easily together, and I quickly assembled them all, laying them on the ground to make a plaque with a crude symbol painted on it. It took me a moment to recognize it. A fish, the simple sort used as a sign of the early Christian church.

I gathered up the pieces and held them in my still-tingling palm. Stepping back, I surveyed the tree. A movement caught

my attention in the meadow grass. Something red and black undulated in a strange, surging motion. My first thought was that it was a live thing in trouble, struggling, and I stepped toward it only to stop cold when it registered what it was I was seeing.

I recoiled. The half-eaten carcass of an animal lay before me. What sort of animal was impossible to tell, for its flesh was nearly stripped, and it lay eviscerated on the soft green of the plain. On it, above it, and all around it were night-black crows, surging over one another, fighting for dominance as they furiously feasted.

At first they paid me no mind, too intent were they to register an intruder. Their shining beaks snapped at the scarlet-stained flesh, at one another—viciously, frantic for each bite. Presiding over this scene, resting on a thorny branch, sat one very large crow. His cold, dead eyes glittered in the sunlight as he surveyed the grisly repast, appearing noble and comfortable in his position of power.

He swiveled his obsidian head to look at me. And then, as if he'd uttered an unheard order, all the birds ceased their tearing and turned likewise, fixing me with calculated calm. Almost defiance.

The macabre tableau froze us all for a moment, they staring at me and I at them. Everything around us went suddenly, icily still. In the silence, I heard some rhythmic sound. My own breathing. Steady, labored under the burden of my rising fear. It was silly to be frightened, but I couldn't help it. They were just birds, I told myself. The scene I was witnessing, although gruesome, was ordinary enough.

And then the sky exploded as the birds took flight. They launched themselves into the air madly, their wings beating a thunder into the sky, and I flinched, falling back in surprise. I felt more than saw the large avian body lift off the tree branch and dive into full flight over my head.

As it swooped down, I threw myself to the ground, cringing as it shaved a low flight over me. I remained low, cradled in a moist clump of grass, even after he'd passed, covering my hair, my face, as the other birds careened in a bizarre dance of fury over my head. The cacophony of their shrieking calls reached a crescendo before they flew off at last, their cries fading into silence.

I raised my head to watch them go. It took me a moment to realize they must have attacked because they thought I meant to vie for their ghastly prize. I waited until they were out of sight before standing. It was then I saw my hand was hurt. The shards of the pottery plaque I had been holding had scored a deep cut across my palm. Blood dripped from it, welling up quickly before falling onto the ground—a tiny splash of crimson against the verdant green grass of The Sanctuary.

I entered the house through the kitchens, as I did not wish to run into any of the family in my present condition—not only was my appearance disheveled, but my thoughts were running wildly. The long room was crammed with servants. I attempted to skirt around the women at the scrubbed oak table, who were working bread dough or cutting pastries with deft strokes of flashing knives. A skinny lad of about ten, a sack of oat flour precariously perched on his slight shoulder, almost ran me down.

"Can you point me in the way of the stillroom?" I asked in a quavering voice. My hand was hurting me badly.

He gestured to a corner and hurried off on his errand. I found

the carefully labeled apothecary cabinet, which was managed by a maid named Betty. I explained what had happened and she saw to the cut, cleaning it none too gently while muttering words such as "infection," and "blood poisoning," effectively keeping my complaints to a minimum.

Back in my room, I redressed my hair as best I could with my bandaged hand. I could not avoid wondering whether I'd imagined the strange circumstances this morning. It seemed the only explanation. The sensation in my hand as I reached toward the tree, the way the birds had flown at me as if in attack—none of it could be real, could it?

I tried to convince myself of this as I stripped off my dress and donned a fresh one. As I washed my face with my good hand, I paused to examine my reflection. The silvering behind the glass had turned cloudy with age, so that looking into it was like seeing one's self in the heart of a storm cloud. In that misty glass, I almost didn't recognize myself. I looked older, more serious. My skin was bloodless, my eyes dark and as round as an owl's.

Was this the madness? Laura's madness? Was this how it began?

I turned away from the mirror. I was being quite reactionary, I decided. My goodness, everyone has moments of confusion. It was all a matter of not getting carried away with it.

With this settled in my mind, I took the package I'd brought for Henrietta from my portmanteau and headed upstairs to the nurseries. The suite of sleeping chambers for the children of the house was attached to a small apartment for the nursemaid or governess. Those, along with a large schoolroom, took nearly the whole of the third floor. It was surprisingly shabby, a fact made apparent by the light flooding in from the row of tall, arched windows along the outside wall, which was in want of paint. The furniture was sturdy but chipped and otherwise ill-used.

It was not inhospitable, however; Henrietta had made her mark. Toys and books were piled in the shelving. In the corner stood a dollhouse with tiny furniture and carved wooden miniatures scattered on a braided rug. On a nearby table, watercolors were laid out and several paintings were drying. Neither Henrietta nor her nurse was in sight.

I saw there was another Latin inscription above the center window. *Tempest Fugit.* I laughed softly, hoping Mary would be able to translate that one correctly.

I spied Victoria, Henrietta's favorite china doll, perched on a chair as regally as her royal namesake. "Hello, Victoria," I murmured to the doll's staring face. The hair, a bit wild from putting on and removing the lace-edged cap she wore out-of-doors, stuck out. I smoothed it down and untwisted the tiny cross that hung around her neck. The simple ornament had been a present from some relative of Roger's to Henrietta, but she had insisted the doll had demanded it for herself. Henrietta liked to pretend Victoria whispered imperious instructions to her, which she repeated to all of us who were not privileged to hear from the doll directly.

I smiled and reassured the china face, "Now you are as lovely as ever," as I repositioned her in her chair.

My hand throbbed. I held it aloft to keep the blood from rushing to it.

"Henrietta, darling?" I called. "Are you here?"

"Cousin Emma!" Henrietta burst from the doorway behind me leading in from the hall. I spun about as she ran to me, her small arms held out and her plaits flying behind her. I caught her in an embrace as she nearly knocked me over. "I knew you would come today. I told Victoria so."

"Look at how tall you've gotten!" I exclaimed, holding her out for inspection.

Her eyes twinkled. "You said that last time, when we came to visit you after Cousin Simon died." Her eyes clouded. "Oh. I'm terribly sorry. I didn't mean to make you sad."

"It doesn't make me sad. How can I be anything but happy to see you? Now, don't you wish to see the present I've brought you?" I held out the package.

"Yes, yes!" As she took the gift, her face puckered. "Oh! You've hurt your hand."

"It is nothing serious. An accident during my morning walk. The stillroom maid assured me it will be as good as new very soon."

Her eyes flickered to me, taking a moment to make certain this wasn't one of those times adults told children things not wholly truthful. "Good." She addressed herself to the package, lifting away the paper to reveal a box of paper dolls in the style of the queen, her prince consort, and several young princes and princesses. "Oh, thank you, Cousin Emma! They are lovely."

She snuggled herself into my arms for a hug. Pulling back to peer at me, she inquired, "Do you really think I am getting tall? Do you think I shall be as tall as you?"

"I hope not. Better to be petite like Cousin Alyssa." I fluffed her fringe playfully. "You'll be as pretty as her."

She studied me. "I'd rather be tall, like you."

A warm feeling suffused me. I would be less than honest if I did not admit I had surrendered rather easily to her insistence to make me her idol.

"Hello, Miss Harris," I said to the young, pretty nurse who was standing behind the child.

"Good day, Mrs. Andrews," she replied, uncharacteristically coolly. Miss Harris was a cheerful companion to Henrietta, which I liked. Henrietta tended toward the serious at times.

"Why don't you have some time to yourself," I told her, "and as I have not yet had breakfast, Henrietta and I can share elevenses. Would you ask the cook to send something up?"

I thought she would be happy to have some freedom, but she seemed reluctant to go. She could not refuse, however. Henrietta and I set to work to clear the paintings so we could use the table for our meal. The child proved quite secretive about her artwork, whisking the paintings away onto a shelf under the open window. We put away the watercolors and sat down.

A servant brought up a tray supplied with tea, sandwiches, and biscuits. "Are you enjoying your new home?" I inquired when we were settled, Victoria presiding over us in a third chair.

"Mama likes it. Papa takes me out driving. Or he used to do so every day." She smiled, her rosebud mouth curving sweetly. "But he's been too busy getting ready for the house party and now he says I have to stay indoors."

"Poor Hen. Miss Harris keeps you entertained, though, doesn't she?"

She nodded, not very enthusiastically. "How long are you going to stay?"

"Well, for a few weeks, perhaps." I was loath to commit to the child and lock myself into a protracted and unpleasant stay should Alyssa and Mary prove difficult.

She rolled her lips in, biting them from the inside, as was her

way when something was on her mind. "Where is your room? Can I come see it?"

"I am on the second floor." The faintest of frowns creased her snowy brow. I leaned forward, touching her wrist. "Why?"

"This house is very big," she stated, avoiding my eyes.

"Oh, darling, does it seem that I shall be very far away?"

She picked up her doll, holding it close as she fussed with her bonnet. "Victoria says the house is ugly."

I could think of nothing to say, save *I heartily agree with her*, which I could not admit aloud. Finally, I compromised with "It is quite all right if you don't like the house, even if it was where your papa grew up. You can tell him, you know. It will not hurt his feelings and you might feel better."

I was disappointed she didn't brighten. Eventually, and after a lengthy rearranging of Victoria's ribbons, she said, "Victoria says there are ghosts here. She doesn't like ghosts."

I nearly sighed in disgust. Some servant gossip, idly spoken, and now poor Hen was frightened. I slipped off the chair and onto my knees before her, so that I could look directly into her face. "She shouldn't worry, though. You should let her know there aren't any such things as ghosts."

Her large blue eyes lifted to mine. "But there are. I saw him." Slowly, she slid her gaze to my left, looking out the window. "At night, he taps on the glass."

I opened my mouth to reassure her, but the words froze in my throat. Gooseflesh pricked along my arms. "Hen, darling, it must just be a nightmare. Sometimes our dreams can seem very real. It's a big step, coming to a new home, and your mother so busy with all the preparation for her party, and your papa not able to take you out for your rides."

Lowering her eyes, she remained very still. "He wants to come inside."

"Darling, no—no one can come in the window."

My reassurances died on my lips as she looked at me solemnly, her small mouth pursed, her eyes as big as moons in her wan face. She didn't look like herself, and for a moment I felt a flutter of alarm.

I forced a smile. "We'll talk to your papa about this. I'm certain he will have a wonderful cure for bad dreams."

She blinked as she considered this. To her, Roger was all-powerful. I'd been very clever in invoking his powers, for she seemed relieved. She even smiled.

"Now let us have our tea." I fixed her a cup, half cream and half tea with three spoonfuls of sugar, and placed a ham sandwich with the crusts cut off on her plate. "Eat this first, and then you can have biscuits."

I had worked up an appetite after the morning's excursion. It took two sandwiches before I felt satisfied. The frosted biscuits I left to Henrietta, watching with amusement as she devoured one after the other.

I sat back and sipped my tea as she enjoyed the treats. A draft blew over us, causing a few of Henrietta's paintings to flutter to the ground. My gaze caught on one, and I felt a sudden jolt. My hand shook, causing my cup to rattle. I clamped it down firmly on the saucer to prevent a spill.

Very aptly made, in dark colors of gray and black, was a stunning representation so accurate that I knew at once what it was. A painting of a tree, but a very particular tree, like a stick topped with a nasty cap of black spun sugar. It was the hawthorn from the meadow.

Henrietta froze, her attention snapping from the painting

on the floor to my face with alacrity when I retrieved the fallen artwork.

"That is an interesting painting," I said carefully as I put the pile of papers back on the shelf. "I saw a tree like that on my walk this morning, out by the place where the old stones once stood."

She cast a look at her doll. Victoria's glass eyes stared back without expression.

"It is Marius's tree," Henrietta whispered in a tiny voice.

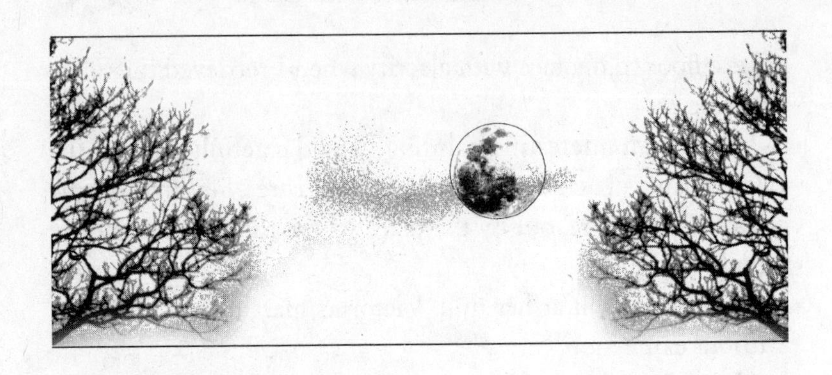

Chapter Three

I girded myself against the tickle of apprehension. "Marius's tree?"

Henrietta pursed her little lips. "I see him there," was all she said before she turned away. I quite got the idea that she didn't wish to speak of it any longer.

I wanted to believe she'd endowed a squirrel or some similar creature with a personality as she had her doll. This seemed a likely solution. Yet there was no denying she was afraid. And she kept glancing at the window.

I was deeply disturbed when I left the nursery, the identity of the mysterious Marius very much on my mind. My disquiet was all the more pronounced at the idea that, whatever this was,

it was attached to the same tree at which I'd had my scare that very morning.

In contrast to its inauspicious beginning, the rest of the day went well. My sister was in a good mood and Mary fluttered happily among her guests, flushed with the success of how well we were getting on. I had the opportunity to speak with Mr. Hess again, listening raptly as he expounded on the long history and lore of the county. I wanted to ask about the tree, but I refrained, fearing I would give myself, and my ridiculous fancies, away.

For dinner, I dressed in a new gown of watered silk, the fitted bodice complimenting my slender figure. As I found myself ready a good hour before the other guests were set to gather in the parlor, I took the opportunity to visit the library, which I'd not yet had a chance to explore. On a whim, I paused outside of the doorway and glanced upward, looking for an inscription.

"Is the roof leaking?" a man asked. I turned to my left to find a stranger standing beside me. His head was thrown back as he stared above us. He glanced at me and I saw amusement dancing in his eyes. "Or are you appealing to God to give you strength to endure the evening? If so, just say the word and I will leave you to your prayer." He donned a look of gravity. "You will no doubt need it."

The man before me was dressed fashionably in a colorful waistcoat with intricate embroidery. His cravat was tied in a wide, snowy-white bow, above which his smirking countenance regarded me steadily under a cap of light brown curls so carefully arranged they had to be the result of curling papers. His cheeks held a flush like a Renaissance cherub. His skin was too pale, the smooth sort which was achieved through a discreet use of powder. He was, I saw at once, what used to be known as a dandy.

But he seemed completely immune to my amazement. "You must be the great and wonderful Cousin Emma." He held out a pale hand. "Can you guess who I am?"

I took his hand. It was surprisingly warm and firm. I suddenly knew who he was, for I'd heard him spoken of in tight whispers. "You have to be Sebastian, Roger's brother."

"So you have heard of me," he purred, holding on to my fingers.

"Mary mentioned you were to be among the guests. She told me Henrietta was counting on it. The child certainly thinks highly of you, by the way. She has spoken of you in the past in the most glowing terms. As we've previously never met, I made a deduction you might be the very guest Henrietta has so eagerly awaited."

"What a logical mind you have!" He gave me a sweeping glance, as if reassessing me. "And so diplomatic. You don't even mention my sister-in-law's apoplexy when my name is brought up."

I laughed and he waved off any denial I might have tried. "Never mind. I am glad we met alone, for I must inform you that I am quite jealous of you." His nose lifted with an injured air. "I was little Henri's favorite until she started talking of 'Cousin Emma' this and 'Cousin Emma' that. She thinks you are quite pretty. Mary doesn't, you know. I suppose it is because you are so unaffected." He tapped his finger on his jaw, considering me once again from the top of my coif to the tips of my slippers. "I agree with dear Henrietta. You are fetching."

He waved his hand around in the air on the last word. Then

he stopped, cocked his head, and asked, "As turnabout is only fair play, you must tell what you have heard of me. I suspect there may be rumors—merely ill talk, mind you, nothing I credit—that I have the capacity to grate on one's nerves. Not all, you see, can tolerate my biting wit."

"I see little evidence of any wit, biting or mild."

"You have a bit of a bite yourself." His slow smile was broad and filled with delight. "Ah. We shall get along famously, you and I. Would you happen to require escort to the parlor?"

"I was going to the library," I told him. "It is too early for the others to be assembled."

"Good thinking. As I never enter a room unless I am most fashionably late, I am in want of a destination. The library it is, though I have never liked the place. Filled with books, you know. Odiously boring things, books. But quite useful for filling up shelves. Think of the dust that would collect if those useful items were not there to take up space."

We fell into step together and proceeded along the corridor. "You do not enjoy reading?"

"Please." He shuddered like a woman. "Reading requires one to be quiet, not to mention sitting for long periods of time. I had enough of that at school. And what do you get for your sacrifice? Some snob telling you what to think, or some convoluted prose that tangles the brain. Just hearing Milton's name puts me into a coma."

"Most think Milton very wise." We had entered the library and I strolled along the shelves. I began to run my finger along the spines.

"Wisdom," he said, his voice losing some of its playfulness. "Is it not like beauty, found in the eye of the beholder? The kind of intelligence that will really do you good in the world one gets from observing. Human nature, now there is a study worth doing."

I slid a book out of its spot. *Gulliver's Travels*. "As you are observing me?"

"I observe everyone, so do not take it hard. I do not, however, always approve. In your case, I do, most heartily."

I placed Swift's tome back in place and continued to peruse.

"Are you looking for anything particular?"

"Mr. Hess has whetted my curiosity about the place." I turned to face him. "You must have run about the countryside as a child, having grown up here."

He made a face. "On horseback only. Too much mud to go about on foot. Imagine the disaster my boots should be if I abused them so."

He pointed his toe to show me his footwear, and I made an appreciative nod.

"There is fascinating history here," I commented with studied casualness. "Particularly The Sanctuary and that strange tree."

"I suppose." He sounded bored, and his casualness was unstudied.

I paused. "Do you know who Marius is?"

He flopped into a large leather armchair. "Who? Oh, Marius—did Henri tell you about him? He's her new imaginary friend. I think Victoria is jealous." He laughed. "See, I know all the gossip, even if it only concerns the manifestations of a little girl's mind. But our Henrietta makes it very dramatic—and I cannot resist drama of any kind."

"What is this Marius like?"

He laughed. "How the devil would I know? I don't see him!"

I flushed and he held out his hand in a gesture of apology.

"Oh, you mustn't worry. When I was young, I played for hours with imaginary friends. Let me see, there was Lady Hatterly. She was an old battle-ax. And the mischievous Miss Penn. She knew how to dress, did Miss Penn. And, of course, Raoul, who was dashing, with a mustache to die for. When my brothers would brutalize me with taunts and pinches he would always swear to avenge me. I had to beg him to let them live. Did you have a cast of invisibles as a child?"

"No, I am afraid not."

As the words left me, something stirred in the back of my mind, as if memories were shifting somewhere . . . The veil parting again, and with it, the sharp pain jutting down from my temple through my skull. I had an impression, a shadow moving in a mist, blurred and indistinct.

I paused, waiting for a revelation that did not come.

Sebastian noticed my hesitation. "What?" he asked.

I smiled abruptly. "Nothing at all."

He allowed his head to fall back as his eyes swept the room. "My God, it is dark in here. I remember my father at that desk, hands folded carefully on the blotter to keep himself from throttling me." He laughed. "Oh, he detested me. Care for a drink?" He gripped the arms of the chair and popped himself to his feet as if shot out by electric current.

"My, you do not sit still for long, do you?"

Waving a hand, he taunted, "It will relax you for dinner. Makes it easier to sit through the squire bragging about the stags he's hunted, and that dratted curate will speak softly but with this quiet little menace that will make you feel guilty for no reason." He splashed brown liquid from a decanter to a tumbler, then threw it back. He held out the decanter. "Are you certain?"

My father drank, and I could not tolerate a man too fond of spirits. I moved before I knew what I was doing, going directly up to him and taking the glass, empty now but ready for a second filling, and putting it on the sideboard with a gentle slap. "I shall face them sober, Mr. Dulwich. And if I must, then you may as well do so with me. Should it become too much for you, then you've only to think of Milton and there find sweet, blissful numbness."

"But . . ." His protest was feeble as he watched me place the decanter back in its place. Then he threw his head back and laughed. "Oh, Cousin Emma, you are the devil. I do so like that in a person."

"I am not your cousin, Mr. Dulwich."

I meant that he should address me as Mrs. Andrews, as was proper, but when he shrugged and said, "Oh, Emma, you must call me Sebastian," I somehow did not refuse. I had found a friend at Dulwich Manor. I was not about to quibble over the terms.

Friendship, I learned, did not come without a price. Sebastian insisted on my accompanying him the following morning horseback riding despite my protests. I told him plainly I was not an able horsewoman and would be more hindrance than companion on a countryside jaunt. But even my wounded hand did not excuse me, and in the end, I had to give in.

Of course, he deviled me the entire time. "Come, Emma, you are taking all day!" he goaded.

"Stop being beastly. I shall find myself sprawled on the ground if I attempt to go any faster. If you refuse to allow me to continue at this stately pace, I will turn back."

He circled around to pass me, maneuvering his horse in a

high-stepping prance. "My dear, you have no sense of adventure."

"Ah. You've found me out. No doubt it is the result of all that reading."

"Indeed," he agreed. "Absolute poison." But he slowed.

He took me in the opposite direction of The Sanctuary. I was glad not to be going back to that place. I did not know what it was I had sensed or seen yesterday, or what I thought about the disturbing confidences of Henrietta regarding her new imaginary friend. I felt a certain desperate desire to dismiss it, to brand it a figment of fancy and turn my thoughts away. Because of Laura, I'd lived all my life with the fear of my own mind betraying me one day. One mustn't entertain fancy too deeply, or too long.

"A storm is coming." Sebastian frowned at the sky, where a tower of thick, gray clouds loomed over the trees. The far-off meadows were already darkened under the encroaching shadow. "It is going to be a monster," he muttered as he pulled on the reins to bring his horse around. "Let us ride. This coat will be in a ruin if it gets wet. Come now, hurry!"

"Go on ahead," I told him. "You shall get a drenching if you wait for me."

"Oh, indeed, and that would make me a knave. I've been called a cad, a bounder, a rascal, and an ignoramus—but never a knave. I won't have it. Come, now, Emma, kick that mule you're riding and simply hold on. You might get your teeth rattled, but we'll make it in."

The first splats of water hit us. He muttered a curse and glanced over his shoulder. I followed suit, and found the clouds had overtaken us. Then I saw something else, and in one leap, my heart bounded up from my chest to lodge firmly in the base of my throat. Faintly, against the smoky sky, one gunmetal-gray cloud appeared to be collecting itself into a shape.

It seemed to be an image of a great bird. I thought of the crow, the large black bird that had menaced me from the tree. But this shape was different.

I turned back around, suddenly infused with terror, and spurred my horse forward. Clasping the reins desperately, I glanced back and saw that the billowing formation had made itself into the suggestion of a large and looming serpent.

"Do you see that?" I blurted, shouting over the sound of the horses' hooves.

"What?" Sebastian glanced back. "Is it lightning? Lud, I hate electrical storms. Come, Emma!"

The thing was now quite distinct. It was not a serpent, for it had wings. It was a dragon. I could make out the coiled tail, the ridges of its back, its head, and the suggestion of elongated teeth protruding from a snarling mouth.

I saw Sebastian look again, saw his eyes aim directly at it, then they shifted rapidly to the left and then to the right. He was merely scanning for signs of flashing light in the clouds. He did not see the figure.

A cold finger of terror, more deep and real than any I had ever felt before this, traced a path up my spine. If he did not see it . . .

"We must hurry, Emma," Sebastian urged. "If those are thunderheads, we will be in real danger out in the open."

Gritting my teeth, I held on as we galloped back to the stables, making quick progress to the fence of the inner paddock. A stable hand came out to grab the reins of my horse, running to get us quickly into the barn. He helped me dismount, and

as I had never gotten into the aristocratic habit of ignoring the staff, I turned to thank him.

There was no explanation for my reaction. He was but a servant, a lower-level stable hand, the short, sturdy kind with a thick form that holds graceless but unmistakable power. As dark-skinned as a gypsy, his thick hair curled in clumps around his head like clawed fingers and a heavy mustache obscured his mouth. There was nothing repulsive about him, not on the exterior, and yet I shrank from him, repelled and filled with sudden fear.

I felt the sudden, vicious stab of pain in my skull, and the sensation of the veil parting assailed me again. Something was there, beyond the reach of my mind, something pressing forward, coming now. Closer. Closer.

The grooves in the groom's weathered cheeks deepened as if he was smiling underneath his mustache. Large, liquid eyes held my gaze boldly, gleaming as if he knew something, something that gave him pleasure to savor, something of which I was ignorant.

"Emma!" Sebastian called. His hair had wilted under his hat, the curls lifeless and sticking to his cheek. "We should make a dash for the house now. Here, put my coat over your head."

I could not get away from the barn fast enough. Grabbing his arm, I raced with him through the fat droplets pelting down upon us, cowering under the shelter of his ruined coat. When we arrived at the garden gate, I glanced back. The gypsy was still there. His teeth showed under the dark slash of drooping mustache. He was laughing.

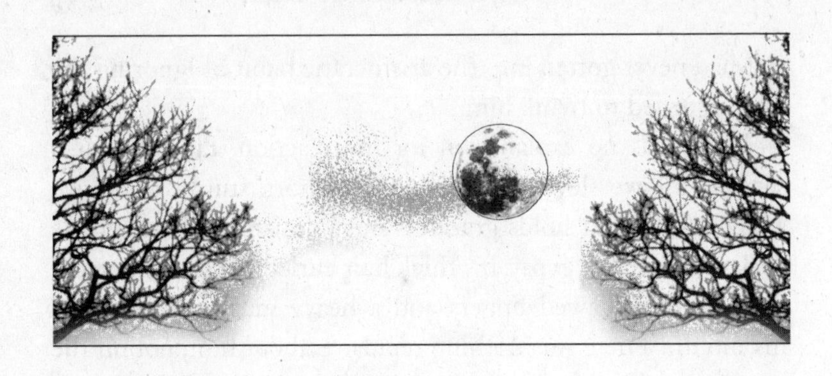

Chapter Four

I took to bed straight away, tired and distraught and fit to see no one.

I dreamt of a woman weeping. In my dream, it was my mother, staring down at me as she bent over my bed. Tears ran in broken rivulets down her cheek, dropping off her trembling chin. Upon waking, I found tears on my own lashes and a hard knot in my throat which made it difficult for me to swallow.

Shivering in my bed, the coverlet pulled to my chin, listening to the steady patter of rain, I wondered if my wits were slipping away. But despite the long-held fear that my mind would weaken as my mother's had, I did not believe this was true. Somehow, I felt something strong and sure inside my breast. As

fantastical as all of this was, I did not think I was insane. I had sensed and seen things that were not real in the strict sense, and yet existed. Perhaps not in normal perception . . .

I paused in my thoughts, wondering if this was how the mad reasoned.

I forced myself out of the bed upon that thought, seeing there was no point in tormenting myself. Struggling against the feeling of heaviness in my limbs, I bent over the table to light an oil lamp. My head ached in a vague, dull way. I padded in bare feet to the window and peered out into the dismal weather. Mists had come in with the rain, floating fingers wrapping themselves around the landscape like a ghost making a fist. I frowned at my fanciful imagination and yanked the drape closed.

Yet I could not prevent the pulse of my thoughts from going to my unhappy preoccupation. I felt in every other way quite normal. Would I know if my mind were becoming disordered? Or would I hold fast to the false belief that I had really been attacked by the crows, that something terrible had truly ridden the storm, that the gypsy in the barn meant me harm?

I missed Simon terribly in those moments. What comfort he would have given me, his wan smile, his distracted pat of affection to my shoulder.

I do not speak of love for my husband, and that may disappoint some. When my father had known he was ill, he arranged for Simon, an older gentleman with whom I had barely a passing acquaintance, to marry me. He told me Simon Andrews was wealthy, amenable to a wife, and a good man. It turned out he had been correct on all accounts, and my married life had been unexpectedly pleasant until Simon's weak heart had failed him just last year.

My husband had liked me, and we had been friends after a fashion. I could have used such a friend now, and I mourned him with the selfish longing of a denied child.

The maid came in and I turned away. "I'm down with the megrim," I told her. She left me with a fresh basin of cool water to bathe my temples. I lay on my bed, letting darkness gather around me as the day waned.

It was fully dark when Alyssa slipped into my room. "How is your headache?" She spoke softly.

"Better," I lied. I was too curious to send her away. It was not like Alyssa to be solicitous of me.

"Would it bother you if I sit?" She had already pulled a chair beside the bed by the time I uttered my assent. "Did you not have even a cup of tea?"

I was suspicious, even wary. "The maid offered, but I was not of a mind to eat."

She seemed astonished. "But you should have taken at least a cup of tea. It can be so restorative."

"I do not wish to be a bother."

"It's too late for that," she said unkindly. She eyed the stack of books I'd brought with me, piled on the bedside table. "I hope you are not taxing your eyes while the headache has you. And why is it so dim in here?"

"I have not felt like reading, no."

Her eyes shifted back to me, narrowed in kittenish vexation. "If you are malingering, I shall be most put out with you, for it is making everyone nervous. Roger is fearful of this dreaded wasting disease."

"I do not have the wasting disease, I assure you. Just the megrim."

"Well, it is remarkable to find you with such complaint. Never was a woman less given to vapors than you. You are hardy, not delicate." Unsaid went the end of that sentence: *like me*.

Her hands were folded neatly on her lap. Yet another difference between us: she could sit like that, like a portrait, so still. "You've been hiding in Devonshire since Simon died," she observed.

"I lost my husband not long ago." I made an effort to sit up.

"Oh, Emma. Do not act as if you and Simon shared affection."

I was stung. "As a matter of fact, we did, Alyssa. Not like you and Alan, true, but deeply felt nonetheless."

But she was right. I was not in mourning. Sad, yes, but not bereaved.

"And you are very wealthy," she observed. She could not keep the tinge of bitterness from her voice.

I sighed. "Please, if you've come for a quarrel, give me some respite tonight. I am not up to my full wits."

She sniffed, drawing herself up. "I know we have never been friends, but we are sisters." Her still hands began to move, restless on her lap.

"We are sisters," I agreed. "Alyssa, is everything all right? Are you and Alan getting on?"

The anxiety in my voice made her smile. "Yes, yes. He is as devoted as ever. That is why I married him. It is why you objected."

"I . . ." It hadn't been that. I had simply been of the opinion that Alyssa deserved something more than calf-eyed admiration. What I had failed to see back then was that Alyssa had not wanted anything more.

Swinging my legs to the side of the bed, I sat facing her. "I always wanted you to be happy. I truly hope you are."

Her smile wasn't sad, exactly. Perhaps a little bit hard. "I am. Brilliantly happy. And . . . I've some news. I am going to have a child, Emma. I'm to be a mama."

"Oh, Alyssa, that is wonderful." I had the impulse to embrace her, but she held herself so stiffly that I hesitated. "You are going to be such a beautiful mother."

"Do you think so?" She stood suddenly and went to the window, lifting the velvet curtain. "The rain is so dreary. Mary is beside herself over the weather. We were to have a tournament of bowling tomorrow. It will have to be postponed."

"Alyssa, come sit down."

To my utter shock, she did. I could not recall the last time she had obeyed me. "Tell me what is bothering you," I commanded gently.

She shrugged. Then she laughed. "It is so silly, really. I . . . I keep thinking of Mama. And Papa. I don't think I missed them so much as now, with the baby coming." Suddenly, she grabbed my hand. "I find, now that we have been apart for so long, that you do not irritate me nearly as much as you once did."

I smiled softly as she went on, oblivious to the insult buried in what she surely saw as a compliment. "When you urged me not to accept Alan's proposal, I thought I would never forgive you. I was so angry with you . . ."

"I have ever had a knack of accomplishing that, always to my dismay."

She looked at me, a smile twisting on her lips but remaining unformed. "Yes, you did." She wrinkled her nose. "But that was

Papa's fault. I may have been Papa's pet, but you, Emma, you were his pride. You knew it, admit it."

"I didn't," I replied truthfully. In fact, this news shocked me to the core. I had always been the outcast, I had thought. I knew my father loved me—that I had never doubted. But I remembered my father's dark gaze on me. I'd never detected a trace of pride or affection. He had always seemed so removed.

I had thought he was ashamed of me, the daughter of a madwoman. A warm feeling of tenderness suffused me and I wished I had realized this sooner. It would have been a comfort to me so many times when I'd felt alone.

For a moment, the old sneer played on her features, marring her perfect beauty. "Imagine, him bringing you up the way he did, with your own tutor and all those unwomanly interests. He could deny you nothing, Emma. It drove Mama to distraction. Perhaps she pointed out your faults too often, but she was only looking out for me. Her great fear was that I'd be pushed to the side." She sniffed. "But it was you, Emma, the clever one, the steady one, the interesting one . . . you he bragged about. He indulged your ridiculous infatuation with books. He never pressed you on your looks and you didn't bother having to dress up. It wasn't expected of you."

"But you were always the shining joy of his life, Alyssa."

"No. I was just pretty. That's what I am, pretty. Mama always told me I had to be pretty for Papa." Her high voice mimicked her mother's advice, shrill and harsh. "'Wear the pink satin, and stand up straight. Don't dare muss your hair.' But you he loved, and you didn't even have to try."

How wrong she was, but I was no longer disposed to argue. "It was Father's nature to hold his affection to himself."

"Papa was a dark man. Haunted." Glancing away, she grew

sullen. "He never recovered from what happened to your mother. Mama told me things . . ."

I did not want to hear them. I interjected quickly. "But you shall do so much better for your child. Your baby shall bask in the affection you'll shower on him."

"I shall," she said fiercely. "But I absolutely determined I am going to have a girl. And you are not to hide away on that dreadful moor. I will not have you abandoning me in that fashion. I shall have need of you to comfort me and calm me."

I fought a smile I knew she wouldn't appreciate. The world had surely changed cataclysmically if my sister was looking to me to bring equanimity to her life. In the past, our encounters could be counted on to send her into fits, for we could never seem to get along well. The difference was that now she needed me. I had never been needed like this before.

"You shall come to dinner," she said, rising.

I felt somewhat revived by my sister's visit, and by the revelations that had come as a result. I resolved to put my troubles out of my mind. I would strive to carry on with an improved attitude. I would no longer lie about and worry.

However, I could not completely dispel the dull headache. It stayed with me as I departed the gloomy safety of my room and again joined the world of the living.

The following morning, after visiting Henrietta in her schoolroom, I joined the guests in the salon. The curate and Mrs. Bedford were among those present for luncheon. Sebastian slipped to my side. "No bowling today. Are you absolutely crushed?"

He wore a gold-and-peacock-blue waistcoat that dazzled my

eyes so intensely I had to squint. He smiled at my reaction at such a costume and began to fuss with his lacy cuff. "You like it? I spent nearly all my quarterly allowance on it, but it was worth it. Is it not marvelous?"

"If there is a better word to describe this apparition, I cannot think of it," I replied drolly.

"Look," he said, jerking his head to where Roger stood in conversation with a knot of men. "A Mr. Valerian Fox." He drew out the name with flavor as I spied a new guest.

"Is he a friend of yours?"

His hand fluttered dramatically. "No, no, dear, I've just made his very intriguing acquaintance myself. He's Roger's friend, someone from London, I think. I took it my brother was rather surprised to see him here."

I peered more intently at the man. He was tall and blade-thin, but his shoulders were broad, filling his coat and stretching the material slightly when he placed a glass on the mantle. Someone made a joke—I'm sure it was Roger, as Alan has no sense of humor—and the deep timbre of masculine laughter filled the room.

"Was he not invited?"

"I do not know the particulars, but he seems to have corresponded with Roger, after some mutual acquaintance provided a letter of introduction. Roger had no choice but to ask him to join us. Which was quite decent of him, but you know how absurdly polite my brother can be."

Mr. Fox half-turned, and I caught his profile. In that first glimpse of patrician nose and intelligent brow over which spilled a spike of dark hair, I don't believe I breathed. Mr. Fox chanced to glance over one square shoulder, and caught me watching him. He merely returned my perusal, his dark, hooded eyes unwavering without being rude.

His face was interesting rather than handsome, composed of angles and planes; pointed cheekbones and a square jaw were balanced by the smooth, swarthy skin of his cheek. There were elongated hollows on either side of a sensuously curved mouth, lending an aspect to his face that was too sharp for conventional good looks. And yet it was arresting. I caught myself staring with what had to appear startling rudeness.

"Come on, let us get you introduced," Sebastian whispered, and I instinctively drew back. But my resistance was easily overcome when he pulled insistently at my elbow and marched me toward the group.

"Mr. Fox," he said, his face alight with excitement, "may I be allowed to present you to Mrs. Emma Andrews."

Mr. Fox's dark head inclined and his gloved hand extended with smart correctness. "Your servant," he said.

His voice was like silk drawn over a rough surface, smooth with a slight rasp. His eyes were nearly obsidian, glittering cleverly as he took my measure.

"Emma, this is Mr. Valerian Fox," Sebastian continued, drawing on the name again, saying it with relish. "Emma lives in Devon," he explained, sidling a touch closer to the man as if imparting something of import. "We are so happy to have her here at Dulwich. Since she lost her husband after last Christmas, we would like to keep her with us as long as possible."

Ah. The mention of my status as a widow meant Sebastian had appointed himself my matchmaker. I would have liked to have struck him with a blunt instrument at that moment.

"I am sure it is desirable to keep such a charming person as Mrs. Andrews as close as one can," Mr. Fox said to Sebastian,

then addressed himself pointedly to me. "I understand you have been under the weather recently, Mrs. Andrews."

"A low place indeed, given the wretched state of it," I replied.

His eyes flickered over me, brushing a light touch down my neck and to the gentle swell of my bosom, encased in steel-blue lace, then back up to my face. His gaze seemed to narrow in on me. "There is sickness in the town, I understand. You must have a care."

"Thank you," I replied, "but you have been misinformed. I am not unwell."

He seemed to appreciate that fact, something he made apparent with an almost improperly bold look. "What a relief."

For some reason, I found myself slightly breathless. His regard of me was intense, and I cannot say it did not affect me, making me a trifle nervous.

I excused myself and turned toward the others, catching my cousin's eye watching me. Mary was wearing an expression of animated interest, and approval. I nearly groaned, for she had seen my exchange with Mr. Fox, and I feared it was giving her ideas. My dread was realized when moments later she announced lunch, and in arranging the procession into the dining room, made certain I was partnered with Mr. Fox.

The promenade was a rather foolish custom, I had always thought. I made a self-conscious overture to conversation. "There are Latin inscriptions all around the house. Have you seen them?"

His movements were economical, even the slight nod he gave me now. "Oh, indeed I have."

"There it is," I said, pointing to an archway as we passed. "*Semper paratus.*"

His heavy eyelids lowered to half-mast, and he translated in a voice deeply resonant. "'Always ready.' Good advice, do you not agree, Mrs. Andrews?"

"Indeed, but the question begs to be asked, sir: ready for what?"

"Why, for anything." He faced forward, his sphinx-like features as immutable as stone. "Anything at all."

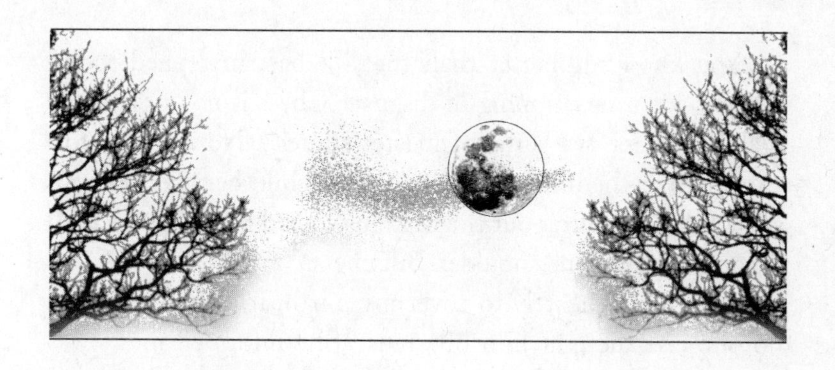

Chapter Five

By the time the soup course was concluded, I decided I did not like Valerian Fox. It was his stillness, as if every nerve were on alert, watching everything. Especially me; even when his eyes were directed elsewhere, I felt his awareness of me. He unnerved me. I dropped my fork twice, making a racket against the Wedgewood plate. My sister scowled at me, and I tried harder to steady my hand lest I overtax our new détente.

Sebastian asked me, "You visited our Henri this morning?"

"She beat me four times out of five at Peggity," I said, carefully spearing a slice of ham. "And do you know what else? The little minx challenged me to chess."

Roger barked. "Chess? Did you teach her, Sebastian?"

"You know me better than that," Sebastian replied to his brother, his tone dripping in disgust. "Chess is not a game for a child. Chess is a game of master strategy. Now, I admit to showing her the important things for a child her age to know, such as how to ferret out the best gossip and the proper way to drape a cape off one shoulder. But chess?"

I coughed delicately to cover my mirth. It amazed me that no one else thought him hilarious. "She informed me it was Marius who taught her," I told them.

Roger chewed for a moment. "Who on earth is Marius?"

Sebastian shrugged. "Her new imaginary friend. Didn't you get an introduction? He seems to be rather a formidable character. Victoria is quite put out at being displaced." He pulled a face. "I never liked that doll. Too haughty."

I did laugh then before I could catch myself.

"Darling," Mary said to Roger, pointedly ignoring her brother-in-law, "do you have an ancestor named Marius? Perhaps she saw a painting in the gallery."

"I'm afraid I do not know offhand," Roger said. "But that still does not answer where she learned chess."

I caught the look on Mr. Fox's face just then. It seemed to me to be chillingly absent of any discernible emotion, and yet his eyes, glittering black as they swept the company around the table, were sharp with interest.

Immediately after the meal was concluded, I returned to the third floor, where I found Henrietta seated by the window with a book on her lap. The puddle of sunlight angling through the leaded panes gilded her curls, setting them agleam like an angel's, but her eyes were steady and somber as I greeted her.

"She's feeling a bit poorly," Miss Harris informed me. "A quiet afternoon is in order, I should say."

"Every afternoon is quiet," Henrietta said, turning back to her book. "And very long."

Hunkering down in front of the child, I took her hand in mine. "You aren't very happy about being shut up inside, I see. Maybe that is what has you in the doldrums."

She lifted a slender shoulder in a pretense of diffidence, but I knew I'd struck on her problem.

Miss Harris's voice took on an uncharacteristic stridency. "Her father doesn't wish her to go outside because of the illness."

"Yes, but maybe if we stay away from the village it will be all right. And we do not have to be out very long, just a nice brisk walk to put some color back in your cheeks. I'm sure your papa wouldn't mind." I considered the dappled light outside, then smiled down at Henrietta. "The day is getting milder, so it would seem the weather is inviting us. What do you say?" Henrietta smiled and nodded.

The nursemaid tried to protest but I cut her off. "It is settled, then. We will not be long. Hen, go fetch your boots and grab Victoria."

Henrietta shook her head. "She's left me."

Miss Harris clucked. "I'm afraid we've misplaced Victoria."

"We shall look for her when we get back," I promised, and went to fetch my shawl. I would take her toward Overton. That path cut nowhere near any crofter's cottage or farm and, as I'd been there before, there could be no question of our losing our way.

We would, however, pass near The Sanctuary. In the broad

light of day, the thought of seeing it again made me feel strangely excited. I suppose I was eager to prove there was nothing to be afraid of, that whatever fancy had gripped me temporarily was quite done with.

We had a happy walk, for Henrietta came alive like a wilted flower reviving in the sunlight. The air held that certain crispness that comes after long rains, and it had a renewing effect on me as well. I inhaled deeply of the sweet breeze and my head felt clear. The sound of Henrietta's laughter floated around me as she skipped and leapt at my side.

When Marius's tree came into view, my heart gave a great surge, and I could not prevent myself from scanning the tall grasses around it to see if the birds were anywhere in sight. Nothing disturbed the meadow, or the wild holly bushes at its edge, not even a breeze. The long, lazy branches of a weeping willow barely made a stir. The grass was thick and deep here, and it was not easy going as we thrashed our way through.

There was no detectable change in Henrietta as we approached, then passed, the strangely shaped hawthorn. Relief swelled in me. It had all been a bit of nonsense.

A patch of early wildflowers occupied us for a while. I showed Henrietta how to string them together to form a daisy chain. She grew bored and wandered off to fetch more flowers. I got rather lost in figuring out the knack of tying the little blossoms. It had been some time since I'd undertaken such a winsome activity.

When I'd finished the first chain, I looked up and saw, to my surprise, that the field was empty. I scrambled to my feet. "Henrietta!" I called, and, at once, my fine sense of well-being evaporated.

The object of my labor fell from my hand. I searched franti-

cally along the top of the grass for a cap of golden curls. "Henrietta?" I called.

Lifting my skirts clear to my knees, I broke into a run. The height of the grass was an impediment, and I was not graceful as I loped through. I had a thought she might have made for the hedgerow and set off in that direction.

Then something touched me, a presence, burning lightly into the flesh of my back. My steps slowed. I stopped. The air grew electric, and the sense of pressure, the terrible stabbing pain inside my head, sprang to life.

I swung about to look behind me. I was standing by Marius's tree. A terrible feeling saturated my flesh, aching a dull pain in my bones—it was coming from there. The feeling was coming from that direction.

The sound of Henrietta's voice drifted over to me. "No," she said in a tone calm and measured, "I do not think it is so."

I felt relief, for I had found her, but it was quickly cut off, replaced by a creeping finger of dread that ran up the vertebrae in the small of my back. She was talking to someone.

I spotted her, sitting cross-legged on the ground among the high grass. Her face was upturned as if there were someone standing just an arm's length in front of her.

She went still, as if she were listening. Whoever spoke to her did so in such a low tone I could not hear it. Then she laughed. "I should like that very much!"

I approached quickly. What trick was this? Was someone hiding behind the tree? I could not see properly, so I cut a wide berth behind the child to trap him. Circling, I stopped short.

The meadow was empty.

Henrietta was even now smiling and nodding, as if in response to words I could not hear. But there was nothing there.

Fear cut into me, a deep, razor-edged terror. When she'd played pretend with Victoria, I understood that she knew it was a game. This looked so real. As if something or someone really were there, speaking only to her . . .

I cried out as a sudden burst of pain descended upon me like a hammer's blow. I went down on my knees with a gasp, clutching my hands to my hair. I felt like I was being wrenched open, as though something inside me were tearing, and then, as I curled forward, mouth open in a silent cry, a sharp final snap burst upon me, as if a twig were rended in two.

And then I felt no pain, just breathless relief. I lay there, unmoving, for only a moment before I remembered Henrietta and made myself rise. Unfurling myself, I found her motionless before Marius's tree, enraptured. She still had no idea I was present.

But now I saw it, as if a veil had been finally ripped aside. A shadow, the suggestion of a male figure, enshrouded in mists, stood in the shelter of the wild tangle of branches of the ancient hawthorn tree.

I stood on shaking legs. "Henrietta!" I cried.

She whipped her head around. The shadow dissolved and Henrietta jumped to her feet, her little body going rigid. I reached her, snatching her by the shoulders and pulling her toward me.

Her head twisted to turn back to the tree. "You made him go away. He was being nice to me."

"Who? Is that Marius?" I grasped her shoulders and shook her, perhaps a bit more roughly than was necessary, but my blood was pumping furiously in my veins. "Is this Marius, Henrietta? Please tell me."

Something dawned on her and she looked upon me with a new amazement. "You saw him."

I was about to reply and stopped. What had I seen? "It was just a shadow, but like a man. Tall, and very dark. Is . . . is that what you see, darling?"

She shook her head. "No. He's very handsome. He talks to me." She smiled, a chilling, ghostly smile. "He tells me things sometimes. I like it when he's nice." Her face went cold. "I'm afraid of him."

My heart plunged into ice. "Isn't Marius your friend?"

She bobbed her head, but her little forehead puckered and she whispered, "But I don't like it when he wants to talk to me at night. He's different then. He gets angry."

He taps on the glass at night, I recalled. "Who is Marius?" I whispered.

A moment pulsed as I gazed into Henrietta's face. In the pureness of her eyes, I could see the agony of indecision, of divided loyalties.

I pulled her away from the tree. "We must never come here again. Your father was right, it is dangerous. I wonder if he knows just how much so. Come, hurry." I left unsaid the remainder of my thought: *Before he comes back.*

We fled that place with me all but dragging Henrietta behind me. We'd gone a short way when I saw a figure framed on a hilltop in the direction in which we were headed. With the low-hanging sun behind him, I could make out a man astride a horse. I thought it was Sebastian. Perhaps he'd come from the house to find us.

I fled toward him, our progress slowed by tiny Henrietta battling the hip-high grass. Finally I scooped her up and carried her, running against the tangle of my skirts and the uneven ground. He saw us, and kicked his horse into a gallop down the hill. As the gap between us closed, I could see the tall, slender figure commanding a huge black beast was Valerian Fox. He reined in his horse directly in my path and peered down at me.

"Are you all right, Mrs. Andrews?" he demanded sharply. His dismount was fluid, controlled. Once he was on the ground, he reached for Henrietta. The act so surprised me, I surrendered her without question.

His eyes lifted and scanned the horizon behind me, his face as inscrutable as ever. "You are too far from the house. It is dangerous out here." His gaze jerked abruptly to mine, and I had a clear, unwavering revelation—

He knows.

Then he drew his horse close and issued a curt order to the beast. It was either some kind of code or another language, but the horse bobbed its head and went stock-still.

"You will have to ride astride," he said. "I'll help you."

I set my teeth edge to edge, grasped the pommel, and turned my mind away from the humiliating business of having Mr. Fox haul me astride. But the process was done quite handily, his strength proving astonishing for one without the excess of brawn. Astride the saddle, skirts bunched around my lap and the hem nearly to my knees, exposing my boots and a peek of stocking, I straightened tentatively, very uncertain at the unaccustomed height I found myself upon the back of his great horse. The gelding remained perfectly still. Fox handed Henrietta up to me, and she curled comfortably in my lap.

Taking the reins, Mr. Fox led us back to the house.

Chapter Six

"I understand that is the second time you have come to some ill near that place," Fox said. We were in the library, where he had asked me to meet him after seeing Henrietta to the nursery. I'd wished to duck into my room to freshen my appearance, and this thought, as soon as it occurred to me, struck me as strange indeed, considering the much more important things I had on my mind.

"What do you mean?"

He reached out and cradled my bandaged hand in his. There was sureness in the way he touched me, as if we weren't strangers. As if we'd known one another a very long time. "You cut your hand out there." His finger traced the line of the cuts, visible through the bandage by the seeping blood. I'd ripped them open carrying Henrietta.

My mouth opened, and I was about to ask him where he could have learned such a thing when it occurred to me that a man like him had numerous methods to gain intelligence.

I disengaged my hand with some difficulty. "Funny," I tossed out with a smile, "but I've never been accident-prone before."

He changed tack. "The child is unharmed?"

"She is fine. I appreciate your concern. And your help. Your arrival was timely."

"Yes . . ." He stood with his feet braced apart, looking like the captain of a ship poised at the prow. "Might I have a word with you?" he asked.

"We are having words now," I replied, trying to be tart and then, hearing how I had just misspoken, blushing.

He smiled slightly and his eyes, too, eased somewhat in their intensity. "Surely our conversation was not that extreme. I meant, might we speak a bit more . . . plainly, you and I?" Moving toward me, he gestured to one of four wing chairs by the unlit hearth, inviting me to sit. I complied. He took the chair closest to me, his long legs stretched out so that his shoe nearly touched the hem of my gown.

Resting his elbows on the armrests, he laced his fingers just at his chin and leveled his black stare at me. I folded my own hands on my lap and returned his gaze evenly.

After an interval, the smile came again, this time a tad deeper. "It seemed from my vantage point that something disturbed you today on the Overton Hill."

"How long were you watching me, Mr. Fox?"

"A while," he admitted without embarrassment. "I noticed the child by the tree. What was she doing?"

"Nothing." My reply was quick and obviously defensive. "Merely taking a rest."

He disengaged a long finger, using it to stroke his lip. He said, "I had just come over the crest of the hill when I spotted you wading through the grass to her, but the child . . . The child was, if my eyes did not mistake me, talking to the tree."

I swallowed first, then made my voice light. "I wonder you cannot find something more interesting to occupy an afternoon."

That elegant finger leveled at me. "And I noticed you had a fright."

My mouth worked a half-second before my voice came through. "I had lost sight of her. I was naturally overset. Let me ask you something, Mr. Fox. How was it you saw so much? You were very far away, and I could barely see from where I stood the outline of a figure of a horse and rider, let alone all this nuance of expression you claim to have noticed."

"I have excellent eyesight," he said.

"It must approach the vision of an eagle, I daresay." I attempted a show of arrogance to indicate my disbelief, but succeeded only in feeling childish. "And you happened to be riding in the area of The Sanctuary this morning? Why?"

A ghost of some emotion passed over his face. "I am most interested in that tree."

"Do you have an affinity for botany, Mr. Fox?"

His laughter came suddenly, an abrupt bark that punched sound into the quiet room. His smile lingered, showing teeth this time. They were very white and even. The fully blossomed smile was devastating on his somber face, and I saw he could very well have been very attractive indeed had he had better manners.

His eyes on me were keen. "I have many interests."

"Including spying on us."

He froze me with that icy calculation of his. "I wonder, was your mission on the hill so clandestine that my observing you creates discomfort?"

"I find it odd that you are so curious about an outing of a widow and a child," I said pertly. I might as well have said: *I find you odd, Mr. Fox.*

Nevertheless, he took no offense. He merely shrugged. "Inarguably."

He would give nothing. Well, neither would I. I had the very strong, very definite sense that he knew something, and he was attempting, in a sly, disarming manner, to pry some sort of admission from me.

And yet I am embarrassed to admit that a small part of me—a part I most emphatically repressed—wanted very much to tell all to him, lay it at his feet and share the dark burden that was gathering across my shoulders.

I rose abruptly. "Well, I need to see to changing for dinner. Good afternoon, Mr. Fox. Thank you again for the generous use of your horse."

He waited until I was at the door. "Mrs. Andrews."

I paused, turning my head enough to see him approach with a feline grace. He drew uncomfortably close. I was forced to gaze upward to meet his eye. "May I ask you a question on a rather delicate matter?"

My heart, for some reason, beat wildly. "I am intrigued. Ask, then."

His cheek twitched. "I fear my manner has offended you."

I said nothing at first, then, "Is that the question? Then the answer is yes, perhaps it has a little."

"No," he murmured with a chuckle, "that was not the question. What I wished to know was . . . well, I was some distance away, but it seemed to me by the way you reacted that you may have seen something at that hawthorn tree . . . Did you, Mrs. Andrews?"

I am no good at lying. I said, "A trick of the light."

"Or the dark," he said, almost to himself, as he turned away. "May I offer something, a suggestion, Mrs. Andrews?"

My nerves, worn raw by now, made me unintentionally snappish. "And pray, what is that?"

"A book. Let me see." He drifted along the shelves, paused, then selected a slim volume. "Here we are. Have you read Coleridge's 'Christabel'?"

"Yes, of course." I was familiar with the poem to which he referred, but it was not one of my favorites. I had found "Christabel" a sinister, uncomfortable story with haunting images of witchcraft and hints of twisted sexuality. I had liked it not at all.

Mr. Fox closed his hand over mine as he handed me the volume. The action was exceedingly improper, and yet I did not balk. There seemed to be electric current in his touch, made skin to skin, for neither of us was gloved, and I blush to admit it was rather stirring.

"Read it again," he said with gentle urgency. And then he left me.

I wanted to flaunt his suggestion, but the hope that Mr. Fox had some insight into my troubles had me secreted in the conservatory, devouring the lines of Coleridge's work within a half hour. Sebastian found me a while later, sweeping into the room with a frown as he looked me up and down.

"That is an unbecoming color on you," he said, collapsing onto a wrought-iron chair. His hand waved dismissively toward the embroidered silk gown I wore, cream-colored with sprigs of pale yellow and green stitched upon it. "It washes out your complexion and renders you pasty. You want to look your best for our Mr. Fox, don't you? What do you have there?"

He was not dissuaded by my impatient look. He peered at the page and read aloud: "The night is chill, the cloud is gray: 'Tis a month before the month of May, And the Spring comes slowly up this way."

Recoiling, he exclaimed, "Good God, Emma, can you not find something more cheerful? This is why I object to the influence of literature. Too bloody dreary!"

"I had a disturbing thing happen this afternoon," I said after a moment's pause. "Hen and I went out for a bit of a walk. I know she isn't allowed, but I thought there could be no harm in taking her into the meadow since it was a familiar path for me. She wandered off and wound up near that tree. Did I tell you about the tree she draws? She calls it Marius's tree, and was just sitting by it, staring up as if she were speaking to someone. She said she was talking to Marius."

"Oh. Did he ask for me?"

"It is not a joke, Sebastian. And what has happened to Victoria, by the by? That doll used to be with Henrietta everywhere she went, and now I never see her at all."

He shrugged. "Good riddance, I say. She was always so judgmental."

I sighed, for once not at all amused at his silliness, and he realized my frustration. "Forgive me, Emma." He sounded truly contrite. Leaning forward solicitously, he grabbed my hand. "What is it?"

I could say nothing more than "Marius."

He lifted his brow.

"Mr. Fox saw us out on the meadow. We . . . we had a fright. He brought us home, actually."

His eyes lit up. "Really? How romantic. Did he make you ride pillion, with his strong body pressed up against yours?"

"Certainly not," I protested.

"Ah, pity. I tell you, Emma, I am absolutely rabid for a scandal of some sort. How dreadfully thoughtless of you not to provide one. Oh, well, perhaps I can stir some mischief at dinner. Which is being served promptly, so we should go."

He gallantly offered me his arm. "Sebastian," I asked softly as we were exiting the room. "I beg you to tell me the truth. Did you teach Henrietta to play chess?"

He was perfectly serious when he shook his head.

After the meal, I sat with Alyssa and Mary while the men lit cigars and lingered over port.

"I think the custom of taking tobacco is barbaric," Alyssa pronounced.

I smiled. "You are put out because it is an aspect of men that excludes women."

"Well, it is a smelly habit, and I do not see at all how it is pleasurable. And all they wish to talk of is politics—how boring. I do not know how a lady such as Queen Victoria stands it."

Mary waved a hand at her, smiling indulgently. "Men must make their power games and play them out. I, for one, am glad they are out of earshot."

"Does anyone have an indication of Mr. Fox's politics?" Alyssa pouted. "Is that how Roger knows him? I know your husband is devoted to the Reform movement. Something is not right with Mr. Fox. He did not speak to me once!"

Mary shrugged, ignoring my sister's petulance. "I am sure I do not know. Roger has not told me much about him, but I do believe he is very well connected. We were pleased to offer an invitation when his correspondence arrived saying he'd be in the neighborhood. Roger admires him."

To this praise I said nothing but I'm afraid my curled lip betrayed me, for Alyssa looked at me strangely. "You are not down with the headache again, are you?"

"No . . ." The headache had been gone since the incident on the meadow, when I had seen the vision of the figure (dare I think of it as Marius's shadow?) that afternoon. But I remained much distracted by the entire matter, and all that had gone on before. I was terribly concerned for Henrietta besides. I felt there was something wrong, something happening that I must put an end to. "I am merely a bit tired," I said at last.

"Oh, please do not fall ill again, or Roger will be overset." Mary appeared annoyed. "He is always going on about illness, as if the poor were not inherently prone to all manner of unfortunate contagion."

"Perhaps that is why he is so dedicated to Reform," I suggested carefully. It was a bad idea to make my social views known, but I simply could not help myself.

She seemed startled. "Well, of course, we all pity the poor, but, Lord, one cannot make them a cause."

"Please," Alyssa wailed, "not politics!"

In deference to her condition, we changed the subject. I slipped away at my first opportunity before the men joined us—I was in no mood for Mr. Fox's enigmatic presence—and went upstairs to check on Henrietta. I found Miss Harris in her nightdress, reading in the sitting room. Behind her, Henrietta's door was slightly ajar.

"She's sleeping," the woman said, putting her book aside and standing, as if to block my path. "Poor dear was quite exhausted."

"I should not have taken her out of doors," I admitted, feeling quite overset with myself. "I understand she has been troubled by nightmares."

The nurse smiled a bit patronizingly at me. "Children go through these things."

"I noticed she has been missing Victoria. Perhaps she will sleep better when she finds her. Do you have any idea where she is?"

"I shall look for it tomorrow."

"I promised her I would help—"

"I will take care of it," Miss Harris said crisply. She turned and went into her room. I stared after her, wrestling with my temper at her rudeness. I decided I very well would have a look for the doll.

In the shadows of the schoolroom, the light cast from my lamp was merely a tepid yellow, too weak to do much against the night gathered densely in the large room. I crept quietly, suffering a stubbed toe and a banged shin without a sound. However, in the end, my determination won out. I spied a lock of shining blond hair behind a pile of books and toys stacked against one wall, and Victoria was found.

I rearranged the doll's tousled curls, happy with the thought of Hen's pleasure when she saw her again. "Henrietta has been missing you," I whispered.

A light, sharp staccato sound came from the direction of the window. I tensed, turning slowly to see it was only a branch stirring in the wind, brushing against the glass. Henrietta's tapping. I sighed and laughed at myself. My nerves were overwrought. I would do well to put myself to bed.

I was almost at the door when Henrietta suddenly cried out in her sleep. The tapping stopped.

I doused my lamp and placed it on the floor, moving slowly toward the window. Tentatively, the summoning noise started again. I peered out into the night, but I could see nothing. In her bed, Henrietta called out again. I heard her say, "No."

I clutched Victoria to me as I strained to see what might be out there. A sensation of heat against my breast made me look down. The doll's blank eyes gave nothing away, but the moonlight caught the cross hanging about her neck in a curious manner, giving it the strange and unnerving aspect of casting it aglow. I touched it. It felt warm.

Just then, a gust of wind kicked up outside. I heard the high-pitched wail of a screech owl, so close it might have been seated on the very branch scratching at the window. It sounded unnervingly like something in pain. There was a great, sudden sound of air rushing past the glass, then all was still.

My legs shook. What was happening? Was this a fancy, too? Did I dare believe the evidence of my senses?

I went into Henrietta's room and stood for a long time, smoothing the hair gently from her forehead. Then I placed Victoria next to her, tucking the doll gently under her arm.

"He doesn't like that, does he?" I whispered. I leaned over and kissed Henrietta's forehead, careful not to wake her. She stirred, clutching the doll closer.

I retreated to my room, thinking of the cross growing hot, of the shadow I'd seen by the tree, of everything collecting around this house, this child. And I thought of Mr. Fox. I believed he knew something. He'd given me the Coleridge poem.

I lit a candle by my bedside and read it through, absorbing its brooding images, the chill sense of danger. The long poem was rife with dark phrases. "Each matin bell, the Baron saith, knells us back to a world of death." His words were haunting as he described a mysterious midnight visitor, Geraldine, and how she seduced the innocent Christabel, thus bringing about the slow demise of her world and all she loved. She was clearly some kind of demon or ghoul. What was Mr. Fox getting at in suggesting I read this?

One particular passage caught my attention.

A snake's small eye blinks dull and shy,
And the lady's eyes they shrunk in her head,
Each shrunk up to a serpent's eye,
And with somewhat of malice, and more of dread,
At Christabel she look'd askance!

It struck me as curious and brought on a vague sense of disturbance. The image of a serpent seemed to be a common thing of late: the Great Stone Serpent of The Sanctuary and the figure I'd seen in the storm clouds. Had that been a serpent? Or perhaps the shape of a dragon? And a dragon was really a serpent with wings, I reasoned, so it was too similar to be ignored. Was this why Mr. Fox had recommended the poem?

When I was finished, I read it again, and with the day's events in mind, ruminated far into the morning hours, and in the end, my credulity was primed to consider the extraordinary possibility that perhaps my mother's madness was not at work here.

But if not madness . . . then what?

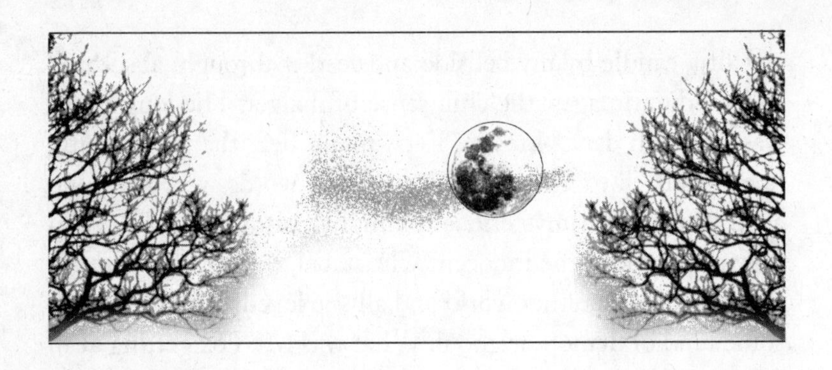

Chapter Seven

I sought Mr. Fox the following day as soon as I could sneak away from my sister and cousin, who were excitedly planning the new baby's layette and I am sure did not miss me. I found him standing in the middle of the second-floor hallway, his brow furrowed in concentration as he stared at the archway over the music room. Upon his spying my approach, his smile of greeting seemed rueful. Waving his pencil, he pointed to an inscription. "I'm writing them all down. Fascinating, do you not agree?" Squinting at the words, he intoned out loud, "*Exitus acta probat.*" He paused to scribble in his notebook. "I shall translate it later."

"The result validates the deed."

He gazed at me, surprised. "You know Latin?"

"I do," I replied coolly. But my ennui was a farce; I was unforgivably flattered that I'd impressed him.

"Hmm." He regarded me with those glittering onyx eyes, then strode away, caught up in his thoughts.

I followed. "Why are you interested in these inscriptions?"

He placed the notebook under his arm and the pencil in the pocket of his pants. "I believe, Mrs. Andrews, these are clues."

"Clues? To what?" I was being disingenuous and he knew it. His eyelids lowered to half-mast. He smiled patiently at me, as if in silent remonstrance that I should know better. He moved along and I fell in step with him.

"Mr. Fox, I read the Coleridge poem last night. Twice, in fact. Please explain why you suggested such a thoroughly inappropriate selection."

He frowned. "But what did you think the poem was about?"

"Christabel meets a stranger and invites her into her home, although the nature of Geraldine's wickedness was not clear. There seem to be more hints of disaster than any real description."

"Did you realize, Mrs. Andrews, that Geraldine is a revenant?"

"A ghost!" I exclaimed. I meant to be mocking, but the sound of my voice was too high-pitched.

"More precisely, a being that is, for lack of a better explanation, undead."

I could barely breathe. "And again I ask you, sir, what relevance do you feel this has on any situation at present?" I feared I knew the answer.

"That, Mrs. Andrews," he said with crisp accents, "is exactly what I intend to find out."

I stepped in his path. "Please do me the favor of explaining yourself."

He hesitated before responding. "Mrs. Andrews," he began,

his tone conciliatory, "might I inquire after the child. Little Henrietta."

Fear stopped me dead in the space of a heartbeat, cooled my heat. "Why do you wish to know about Henrietta?"

"You are close to her. Surely, you would notice any changes in her behavior of late. Unexplained fatigue, a pallor that seems untoward."

Suspicion crowded my thoughts. "Are you referring to the affliction in the village?" I asked.

He inclined his head.

The cold fear that had doused my annoyance now chilled me. "Mr. Fox, again I implore you to tell me what it is you know. Or, at least, suspect."

His eyes flashed, a brief glimpse of anger, and then I saw his emotion shift into something bleak and . . . And if I did not know better, I might have thought I saw real regret there. His response was simple. "No, Mrs. Andrews. For your own good, no."

My vision blurred and I fought for my self-control. "Mr. Fox, we both of us know something very wrong is in Wiltshire. If Henrietta is at any risk, you must tell me what it is. You must trust me with your thoughts."

He drew in a slow, thoughtful breath. "And do you trust me?" he queried gently.

The soft-spoken question was like a slap. Would I trust him—indeed not! What would I sound like, speaking of talking shadows and clouds and tapping at the window? Yet I wanted to tell him. Holding all of this inside me was becoming unbearable.

"So we are at an impasse," he murmured somberly.

I pushed past him, rubbing the palm of my right hand against my skirts to minister to the itch there, so great was my desire to strike him. If I had thought violence would have served any purpose, I would have. And I would have enjoyed it.

When I was a child, I would sneak into the spare bedroom to which my stepmother, Judith, had banished my mother's portrait. I'd lie on the bed for hours and stare, trying to capture one small recollection of Laura's face, her scent. One memory.

As I studied her painted likeness, I had asked myself what would her laugh be like? Perhaps she might look down at me fondly, brush my hair with the palm of her hand, or lean in to whisper something secret into my ear, something for just us alone. I had no real memories, for I was only three when she died, and no one spoke of her. The only knowledge I had of her was the furtive gossip of the servants. That was how I learned of her madness—and I learned, too, that they all expected me to follow suit one day.

In my room, where I was attempting to read in the middle of another dreary afternoon, I thought of the flash I'd gotten, the memory of my mother's weeping. One precious memory at long last, but it was disturbing, not the kind of vision I'd longed for as a child. I wanted to know more. I deserved to know more of what had happened to her.

The only other person who had known Laura then was leagues away. Uncle Peter, my father's dear friend and my godfather, had known my mother; he'd visited frequently in my childhood and through my youth. He was a magical influence on me when I was a child, for he exuded old-world culture and a quiet air of wisdom. His accent and exaggerated manners—both a result of his Romanian birth—made him exotic and romantic. He had been my idol and my first infatuation, a dashing foreign-born man with heavy mustaches lying luxuriously over a smiling mouth, the crinkles in the corner of his eye sparkling with delight in me, for I had been his favorite.

Had he been here, I would have laid my burdens on his capable shoulders and sighed with relief. I had his direction in London, where a letter would find him even if he were out of the country. As a member of Romania's diplomatic delegation, he was meticulous about forwarding his correspondence.

I put aside my book and took pen in hand. It was only a letter, but it provided catharsis, and my head felt clearer after writing that I was thinking of my mother of late and felt, as she had been particularly on my mind, that I should know more of her illness, and what had happened to her.

It was a bold thing, but I was glad I did it. I instantly felt better. While I had my ink pot out, I attended to some other correspondence to old friends which I'd neglected, sealed the letters, and put them on the table to be taken to post. It was good medicine; for a moment I felt almost normal.

It did not last. That evening, after dinner, Mary and Roger were summoned to the nurseries, for little Henrietta was inconsolable. It seemed that after a too-brief reunion, Victoria had gone missing again.

I was awakened at dawn a few days later to the sound of church bells tolling in the distance. Hampered by the heavy mists, the low chime was dull and full of mourning. I knew what it meant. The strange illness in the village had claimed another, and the latest to die was to be interred.

After checking on Henrietta and finding her sleeping safely and peacefully, I went straight to the library. The house would

sleep in, for we had been up late last night playing parlor games, and I would have a good deal of time alone.

I had been doing more reading of the sort Mr. Fox had directed. I had already discovered Keats's "Lamia," a dark tale of a female demon that repeated the misogynistic theme found in Keats's other, more famous work, "La Belle Dame Sans Merci." I also found an interesting short story, entitled "The Vampyre," by an unknown author, one Dr. Polidori.

I recalled Mr. Fox saying that unique and disturbing word: *undead*. I was convinced he knew something, and as I had no other avenues of investigation, I sat down to read it. Then I caught myself. How swiftly I'd thrown myself into the Romantic Era literature, caught up in the vagaries and sly hints Mr. Fox had thrown to me. Annoyed with myself, I put down the tome. Mr. Fox was leading me on a merry chase. And I followed along like a puppy eager for a morsel of meat. I did not need to play literary detective; I needed to confront him, I suddenly decided. Enough with his evasiveness and intrigue.

Not for the first time, I considered going to Roger about Fox. About everything, for if there was danger to Henrietta, I must tell him. But here was the rub—what exactly could I tell him? Of the shadow at the tree, of the clouds advancing like a spectral invasion?

The sound of the front door closing took me to the window, where I observed Mr. Fox trotting down the sweeping front steps, a sack over his shoulder. It was still very early. Now what was he about?

Snatching my light cape from its cloakroom peg, I followed. Not a ripple of conscience plagued me as to the rightness or wrongness of what I was doing as I slipped outside and made my way through the fading mists, keeping a careful distance from the tall figure striding purposefully in the direction of the village.

We came to a church, an engraved sign informing me it was known as Sarum Saint Martin. Built in the Norman style, it was a small but imposing square of iron-gray granite with an artless, pointed spire. I paused, thinking myself a fool as I hovered at the gate of the churchyard. But I could not refuse the impulse. I was mad with worry for Henrietta, and I knew—I *knew*—Mr. Fox had some knowledge of what ailed her.

I paused among a cluster of alder and larch. Mr. Fox faded into the fog that clung stubbornly among the gravestones, a ghost moving among ghosts. The markers were very old, some of them leaning to one side and streaked black with coal smoke, giving the appearance of a phalanx of weary sentinels. Among these, a man materialized beside a fresh mound of earth. He was standing quite still, head bent and hands clasped.

Fox saw him, too. He hunkered down, instantly swallowed by the low-lying mist as he hid behind a large carved stone cross. I did the same after scooting forward for a better vantage point.

The figure by the grave was hugely wrought, with massive shoulders and strong legs, arms curled under the weight of his muscle. He was dressed in a flowing cape. The dreary day was my enemy, for the light was too suffused to allow me to see plainly, but if my guess was correct, he was praying. Indeed, I was proved right when he grasped what I now saw was a large, laborious cross hung from the beads—rosary beads—and used it to make the sign of the cross, finishing with a slow, lingering touch to his lips.

I realized now the short cape draped over his broad form was a surplice. And the white of his collar too small to be a cravat. He was a priest.

Fox retreated, moving past me and on back to the house. He'd apparently been thwarted in whatever business had led him to the graveyard. I left as well, making fast for my room, once I gained the house, to change my ruined shoes and dress, for the hem was damp and spattered with mud.

I now had one more mystery to add to my burden: what the devil was Mr. Fox about in a graveyard just after dawn? And why would the presence of a priest drive him away?

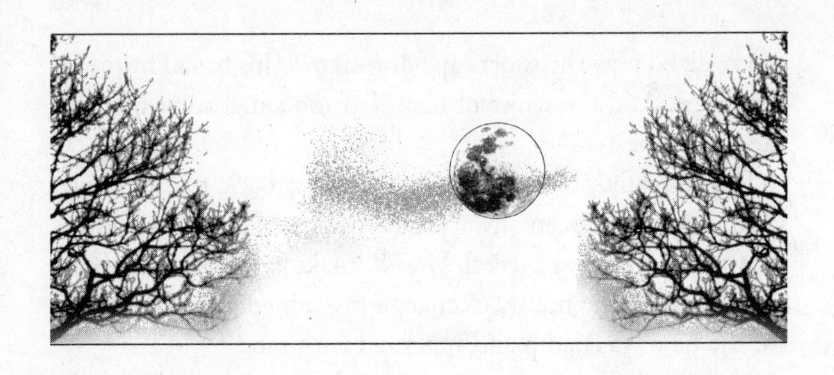

Chapter Eight

Henrietta and Miss Harris were at the breakfast table with the family when I arrived downstairs a half hour later. "Mama promised I could join the adults as a treat since I had a lovely sleep with no nightmares," Henrietta boasted. She fairly bounced in her seat with pride. "I know you are riding out today for a hunt, and Papa said last night I might watch from the veranda." She frowned at me. "But you are not dressed for riding."

I gave her a quick kiss on the forehead before taking my seat. "Indeed, I had quite forgotten today was the hunt."

"But you are going, aren't you?" She looked at me eagerly. I saw admiration shine in her eyes that I, a woman, was to be included.

"I shall change my dress immediately after breakfast," I promised as I placed my napkin on my lap. "I would never disappoint you, Hen."

"Imagine," Sebastian said. "We've a Hen and a Fox. Shall I change my name to Horse?"

Roger grinned as he dabbed his napkin to his mouth. "If my daughter were not in earshot, I might make a suggestion along the lines of a certain kind of mule."

Mary made a disapproving tsk at him. But we were all in high spirits. Henrietta was so bright, so much herself, that her happy, shining face filled me with relief and joy. *Whatever has been troubling her is done,* I thought. If there was ever anything at all.

We were soon joined by the others from the neighborhood. Mr. Hess was in high color, ready and eager for the day's activities. Brooding Ted Pentworth had brought a chum with him, a very dashing Mr. James Farrington, and Sir William bored them with his lectures on the best way to bag game. Everyone was anxious to be off.

Mr. Fox made an appearance, but he seemed sullen and removed from the rest. He declined to join the party. I made it a point to ignore him. "I'll collect my mount and join you after I've changed," I told Roger as I hurried toward the stairs. "Really, I promise I'll be quick as a wink."

I was better than that, and not ten minutes later, I dashed across the back garden toward the stables. Sebastian was about to canter out of the paddock, but paused to laugh at me. "Have the stables furnish you with an old roan mare, or a pleasant doddering nag so you will not get thrown."

Offering a haughty toss of my head, I replied with equal good humor, "I may be a wretched horsewoman, but you have not seen me shoot. I will best you, I promise."

"Is that a challenge?" he declared, clutching at his chest. His horse high-stepped backward artfully, as if performing a dance. "Ah, I see another quality I like in a friend. Emma, you have a wicked streak. No wonder Mr. Fox is so intrigued with you."

I turned away from him, my humor gone. "Hush. Someone will hear."

He laughed, enjoying teasing me. "Admit it, he is an interesting man."

"He is a boor," I said, and picked up my pace, striding purposefully toward the barn.

I told a rushed stableman I required a tractable mount and he brought me the sweetest-tempered mare he had. "She'll do you fine," he said as he tethered the reins to a post. "I'll send someone out right away to saddle her for you, ma'am. I've got to run these boots out to Mr. Farrington. He just tore his heel and must borrow these."

It was a few moments before a groom emerged from the tack room. "Oh, thank goodness. We must get her saddled . . ." My voice died.

The gypsy strode out of the shadows, carrying the tack. I froze, a dark, hot feeling crawling up the back of my spine. As he laid the saddle on the mare and cinched the strap, his gaze stayed on me, his eyes alive with the insolence he'd displayed before.

I was acutely aware that he and I were alone. Everyone else was too far away and too busy with their preparations to hear any call for help I might make. Had I possessed more sense than pride, I would have fled.

His lips curled under his mustache as he grabbed the reins he'd just buckled into place and, twisting the horse savagely, pulled them down and over with great and sudden strength. The beau-

tiful creature surged forward and I jumped clear as she danced nervously in my direction. The maneuver took me deeper into the dark stable as the restless mare, her high-stepping hooves pawing the ground as her eyes rolled in the aftermath of such rough treatment, effectively blocked me from the open door.

"Have a care," I said sharply. My heart was now beating furiously. Behind me, the inner corridor of the large barn was dark. It was empty, all stablemen being needed on the lawns with the hunting party.

He pulled on the horse roughly again, drawing her forward to crowd me. She reared slightly, and I was afraid she would strike me. I heard him speak in a low tone. The syllables were strange, clipped and guttural. He was speaking in another language.

He smiled at me, and spoke so I could hear. *"Tu vei nu interfere cu Draculae avion."* Then he jerked the horse, who skittered, swinging her flank toward me.

Terror and rage mingled to make my voice sharp, imperious. "What are you doing? Stop it. Stop it at once."

He murmured again to the horse. The mare grew more agitated, and I retreated further into the barn to get away. To my great relief, he did not follow. He continued to murmur in his foreign tongue, teeth flashing as his laughter joined in, and he nodded to me, as if I'd pleased him.

I started down the row of stalls into the dimly lit barn. The air was different here, thick and cold. It shouldn't be so cold, I thought. It was like an icehouse, or like passing from summer to a frigid January night in the space of a step. Behind me, the gypsy led the horse outside and closed the stable door, and I was cast into darkness.

Now I could smell the rank odor of the air around me, as

if no one had mucked the place out in weeks. The few horses left were as agitated as the mare had been, moving restlessly in their stalls, whinnying to each other. Then, underneath it all, I heard a whisper, like the sound of a soughing tree, and they fell silent.

My eyes had adjusted so that even in the darkness I could see the ash-gray collection of blackness coalescing in one corner. I threw myself against the stable wall. The sense of something putrid, something terrible, raised the fine hairs on my arms and the back of my neck.

The gypsy hadn't been threatening me. He had been driving me in here, to the dark thing that I'd sensed before. And now I was alone with it.

Everything was so still.

The sound came first, the slick noise of muscled bodies scraping across the floor. I whirled wildly, primitive recognition shooting into my veins. I looked and found them, a phalanx of snakes slithering among the straw, all rushing toward me.

My mind, shocked for only a fraction of a second, sharpened with a sudden clarity of senses heightened by fear. I picked out four snakes on my left. To my right, I spied three more. Their attack was swift, direct, and, I could only assume, intended to be deadly.

The first snake rose and tensed to strike. Its mouth yawned open, and I watched in fascination as a sliver of light fought through the gloom to set the long, pointed fangs glowing like luminescent pearl. This could not be a species of earthly origin. As it hovered, I felt a preternatural sense of intelligence emanating from the creature.

As the thing lashed forward, I hauled up my skirt, without thought or a plan, and struck at it with my foot. The thickness

of my boot was a gift, for I had no fear of a bite. I did not miss. My foot, snapping with a force I had not known I possessed, connected with the head and cast the serpent back.

No revulsion registered as I pressed my heel down on the stunned creature's flat skull, leaving the thing twitching on the ground. But the demise of this first did nothing to discourage the others. The next reared in front of me while a second coiled itself into a tight spiral to my right, eyes slit with eerie consciousness.

The only weapon at hand was a pitchfork. I could hardly hope to spear the swiftly moving targets on the slender tines, but I grabbed the thing anyway, my arms moving almost of their own volition. It felt good to hold the weight of some barrier in my hand, even if I had no concept of how to use it effectively.

When the second snake opened its mouth, showing its fangs in a wicked display, I struck first. But it was a trap; I saw three other snakes rushing toward me, an unearthly odor coming off them. Suddenly, the pitchfork was in motion, sweeping first to my left, then to my right. When I looked, two ropes of dead flesh hung from the tines. The third lay struggling under my boot. I snapped it with a twist of my ankle.

I had not a moment to consider my unexpected ability, for three other snakes remained. Two circled, while one hung back, watching as if to see what I would do next.

Again, I did not wait for the attack. I spun the pitchfork, using the wooden tip of the handle to sweep the ground, hooking the snake I was aiming for and sending it against a wall with sickening force. It fell to the ground with a dull thud, leaving behind a wet smudge on the wood. Shifting the weapon in my hands, I bore down on the second. It hesitated, feinting to one side, but my reflexes resisted the trick and I flung the pitchfork with effortless aim, watching as it landed, tines down, with the snake writhing in its death throes under two of the three points.

The quiet rustle of retreat spun me around to see the last snake fleeing into deeper darkness. In defiance of reason, I charged. I did not even bother to retrieve my weapon—such as it was. I simply dashed forward, intent on not allowing that last one to escape, when suddenly a dark figure cut me off.

It was the gypsy. And this time he was not smiling. His eyes burned above the shining bare edge of a wickedly curved saber. My eyes fixed on that blade. It was foreign, ancient, etched with scrolled designs that made it beautiful.

He said something in his language, his words broken and sharp. My reflexes failed me, and I had a sinking feeling of defeat as I saw the muscles of his hand tense and his knuckles whiten on the hilt of his blade as he drew back to strike.

In thickly accented English, he said, "Your mother will weep, Dhampir. You should have stayed asleep."

The sound of an explosion startled a cry from me, and I jerked back. The gypsy convulsed, his eyes wide and furious for a terrible moment before they rolled back and his body collapsed on the floor at my feet.

Dazed, I could only stare down at him. I saw the dark stain of blood saturate the dirt creeping toward me. Repulsion drove me back. I raised my gaze and turned to look behind me.

Mr. Fox's pistol was emitting an acrid thread of smoke, behind which his dark, shrouded eyes regarded me with calmness and curiosity. "Mrs. Andrews," he said, his voice as rough as sand. "Are you quite all right?"

It took several tries to find my own voice. "Yes. Yes, I am."

He lowered the weapon. Stepping closer, he gazed down at the body. "Do you know who he is?"

I shook my head. "He is merely a stable hand. I don't know why he tried to harm me."

I could hear shouts, and the sound of people running toward us, most likely summoned by the sound of Fox's shot, but Fox and I simply stared at each other, a silent bounty of words unsaid. Just before chaos descended, he spoke, his tone low, urgent, resigned. "We must talk."

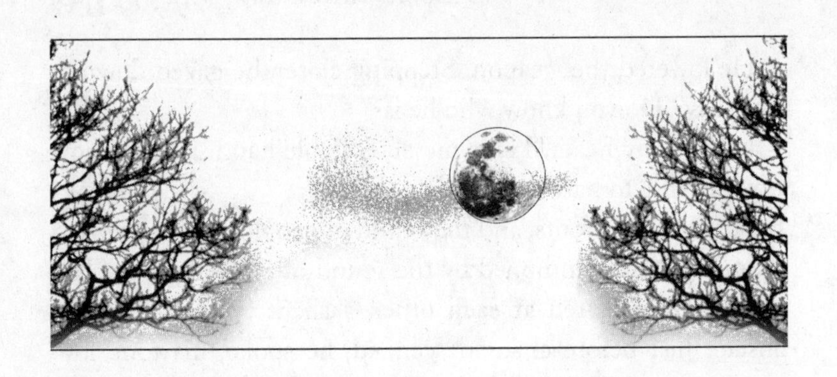

Chapter Nine

I was bundled away by Sebastian, who held me close to him, as if to shelter me from any further harm on the short walk to the house. He could only mutter, "My God, Emma," and shake his head. I was capable of even less. I was in a stunned state, moving numbly as he directed. I did not want to go back to the house. I wanted to confront that damnable Valerian Fox and demand—finally and forcefully—he tell me everything.

Sebastian deposited me in my room, ignoring my pleas not to summon my sister. Though I knew this was not the sort of affair one could keep secret, I nevertheless dreaded her reaction. As predicted, Alyssa arrived in full panic, flying at me and flinging her thin arms around my neck. "Emma! How could you possibly be involved in such a sordid, distasteful affair?"

I did not have the strength to be angry with her. Mary, who was just behind her, gently extricated me from my sister. "Now, Alyssa, it is not good to upset yourself. And we must think of Emma."

"I am sorry to be so much trouble," I muttered. I lay my hand over my eyes, warding off the echo that had been playing relentlessly in my head. *Your mother will weep, Dhampir. You should have stayed asleep.*

I suddenly felt ill.

Mary led me to the bed. I rolled my face toward the wall. "I think I should rest. Would you please excuse me?"

My sister promptly burst into tears. "My Lord, you are so wretched brave, aren't you, without a thought to me. What would I do without you? Did you consider that?" Covering her face, Alyssa fell to weeping.

I was moved by pity, sitting up and taking her gently into my arms. "There, darling, we've all had a fright."

"It should be you sobbing!" She said it like an accusation.

"Why should I, when you save me the bother?" I smiled, and she sniffed, her shoulders shaking. "You let me be the brave one."

And, in a way, it was true. I was the practical one, strong, reliable, sensible. And she was free to come down with the vapors at the slightest provocation. If she envied me my strength, then I could admit I thought it might be a blissful release to let loose with just a bit of emotion, a few sobs once in a while.

Now, for example, would be an excellent time for such an indulgence. A man had tried to murder me today. What an impossible reality to try to absorb. And if that weren't enough, what had come over me? I'd crushed snakes under my heel. I'd pinned them with a pitchfork, using the weapon with precision that was nigh-unfathomable. No one could do what I'd done. Yes, I was a good marksman—an instinctive shot, my father had called me—but how could I have possibly wielded that weapon as I had done?

The knock on my door came just before dawn. I'd been expecting him all night, knowing he would not allow too much time to pass before he sought me out. I had no hesitation of opening the door, and no thought for convention. My night rail was modest enough, and I'd drawn a wrapper around me.

Fox was fully dressed. He said nothing until he'd closed the door softly. "I trust I did not wake you."

"I could not sleep."

He nodded. "I apologize for the intrusion into your bedchamber at this hour."

I laughed, then caught myself. "Mr. Fox, really, can we dispense with such useless observances of propriety. Men and women have been creeping in and out of bedrooms for centuries with less provocation than we two have between us this night." I crossed to the bed and sat on its edge. "Go ahead," I said, indicating the wing chair in the corner, "you might as well be comfortable."

He did as I requested. He studied me for a moment, then asked, "Mrs. Andrews, did you truly kill six snakes with nothing more than a three-tined pitchfork?"

"Oh, Lord! Did they see?" It was bad enough *I* did not understand what had taken place—what would the others, who had rushed in upon hearing Mr. Fox's shot, make of it?

He shook his head, making a calming gesture with his graceful hand. "I did away with the carcasses before anyone noticed. I must say, some of them had been pinned, and quite smartly.

I can only imagine the skill . . . Roger had bragged about your marksmanship, but this was beyond the pale."

"I'd no idea I was capable of such accuracy." I thought of how my hands had grasped the handle of the weapon with expert balance, my shoulders easy with the weight of it, and I shivered.

"You are uneasy," he observed calmly.

To my disgrace, tears stung my eyes. "I am terrified." I jerked my head to confront him. "You must tell me everything you know. I am quite desperate."

He nodded. "Indeed, it is time for us to be honest with each other, I think. I regret caution has required me to refrain from speaking freely with you, as I wished to do, but I had to make certain that you were friend and not foe."

"Surely, you could not think I would ever intend any harm to a living soul."

"I have found that people do not often live up to appearances. I have also found that it is best to expect nothing from others, and anticipate everything."

"And you trust no one."

He inclined his head, pausing for a moment. "You did something utterly astonishing today. And I know you saw something at that tree when I found you and Henrietta near The Sanctuary, did you not? Yes, Mrs. Andrews, you are part of the disturbance here at Avebury. But I do not think you are at the heart of it. You are a bystander, like me, but connected all the same."

"I have the same sense," I confessed. "The idea that this has something to do with me, or something about me. Why is it I see things, sense things, when no one else does? I thought I was going mad."

"You may wish you were," he muttered. "My coming to Avebury is not by chance. Through means far too lengthy to go into at the moment, I became aware of the thing you refer to as Marius. I have been hunting this thing for . . . many years."

"What is it?" I said. "What is this thing, Marius?"

"I could explain," Fox went on, "but that is not my preference. I have come here to request you come with me, now. With what you've already seen, showing you what you need to know will serve my purpose better than words that, I fear, will be too fantastic to digest and too easily dismissed as error, or my insanity, or pure malefaction. Will you dress and meet me outside your room?"

"Where are you taking me?"

He hesitated. "Dawn is nearly here. I would like to be underway as soon as possible."

I drew in a shaking breath, considering his unusual offer. I did not entirely trust him, but I was too intrigued to refuse his request. "All right," I said at last.

I donned an old woolen dress, for the chill of early spring was heavy on the ground, and wrapped a cloak around my shoulders. He met me in the hall and took me out through the library doors, onto the flagstone terrace. "Stay close," he murmured, grasping my arm.

We ventured into the thin, gray light, down toward the barn. He glanced at me. I guessed he was wondering if I would balk at returning to the scene of the attack. I did stay close to his side as we entered the stable. The acrid odor of horse sweat and manure assailed me, but it was at least pure. Not the putrid scent that had permeated my nostrils before.

I proceeded close behind Mr. Fox, who paused to turn up his lamp. Placing a finger to his lips, he led me inside a stall. My boots crunched a fine dusting of small stones underfoot. A

thick rope of something banged against the door, writhing like a snake and causing me to flinch. Fox saw what had startled me, and the corner of his mouth jerked down.

"Sorry. Merely garlic," he murmured.

Garlic? I hardly had time to assimilate this when the light that spilled into the stall illuminated a shrouded figure laid out on a long plank set between two barrels. I stepped back quickly, slamming against the closed gate as I realized where he'd brought me. And who that was.

"No!" Fox held his hand up to stay my panic. "Mrs. Andrews, please trust me."

"I most emphatically do not trust you, sir!"

When I would have let myself out of the stall, he grabbed my shoulder. "For God's sake, Emma, do not turn your back on it!"

The use of my Christian name was perhaps more disconcerting than what he said. In any event, I froze, and my gaze connected with his through the light cast from the lamp he held in his hand. The shadows and planes of his face were like a mask. But his eyes implored me, and my body relaxed.

"It?"

"The man known as Wadim."

"What are you talking about, Mr. Fox? He is dead. You killed him."

The way his head moved slowly from side to side in denial caused my temperature to plummet. "I did not kill him. I merely dispatched him from one revenant form to another. Come and see."

Knowing full well I should have fled, I crept behind him as he lifted the covering from the body. I expected to see the gray-green pallor of death I'd looked upon before, when my father and Simon had lain in the parlor amidst the cloying scent of flowers; lips that would never speak or kiss faded to a shade of white tinged with violet.

But these lips were scarlet, bright under the silky black of the groom's mustache. The cheeks were flushed with vitality. I sprung back. "He is not dead!"

"No, not in the sense you mean." Taking me by the shoulders, Mr. Fox turned me to face him. "Do you know yet what I am about to confess?"

I did. A part of me already knew. But the mind cannot fathom such a reality; it resists, as mine had done. It pleads a trick of light, a fanciful perception, even madness. It longs for reasoned explanation, it mutinies against the plodding advance of what is sensed and felt and, ultimately, realized.

Of course I knew.

"He is a vampire, Emma. This is a vampire, and we are going to kill it tonight."

The ridiculous statement was spoken aloud, heard by human ears, and now it existed as more than a thought. Or a fear. *This is a vampire.*

"I saw him in the day," I said, my voice strained. My eyes cast nervously to the body. "He cannot be what you say. They . . ." *Say it.* I swallowed. "Vampires cannot emerge in the daylight, isn't that so? I mean, everyone knows this . . . the legends, I mean."

Fox bent to the satchel in the corner. I recognized it as the one he'd brought with him to Sarum Saint Martin's churchyard. "The Romanians call them *strigoi vii.* Living vampires. Human servants, bound by a vampire master, to serve as minions while they are alive. They feed like any other revenant but

do not have full power. They gain that, and immortality, when they die." His tone was crisp, businesslike, and he spoke rapidly as he hefted the weight of a mallet in one hand. Then he straightened, his quick eye examining a long, sharpened stick double the width of my thumb. His head swiveled to his quarry. "Wadim will rise, now *strigoi mort*."

My mind screamed in rebellion against what he meant to do. I was shaking so violently it was like a palsy. *He is wrong!* I thought suddenly. What was I doing here? This man was going to drive a stake into this body under the absurd belief that he was killing a vampire.

The body had not stirred. Fox approached it with his weapons in hand. "I did not kill this man, Wadim—if that is his real name," he said. "He is not dead, but neither is he alive."

"If he is truly what you say," I said, backing away, "then why is he lying there like that? Wouldn't he defend himself?"

"When he wakened tonight, he could not feed because I sealed him in with garlic and salt, trapping him here."

Salt, I thought. I had not crushed rocks underfoot earlier, but salt.

"He is young," Fox continued, "that is, newly made. He might have received the three bites years ago, but in death, he is a child. He is not strong enough to break the seal, as flimsy as it is." He glanced out of the gate, down the corridors to the doors we'd left open. The sky was not much lighter. "I would have preferred to wait for full daylight. There is no sense taking any chances, especially with you present. But the servants rise early. Stablemen will be about their work when the sun rises. This was as late as I dared."

I said nothing. He glanced at me. "Are you all right, Emma?"

I opened my mouth, but said nothing. He spoke more softly, as if sensitive to my incredulity. "He is what I have said. You will see."

And although I wanted to flee from this madness, I felt he was right. I did believe. Slowly, I nodded.

He solemnly held my gaze for a moment, then turned to the body, raised the stake, and placed the point of it on the man's chest. "You will see everything in a moment."

The hiss of my indrawn breath cut through the air as he raised the mallet. Sharp-edged sanity reared one final time, and I was struck with a deep sense of horror. I wished to scream, and to stop the sound, I stuffed my fist in my mouth. But I did not shut my eyes, and so when the body animated, I saw everything.

There was no twitch of muscle, no stirring of breath. The eyes of the gypsy simply opened, the hands flew up, fingers clawed, as he sprang into attack. The action was utterly unexpected, and it took Fox by surprise, which allowed the vampire to throw off the stake. As the weapon hit the floor, rolling beyond the pool of the lamplight, Fox staggered back a step, brought the mallet up, and swung the massive head with an audible whoosh as the corpse rose.

There was no question the fiend was, in truth, alive, not when I saw it draw back its blood-red lips. Fangs—nothing less than this term can suffice to describe the unnatural canines protruding from under the heavy black slash of the vampire's mustaches—gleamed. Its eyes glowed malevolently, and it reached for Fox.

Fox slammed the head of the mallet into the creature with a force that stunned it, but did not repel it for long. Catching its balance with shocking agility, it lunged forward and grabbed Fox by the throat. Fox did something with his hand, a sharp jab to the neck made with dazzling and seemingly unnatural swiftness, and the gypsy hissed and sprang back.

"Fox!" I shouted, and snatched the rope of garlic from the peg, tossing it to him. His hand lashed out and caught it in midair. The gypsy grew more wary, eyeing the herb.

"Get the stake!" Fox barked, but I was already on my knees, feeling around in the dark. I kept one eye on the creature. Its empty black eyes, when not fixed on the garlic, flickered to me. Its hateful mouth worked over those hideous teeth, and my fingers went nerveless with fear.

"Here it is," I called, standing and turning in one motion when suddenly the gypsy lashed forward. I dropped the stake as Fox and I jumped apart to avoid the strike. Now the gypsy was in the middle of us. He immediately turned toward me.

His face was eager. The words he had spoken earlier drummed in my head. *Your mother will weep, Dhampir. You should have stayed asleep.*

It was not a moment later when the pointed tip of the stake burst through the gypsy's chest. There was no fountain of blood, no thrashing protests. He—it—simply fell to the ground, first to its knees, then back, the stake protruding squarely in the middle of its chest.

I gaped, awed by the sudden transformation as the pall of death leeched the color from the creature's face, bleaching it rapidly before my eyes. The point of the stake was rusty with dried blood. Fox had pierced it straight through, spearing the revenant with astonishing force. His strength took me by surprise, for he was lean, and though by no means frail, his lithe, elegant form did not give the impression of being capable of such power. But then I called to mind how he had lifted me so easily onto his horse when he'd carried Henrietta and me away from The Sanctuary. He had surprised me then, too.

The gypsy's mouth worked vaguely, and I imagined it was trying one last time to sneer at me, as if it weren't defeated at all. As if it knew some secret that consoled it as it slipped into death.

I felt numb. Over and over, I told myself that we together had not killed a man. *It was already dead*, I repeated in my mind, hoping to make it real.

Fox went down on one knee beside the body. "Quickly. The servants will be up soon."

I did not move for a moment. My world had tilted, and I was off balance. Disbelief—despite the evidence of my eyes—held me in its fist. It is the nature of human love for predictability, safety, and the comfort of the known to want to deny that which threatens those things. At this moment, my every instinct wanted to flee from what had just happened. Had there been a retreat, some method to coil myself into a safer reality, I would have fled gladly.

No such blessing came, however, and eventually I recovered slightly, and fell in beside him. Moving mechanically, furtively, I worked together with Fox to perform the laborious task of extricating the stake, then rolling the body on its back.

As we did so, I noticed a small design on the corpse's arm, what appeared to be a serpent's tail. "Look at this," I said, pointing to it.

Mr. Fox frowned and peeled back the sleeve to expose the entire forearm, revealing a tattoo of a dragon rampant, its tail

coiled around its body, its jaw open to show prominent teeth, and its forearms bristling with claws. Something about Fox's reaction made me look at him, startled.

"Do you recognize it?" I asked.

"It is a dragon," he said simply.

"I see that. Is it important? You reacted strangely."

He seemed reluctant to say. "It makes me wonder about something, a legend. I do not know much about it. But perhaps this is something to do with the Dragon Prince."

Perhaps it was how he said it, but my blood suddenly went cold. "The Dragon Prince? What is that?"

He snapped his gaze to mine, as if he'd been caught in his own thoughts. "I have heard whispers of the Dracula, but most do not dare to speak of him. More than the name, I do not know. I have seen others react to this symbol. The dragon is greatly feared, and the legends around it are shrouded in a great deal of mystery."

"And you think . . . this was him? I was attacked by this . . . Dracula?" I asked. The name was frightening. I could not understand why, but just the sound of it spoken aloud called forth a primal kind of dread inside me.

He gave a dismissive laugh and a shake of his head. "No, surely not the Dracula itself. I am no doubt mistaken. Come, help me put him back onto the planks."

I did what I could to aid him in placing the body back on the slab and adjusting its clothing to cover the chest puncture. Then we draped the tarpaulin over it once again.

"I will have to return to the corpse once it's buried, to take its head." He gathered up his tools, stuffing them into the sack. "The old Kashubian method of laying the severed head between the feet and anointing the whole with millet seeds will be enough for a revenant of his magnitude."

One would not think I could still be horrified after what I'd just witnessed, but the brutal method of dispatch he'd described and his casual tone shocked me. "My God," I could not help but utter.

He gave me a curious look. "It's what I've done to every victim of the damnable 'wasting disease.' It is no illness, Emma. The damned master vampire I've hunted here is feeding, although I do not understand why. He just glutted himself in Amsterdam . . ." He bowed his head under the burden of his thoughts. "I do not know if his intention is to make others like himself. Perhaps he seeks to raise an army. I've heard rumors to that end. He has come to Avebury for a specific purpose. Something about this place is special. It is not one of his usual haunts, and vampires are creatures of habit."

I was somewhat dazed by this information. "Make others? Other vampires?"

"Of course. It taxes his strength, but he may have need of reinforcements." He might have been discussing the habits of sheep for all the emotion he put into his words. And yet, each one fell like a brick, pelting the thin veneer of my old world and exposing me to a great and terrible knowledge I was suddenly sure I did not want.

Oblivious to my horror, Fox continued, "That is why I have dispatched all of the dead, just in case." He peered at me, half-smiling. "You did not think every vampire victim becomes one himself, do you?"

"I . . . I can't say I've given the matter much thought."

He was finished packing the sack, and began to scatter the salt with the toe of his boot, grinding it into the dirt, erasing

all evidence of what we'd done. "If that were the case, vampires would have taken over mankind a long time ago. They'd keep us to feed, as we keep cattle."

I wrapped the cloak about me more tightly and stared at him. Fox shouldered his bag, and said, "That is it, Emma. The night's work is done. But the battle is far from over. Marius will not like to have lost this one."

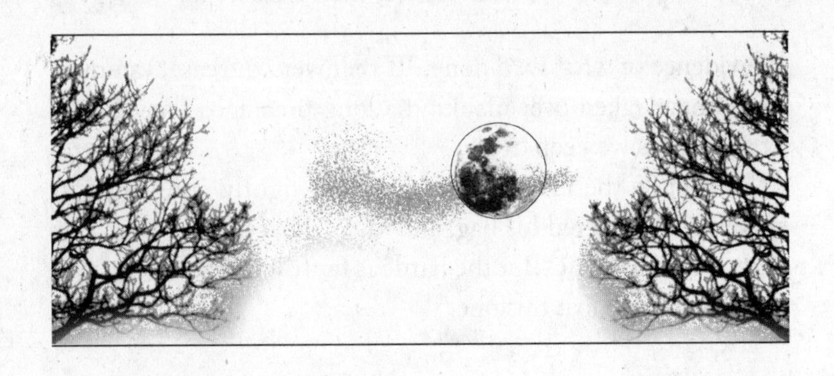

Chapter Ten

We returned to the house under cover of the last vestiges of night. A gray vapor crawled knee-high along the ground, a cloying, choking mist, and I felt stifled, needing air. I stumbled, because my knees went weak, I think. My strength was gone.

Fox's hand was tight on my arm to steady me, and a strange thrill caught me, caressing its way under my flesh in a way that was not unpleasant. It occurred to me that despite having been a married woman, I had never shared anything as intimate as this night with Simon or any other man.

I gathered my wits. "What happens now?"

He was grim as he explained. "There is a sophisticated vampire hierarchy based on power, age, and how a creature feeds.

Wadim was among the least of them. Marius is a great lord, a master of others and one of the most powerful among his kind. The loss of his servant is only a minor setback, but one that will not please him."

We waded through the fog, our footsteps muffled. A sense of unreality pursued me like a stubborn shadow. I thought, *Vampires?*

I did not know if I wanted to believe it or not. I looked at Fox. His stoic face in profile, seemingly so confident, calmed me. We could not both of us be mad. "How is it you know of these things?" I asked.

He did not answer at first. Then, carefully, he said, "Sometimes we are exposed to things we would never choose to know. If we survive, we gain experience. If we are lucky, we gain expertise. I've traveled to the eastern regions of Europe, visited Istanbul, and even gone all the way to far Egypt. I've spent a long time learning what I could."

"Egypt!" I was amazed. "That is a very long way."

"It was the only means to know the things I sought to know. There is no study of revenants and ghouls to be taken at university." The smile he wore was a mixture of self-deprecating humor and sadness. "One has to carefully trace the plethora of legends to find the truths in them. It can be tricky, for they are mingled with useless superstition and outright lies. But I have learned that a vampire reliably moves within a cycle of hunting grounds. He will set up in a location, a town or village, and make a few like himself, either *strigoi vii* or minions to aid him. He cannot do this easily, or often, and he must be at his full power."

He stopped in his tracks, and his voice changed. "It takes three bites of a special nature to make a vampire," he said, a leaden rasp to his voice. "And each costs the host dearly, for the victim is transformed farther and farther from his human nature with each bleeding. It costs them their very blood. Some die trying to make another, especially on the first bite, which is the most draining for them. Others can do, and even become adept, so always with great taxing of their power."

"Then why do they do it?"

"The undead are social creatures. They crave their own society." His gaze drifted away as dark thoughts clouded his features. "Often they hunt together. It is play to them, you understand. Sport."

These terrible words hung in the air, suspended in the mist. Fox took my elbow and we resumed walking. "When they have fed their fill from a place," he explained, "the vampires move on. They are nomadic, visiting the next hunting ground in turn. It will be a generation or more before they return to a particular one. This is how I know Marius has not come here before to hunt. There are no legends, no past plagues or supernatural lore here to hint of his past visits."

"He is killing. Those deaths, the bloodless corpses, they have to be his work." My head shot up with a thought. "I thought the vampire bit here," I said, touching my fingers to the soft, warm spot on my neck, just behind my earlobe. "The artery that supplies the blood to the brain. Would there not be evidence of such a wound?"

He nodded. "None of the victims of this local plague have displayed such signs of an arterial wound. If it had, talk of a vampire would have generated well before this, even here in England."

"Then how does he . . . ?"

He made a motion with his hand, a gesture of pure frustra-

tion, then stalked a distance and stopped. "One such as Marius has special charms to seal the wound with a drop of his own blood, for vampire blood is imbued with magical properties. When he is at the proper strength, and with enough time after the kill, he can cover the evidence of his crime."

He glanced at me. I had the feeling he was trying to gauge how I was taking all of this. When he saw I remained calm, he appeared to relax. "There is another subject that has been on my mind," he ventured. "The time, or rather the season, is important, I am convinced. Certain seasons, I have heard said, affect the power of these creatures. This is spring, and there are important feasts coming that have long been recognized as times when evil is strong." His steps slowed as we neared the house. "In fact, Beltane is nearly upon us."

"Is that not May Day?" I asked. The tradition of going Maying was very much in fashion among villagers in the countryside where I grew up, if nothing more than for an excuse to drink and act bawdy. It was a night in which girls like Alyssa and I were tucked into bed early. "The traditions of May Day have to do with fertility."

He paused. We'd reached the back gate but did not go further. "Did you know it is the custom at Eton for the boys to collect hawthorn switches on Beltane? They use the boughs to ward off evil, for hawthorn is considered holy."

I froze momentarily, then recollected myself. Had he meant to catch me off guard with the mention of the hawthorn? He knew about the tree, I was certain. "May is a mere five weeks away," I observed.

"I believe that is all the time we have to understand Marius's purpose here."

My heart leapt to my throat, beating so forcefully it nearly choked me. "My God. Henrietta. She thinks he is her friend." Several beats of silence passed, after which I asked in a small, frightened voice, "What do you think he wants with her?"

Fox spread his hands in an open gesture. "I cannot assure you of much, but I feel safe to assume he does not mean to feed from the child, for the simple fact that if he did, he would already have done so. He must intend to fool her, trick her into doing something he wants or needs."

"But what could he want, or need, from a child?"

He appeared genuinely regretful. "I wish I could tell you. To have a child in the sights of such a creature, it is unspeakably horrible. And I know you love her a great deal."

I nodded numbly. I was not reassured that we had discovered anything in our discussion to help Henrietta.

"I will attempt to help you safeguard her," he said, and his voice had a new quality. It was softer, gentler, as if he were sensitive to my fear. "I know you have sensed, or seen, things, haven't you? Can you tell me what these are? It might help."

I had resisted trusting Mr. Fox previous to this, but no more. I believed him when he said he, too, was concerned for Henrietta. Thus, I surrendered my reservations and told him everything, from my first twinge of headache upon arrival to a detailed account of the serpents' attack in the stable.

"It seems it all centers around Henrietta," I said in conclusion. "Do you not agree?"

"It appears to be the case. Perhaps he is merely using her to gain entrance to the house," he said contemplatively. "Children are easily beguiled because of their innocence, and they trust so easily."

"So it is true a vampire cannot enter a house unless invited?" I asked.

"It is one of those superstitions that turns out to be true."

"I cannot say I know much of vampires."

He cut me a look. "You will need to learn quickly."

I clutched my cloak about my shoulders. The chill of the morning finally penetrated my numbness, and my teeth began to chatter. "I think she is resisting him for now. That explains the nightmares. Do you think he will give up and leave her alone?"

"He shall try some other means," Fox said darkly. "If he wants something in this house, he will not relent. With a house that size, it will not be difficult to find someone else to aid him if he wants entrance. I wish I could tell you a better hypothesis, but it seems he wants that child, Emma."

So Henrietta was not safe at all, nor were any of us.

"I think you should go inside now," Fox said. "You are getting cold."

The household was already awake, we found as we passed through the garden gate. Cook was bustling in her kitchens. A yawning lad of eight tottered off with his bucket to the chicken house to gather the freshly laid eggs.

We used the French doors in the library, and I was able to slip upstairs unnoticed. I crawled into bed, my exhaustion sudden and complete, closing my eyes tightly. I tried to remember what it was like when Simon was alive, the sanest time of my life. In an effort to find some comfort for myself, I imagined he was here with me, sleeping silently beside me. I had but to turn on my back, and upon the pillow would be his silver hair, his bold features in repose.

What would he think of what I had done tonight? As indulgent, as doting as he had been, I doubted even my dead husband would find any understanding for the driving of a stake into the heart of a revenant.

But I had done such a thing with Valerian Fox, and I was not ashamed. My shaking eased. I had helped drive an evil creature back into the realm of death. I thought of that, then, and in time my sleep came, dreamless and deep; what my stepmother used to call the sleep of the just.

The world, upon my waking late in the morning, was different. I lay abed, wondering if I'd dreamt the early morning's mission to the stable. If I had, it had been the most frightening nightmare imaginable, for it had seemed real. Could I truly accept the existence of vampires? Such things were mere legends, terrible creatures fantasized in superstition. But I had seen the creature Wadim come back to life. I had battled the serpents and through some spectacular, completely unanticipated skill, killed six. These things were not my imagination.

Those were not the only reasons that convinced me that what was happening here in Avebury was real. The other I can only name as instinct, although that is not an adequate way to describe it. More my nature, I think, unfurling slowly, jerkily, incrementally aware that there was a world beyond the safe, ordered existence of the human race, and that, for some reason, I had acquired a particular glimpse into it.

I rose with a sense of purpose and dressed quickly, anxious to meet with Mr. Fox. We had much to discuss.

However, Alyssa was waiting for me, casting aside her cards when I entered the drawing room. "Emma," she cried, indicating the seat next to her on the couch. "I have to talk to you about the embroidery for the baby's layette. We must get started right away and I haven't decided if I'm going to do daisies or roses."

I almost quipped that either would be inappropriate if the child were a boy, but realized such an observation would not be

appreciated. I adopted an indulgent manner. "I am sure whatever you decide will be lovely."

Mr. Hess was holding court, and I overheard him mention The Sanctuary and something about a Catholic church. "Saint Michael's was never taken over, either by the Tudors or Cromwell, which is remarkable as it is quite a wealthy holding."

Mrs. Bedford said, "This is the parish up past Overton Hill, and you say it lies directly upon this line?"

"What do you think is the right time to begin letting out my dresses?" Alyssa asked, pulling my attention away. "I shall hate being fat and misshapen . . . Emma. Are you listening?"

"Indeed, yes," I answered, although this was only partially true. I regretted I could not be more attentive now that Alyssa finally needed me to provide the kind of companionship she required. "Maybe some new shawls will be the cure," I said, thinking quickly. "If you collect some really interesting pieces, you can wrap yourself in them in any dress and they will draw the attention from your condition."

Her mouth made a small "O" of delight. "I have the Chinese silk, of course," she declared excitedly. "I could embellish some others. I am skilled with a needle."

I was delighted with my cleverness. She and Mary began to discuss the possibilities, and as the two of them were amply distracted, I was able to eavesdrop once again on the group behind me.

Mr. Hess was speaking. "So our Saint Michael in the Fields is part of the Saint Michael Line, you see."

"Not our Saint Michael's, surely," harrumphed Sir William, rolling his eyes, "as we are no papists."

Hess's previous profession as an Oxford don became evident as he warmed to his subject. "The power meridians of which I speak have to do with ancient beliefs in forces that flow naturally through the earth's body."

"Pagan nonsense!" declared Sir William.

"Indeed," said Mr. Hess, "that is the popular opinion. I have been trying to get a paper published on the subject for an eternity, but the obvious is all but ignored. That does not change the fact that there is ample evidence of forces scoring the surface of our earth, spiritual paths where things out of the ordinary are common occurrence."

"What are these forces?" I asked, twisting in my seat, abandoning the pretense of attending my sister.

"The sort of thing the old religions of the area used to know," Mr. Hess said with a warm smile for my interest. Behind him, Sir William scowled darkly at such talk, but Mr. Hess, bless him, was immune—if not unaware—of the disapproval directed at him.

I was intrigued. "This meridian, then, what exactly does it do?"

"Well, that is the thing, isn't it—how can we know? All that is known is that when the Christians came to our fair isle, Rome made it a priority to take possession of the pagan shrines along the line that stretches from Land's End to East Anglia, and each one, including newer churches and chapels, is dedicated to Saint Michael the Archangel. And the line cuts directly through the heart of our village of Avebury."

Mr. Bedford cleared his throat. "Saint Michael being the great archangel, God's general, you recall. It was he, in fact, who defeated Lucifer, and cast him straight into hell for the sin of pride." He was using his pulpit voice, and the final three words rang with victory.

His wife leaned in eagerly. "My husband's point is interesting. Think of this, Mr. Hess. Saint Michael defeated the devil and this same fallen angel appeared to Adam and Eve in the form of a serpent. Can this be the connection to that stone serpent figure laid into the downs?"

"Just so," Mr. Hess agreed with a smile that bespoke he was of the same mind.

"Indeed," Mr. Bedford interjected, adopting his sermonizing voice, "it was to tempt a weak-willed woman that the serpent appeared in Eden. He appealed to Eve's vanity."

Mrs. Bedford did me the favor of a silent reprimand in a manner only a wife could deliver. At her scowl, Mr. Bedford appeared alarmed and lapsed into silence.

"Emma!" Mary's voice was sharp, bringing me around with a start. I realized I had forgotten my sister.

Alyssa had tears in her eyes. "I see you can scarce be bothered with a word I've said. Well, if I'm boring you, I'll take myself away. I do hate to be trying."

She fled the room. My conscience flared.

Mary leaned forward. "I know she is difficult, Emma, but think of her condition. Pray hurry to console her before she becomes overset."

Any other time I would have rushed to do exactly that. In fact, I rose, poised to follow my cousin's advice, but at that moment Mr. Fox appeared. He caught my eye meaningfully.

I realized my unhappy choice. Of all the times I'd wanted to take Alyssa into my arms and comfort her, now that she needed me I could not capitulate.

Mr. Fox was waiting.

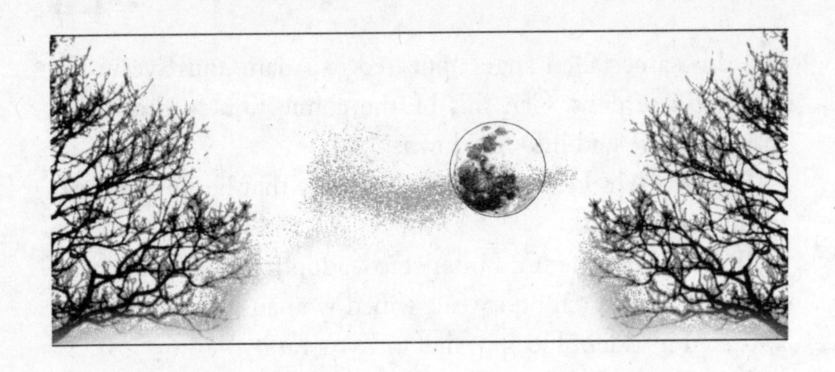

Chapter Eleven

We arranged to meet in the small room across the hall, a formal drawing room unused at the moment. Pleading different excuses, we slipped out—he first, then I—and tiptoed across the parquet of the center foyer.

When I entered the room, he crossed to me, and took my hands in his. "Are you . . . well?" he asked, peering at me deeply.

I daresay, I was not unmoved by his sincere manner, nor the warmth of his hands folded over mine. His nearness, too, made my head feel a bit light, and I was unnaturally affected by the scent of his soap, some exotic, spicy aroma that hinted of the travels to Turkey and Egypt he'd mentioned.

"I seem to be," I said, somewhat dazed. I was used to his

being aloof, even rude. This attentiveness was disconcerting.

One corner of his mouth jerked in a semblance of a smile. "How many times have you decided that you are insane, or that I am?"

I smiled. "Too numerous to count."

"And it is not yet a day. It is not something one takes on easily." He was closer than he needed to be, but it felt comforting. "You have, I must say, responded amazingly well. No shrieking or pulling of hair. You are of an astonishing constitution."

Yes. I'd noticed that, too. "I suppose I have," I replied.

"I wonder if you've experienced phenomenon like this before. The sightings you described, the shadows and such?"

"No. Never." I disengaged my hand and walked stiffly to take a seat. "I found the source of the quote carved into the trunk of the hawthorn tree. I told you it reads 'The Blood is the Life,' if you recall. That comes directly from the Bible, the Book of Deuteronomy, to be exact, which says . . ."

I closed my eyes and concentrated, bringing forth the words I'd committed to memory. "'Only be sure that you do not eat the blood: for the blood is the life; and you may not eat the life with the flesh.'"

"How extraordinary," he murmured, pacing the width of the expensive Aubusson carpet, then back again. "But if I recall that portion of the Bible, these were just dietary laws for the Jewish people."

"Yet it reads like an uncanny prohibition against the evil temptation to drink blood and live into eternity. Do you see? It further links the tree to Marius. That place must have a particular significance."

He paused, staring. "Indeed."

"Marius is drawn there, and it is located in a rather unique spot. Mr. Hess says that ancients have built an immense temple to the dead here in Avebury, as represented by the stone monument stretching along the entirety of Overton Hill. He was just now expounding on his belief in something called a power meridian, which runs through this area, as well as other spots significant in the lore of pagan mysticism. This was something he called the Saint Michael Line."

Fox grew thoughtful. "I must find an opportunity to speak with Mr. Hess. But for the moment, I wish to ask you something which has been much on my mind since yesterday. It is about what you did to the snakes in the barn. You described that they attacked, an event which would disconcert any person—to say the least. Yet you dispatched all but one with alacrity, using only a pitchfork and ingenuity." He was assessing me with his dark, dark eyes. And there was something there, a suspicion glimmering just below the surface as he asked, "Exactly how does a gently bred lady such as yourself come to possess such skill?"

"I am sure I do not know, Mr. Fox, and that is the truth." I was not about to discuss the deep grip of tension I felt over this very matter. For all of the madness of the past week, this was the thing I could not quite assimilate. How *had* I done what I'd done?

Wishing to change the subject from me, I asked, "Do you have any idea where Marius has his . . . well, I hardly know what to call it—bower? I assume the folklore of a vampire needing to return to his grave is true."

He knew my ploy, but went along with it. "I have not found it. In all my years of tracking him, I've succeeded in locating it only once, when it was guarded by a very capable minion, a particularly vicious Punjab fellow I hope you never have the misfortune to meet."

"It must be on The Sanctuary. He favors that place."

He cocked his head as a thought struck him. "I've looked, I assure you. But only the most outrageous stroke of luck will help us uncover it. He has not lived for centuries by being careless when he sleeps, for that is when he is most vulnerable. The cleverness in concealing his bower is nearly impenetrable. I know of no way to locate it other than to follow him to it, which happened under extraordinarily singular circumstances when I accomplished it the one time."

I mulled over what he had said. "So if he must burrow in his grave during daylight, how is it he appeared to Henrietta, and to me?"

He folded his arms over his chest, stretching the seams of his coat over his broad shoulders. This must have been uncomfortable, and he asked, "Do you mind?" indicating he would like to remove the garment.

I waved him on and when he had doffed the confining thing, he explained. "Keep in mind he did not emerge from his slumber, but merely sent a shade of himself to communicate with the child. In this form, the creatures are quite literally invisible. Except to some." He narrowed his eyes and considered me for a thoughtful moment. "Children are sensitive to these things, for their innocence makes them vulnerable. And perhaps your love of the child made you equally so."

Not a bad theory, but I did not quicken at consideration of it. Nor did he. I could see how he was watching me, a close scrutiny that was far too intense. Disconcerted, I rose and paced to the window. I was annoyed, although uncertain whether the object of my irritation was he or myself. “The dreary weather wears on one’s nerves,” I said idly. “I’ve never seen a more dismal spring.”

“He commands the elements, you know.”

Yes. I had heard that long ago, listening to dark, frightening tales as a child. A vampire can summon a storm. “You make him sound invincible.”

He said nothing, not even when I turned to face him. I wished he had. Mr. Fox was looking at me with a peculiar and decidedly uncomfortable fierceness of concentration. “There are those who are born to fight the vampire. Those with innate powers. Gifts. Even a master vampire such as Marius fears them.”

A strange sensation bubbled up inside me. Fear and excitement. Fox blinked, as if catching himself having given up intelligence unwittingly. He made to turn away, saying, “We should get back to the others. They will come looking for us soon.”

I grabbed him by the arm and turned him forcefully back to me. My strength was no match for his and had he wished to leave, he would have done so. Yet he was kind enough to attend me with a patience that surprised me.

“Mysteries and riddles again, Mr. Fox? Have we not gone past this point?”

There was a fine dew of sweat on his brow. “You will not thank me for the question I am about to ask, but very well, Emma. Tell me, what do you know of your mother?”

My head snapped back, as if I’d received a slap. “What?”

His gaze was sly—or was that my imagination? I was never quite rational on the subject of my mother. For too many years, I’d suffered innuendo and avoidance.

He leaned forward. "Your mother, Mrs. Andrews. Who was she?"

"Her name was Laura Newly. Why?"

"And what do you know of how she died?"

"She . . ." It struck me that he had not asked if she were alive or dead. I began to feel a vague disorientation, such as when extreme anxiety dulls the wits. "Sh-she was ill."

"Ill, was she? A wasting disease?"

The implication nearly felled me to my knees. Rage and horror rose up in me, licking at my nerves like flames. I stood breathless and seething as I stared back at him. "That obscene suggestion does not merit a reply."

"It was not a suggestion, and you mistake me, Mrs. Andrews. I am not implying what you think." His sharp eyes narrowed. "Yet I am interested why it riles you so."

"Because she was . . ." I broke off, the words damming up in my throat, nearly choking me. Did he know of her illness? Had Mary or someone else mentioned it?

I took a moment to compose myself. "Why are you asking about her? Just what are you saying, Mr. Fox? And what, if anything, does it have to do with what is happening now?"

He clearly regretted having spoken. What was most maddening was that I knew from the tension coming off him that there was good reason for his strange interest in Laura, but he was not ready to tell me what it was.

"I think perhaps I made a mistake," he said slowly. "I should not have ventured into such a distressing topic. It was insensitive of me, and is clearly none of my—"

"I thought you wished to help me!" I accused.

He frowned. "Emma, I do not wish to overset you."

It was far too late for that. "Why do you not simply speak plainly, Mr. Fox?" I said.

He hesitated, hovering in indecision a moment before inclining his head. "I think my error was in doing exactly that," he murmured. "And I have spoken out of turn. Do pardon me."

The sense of betrayal hit me. He was no ally. His brief period of honesty with me was over. I whirled and stalked out of the room, furious.

Then I remembered what Wadim had said—he, too, had spoken of Laura. I felt dizzy for a moment, a slow, creeping sense of fear settling over me. What had any of this to do with my poor, mad mother?

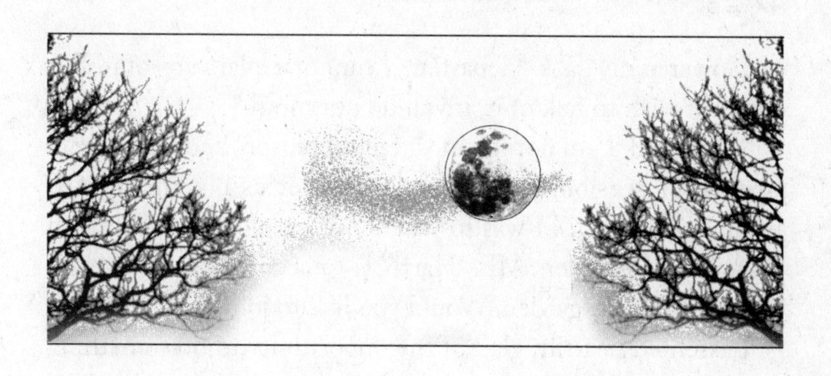

Chapter Twelve

I am not speaking to you, of course," Sebastian said on a sniff as he passed me in the hallway. "You have been ignoring me all day. You gave us all quite a fright yesterday, after all."

I altered my path and followed him. "Shall you refuse to accept my heartfelt apology?"

He sighed, pausing with his hands folded and laid across his chest. The pose of mock hauteur meant I was to be permitted to make my case. I played along. "It was thoughtless of me to neglect you. Even though I had nearly met my end, I should have realized you needed my attention."

His eyebrows rose and he smiled. Then, his mask broke, growing serious. "Emma . . . What happened out there?"

I lowered my gaze. "Sebastian, I cannot explain any of it. But I do not wish to talk of it, if you do not mind."

"Very well. I am not the most tactful person, and if I've tread upon your sensibilities, I regret it. So, let us put the dratted business behind us. I was to take Hen for an outing, although under Roger's orders Miss Harris is to accompany us. We are just going in the garden. Would you like to join us?"

I assented heartily, glad of the opportunity to do something other than brood on the swirling confusion of my thoughts. The moment I was out of doors, the scent of earth, moist and soft after the winter's thaw, enveloped me like perfumed arms. The sun was out, but the air held a slight chill. I could have used my shawl, but didn't wish to go back into the house for it.

"How is the mysterious Mr. Fox?" Sebastian asked companionably as we walked.

"Mr. Fox is the kind of man who follows a solitary path," I replied sourly. "One will never plumb his depths."

Sebastian snickered. "But one tends to want to try."

"Not I," I vowed.

Sebastian sighed. "Lud, it is so utterly *provincial* here. I am reduced to squeezing a paltry scandal over you and Fox, and I know full well you are doing nothing improper." He paused and peered at me hopefully. "Are you?"

I laughed and laid my hand on his arm. "Pray bear the inconvenience a while longer. I fear my boredom would become intolerable were you to leave."

He patted my hand. I had the sense that he was touched. "I suppose if it matters so very much."

It did matter, I was surprised to discover. "You are very good to indulge me," I countered with a touch of sarcasm he appreciated.

Henrietta was waiting for us with Miss Harris. The four of us played Pass the Slipper, which was our little girl's favorite game. As Sebastian was fond of Blind Man's Bluff, we played that next. I was chosen to be "it" first and Sebastian conspired with Hen to torment me with evasion until the poor child felt sorry for me and let me catch her.

Afterward, we lolled on a blanket spread on the lawn. "In the summer," Sebastian said as he looked about the garden, "the air is scented with lavender, a favorite of mine. There's feverfew, dianthus, and catmint. It is quite beautiful."

The day was so very pleasant, an anathema to the darkness that had surrounded me of late. Henrietta jumped up, exclaiming, as a black-and-gold butterfly danced across the lawn. She skipped off in pursuit, Miss Harris behind her.

Sebastian leaned back and sighed contentedly. I regarded him thoughtfully. "Why is it you enjoy Henrietta's company so?"

He laughed. "There is a freedom being with a child. Maybe not any child. But Henrietta is unique. She is . . . well, she is quite perfect. She is simply the most pure human being I've ever met."

"She is very special," I agreed.

"Why do you?" he countered. "Shouldn't you be concentrating on having babies of your own?"

"What a personal question. However, I shall answer it. I do not expect to have children of my own, for I shall never remarry. I like my independence too much. As for Hen, I adore her. It's that simple. And she doesn't disapprove of me, which has been a rare thing in my experience."

"Just so," he murmured, then lapsed into silence, closing his eyes for a quick nap. I sat beside him while he slept, contented with my thoughts until the grass moved unexpectedly. The thought of snakes sent me leaping to my feet with a small cry, but I saw quickly that it was only the wind.

Nevertheless, I was reminded of my uncanny accuracy in battling the snakes in the barn. I wondered if I could do it again. I had heard that people were capable of amazing feats in moments of crisis. Perhaps that was all it had been. I had always possessed excellent aim anyway.

To test myself, I picked up a rock, took aim at a low-lying leaf, and let the stone fly. The trajectory of the missile was a blur, but the leaf I'd selected disappeared with a barely audible snap. I stared, amazed at my accuracy.

Maybe that was too easy. I tried again, this time aiming higher, to a leaf buried among others. My eyesight was keen, but even I could barely pick it out. I threw the rock, this time aiming less with my eyes than with some inner instinct. As before, the leaves around the one I'd selected were undisturbed, but the one I'd tried for was gone.

I began to grow excited and I raised my gaze to the topmost branch. Taking a moment, I chose the target, a jutting twig as thin as my finger. I'd have to hit it at just the right point. The weapon I chose was a fist-sized rock, perhaps too much of a challenge to throw so far, but I'd need weight to break off the branch.

I felt something happen within me this time, a weird, lifting feeling inside me, an increasing of certainty, a narrowing of focus. Throwing the stone, I heard the sound of breaking wood follow immediately.

I retrieved the branch to study it. It had been severed clean, a seemingly impossible accomplishment. My hand trembled as I studied my work, dazed with incredulity. I carried it with me

back to where Sebastian dozed, fingering the cleanly cut pulp, my head swirling with disbelief, exhilaration, and worry.

I did not have much time to reflect on my unexpected abilities before Henrietta and Miss Harris appeared. I tossed aside the branch, as if it somehow gave me away, and fixed a bright smile on my face. But my expression of welcome never materialized, for my body seized up, frozen solid by what I saw.

Something was tangled at Henrietta's skirts. I blinked in an effort to focus on the strange, shifting shape. It seemed to be some kind of mud or . . . mist of some kind. Black mist, twisting in elongated tendrils, slithering in her wake and around her ankles.

I opened my mouth but caught myself. An inner sense told me neither Miss Harris nor Sebastian would see anything amiss. But I could see it, as clearly as I saw the ribbons on my little cousin's shoes. And I saw something else, as well. Behind her came the tall, masculine shade I'd spied once before, at the hawthorn tree.

It loomed above her, keeping just behind. I could feel its malevolence, that sense of something putrid and foul in the air—not a smell, exactly, but affecting me as noxiously as the worst stench, the same odor I'd detected in the barn.

Oblivious, Henrietta walked contentedly with her nurse, her smile as untroubled as the stretch of azure sky above us. She did not know he was there. She'd seen him before at the tree, but today she was unknowing of the shadow that slipped greasily over the newly greening trees, doggedly in her wake.

Panic rose violently inside of me. Henrietta was not safe at all. Marius was still with her.

* * *

Trembling with the aftereffects of what I'd seen in the garden, I battled an unreasonable sense of betrayal as I entered the house, for my first instinct was to go to Mr. Fox and tell him. But Mr. Fox was not my friend, nor my ally. His surreptitious questioning about my mother had brought that starkly into focus. Whatever terrible danger threatened Henrietta, I would be the only one to face it, defeat it. But how? I did not even understand the first thing about what was happening.

So deep was I in my thoughts that I did not notice Mary until she was upon me. "Emma, I need to speak to you about Alyssa. She is in a state over what she views as your neglect of her lately."

"Yes, yes," I said, but my attention was leagues away. Marius had done away with Victoria, and I knew why. The cross around the doll's neck had glowed the night I'd heard the tapping. I remembered that the priest in the graveyard had held a large cross, the anchor to a large row of rosary beads, and this remembrance put me to mind of the little church nearby, Saint Michael in the Fields, which Mr. Hess had spoken about.

Crosses and churches and priests. The old legends pitted these icons of Christianity against the revenant world. Yes, there was power in these holy things.

Mary laid a hand on my wrist. "I know you've always longed to be close. This is the time, Emma. Alyssa is older now, a woman, about to be a mother. You and she might find the friendship you've always sought."

I blinked, trying hard to concentrate on what she was saying. "Oh, Mary, you know I love my sister. You and she are all the family I have, and I would do anything for either of you. But I cannot do what you ask, not now. There is something very

important, something vital I must attend to. I cannot explain." I brushed past her.

She called after me. "Will you—?"

I did not hear the rest. I found my bonnet and put it on hastily, stopping in the kitchens briefly to ask the direction of the church. I set out on foot. It was late afternoon, and as I had no idea where I was going other than generally in the direction of the "old circle" on Overton Hill, I was wary of the time. If Marius were still seeking Henrietta, night would be the time when his powers would come into full. I needed my answers before the sun set.

I was able to locate the church and rectory without trouble. The difficulty came when my knock on the rectory door went unanswered. A reasonable alternative to the priest being home was his being in the church itself, so that was where I went next.

The outside of the building was unassuming, but inside the cave-like structure, dimly lit magnificence opened under a row of high, pointed arches of the nave. The fading light broke into color as it passed through the stained-glass windows, falling on me as I strode the marble aisle.

The silence of the place swallowed the sound of my footfalls. I had never been in a Roman Catholic church before. Everything was ornate and alien. I swallowed, the hallowedness of the place overwhelming me. Everywhere I looked, bold images of Christ, his mother, his apostles, his saints, stared at me with solemn, pitying eyes.

"May I help you?" a woman's voice inquired.

I started, leaping about to face a diminutive woman dressed in black. She smiled in apology. "Oh, dear, forgive me for frightening you. I thought you would have heard me coming. One cannot sneak around this place, with the echo. That's how I knew you had come in, I heard your footsteps."

"I . . . was . . . looking . . ." I indicated the paintings, the statues, the windows.

She nodded, as if she understood how awesome it could be to the uninitiated.

"May I see the priest?" I asked quickly, recovering my wits.

"Oh, Father Luke is not here, dear." Her eyes held genuine sadness. "May I help you with anything? I am Mrs. Tigwalt, the good father's housekeeper. I keep the church up, too." She looked about proudly.

"Goodness, surely you do not do all of this cleaning?"

"I oversee a small staff, a family of sisters from the village who do most of the dusting and polishing, and their father who keeps up the gardens." She folded her hands in front of her. "It's a modest parish, but we who worship here love it."

"It is magnificent." For its size and its humble appearance from the outside, I had not expected Saint Michael in the Fields to be so grand.

"I can show you," she said eagerly. "The church has been here for more than four hundred years, you know." She pointed to the painting behind me. "Here is our Blessed Mother, cradling Jesus taken down from the cross."

I stared at the pathos painted into the beautiful face of the Madonna, and in this place, the rendering of her suffering might have made me weep had not Mrs. Tigwalt hurried me on to the next exhibit.

"And here is Saint Michael, casting Lucifer into the bowels of hell," she said, leading me to a more primitive painting. The halo and wings of the angel might have been drawn by a child, but the face of the fallen angel was hideous, perhaps because it was so crudely wrought. The demon had never looked more vile, its visage seethingly malevolent, while the angel, not quite as majestic as he would appear in later Renaissance art, wore a bland expression, as if his duty meant to him no more than ridding the world of a fly.

"The Stations of the Cross were done in the late seventeenth century." She indicated a panel showing Veronica wiping the blood from Jesus's face, a crowd of leering onlookers behind.

I peered closer, something having caught my eye on the wooden faces of the ugly mob. My heart quickened. Was it my imagination or was that a suggestion of protruding canines on one of the faces?

My heart lurched in reaction. I peered closer, but could not make out the details. I wondered if having thoughts of vampires teeming in my brain was causing me to see things. The religious iconography was indeed suggestive to my imagination, and as the light was bad, I concluded I could not be correct.

I drew back, composing myself. "Is Father Luke usually home for dinner?" I suddenly wanted out of this church, to conclude my business and get back to the manor.

"Oh, he'll be along, although sometimes he is gone until late. I can give him a message if you like."

I thought of the message I might entrust to Mrs. Tigwalt and felt a giddy rush of hysteria. *Yes, please inquire as to the proper vampire remedies, as a very beloved child is being currently afflicted by a higher-order lord of the undead.*

What I did say was, "If you would tell him I called, and would like to speak with him. He can send a message to Dulwich Manor with a time that would be convenient."

"I can do that, dear," she said, smiling cheerfully.

Over her shoulder, I spied another depiction of Saint Michael's great triumph over his brother angel, Lucifer, but this time, the devil was depicted as the wily serpent who had stolen paradise from mankind. The image made my breath catch, for I was becoming increasingly certain this symbol was of some significance. Its frequent occurrence could not be coincidence.

I saw that in the broody, finely wrought painting, which was done in a much more detailed and formal style than the previous one I'd viewed, there was a disturbing suggestion that this creature was more than a mere snake. The serpent seemed to have clawlike hands that were raised to attack the archangel, but these were nearly obscured by foliage the painter had placed around the image. There was no mistaking the scales on the spine which tapered down to a pointed tail. And there was a shadow behind it that could have been, if one were looking for it, a hint of wings.

I swallowed hard, digesting the implications of what I was seeing—or thought I was seeing. Was this indeed a dragon? More important, did it have some significance to the dragon tattoo Wadim had borne, something to do with what Mr. Fox had referenced as the mysterious Dragon Prince? What had he called him?

The name came back to me. The Dracula.

Then my attention was stolen by something else in the background. I heard my own sharp intake of breath hiss in the reverent quiet of the church. Mindless of how I must look, I rushed forward, pointing to an object in the upper right-hand corner of the painting. "That tree. It is the tree on the meadow, by The Sanctuary."

Mrs. Tigwalt came up behind me. "What is that, dear?"

I was not mistaken. The slender trunk, the dome of tangled branches—it was a unique and instantly recognizable shape. However, I realized how I must sound, so I forced myself to smile and say casually, "What a coincidence."

"Oddly shaped, isn't it? It must have been done by a local artist. He obviously used the nearby landscape as the model for his work."

"Of course." It was a reasonable explanation, I told myself. It could all be mere coincidence, made to seem more by my overexcited imagination.

"Sometimes, artists use symbols to represent meaning in their painting. Oak trees, being strong and lasting, would be an excellent representation of Saint Michael's powerful position as God's right hand."

Her earnestness made me smile. "It is a hawthorn," I told her softly.

"Oh, well, then that is even more significant." Her eyes widened and she nodded sagely. "Hawthorns are holy trees. They are the only tree that blooms at Christmastide as well as spring, which indicates God's special blessing through that tree in the season of His son's birth."

I recalled Fox telling me about the May Day ritual of the Eton boys, using branches of hawthorn to ward off evil. "So it is a symbol of good?"

"Indeed, yes. You know, of course, the story of Joseph of Aramethea at Glastonbury Tor?"

"I . . . I'm afraid I do not."

She tsked, shaking her head as she took my arm and led me along the wall, down to a particular carved panel depicting Jesus being taken down from the cross. "Joseph was Our Lord's friend, a wealthy patron, and it was in his tomb that Jesus was laid. You did not think a poor carpenter could afford a stone tomb such as that, did you?"

"I recollect him now," I assured her.

"He became one of the first Christian bishops. He sailed north, landing on our island at Glastonbury, back when all those marshes were under water and Glastonbury lay on the coast. There he struck his staff on the ground upon setting foot on land, and a hawthorn tree sprouted from it. This is the Holy Hawthorn." She smiled triumphantly, her eyes glowing. "It is still there today, some say, for being holy, of course, it has survived the ages."

"What a very interesting legend," I managed to say.

Her look soured. "It is not legend. It is the truth. And he put the chalice of Christ in a deep well very close to it. You know, the Holy Grail. Why, the water still runs red with Christ's blood even today."

"Of course," I murmured, though my credulity was strained. "Thank you for showing me your beautiful church."

"Oh. Well, come back any time, dear. My, look at the hour. It's long past when I should be starting the father's supper. Would you like to stay and eat with us?"

"I am afraid I cannot. They are expecting me at the manor. But I will come and see you again."

She tried to be cheerful, but clearly she was disappointed to be losing me. "Come early, dear, and we'll have a nice tea."

I paused at the doors of the church, my gaze straying to a silver bowl set upon a table against a wall. Above it a crucifix hung, and I swallowed at the sight of that broken body.

On impulse, I turned back to the housekeeper. "Mrs. Tigwalt, as you know, I am not a Catholic. But I came here today

because I am having some difficulty, and I think this church has given me solace."

Her eyes glistened instantly. "Oh, dear, that is so very good to hear," she said with passion.

I felt guilty for my deceit. Except it really wasn't completely untrue. "Might I trouble you to ask for some holy water?"

"My goodness, of course, dear. I have only to get a jar for you to take it away in." She began to rush toward the back of the church where a door stood at an angle from the main exit doors. "There should be something back in here. People do like to take the holy water. Let me see, what can we use as a vial?"

The room contained a stock of priestly vestments and an assortment of objects—cruets for the water and wine and dull flat trays with handles. While Mrs. Tigwalt was distracted rummaging about, I slipped quickly to the other side of the nave where it opened into the narthex. The symmetrical design of the church demanded another font.

I took the matching crucifix from its nail, muttering a quick prayer of forgiveness. The urgent and secretive need that pressed upon me was not logical, but I felt desperate. I secreted my boon in my reticule and resumed my position in time so that when Mrs. Tigwalt emerged with a tiny vial and dipped it into the basin, I appeared to have gone nowhere.

"Thank you," I said, offering a coin as she pressed the talisman into my hand.

"Oh, my dear, no!" she declared, clearly horrified that I would try to pay her.

I could not have her refuse. For my own conscience's sake, I would insist on remuneration for what I'd stolen. "For the poor," I urged, and she relented.

“All right then. You had better hurry, missus, if you are going to make it back to the manor before dark,” she urged.

“Please remember my message to Father Luke.”

“Oh, my dear, I am going to tell him all about you.” She beamed. “He adores this church as much as I do. He’s absolutely devoted to it. He’ll be so sorry to have missed a chance to show it to you.”

I waved weakly, realizing I had just made a grave error. I’d needed the crucifix. But, now, when my theft was discovered, I would no doubt be a persona non grata with Mrs. Tigwalt and Father Luke, generous donation aside.

And I needed Father Luke to tell me what he’d been doing in that graveyard.

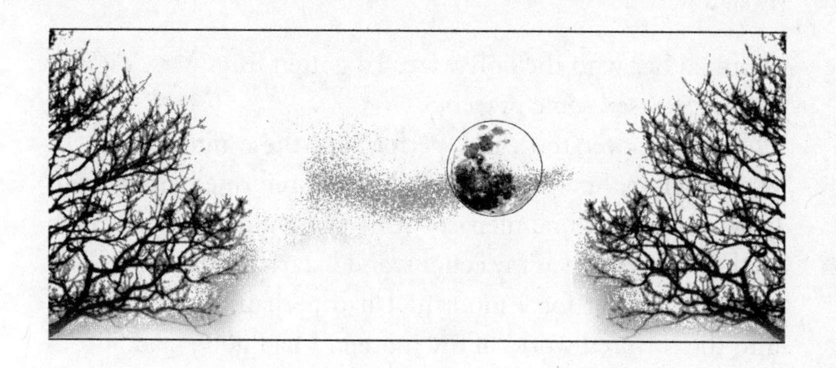

Chapter Thirteen

That evening, after a tense supper, I played cards with Alyssa to make amends. She was sullen, but allowed my penance.

I did not permit myself even so much as a glance in the direction of the brooding Mr. Fox. He sat amongst our company, wrapped in the dark thoughts he'd never share. He had made that very clear when he'd refused to explain his inordinate interest in my mother. Whatever strange path Mr. Fox walked, he walked it alone.

As did I. And though perhaps I did not know all, or even enough, I knew something. Thus, when everyone was abed, I stole into Henrietta's room as silently and stealthily as a thief. I anointed her with the holy water I'd gotten from Mrs. Tigwalt and improvised some prayers.

Standing over the child, performing these ministrations, I was struck by how easily my reality had reformed around this belief in supernatural menace. Tears pricked my eyes. My own credulity marveled at my actions, and I stared at the vial of holy water. I thought for a moment I had perhaps indeed slipped into the tortured world of my mother. I had gone mad, just as everyone knew I would.

There was a certain freedom in believing this, if I could. There would be no shadowed fight to be waged, and Henrietta would really be safe. I would trade my sanity for that, I knew. I would lay down my life and more for the child, embrace madness if it meant I could see her live free of the evil I felt around her even now, for my senses seemed sharpened toward it.

Henrietta lay undisturbed, her full, rounded cheeks flushed with the kiss of untroubled sleep. An impulse bade me touch the stolen crucifix against her skin. What else could I do to safeguard her against the night? Should I spread salt about, as Fox had done? And garlic—was that a powerful repellent, as superstition held? I needed to research what kinds of things were held by tradition to ward off evil.

I fell asleep in a chair by Henrietta's bedside until a breeze rifling through the room woke me. I was sure no window had been left open. Immediately alert, I leapt to my feet and rushed into the schoolroom. The furniture, blanketed in the deep coal-gray of shadow, appeared as strange, disjointed forms, taking on sinister aspects in my unsettled state of mind.

I noticed a sudden drop in temperature, more than could be accounted for by the breeze. I followed the bank of windows to discover the last one at the far end stood open. The pitch of the

moonless night lay silent this early in the spring. Somehow that silence was eerie, unnatural.

I put both hands on the sash, pulling it down with all of my strength. The heavy frame of glass rumbled in its tracks so that the sound I thought I heard behind me was almost swallowed by it. But not quite. I heard, distinctly, the scrape of a shoe on bare floorboards.

I whirled to find the room empty. Despite the evidence of my eyes, I had the strangest feeling it was not vacant at all. I waited, my hand gripping the purloined crucifix, until all was quiet once again.

"You are avoiding me," Fox said to me immediately after breakfast. He stood close to me because he did not wish to be overheard. However, I found his proximity strangely and disturbingly distracting.

Mary's shrill call saved me from having to make a reply. "Come, now, everyone, we are to have a croquet match!"

"Do you play?" I asked Mr. Fox, assuming an arch tone as I moved past him.

He narrowed his eyes as he fell into step with me. "Admit it. You are put out with me."

"I am merely accepting of the state of affairs between us. I realize we are not friends, not even business partners, but only had a common purpose for a time. That time is over."

He lifted his head, an arrogant gesture I was not sure whether I despised or admired. I held my tongue, although I wanted badly to tell him what I thought of his cryptic references to my mother, for our last interaction was still firmly lodged in my craw.

Had I thought he would give over one small detail of why he had found the topic of my mother's fate relevant, I would have pursued our conversation, but I'd despaired of his being forthcoming. "I am going to play croquet," I said as I brushed past him. "May I proceed?"

I picked up my pace, joining the others gathered on the lawn. A few moments later, he departed, and I was annoyed at the pang of regret I felt at his absence.

Putting matters of Mr. Fox firmly out of my mind, I applied myself to my mallet and ball. As I tend to excel at sporting activities, I did well in the match; Roger crowed at his cleverness in selecting me for his partner.

"For me," he announced to a glowering Sebastian and bored Mr. Farrington, who were our opponents, "the game is not so much here"—he swung his mallet smoothly—"as here." He tapped his temple, then looked meaningfully in my direction.

"Roger, please do not provoke our guests," Mary chided. She and Alyssa were seating in rattan chairs that had been carried out to the lawn in preparation for our eating luncheon *al fresco* later. "You are being a beast."

"But I am winning, my love," he called cheerfully.

He howled with pleasure when I struck Mr. Farrington's ball and, placing my foot on my ball, delivered a steady stroke that sent his far into the rough. Sebastian groaned and threw himself into an empty chair. "That is the end of us!"

The game quickly transformed into a rivalry of the two brothers. When it was concluded and we'd won, Sebastian groused while Roger gloated. We rested afterward under the shade provided by the Grecian-style folly and refreshed ourselves with glasses of lemonade so cold it made my teeth ache.

A maid came from the house and whispered to Mary. My cousin's head came up sharply, and she turned to me, her eyes very wide. "But, of course, Beth, show him in."

She waved to Roger, who bent his head for a moment before jerking it back up to stare at me as well. "Well, well," he said, and smiled broadly.

The momentary mystery was solved when a lean figure, walking slightly bent over a silver-topped cane, emerged onto the flagstones and made his way down the three wide steps to the lawn.

I recognized him at once and stood, exclaiming, "Uncle Peter!"

His smile upon his seeing me bent his eyes with deep pleasure into half-moons. "Emma, my love," he purred in his heavily accented tones. He folded me in his arms, neither one of us caring about the spectacle we provided for the others. "I am so very glad to see you."

Emotion welled inside me. The man had been my Prince Peter in all of my stories, and my Sir Peter when I needed a knight to rescue my imagined imperiled self in a daydream. His patience and attention had given me reason to suspect I was, after all, someone of worth, even if only to him.

"Whatever are you doing in Wiltshire?" I asked, pulling back to look at him. His face was lined more deeply than when last I had gazed upon it.

"Why, I've come to see you, of course." He paused meaningfully, his gaze boring into mine—never losing his smile—before lifting to include the others. "And Alyssa and her new husband."

On cue, my sister drifted forward, presenting her cheek coolly. She was miffed at the slight, which had been rather obvious, of his having taken special notice of me first. "Hello, Uncle Peter. It is good to see you."

"You are as lovely as ever, dear Alyssa. And Mary, my dear,

you grow as regal as your great queen. I hope you do not object to my descending upon your house party."

Mary greeted him with genuine warmth. "Indeed not, Mr. Ivanescu. You do us an honor."

Mary had loved him, too, I recalled. Alyssa and I had made her a third daughter-in-residence when Uncle Peter visited so she wouldn't miss any of his perplexing riddles, the amazing sleight of hand he was apt to produce to surprise us, or the thrilling stories that were his specialty when he was in the right mood.

"I am staying in the village inn, of course. I would have sent word, but I could not resist seeing the surprise myself." Again, his gaze rested upon me.

Mary was appalled. "But you must stay with us."

He held up his hand. "No, I will not hear of it. Besides, my man is unpacking my portmanteau even as we speak, so the matter is quite settled. But I will not quibble if you were to offer me some of your lovely English tea."

"Yes, yes, come in, please. You must meet everyone."

I followed, dazed and deliriously pleased. Mr. Fox had materialized again, and he tried to catch my eye, but I was not of a mind to tangle with him at present.

Within moments of Uncle Peter being introduced to the group, his old-fashioned elegance worked its magic. He must be near seventy, I thought, but he was still handsome. His hair had gone gray years ago, but it was thick and swept luxuriously from his high brow. A hawk-like nose gave his face the aspect of keen intelligence.

After he'd taken refreshment, Mary tried to press him into the parlor games she had planned for the afternoon. He refused

politely, and I picked up on the cue, offering to take him for a stroll in the garden if he desired.

"Splendid," he announced, coming to his feet with a rather laborious effort and use of his cane. The silver snake head glinted in the light. I thought of the serpents in the barn and shivered.

When we were away from the others, I steered him to a stone bench, and he took his ease gratefully. "Now we are alone," he said with satisfaction. "And at last you shall tell me, child, what is wrong?"

The cadence of his words was both familiar and exotic. He spoke with a "v" in place of the "w" and the "i" long. The comfort in his invitation, spoken musically in those exquisite foreign syllables, was like a warm rush of air after a long stay in the cold. It brought back such wonderful associations of happy times, and I almost missed the significance of his question.

"Wrong?" I was taken aback, gaping at him at this show of prescience.

He took my hands in his. I remembered them as large, capable, and strong, but they felt frail to me now. "I received your letter." His eyes were searching. "And I suspected that you were in some kind of distress. I had the feeling I should come."

"But how did it reach you so quickly?"

"As it happened, I was at my London house when your post arrived. I set out immediately, for you seemed distraught, although you tried not to be obvious. And you asked about Laura. You mentioned she had been on your mind." He peered at me intently. I wondered if I was imagining the caution in his gaze. "Can it be you are remembering the past?"

I replied, "Only a little. I have been . . ." I paused, not sure how much to reveal. "I have been in a strange state of mind of late."

His gaze grew piercing. "Did this upset you, to think of your mother?"

"I remembered something at last. I never had any memories of her before."

"And what did you recall?"

I was *not* imagining the tension. He remained very still, as if braced for what I was about to say.

"I saw her weeping. It was very clear in my mind. It still is, in fact. It is like I can hear it as if it is happening now, it is all so vivid."

"Laura was very unhappy for many years." His brow folded with deep thought. "You must think it strange I would rush here to discuss your mother, but it was not only that. I heard you were recently attacked, my dear. A man was killed?"

My head snapped up in surprise. How had he heard about Wadim? It was almost as if he knew something more than what Fox and I had told the others, but I could not imagine how. No one knew the truth—that Wadim had been a vampire.

I was so overtaken by shock I could not think of what to say.

"A gypsy, they tell me," he prodded.

I recovered from my dismay. "I was never harmed. It was Mr. Fox who happened in when the man threatened me, thank goodness, and shot him dead."

"Yes," Uncle Peter purred, "thank goodness indeed. Then we all owe a debt of gratitude to this Mr. Fox. I shall find him and convey my most heartfelt appreciation."

I smiled, laboring to shake the strange feeling that there was something amiss in his interest. What was this paranoia? Why

could I not quell the sense that there was an undercurrent of meaning below the surface, just out of my grasp?

"Miss," a new voice cut in, and I looked up to see one of Mary's staff standing nearby, "Mrs. Dulwich has asked that you join them."

No doubt, Alyssa was put out that I was monopolizing our cherished uncle. I sighed and glanced toward Uncle Peter. There was regret in his face. He patted my hand gravely. "We shall speak together soon, do not despair."

I was left with the distinct impression that he felt this was imperative. And that there was more to his visit than he had told me.

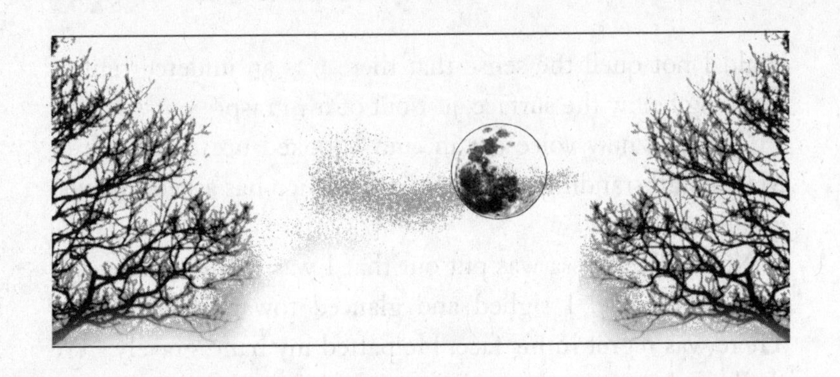

Chapter Fourteen

As soon as I was able to slip away unnoticed, I returned to Saint Michael's. This time, Father Luke was in. A decidedly less friendly Mrs. Tigwalt showed me into the kind of room in which you would expect a cleric to be busy at work, crowded with books and papers, various religious artifacts of no especial beauty, and furniture well worn to just a shade under shabby. A large desk was positioned in front of a mullioned bay, so that the large man seated behind it, hunkered over a pile of papers, was bathed in the ample backlight of the sunlit afternoon.

"This is Mrs. Andrews," she said, pronouncing the syllables with meaning.

Father Luke raised his head, an action that reminded me of

a great lion rousing from a nap. He was a man of no particular handsomeness, with a square face. His lips were thin but not cruel, his nose prominent, and his chin rather broad, but these strong features were balanced by a wide, scholarly forehead above and an incongruous assemblage of musculature below. His eyes were quite hot right now, watching me closely, but then he would have heard of the missing crucifix and would be suspicious of me.

He looked first at me, then at his housekeeper, nodded, and she departed with a cool gust of air. It was on my mind to say something about my theft, offer an explanation—or, rather, partial explanation, for I surely could not confess in full—but I knew it was a bad idea, guaranteed to put us at odds outright. I had more important business to which I had best attend.

"Mrs. Tigwalt had mentioned you'd been to see me," he said. He extended his left arm, indicating the chair. He had thick, strong-looking fingers, a gold ring encircling the third finger of his left hand, precisely where a wedding band might be placed.

I said, "She was kind enough to show me your beautiful church. I was quite overwhelmed by the art."

I had no great claims to charm where men were concerned, but neither did I think I was completely without any appeal. My sweet smile and ingratiating tone, however, did nothing to move the priest from his detached, almost cold, perusal of me.

There was silence, awkward silence that stretched on far beyond my forbearance. That dense, powerful frame was intimidating enough to make me blurt, "I am not a Catholic, Father, but I wish to know if you will hear my confession."

Father Luke blinked, but recovered himself quickly. "Of course. We can adjourn to the confessional. I'll need a few moments to prepare."

"Can I not simply make the confession here?"

He offered me a chilly smile. "It is not usual."

"I hardly need the anonymity of the confessional," I said. "Is that not the function the alcoves serve? I think I would prefer not to go in there. Forgive me, please, I do not mean to resist your traditions, but I am not good in small spaces."

His eyebrows crept upward. "I suppose there is no harm in adjourning to the church. We can simply take a pew. But there are certain vestments I need, and prayers to be said before I administer the sacrament."

"Of course." I rose quickly, suddenly infused with a liking for this rash idea. I crossed his small yard and entered the church, hardly knowing what to do. But I figured a few prayers of my own were in order, and perhaps overdue.

I sank to the kneeler, hesitated as to whether I should make the sign of the cross—deciding against it since it felt like pretension—and raised my eyes to the large rendering of suffering Jesus hung over the altar.

I cannot report what communion transpired as I contemplated the savior. I am a Christian woman, of course, but I have never been particularly religious. I do not think the experience I had was because I was in the midst of the Catholic tradition, nor even because I was enveloped in the hallowed space of a Christian church. It was my state of mind, that special state of openness one has when all else is not sufficient. Although this will displease those materialists who will fashion me daft or delusional, I will say I felt a stirring, a settling, a sense that something good was offering me a measure of peace.

In any event, I knew I had come to the right place.

When Father Luke came out and took the seat in the pew in front of me, turning toward the altar so that he was not facing me, he said, "Now, please say, 'Bless me, Father, for I have sinned.' And then you may begin your confession."

I stumbled over the phrase, not only because of the unfamiliar humility of placing myself before a stranger in contrition, but from the swell of emotion. Freedom flowed in the wake of those words, throwing open the doors and leading me to say, without any preamble whatsoever, "I stole the crucifix from the holy water font. I needed it, you see, and could hardly have asked for it. I had not planned to steal when I entered the church. It was not a part of any preconceived scheme, please be assured. But as I was waiting for Mrs. Tigwalt to bring me the holy water, I saw it and impulse overcame me. I tried to make it right by giving a donation to the poor. But it was hardly compensatory to having taken it without permission."

He turned slightly, so I saw the curve of his cheek. "Why did you take it, my child?" Being called "child" was entirely incongruous coming from this youthful, vigorous male who happened to be a man of God.

"Am I protected by the sanctity of the confessional?" I asked.

He nodded.

"I needed it to protect a child." I closed my eyes, girding myself against all the reasons why I should not go on. "I believe, with excellent and abundant evidence, that she is being attacked by a vampire."

All right then, I thought, *let me see if he turns to me with pity in his eyes.* Or perhaps horror. Maybe he would throw me out of this holy place, a person who would speak of such things in the Lord's house—worse than mad.

He said nothing. When I could stand his silence no more, I exclaimed, "I saw you in the graveyard at Sarum Saint Martin's, praying over the new grave."

His head jerked; he was startled. "You are mistaken."

"You are hardly a person I would easily take for another, Father, if you will forgive me for saying so."

He turned a bit more, presenting his profile so that his pinched brow was visible, as was the hard slash of his mouth clamping down on his copious jaw. "Do you have other sins you wish to confess?" he asked.

"Yes. I have witnessed a man being killed. Twice. The same man."

His gaze jerked toward me although his head did not move.

"I have seen and felt evil," I went on. "I wish to fight it, but I do not know how. I have used religious artifacts and icons for functions for which they were never intended. I do not know if that is blasphemy."

"What evil have you seen?" he asked, his voice hushed now, almost a whisper.

"A shadow. A smell—a stench, really. I heard a screech owl once, and I thought it sounded like a creature enraged. I think it was the vampire, after I drove it off. I saw, in my hand, a Christian cross glowing, emitting heat. I killed six snakes that attacked me as if of one mind."

I squeezed my eyes shut to brace myself, then opened them. "I somehow see things others do not. I seem to . . . feel somehow that which is there but not there. I believe something foul is presently loose here, in Avebury."

He was very still, then collected himself and turned back toward the altar. We stayed like that, sitting together in silence, the church's grand art, overly wrought and nearly hysterical, all around us.

Finally, he asked, "Have you spoken of these things to anyone?"

"I have, but I cannot tell you whom." It stung whenever I recollected Mr. Fox's inquiries. "He cannot, or will not, help. I cannot explain further."

"Is he an agent of this evil?"

"I believe he is not. I have seen evidence that he wishes to defeat it. In fact, he was the one who saved my life by killing this . . . creature."

"Twice, you said."

"Yes. Once when the revenant was as a man and then again later, when it rose after death."

"That is heresy," he said, but there was no condemnation in his tone. The words were spoken flatly, as if merely stating a fact.

"He does not confide in me. I know only that he, too, believes a child is in the sights of an evil being."

"A child?" he whispered, visibly stricken with grief. "Little Henrietta Dulwich, is it? Your cousin's daughter?"

"Yes," I said. I found I was trembling. "It is Henrietta."

Bowing his head, he contemplated this. And I realized, with a sudden shock and relief, that he was not disbelieving me. He had not laid his hands on me and compelled the demon of madness to depart from my soul. He had not vacated me from his presence in rage or indignation. And he had not so much as flinched when I spoke the word "vampire."

"I will tell you your penance, my child," he said, his voice restored to its baritone crispness. "Three Our Fathers, a heartfelt Act of Contrition, which you can find written out in one of the pew missals, and a decade of the rosary."

I was deeply disappointed. "And in addition to these prayers, can you offer the benefit of any particular council?" I asked wanly. "I could use some practical aid."

"That you cease such talk." He turned to look at me, his expression serious and a warning in the depths of his eyes. "You shall find yourself contending with consequences no one would desire."

"Wise words," I agreed. "But what if it is a matter of life and death?"

His expression was reminiscent of that which I had seen so often on the face of Mr. Fox, the look of a man willing to take but not to give. Behind his Roman collar, Father Luke regarded me with unfathomable, but not undisguised, calculation. I'd been a fool to reveal so much, I thought dispiritedly, for again I had gained nothing.

No, not nothing. Absolution. But that would not save Henrietta.

"I am but a priest," he said, as if reading my thoughts and offering some explanation.

"But not my priest." I turned, then hesitated. "I cannot return the crucifix. I have need of it. However, I can pay to have it replaced."

"We are not a poor parish." His smile was mysterious. "The item will be replaced. If you still see the need, you may make another donation to the poor." He rose, resting his hand for a moment on the back of the pew. His ring was illuminated in a clear, uncolored pinpoint of light coming in through the painted windows, and I saw there was a symbol on the flat surface flush with his knuckle.

"Your ring," I said, staring. "The fish."

He dropped his hand, taking the insignia out of sight. "It is the early Christian symbol for Christ. You must know it."

"I saw the same on a plaque by the tree near The Sanctuary." I indicated the direction of the painting I'd been shown on my

earlier visit. "The tree is represented in that painting of Saint Michael casting out the devil. What is the significance?"

His ample jaw swelled with belligerence. "I have already told you. Now, Mrs. Andrews, you may leave your donation in the poor box and then I will see you out."

He was not going to leave me alone in the church. So I made my donation, which was twice as large as I had originally intended, because of the slender missal I'd slipped in the folds of my skirts.

Chapter Fifteen

Father Luke was aware of Marius. Of this I was certain. I would even go so far as to say he was engaged in fighting the vampire, for I recollected his furtive appearance in the graveyard, clandestinely praying for the departed soul of one of Marius's victims.

He had not been shocked by my confession, true, but neither had he been interested in helping. No, indeed, he'd seemed more interested in keeping me silent.

It was well known the Church practiced exorcism of demons. Was the belief in vampires so much further into the realm of the unreal than the idea of demonic possession? Could Rome itself be aware of the existence of the undead and of how they preyed on human blood?

The Blood is the Life. The holy tree, right there in the sacred spot of The Sanctuary, along the Saint Michael line and sealed with the sign of the fish. And the little church stood just beyond, a tiny jewel intact and unmolested through hundreds of years of religious strife and strong anti-Catholic sentiment.

I caught myself. I was making a conspiracy out of coincidence. And yet I could not stop worrying it, my thoughts running in roads and lanes that accelerated to dead ends. I walked about in something of a daze the rest of that day, only half-attending to the happenings around me and keeping my keen eye on Henrietta. I had secured her room again this morning, the way Mr. Fox had done in the stable to seal the stall to prevent Wadim escaping. I liberally used salt and garlic and sprinkled the holy water Mrs. Tigwalt had given me. Still, I was ever-anxious over the child's safety.

One thing penetrated my distraction. The normally nattily dressed and meticulously groomed Sebastian emerged from his bed at midday in a state of dishabille. "You look wretched," I told him, taken aback by his appearance.

He touched his hair self-consciously. "I had no patience for a toilette today."

"No, not just that. How pale you are! Do you have fever?" Like a mother, I pressed the back of my hand against his forehead.

He ducked it, playing, in turn, his role of a guilty boy. "One does not acquire fever from too many spirits. I am afraid I imbibed overmuch last night."

He sank shakily into a chair. I viewed him with concern.

"Oh dear, will you leave off!" he barked at last, impatient with my hovering. "I am not dying! It's a man's prerogative to tipple a bit now and then."

I admit my mind had gone to dark ailments, of diseases that waste the body away and whose cure would not be found in an apothecary's cabinet. I was overwrought, I realized, and it was not doing anyone good for me to walk about in such a show of perpetual anxiousness.

Uncle Peter was to join us for dinner. I was most eager to talk with him, but when I entered the drawing room, he was engaged in the telling of one of his stories. Hess and the Bedfords were enraptured. The young Ted Pentworth, however, together with his chum, Mr. Farrington, were bored as schoolboys at a philosophy lecture. My brother-in-law, too, was not engrossed. I guessed Alan would rather be at billiards or faro than listening to the wisdom of an old man.

I tried to look at my sister's husband with new eyes and a charitable spirit. I suppose I should admire his devotion, for he sat dutifully by Alyssa's side. When they had announced their engagement, Simon had tried to counsel me not to interfere, but I had not listened. I had thought she would tire of him, that her more sophisticated interests would come into being once she matured, and she would regret her choice. But my husband had been correct; I should not have spoken against the marriage. It had driven a wedge between my sister and me, and ours was an already fragile relationship. Now she was bearing his child.

My gaze strayed to where Mr. Fox leaned an elbow on the mantle. He pretended to listen to the conversation around him but I could tell he was not paying attention. His hooded gaze lit on me and I tensed. Must he always stare so? What was he thinking?

The timeliness of the dinner bell was a relief, and I was pleased when Uncle Peter took my hand and pulled it through

his arm, disregarding Mary's intended pairings. "Walk with me, my dear," he murmured. His slower gait, exaggerated for his purpose at the moment, gave us an excuse to lag behind the others as we all made our formal procession in to dinner.

"Have you noticed the Latin written up there?" he asked me, and as we were just passing through the doorway from the salon, we both glanced at the carved words.

"They are all over the house," I said.

"Indeed?" His heavy eyebrows twitched. "Do they all say the same thing?"

"No, they are all different. I've been meaning to ask Sebastian to give me a tour of them and write them down." Then I remembered that Mr. Fox had done just that on his own.

"The corruption of the best is worst," Uncle Peter said contemplatively as we moved slowly down the corridor.

"Uncle Peter," I said suddenly. "I need to speak to you, soon. I have questions . . . I want to know about my mother."

His look was suddenly sharp, almost angry, and I felt something fiercely disturbing rise up inside me.

"It is gravely important," I said, and added a heartfelt "please."

He thought for a moment, and seemed to come to a decision. "Yes, my dear. Indeed. I suppose it is time you and I had a very lengthy conversation."

My heart kicked with excitement at this agreement, but I was not completely at ease. It was perfectly plain that the prospect did not please him.

Uncle Peter returned to the inn with the promise to join us for dinner the following evening. In my disappointment at being robbed of him so soon after his arrival, I sought out the company of Mr. Hess.

I had grown fond of the gentle older man, not only for his kindness but also because his great enthusiasm for learning made him something of a kindred spirit. And I was most especially interested in hearing about the local legends, which was one of his favorite topics as well. Thus it was I was able to steer an innocent exchange on the status of Dulwich Manor's garden into a more interesting vein by observing, "I am put to mind, seeing the buds on the trees, of how myths over the centuries—even unto our own religion—affirm the human belief—or is it merely a hope?—that life will always triumph over death."

It was, to me, an obvious ploy, and I hoped to direct the conversation to matters of traditions regarding life, death, and now this new and terrible alternative of living death. But his complex mind took a surprising turn.

"Spring renews," he said with a sage nod. "And it never fails to reassure me. A time of life, and of beauty, although there is beauty in the other seasons, too. But I am most fond of spring, for it is when goodness and life are strongest. Though creation has its own terrors; consider the customs of Maying."

Mr. Fox had also mentioned the pagan feast of May Day as a particularly potent time, I recalled. "I understand it is an old celebration."

"Even druids and the ancients beyond them understood there is danger in the creation of life, for all things in nature are in balance. We think spring is the natural enemy of evil. It is the month of birthing. Lambs, calves, foals, all the flowers and trees—new life, my dear. The anathema to death. But there is another side—a dark side to creation." Mr. Hess raised his index finger, as if anticipating an objection. "You may ask how that can be when spring is the season of resurrection, when our very own Lord triumphed over death, eh? The theme of rebirth,

of holiness and life, is heralded as far back as Greek mythology and beyond, when Persephone is returned to Mother Earth at the conclusion of each winter. Each culture throughout the history of man has venerated the fertility and life renewal of the seasons."

Out of the corner of my eye, I noticed Mr. Fox draw closer.

"Although autumn is the natural time of death and thus, it is assumed, evil, please recollect what I cautioned about the rule of balance. Even within spring, the season of life and therefore goodness, evil must have its reign, however brief. And what is more—and this is very important, dear—how much more intense that brief period of darkness is made by the inherent life-giving nature of the season. Thus, for spring's very goodness, the corresponding evil must be equal. Equal and opposite, for balance as all things must ever and always be. And so tradition holds that on the Eve of Saint George, evil reigns, just as it does on the Eve of All Hallows. May Day, too, is considered a time when the undead roam free and mischief abounds. Evil must have its reign for goodness to come."

"The corruption of the best is worst," I said slowly.

Hess leaned in closer to me. "What is that you say? My dear, how very intriguing. The inscription—you know it? Why it is the very thing I am trying to explain." He bustled to the escritoire in the corner and opened the ink pot, dabbing a quill and quickly scrabbling down a line. After blowing on the paper, he brought it with him as he resumed his seat. Folding it, he placed it in his pocket. "I've discovered something absolutely fascinating about The Sanctuary, and this might be a clue—"

Mary cut in, annoyance in her voice, for she did not want me monopolizing her guest on esoteric topics. "Mr. Hess, do have a raspberry biscuit. My cook is known for them."

"Oh, indeed!" he exclaimed, selecting one from the tray his hostess proffered. Alan caught my eye at that moment, a scowl on his perfect features. I felt the barb of guilt he meant to send, for I could see that Alyssa was sulking. I sighed. I'd neglected my sister, and Mary was now occupying Mr. Hess in a conversation of horseflesh which presently animated Sir William, Roger, and Mr. Bedford.

I slipped next to Alyssa, smiling bracingly at her and taking her hand in mine. "What they say about women in your condition is true. Your face seems to beam with happiness."

"You are a terrible liar, Emma. I feel wretched," she murmured, but grasped my hand back and smiled a moment later at an amusing story told by Ted Pentworth.

I laughed as well, without paying much attention to what was being said. Mr. Hess had given me plenty to mull over, and the faint buzz of some disturbance, stronger than disquiet but lying just under fear, hummed in my head.

My frequent visits to the third floor had made a friend of Miss Harris, and thereby I gained myself an ally in keeping my eye on Henrietta's condition. After playing checkers or paper dolls with Henrietta, I typically concluded by sitting with Miss Harris in the little nursery kitchen, munching on lemon biscuits from her secret tin and drinking tea while we chatted. Henrietta seemed the pleasant, happy child I had always known her to be; I could not have asked for more assurance that all was well with her. But I knew it was not.

Victoria was gone. I searched the schoolroom from stem to stern and found nothing. And when I mentioned Victoria's absence to Henrietta, she grew quiet and lowered her eyes. No amount of clever cajoling on my part would get her to confide anything to me.

Of the shadow I had seen, I spied nothing more, not even a hint. If I asked Henrietta where her friend Marius had gone, she would simply say, "He is sleeping," and nothing more. Yet my mind was not at ease.

One afternoon, we were sorting through the puppet box while Miss Harris was having some time to herself. "Let us select a Henrietta," I suggested. I pulled out the pretty one, with long, painted eyelashes and blond curls.

"And Emma," she said eagerly, rifling through the options. The one she chose made us laugh. It was rather silly-looking, with wide eyes and very red lips. "She's the next prettiest," Henrietta explained.

I waited until she'd chosen a second, a male puppet, whom she named Joseph, after the master gardener who always produced a sweet from his pocket for Henrietta. "Joseph is her friend," she said, pairing off her two puppets.

I, in turn, fished out an older puppet, with a chipped and faded painted face. "And let us make this one Marius."

Immediately, she grew guarded. Doleful eyes flashed to mine. "I don't wish to play with Marius."

"But he is your friend, too, isn't he?"

Her brow furrowed. "I can not talk about him. He is gone now."

"But he is not a secret, love. Not any longer," I said as I carried the puppets over to the theater. "I know all about Marius. I've even seen him. Remember, when you were talking to him up at The Sanctuary?"

She nodded, solemn and watchful. Following me to the theater, she knelt and quietly arranged her puppets. I saw by the square set of her shoulders, the ramrod-straight posture of her back, that her body was gripped with great tension.

With her gaze firmly on the Marius doll I'd chosen, she spoke softly. "He told me you cannot see him."

"But I did. And I saw him again, just a few days ago," I said gently, arranging my skirts as I joined her on the floor. "He was walking with you and Miss Harris in the garden."

She jerked her head up, and my heart plummeted at the look in her eyes. She was terrified. Dropping the puppets, she shot to her feet. She nearly collided with Miss Harris, who was entering just at that moment, as she dashed out of the room before I could react.

The nurse gazed at me in puzzlement, a bit cross with me, I noticed. I understood. We were all protective of Hen, especially these days. Biting down hard on my bottom lip to keep it from trembling, I simply shrugged.

Mrs. Bedford accompanied me on a visit to the village. The pair of us set out by open trap from Dulwich Manor down the road with which I had some familiarity. We passed Sarum Saint Martin's; I shivered to see the high iron gates of the churchyard to which I had followed Mr. Fox, and a pang speared my sternum to think of him.

The weather was drizzly with that sharp-edged damp that permeates the month of March. I was bundled in a winter wool, which warded off the worst of the cloying air as we rode down the country road toward the village. The road wove through fields where the large sarcen stones of the Great Stone Serpent were cast about the landscape like some gigantic child's playing blocks. It was so peculiar to see them peppered in among the living, with cottages in the foreground and farm animals grazing unimpressed in their shadow. Somehow, the contrast only increased their splendor and mystery. Two worlds, the old and the new, existing together.

Two worlds. The living and the dead meet here on the lay line of Saint Michael. Mr. Hess had told me that.

Once we arrived in the village, Mrs. Bedford suggested we share a comforting cup of tea in the inn. The gas jets were ablaze in the common room, and a fire had been lit in the massive hearth to banish the gray damp from the air. I sent word to Uncle Peter's rooms that I was awaiting him, and could he join us at his earliest convenience? He appeared not long after, immaculately dressed and beaming with pleasure to see me.

"You are just in time for our second pot," I told him after accepting a kiss on each cheek. He bowed to Mrs. Bedford.

"Ah, English tea. There is nothing like it in all the Continent." He surveyed the tray with relish, wasting no time in helping himself from the assortment of sandwiches and biscuits arrayed before us.

Mrs. Bedford did not linger after we'd taken our meal. "I am most anxious to visit my friend Mary Linden. Her daughter, Margaret, is ill," she explained.

"Let me walk you," I said, rising with her. She protested, but I assured her it was no trouble, and went with her the short distance to her friend's home.

"I trust the child is not too ill," I ventured. I was concerned, and she sensed it.

She patted my hand. "It is a strange malaise, but not this wretched plague, I am sure. Probably no more than a common ailment of childhood. The ague, I suspect." She suddenly waved, and I spied a woman in the door with a small child in her arms.

The little girl, probably four years of age, had a solemn face with large eyes and a cascade of dark curls.

"I hope she gets well soon," I murmured as Mrs. Bedford joined her friend. I hurried back to the inn to Uncle Peter, who was waiting for me.

"Well, then," he said when I was situated at the table again. He reached a hand across the table to touch his fingers to mine. "Am I correct to assume you are here to speak with me about what you mentioned before?" he asked in his thick accent. His expression was sad but kind. "You wish to talk of Laura."

"I must know about my mother." I braced myself. I was used to being met with resistance, and I was prepared for it now. "I realize it is a difficult subject, but I've waited a very long time to ask someone who knew her to tell me the truth of what happened. And I need to know now more than ever what it was that killed her and what her madness was like. Do not spare me."

His eyes flickered with doubt, and I drew myself up, ready to meet any objection head-on. "I am not a child any longer. I am a woman now set upon my own path in life. I no longer need to be protected."

He regarded me for a moment, then sighed. "This is true enough."

"You and my father were friends for many years. You knew my mother."

"I was half in love with her myself." He smiled, making the statement benign. "It was the same with every man who knew her. It was difficult not to adore Laura. It was not only her beauty. There are beautiful women all over this world—I should know, I've traveled much of it. But Laura, she was special. There was light in her . . ." He trailed off. Nodding,

he then brought himself back with a renewed smile. "And she loved your father. Very much."

The lump in my throat had risen fast. Suddenly it was too large to allow me to speak. I swallowed, but it would not move.

"They were very happy, you know." Uncle Peter's smile was of a man lost in the past, and I saw the love shining from his face.

I found my voice. "How long did they have before she became ill?"

"A few years, that is all. But it was enough, I think. Stephen—your father—he never regretted anything. Perhaps that is the first thing you should be told. When she became ill, he did not feel sorry for himself. He did not despair."

I had never really considered my father in this. I don't know why this was. Perhaps, drawing a conclusion from how he'd looked at me, the watchfulness and tension I'd imagined in his gaze, I had seen him only as a sentinel, an emotionless witness to my mother's suffering. Of course, I had never before known how much they'd meant to each other.

"He was true to her, even when the madness was at its worst." He stopped here, taking in a long, labored breath. "And before. This I believe."

"What do you mean, before?"

"Before your mother fell ill. Her illness was provoked, you see." He shook his head, as if remembering still made him angry. "A baronet's daughter named Astrid Laforge had made her debut that season. As her parents traveled in the same social circles as Stephen and Laura, she was at every dinner party, every dance. Ah, but she was a fiendish little fox, for she was jealous of your mother. Everyone could see how she pitted her youthful beauty against Laura's more cultured air of loveliness. Your mother was beloved by her friends, and the little fox could not stand it. She wished to be the one all admired, and a very thinly disguised rivalry emerged." His jaw worked. "And Astrid had a passion for your father, Emma."

I heard the dark undertone, saw the hardening glint in his eyes, and my heart did a queer leap. I had the first inkling of how difficult it was going to be to hear this tale I'd waited so long to hear.

"Laura laughed over it at first, thinking Astrid silly. She dismissed her. We all did. I can see, in my mind, the way she'd smile when Astrid would ply her wiles on Stephen; I am sure they laughed about it in private. Her eyes would shine with humor when they caught mine, as if to say, 'Are you enjoying her little show?' Ah, her eyes. They were an extraordinary color, a very unique shade of blue. Really violet, in certain light. It was a haunting effect . . ." Uncle Peter trailed off momentarily, then resumed. "Your mother knew her appeal, and she was confident in the love she and Stephen shared. But Astrid was clever, and when she saw she could not lure Stephen into her bed, she did something diabolical. She ingeniously planted seeds of uncertainty in the mind of her rival."

"What do you mean?"

"For example, she would make certain to be noticed coming out of a room moments after Stephen had emerged, and she'd look flushed, acting uncomfortable at having been spotted, as if . . . well, you get the idea. It was all very subtle, but effective. Soon rumors started to circulate."

"And my mother began to doubt my father," I said, knowing this had to be what happened.

Uncle Peter spread out his hands helplessly. "Laura began to listen to the doubts Astrid put into her head. No doubt Astrid delighted when she saw how the seeds slowly unwound, claiming Laura's thoughts and becoming an obsession."

"Did my father not deny it?"

"That was the entire trouble, darling. Your father made a terrible mistake. He knew himself to be a man of honor. He was too proud to answer for his fidelity. When Laura needed him most to defend himself, he stood on principle and refused to speak to her on the matter."

I knew my father to be proud. He had a temper, and it was not hot or passionate. When angered, he went cold, remote, aloof. I had been frozen by that frigid blast myself. How devastating it must have been to a woman hungry for reassurance. "So it was jealousy that destroyed her mind?"

"No, no, my dear. This was only the beginning. You see . . . Laura changed then. She withdrew, became melancholy and secretive. I grew concerned for her, and for Stephen, whose stubbornness I feared would destroy him. They went different ways, each wrapped up in their resentments. Laura became very active tending to various charity work, and when illness struck in the village, she worked tirelessly to help the afflicted. I often thought it was her way to forget how miserable she was."

"And my father?"

"Stephen began to travel. But when Laura fell ill, it all ended abruptly. Give your dear father credit, my child—he realized his bull-headed ways and flew back to Castleton House at once. Laura was struck by the same illness she had fought in others. Stephen, contrite and riddled with guilt, never left her side."

I spoke in a whisper. "This illness . . ."

He seemed surprised by my somberness, then shook his head, waving an expressive hand. "No, no, my dear. This was the first time. She recovered. It was a little while later that she—"

"Describe it to me," I asked abruptly.

I told myself I was being foolish. Villages were afflicted with contagions all the time. There could be no connection to the otherworldly plague now raging in this very hamlet.

Uncle Peter blinked. "Very well. I recall it began with Laura becoming very, very weak. And so pale. She was listless to the point where she barely responded to anyone. We did not suspect any insanity then. Stephen— My God, he was a man possessed. All the others who had sickened from the illness had died, but he refused to let her go. He sat with her, in the dark room, for she could tolerate no light, every hour of the day and all through the night. He thought he had lost her. It was what we both believed."

It sounded similar to the wasting disease, but I was no doctor. "Were you there with him then?"

"I was glad to be helping when I could. The few times Stephen dozed or left her to see to his own needs, I was the only one he trusted to stay with her. She was never without the one or other of us at her side. When she began to slowly revive, she . . . Lord, child, it pains me to tell all of this ugly business."

My throat constricted, for there were tears in his eyes. "That was when the madness came?"

He forced himself to go on. "It will not do you good to know this, but she suffered. She understood she was going mad. The way she spoke, the things she said. Her ranting was vile. I . . ." His voice, creaking on this last, seemed to fail him. He was silent, and very still for a long time. Then, he said, "To witness this was . . . it was a terrible thing."

To my horror, he suddenly appeared old to me, and I felt the weight of my selfishness in putting him through so much. Still, I had to ask my final question, almost against my will, and in a voice so quiet he could pretend he did not hear me, I said, "Did she ever love me?"

His eyes closed, and I saw his jaw tremble. "Oh, yes, my dear, dear Emma. You were the shining light to her, I promise you." His lids raised and he looked at me with pity, causing the lump in my throat to rise again. "You were her child. Stephen's child, whom she loved more than life itself. And she did recover, for a while. They were happy once again. They had you and a few years before the madness returned." His face twitched and he gave a quick, final shake of his head. "But this is overwhelming for one sitting, you will agree."

There was more here, I knew, but I'd lost my nerve. It was too much for Uncle Peter, and too much for me. This intimate view of my mother's suffering, the unimaginable robbery of her reason, of her happy life, was surprisingly unbearable. It was not fair, I thought, and though it was a childish protest, it filled me, nearly crushing me with emotion.

"What do you remember of your father?" Uncle Peter prodded me gently.

"He was quiet. His eyes would light up when he'd look at Alyssa."

"Ah. Yes, your sister was a great comfort to him. It was like he could make himself a different man with his new family."

"He wanted to forget Laura," I said, surprised at the bitterness in my tone.

Uncle Peter's gaze was level and serious. "He never forgot Laura. And you, dear Emma, were her gift to him, and he treasured you."

"He feared me," I stated flatly. "He watched for the madness."

Peter bowed his head, his shoulders slumping under the undeniable fact. "It would have destroyed him had you been afflicted as well." He paused, then said slowly, "And now, may I ask you a question. I pray you will be as honest with me as I have been with you."

I blinked, a bit taken aback. "Of course."

"I do not know that you have been completely forthcoming with me as to why you wish to know of this now."

"I have always wished to know more of my mother," I answered truthfully.

"Yes," he said, waiting for me to go on.

I gave my answer several moments' consideration. "I feel something changing in me, Uncle Peter. I have been married and widowed, but I do not think I've ever really known myself. Now . . . I am learning things I never before suspected I was capable of, and I cannot help but wonder if any of it is connected to my mother, to what might have happened to her or to me as a child as a result of what she endured."

I do not know why this upset him, but I saw his face twitch with tension. His fingers idly scratched the point of his chin. "A strange idea to have—that you were affected by Laura's condition. You were just a child. What could it have had to do with you?"

Was he being coy? I evaded by answering a question with my own. "Do you think it could have? Affected me, that is?"

He lowered his gaze, ignoring my query. "May I ask you

about that dreadful affair in the barn? Is it upsetting to speak of it?"

"I . . ." What could I tell him? Not the truth, nor could I bear to lie to him. And yet there was something very guarded in his manner, as if he already knew what I would say. But how could he? My paranoia was getting the better of me. "It was a strange affair. I barely know what to make of it." I shook my head in confusion. "So many things have been happening around me, and to me. I . . . I feel *different*, somehow. There are changes . . . I am struggling to understand all of it."

He leaned in slightly. "And these changes . . ."

I saw he was thinking of the way my mother's mind had betrayed her. "I am fine, I promise you. If there is one thing of which I am certain, it is that I am not insane."

He looked at me so strangely that for a moment I thought perhaps he would not believe me. He had seen the horror of my mother's raving firsthand. Like my father, would he not live in fear that I would develop the same affliction? But his eyes were true, dark pools of unfathomable emotion as he slowly nodded his head, murmuring, "I know, my darling. I know."

"I am sorry to trouble you with these things," I said, now noticing how haggard he looked. "I realize now how difficult it is for you."

He waved off my apology. "It is I who should beg your pardon. I know you are anxious to have the entire tale, but your patience with me is very kind. Come here, child, and give me a kiss and I shall know you forgive an old man."

Being a properly bred Englishwoman, I had always been slightly uncomfortable with this European custom, but there was a part of me that secretly liked the ceremonial show of affection. I had gotten so little of it elsewhere.

As I leaned to offer first one cheek and then the other, I saw his eyes dart to my neck, unmistakably sharp with concern and undeniably focused on the spot under my ear where the pulse beat with the pressure of my blood. Like a firebrand struck to my heart, I knew exactly what it was he was looking for.

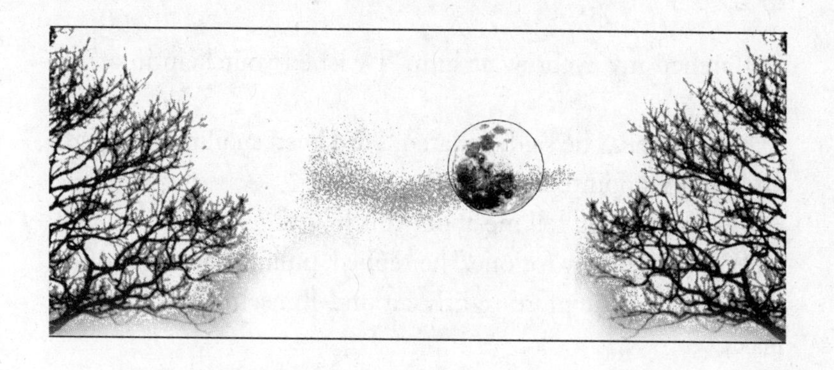

Chapter Sixteen

Sebastian was feeling poorly again. His complexion was pasty and there were shadows encircling his eyes, which were heavy-lidded from exhaustion. I drew him away from the others when the men were making for the billiard room and the ladies to a sewing clutch, dragging him with me into the library.

When he saw my expression of concern, he held up a hand. "I will not have any wailing and gnashing of teeth, thank you very much, I have had my fill of it from Roger. Rest assured I am not stricken with this wasting thing he's always going on about. I am drinking too much, I admit it, and staying up late as well."

I arched my eyebrow at him. "I wished your help in something."

"Oh, bother," he said, deflated. He'd been spoiling for a fight and I'd disappointed him.

"What can you tell me about this house?"

"Well, 'tis drafty for one," he replied, pulling the edges of his velvet frock coat more tightly around himself. "And the roof leaks."

Really, he was in a foul mood. But I was dogged. "Do you know anything of its history? Mary mentioned it was built by a Catholic bishop who had the Latin inscriptions carved into the place. Do you know why?"

Sebastian found a comfortable position on a leather divan, with his feet, sporting a pair of gleaming boots, propped up and his arm cushioning the nape of his neck. He closed his eyes, then cracked the left one open to give me a droll look. "Why don't we have a spiritualist in and we can have a séance, conjure up the old boy and you can ask him yourself. He's around here, you know. I've seen him."

"Sebastian, be serious. Could you at least tell me where all the inscriptions are located?"

"Now? I've just gotten comfortable." His eye shut again.

"I think they are clues," I mused aloud.

He scoffed. "Now you sound like my tutor when I was a boy here. The old fellow was convinced the house contained a secret treasure, and that was why the Latin was all around the place. He was going on and on about how Cromwell's men, in their fervor to erase all traces of the Catholic faith, had seized this house from the bishop who built it. He reasoned the cleric had hidden away his fortune—for the clergy in those days were some of the wealthiest men in the land. It was all bunk, of course.

Oh, not the Cromwell thing, that was sure enough. But the treasure, that was just wishful thinking. Cromwell and his men took every gold chalice, every painting, every silver candlestick, and my ancestor, whoever he was, became the happy recipient of this fine country home. Rather like a vulture."

"Is it not strange Cromwell did not seize the church?" Talk of treasure reminded me of the wealth of art under the roof of Saint Michael in the Fields, and I again wondered how or why the greedy legions of Roundheads had neglected to strip the small parish. "And if they are not clues to treasure—which I agree is preposterous—then what could the inscriptions mean? They must have been very important, for they are not so much decoration as . . ."

I flashed on a memory of the Germanic tradition of painting symbols on their houses to ward off evil. Yes, this reminded me of that—but different. These sayings were warnings. "Do you think it could be a sort of protection?" I asked. "Such as an amulet or talisman might be?"

"Against what?" He tilted his head up to peer at me. "You are not referring to ghosts? Are you afraid of ghosts, Emma?" He hooted, enjoying this. "Oh, my, what is it you've seen? The Gray Lady? The Wailing Child? Oh, Emma, this is delicious!"

"Oh, I do not know why I bother," I said, irritated with him.

He fell back, laughing and hugging himself. "Now, as you have managed to trap me here and I am unwell, I beg you find me something entertaining and read to me."

I dropped the subject of the Latin inscriptions, stung by his mockery. To amuse him, I chose Byron, of course. That scoundrel, with his rapier wit and flouting of all convention, would be exactly what Sebastian would love.

"'Dear Doctor,'" I read, "'I have read your play, which is a good one in its way, purges the eyes, and moves the bowels, and drenches handkerchiefs like towels . . .'"

I paused. Sebastian's head cocked to one side and his mouth twitched.

"'. . . I like your moral and machinery; your plot, too, has such scope for scenery! . . .'"

He barked out loud and I had difficulty pronouncing the next over my own giggles. "'. . . Your hero raves, your heroine cries, all stab, and everybody dies . . .'"

His laughter rose to gales so loud I could not go on. But then suddenly—and abruptly—Sebastian fell silent. I glanced at him sharply and saw he was looking past me at the door. Twisting around to follow the direction of his stare, I found a very serious-faced Mr. Fox.

It was as if a thundercloud had invaded the room. The happiness of a moment ago melted, for Fox's angular face was closed, forbidding, devoid of humor.

Something was wrong.

Slowly, Sebastian shifted to a sitting position. "Why hello, Mr. Fox, have you come to join our poetry reading?"

Fox's smile was tight. "I was searching for Mrs. Andrews," he said.

"Ah. Well, there you are, she is here with me." Sebastian came to his feet. "But I sense three is a crowd. Emma, dear, thank you so much for the lesson in literature. I am not converted yet, but that was good enough that I have decided you may keep trying in the future. Now, I really must be going. No, please do not press upon me to stay, Mr. Fox, I cannot spare the time at the moment. *Au revoir, mes amis.*" He disappeared through the library door.

In his absence, the air in the room grew viscous.

Fox said, "George Hess is dead."

I came slowly to my feet. "Is it . . . ?"

He nodded. "He was found this morning by his housekeeper. Indeed, our friend has become another apparent victim of the mysterious wasting disease, albeit an acute case. He was only taken ill yesterday, I have learned. And this morning, he was dead." He waited a beat, his eyes boring into mine. "He was found bloodless. As the others."

I struggled to drag air into my lungs. The loss of the man I had liked and admired was one thing, a sharp grief. But if he had fallen prey to Marius . . .

"Pernicious anemia, the doctors say," Fox went on, seeming more rational now, his voice losing some of its leaden quality. "It is what they always say. The absence of blood cannot be given any other rational explanation."

"And what of the marks? Was anything found on his neck?"

"Of course not. The same as the others."

"I don't understand," I stated irritably. I knew I was succumbing to the irrational anger at losing someone dear. I was familiar with it, the tumult that arose from the unfairness of death. "Why did he target Mr. Hess? Why him?"

"Can you not guess? Think of his great imagination combined with his intellect and scholarly mind. A vampire absorbs the qualities of those upon whom he feeds. This is important, for one can learn much from whom a vampire chooses to feed from."

"What about those who have died in the village from the wasting disease?"

"They were not drained at once, which lessens the impact on the feeding revenant. Nonetheless, we can assume they were carefully chosen. Marius would not have killed Hess unless his intellect was an enhancement, for to feed indiscriminately on a dull mind would lessen him, at least temporarily. But more than this, I believe Hess had to have become some sort of threat. Marius has, up until now, been careful to keep his feeding far away from this family."

"Poor Mr. Hess. He was just an old man." My voice wavered. "A very kindly old man."

Fox grew somber, and my sadness penetrated his cool exterior. His tone softened to comfort me. "He knew much about the lands hereabouts. He was researching the old legends, you know that yourself. Perhaps Marius feared he would uncover something." He straightened. "A vampire will feed off prey for several bleedings, until the body is drained. Mr. Hess was taken in a day. This indicates Marius did not wish him on this earth any longer. He acted quickly—perhaps even rashly. He took the time to seal the punctures as he did with all the others and even this small spell to heal the wounds with his blood taxes him. It is an extraordinary measure, one I have not seen often—and I have been thinking a great deal about why he would take the trouble to hide the evidence of his bite."

His unease was deep, and frightening.

"I keep coming back to one simple conclusion," he continued, deep in thought. "He desperately does not want anyone to know of his presence. He has come here for something—something quite vital—and he does not wish to be interfered with."

"What do you think it is he wants?" I whispered.

"I know one thing he does not want, and that is to alert anyone that a vampire is at work."

"Surely, that cannot be a great concern. We live in a very

modern age. Who would believe it? I scarce trust my own perceptions."

"Modern? Yes, desperately so. We grasp toward reason, but we have not yet wholly succeeded, Emma. Modernity is a thin veneer, and for all the inventions and intellectual developments, the old ways have not been banished. You would be surprised how quickly the old folklore catches fire again, especially here in the country, in a village as old as Avebury. I have seen it. When people are dying—loved ones—the barrier between rational and irrational dissolves. It is ironic, but what is seen as a kind of group madness is in fact quite effective. And such a thing would put Marius in danger, even as powerful as he is."

"Then he does know fear," I said, half to myself.

"He does have weaknesses. He would not have taken Mr. Hess as he did if he did not want to keep something hidden. In any event, the fact that he wishes to avoid detection means he is planning on staying for a while. I would imagine at least until May Day." He stared at me meaningfully. I had a start realizing that March was almost done and the date of which Fox spoke was not far off.

"But what will he do? What can a vampire want here, on such a night?"

He shook his head, exuding frustration. "There is far too much about this business I simply do not know."

"And far more you refuse to tell." He gave me a warning look, and it triggered my temper. "You have never given me a proper explanation for how it is you come to be here, hunting this thing. What is Marius to you?"

His sharp features snapped into that still, secretive mask with which I'd become familiar, and I thought he would retreat again. Instead, he said, "Marius? I am not used to the name. I always think of him as Emil. That was how I met him, in France when I was a boy on holiday, traveling with my father."

His sudden explanation stunned me. He knew it, and gave me a smile I could have sworn was intended to disarm me. I was chagrined to note it was not ineffective.

He took a seat, leaning forward to rest his elbows on his knees. "I met him one night, face to face, in a squalid Parisian alleyway while he was taking one of his victims."

He let that sit in silence, then tilted his head upward, drawing in a breath, and began. "My father traveled for business, and I sometimes traveled with him, on school holiday and such. That night, while he was having dinner with business acquaintances, I snuck out of our rooms and crossed the Seine into Montmartre."

He squinted at the tips of his shoes. "It was the first time I had done such a thing. I had reached an age when I was curious about . . . certain things. I saw painted women, although I did not have the courage to speak to any of them. I took my first taste of real spirits. For that reason, I would later be very uncertain about what happened. You understand how it is, how the mind fights it."

I did. My own credulity at what I'd seen had been a struggle.

"I found myself lost in the squalid streets—close, dark streets where music and laughter and screams and shouts mingled in a blaring noise that made me disoriented. Or perhaps that was the absinthe."

He laughed, and I was amused to see he was a bit sheepish, as if he were embarrassed.

"I . . ." Tension took over his features. "It was just a scream at

first." His eyebrows drew down, as if he were in pain. "It was . . . unearthly. I have never heard anything like it before. Or since, I suppose." He closed his eyes for a moment. "I hope never to again."

"What did you do?" I asked, my voice barely a whisper.

The flash of his smile was there and gone in an instant. "I was young, remember. Young and full of myself and unaware of how foolish it was to become embroiled in a stranger's matters when in a strange city, especially in an area such as Montmartre. I was filled with noble purpose and rushed toward the sound. Sometimes . . . No. Often. I often wonder how things would have been different if the idealist in me had been a little less and the craven reprobate a little more."

He paused, and I felt my insides tense. To my credit, I said nothing, simply waited for him to go on. It took a moment.

"What I saw, I believe I will not describe to you." His eyes lifted to meet mine in almost challenge, baring something he did not need to speak.

I shifted in my seat, and the crisp rustle of my skirts seemed very loud. "I want to know," I told him. "Everything."

His eyes narrowed, and he thought for a moment before giving a nod. "Suffice to say it was a vampire, fully engaged in the act of feeding. I saw him . . . And I saw the . . . the girl. She was . . . very young. I saw her eyes." His jaw flexed. His voice lowered to barely a whisper. "They were terrible eyes. Ecstasy and pain . . ."

His hand jerked toward his mouth, wiping the sweat from his lip, scrubbing at it even after the moisture had been erased.

"Was she dead?" I asked softly.

His elegant fingers fluttered, restless and jerking. "Not . . .

not yet. It is an unspeakable thing, to see a vampire take a life. I hope we destroy this thing before you have to witness anything like it."

But I wanted to hear. I needed to hear. "This was Marius you saw. And he was . . . feeding?"

"I saw him." The whiteness of his mouth, the hardness of his eyes spoke of an immeasurable rage. It took a while for his voice to come again, and when it did, it was dry, like the sands of Egypt. "And he saw me."

His jaw worked with emotion and I had to stifle the urge to lay my palm along that sharp line in a gesture of comfort. He said, "Vampires fall into a dreamlike state when they feed. That saved me. I fled. I was terrified, hardly daring to believe what I'd seen. Some part of me did, luckily so, for I purchased a gold cross the next day and wore it around my neck. It saved me when he came for me the following night."

"What happened?" I asked eagerly.

He shrugged, turning his shoulder to me to hide his face.

"Mr. Fox," I said gently, changing the subject as I saw he did not want to relive any more of that terrible memory, "how can you be certain that Marius is Emil?"

His back straightened and his tone resumed the crisp, almost strident pace I was used to. "I know him," he said. "I have learned about that world. Vampires are creatures of habit, nomads. I have explained this to you, how they travel among familiar hunting grounds. This is why legends—hauntings and tales of monsters or such—are valuable. The memory of the vampire and its deeds lives after they've departed."

Emotions passed fleetingly over his face, entertained by his features for only a moment before dissolving away to the hard mask I knew. I had never, up to that point, understood the

severe control under which he held himself. I had thought him cold. But I now realized there was warmth there, the heat of a sun sealed behind that steely self-control.

"As clever as vampires are, as powerful and cruel as they are, they do have weaknesses," Fox continued. "One is that they must transport themselves in some manner to each hunting ground, as they cannot cross running water or be exposed to sunlight. Therefore travel must be done very carefully, to avoid exposure."

"Coffins?" I smiled humorlessly.

"More or less. You can imagine, there are particular needs involved in their transport, and they require humans to help them."

"What you refer to as minions."

"Yes. Emil has a few very notable of these. The Punjab, whom I've mentioned, is one such. It is possible to track them and the methods they use to transport their master. In addition, it has not become too difficult to read the signs of vampiric presence. It frequently comes as a report of plague. The problem is traveling swiftly enough to catch the fiend still at work. Last fall, after months of searching, I located him in a small village outside Amsterdam, but he was gone by the time I arrived in the city." He rose, going to the hearth. "On a visit to a dockside pub, I found some information on a curious cargo going to a small cottage in Avebury, Wiltshire."

I shot forward, excited by this news, but he held up a cautioning hand. "Which, by the time I arrived, had been burnt and the trail of Emil—Marius—had gone despairingly cold. But I knew I could pick it up again if I spent more time in the area. I happened to know Roger, having met him in London, through mutual friends. The association is not a close one, but

I can be quite bold when on the hunt. It was my object to impress upon his hospitality, buy time to wait, watch, and see what might materialize."

I sat silent for a long time, surprised he was suddenly so forthcoming. "Mr. Fox," I said at last, "you have saved my life. Twice. My gratitude goes without saying. However, though I have no wish to appear peevish, you made some pointed inquiries upon our last meeting that were uncommonly offensive."

His eyes narrowed. "I asked after your mother, which seems to have put you in something of a snit. Has it not occurred to you that I was trying to protect you?"

"Protect me from what, Mr. Fox?" I challenged. I rose, squaring my stance combatively. "From fiends who would send vipers to attack me? Or perhaps a leering minion who would attempt to separate my head from my neck with a razor-edged scythe? Yes, I see how your inquiry would save me from whatever drained the living blood from our friend Mr. Hess."

"You are working yourself into a state," he warned.

This, of course, sent my blood higher. "Yes, a woman's temper always puts her into a state. A convenient way to dismiss it."

"I merely wish you to calm yourself. You have become uncomfortably emotional."

This sobered me instantly. With as much dignity as I could muster, I walked to my chair and resumed my seat.

Rubbing his palm roughly over his jaw, he turned away. As I watched him, deep fear stabbed into my heart. What could be so awful?

I heard the far-off sound of voices. People were coming.

He turned to me, his gaze darting to the doorway. "We have a duty to Mr. Hess, and I would have your help, as much as I wish I did not require it. We have to dispatch George Hess's body in case it has served Marius's purpose to make him a foul creature such as himself. I doubt he has done so, but I must take the same precaution I have with every victim. He should be shriven. He deserves that."

"Of course he does," I agreed with deeply felt emotion. "But we have not finished our discussion, Mr. Fox. We have no more time to go into it now, but I must insist: when we return, you will give full disclosure. Full disclosure, Mr. Fox. Can you give me your solemn word?"

Mary's voice engaged in conversation grew louder. They were coming.

Fox sighed. "Indeed, it is most likely a long time coming. Agreed, then." He began to speak rapidly, mindful of the impending interruption outside the door. "Hess will lie in state. The viewing of the body before burial is open to friends and neighbors. There will be no opportunity during daylight hours to do what we must."

My breath caught. "You mean for us to go at night?"

"I doubt very much the staff and any mourners who are about would take kindly to seeing us pound a stake through the corpse of their friend."

"Are you making a joke?" I tilted my head at him, as if to consider him from a new angle. "I did not know you had a sense of humor."

I do not think it was my imagination that his expression changed. His voice was gruff when he said, "There is much of me you do not know."

Drawn forward, it was all I could do to keep my bearings. "Indeed, Mr. Fox, it is my chief complaint."

He arched a sardonic eyebrow. My heart beat rather fitfully. I did not like to admit it, but Valerian Fox had a strange, deeply unsettling effect on me.

The door opened, and our encounter was abruptly terminated with Mary's exclamation, "There you are, Emma. I thought we might find you in the library— Oh!"

Her gaze caught Valerian Fox, and she hesitated. Her look, when she glanced back at me, was sly. "Oh. Yes, well . . . Mrs. Bedford has some wonderful shawls she wants us to embroider for Alyssa. You know your sister loved your idea, and we thought we would get started right away on the project."

Fox murmured a perfunctory "Your servant" to us all, then exited the room.

Mary raised an eyebrow, but I cut off the inquiries I knew she wanted to level at me, clapping my hands together and donning a wide, winning smile. "Let's begin right away!"

When I could break away from the sewing clutch, I wanted to spend some time on my own. I stole from the house, needing to walk, to swing my arms and move fast across open land. Once out of doors, I traveled swiftly, savoring each labored beat of my heart as it did its work, thrusting thick blood through my body as I put distance between myself and Dulwich Manor.

I came to the hawthorn tree, having obeyed the instincts that were beginning to flourish inside of me. Mr. Fox had promised to tell me what it was he knew of my mother. Of me. Of this, this driving urge that was not a voice, nor an impulse. It felt like quiet and confident knowledge, and I prodded it with my mind, like a tongue prods a sore tooth.

I had speared snakes on the tines of a pitchfork. I had seen invisible figures, heard an invisible presence cry out in anger and frustration when my presence had barred it from entry. I had read portents in the very atmosphere around here, and shed my blood on its ground.

I stared at the tree, and felt a certainty that its enigma and I would meet. For no reason I knew, I ripped a small branch from it, staring at the wicked barbs curving on its surface. One touch would draw blood. I stripped the thorns and put the switch in my pocket.

When I returned to the manor, I sat in the cheery elegance of my cousin's dining salon and ate heartily of beef and potatoes and crisp green beans. Among this resplendent show of civilization set to light by candles and gaslight—our tools to banish the dark—I fortified myself to participate in a ritual of old-fashioned superstition, of primitive survival against ancient evil. And after I'd eaten my fill, after I'd sat in the company of my sister and cousin, debating the merits of chintz over cotton, I did not even marvel at how easy it was to leave the cultured company and slip up to my bedroom to rest, read, and prepare for the grisly duties that lay ahead.

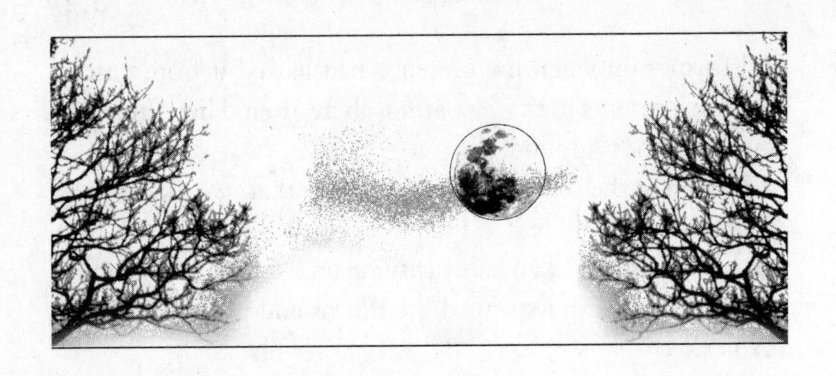

Chapter Seventeen

Thus it was night when we set out to kill Mr. Hess again.

I dressed in one of my older dresses since its skirt wasn't as wide, and the less voluminous folds of the dark lightweight wool would not impede my progress quite so much. I longed for the freedom of trousers but I did not dare. It is strange how one, even in the face of such extraordinary circumstances, clings to convention.

I laced up my heaviest boots and pulled my hair into an untidy knot at the nape of my neck. Thus attired, I stuffed a few items into a reticule and hurried to the appointed place.

Mr. Fox came along presently. He glanced pointedly at my bag.

"I have some holy water, and the crucifix from the church I told you about," I said. "In case Mr. Hess is . . ."

An ugly vision of Mr. Hess's kind face twisted in the horrible mask I had seen on Wadim afflicted me just then and I could not go on.

Fox held up the rucksack I had seen him carry before. "I am always well protected, as you should be. Put the cross on your person, Emma. You are a prize, costly perhaps, but the temptation for Marius will not be small."

"Prize? What do you mean?"

"You already know you are different. There is power in you, and Marius craves power."

I blinked, startled by the thought. I knew he was right, however. I simply felt it. I was strong, somehow, and perhaps I was brave. That was why he had come after me. I had been so intensely worried for Henrietta, of what Marius could do to harm her, that I had not realized I was in danger myself. Why had I not thought of it before?

My stomach felt a bit queasy. I hurriedly fastened the crucifix about my neck.

"This will be different than Wadim," Fox told me. "If Marius made a vampire of George Hess, we can assume it was not voluntary, and that counts for a great deal in the revenant world. Should Hess waken, he will be in a confused and horrified state. It will be beyond terrible, and you must gird yourself for this."

I gulped and nodded. "I am ready," I said. My voice shook. He did not challenge my lie.

He had saddled two horses, and tied them to the post at the base of the stone staircase leading down from the front door. After helping me mount, he led us through the moonlit night, the two of us silent and reflective as we proceeded to Hess's house.

"I would keep you out of this if I could," Fox said into the darkness. There was apology, even self-recrimination in his voice.

"I feel strongly that . . . that I should be with you in this."

He nodded. He did not like it, but he did acknowledge my place here.

We gained entry into the Hess household easily. We were able to climb to a small balcony with the aid of a young ash. From there, it was merely a matter of forcing the handle of a French door.

"Such skill," I murmured as he held the door open for me, a courtesy that might have seemed frivolous under the present circumstances but, in fact, felt quite natural.

He appeared embarrassed as he met my eye. His aptitude at breaking into people's homes spoke of past deeds such as this, nocturnal missions to do unspeakable things to the dead. However, I must admit it was quite handy.

"Here," he whispered, and led me deeper into the house.

It was pitch-dark as we moved away from the windows of the small library in which we'd entered. The deep shadows suggested a room teeming with books, piled on every surface and even on the floor. This proved no hazard, for Mr. Fox seemed not to have any trouble maneuvering in the thick darkness.

"You really do have excellent eyesight," I murmured, remembering all he'd seen from horseback the day he'd rescued Henrietta and me from The Sanctuary.

Mr. Fox took my hand and I pressed rather shamelessly against his side. His warmth and strength were reassuring, and

I felt a surge of something close to joy. I again experienced that sense of intimacy, of being united with someone in a deeply vital cause, just as I had the night we'd killed Wadim together. It felt, if I might be vaporish enough to say so, like destiny.

We turned off into the salon, where the perfume of the flowers hovered stiflingly thick in the air. The drapes had been drawn at dusk, as was custom, so there was no chance for moonlight to aid us. In the quiet of the house, as we approached the remains of George Hess, I could hear only the sound of Fox's breathing, and my own; all else was still.

"Stay here," Mr. Fox whispered. "I shall check the draperies are sealed tight before I strike the match."

"Yes," I replied, taking infinite care with the door so that the click of the latch as I shut it was as quiet as I could make it. A match flared, and a meager light emerged. His features above the lamp were in sharp relief, an eerie effect. We turned together to view the body of George Hess. The pale, ghastly face glowed in our lamplight. He was laid out on a crepe-draped table, looking peaceful, I suppose, for his face in death held no expression, his hands were clasped demurely on his chest. Behind him, the large mirror mounted over the fireplace was also covered in the same black crepe. Before it stood a mantle clock, the glass door still open from when the servant had performed the solemn duty of stopping it, in reverence of the dead.

We approached, and I was happy to see the waxy countenance of true death. "Thank God," I said, glancing at my companion. "We don't have to . . . what was it you called it? Shrive? We do not have to shrive him."

"You have noticed the difference between his appearance and how flush Wadim appeared, but do not trust that. Always remember, Emma—the vampire has many ways to deceive."

"But Mr. Hess—"

"Hush!"

His eyes lifted, and without moving a single other muscle, he swept the room from one end to the other with a hard stare, his eyes like twin points of coal.

There is a cold that is not the fresh, clean, pine-tinged scent of deep winter. It is the cold of the crypt, and it is stale and malodorous without any particular scent. It is the smell, perhaps, of great age. Of rock and earth and dried flesh that had long since ceased to hold life's warmth.

That is what I sensed suddenly. It whispered around me, like bony fingers plucking delicately at my nerves. Looking to Mr. Fox, whose body was as solid and still as the sarcen stones of Avebury, I whispered, "Do you feel it?"

I had only a moment to register the tightness winding itself around Mr. Fox, the way his lips curled as emotion gripped him for one fleeting moment. Fury and fear. He was afraid—that surprised me—and more than a little. I could see it or sense it, I didn't know which. It was his fear that struck my blood cold.

Something came in swiftly between Mr. Fox and me, and flung me against the far wall. Darkness blurred my vision but I fought for consciousness. Mr. Fox shouted something to me, a belated warning, and then there was a terrible sound as he was thrown violently to the ground.

I lay stunned, but it lasted only a second or two before my mind flew to the things I'd brought with me. I searched for my bag, but found that both it and Fox's rucksack lay out of my reach.

The lamp had fallen, but it somehow remained lit, creating light and shadow that fought for possession of the room in a harlequin battle of black and white. I could only see glimpses of

the large, hulking form of the lord vampire hovering over Mr. Fox, a phantasmagoria come to life.

Fox scrabbled ineffectually against his attacker. Marius had him by the shoulders, holding him pinned to the ground. I glimpsed talon-like fingers, hooked like claws tangled in the dark cloth, and the vicious profile of a beast, skin pulled back, sharp teeth bared in a leering grin of triumph. The aspect of the vampire was horrible, stealing my voice as I watched through a vortex of dizzying terror. Fox's hands were at the fiend's throat, thrusting him away, but his strength was no match for the great lord's. Marius bent closer, jaw opening like the maw of a wolf.

"Emma, run!" Fox choked.

"No!" I cried, and this seemed to snap me into action. My legs moved, my hand reached, and I grasped the iron candle stand. But when my fingers touched the cold metal, I drew away and picked up instead a smaller pillar of silver. Throwing off the wax taper, I weighed it in my hand with satisfaction. It was heavy and substantial; it felt good. It felt right. Standing, I took a moment to aim, to focus and solidify my will on what I wanted, and then hurled it across the room.

It struck Marius on his temple, and he reared. But Fox's hands went limp, his strength gone at last. Marius froze, holding the listless Mr. Fox for a moment before letting him go. The body hit the ground with sickening impact, and I cried out in despair, for I feared I'd acted too late.

Marius now turned toward me. His movement was strange, or perhaps I was still too dazed to see how he closed the space between us. It seemed to happen in an instant, as if he floated over the intervening space; he was suddenly upon me without taking a step.

I fought my terror, digging into the deepest part of myself

to think, remain calm. But my mind screamed for Valerian Fox. And then I could not spare my fallen companion another thought, for the beast was here, over me and before me and to the left and right of me. I did not know where to turn to face him. I seemed surrounded, swallowed, the figure everywhere and the haze of its stinking energy plummeting me into darkness.

"Our Father, who art in Heaven," I stammered, "hallowed . . ."

But the prayer died. I was not ready to relinquish my life. If it came to it, I would pray, with all my soul and all my heart, for both Mr. Fox and myself. But now—now I would fight. If I could understand how.

The sensation of arms enveloping me slithered over my skin. I opened my mouth to scream, but no sound came out. Blistering cold bit deep into me and I knew the fight was lost already. Lost before it was even begun, and then . . . and then I heard Fox move, and, glancing down, I saw the light catch the dark planes and angles of his face as he turned his head toward me. "Emma," he rasped.

Marius was here with me, in front of me as his form materialized out of shadow. I could see him as plainly as I could see Fox, a monster no more. The vampire's face was handsome now, made up of strong features. I saw his lips were thin and cruel, his eyes bright and alert. Dark, straight hair gleamed with pomade, pulled straight back from a wide, intelligent forehead. His nose was sharp, large, and matched by a prominent, clean-shaven chin. It was a face one would notice in a crowd, the face of a man who wielded power as his due. A face that would haunt, deep and cloying, even if you never suspected what abomination lay beneath the enticing surface.

He tightened his grip, and his voice now spoke my name, echoing Fox. "Emma." His breath was like woodland earth,

rich and loamy, unpleasant but not repugnant and I did not twist away. I allowed it to fan across my face, caressing images of age and unspeakable mastery. A kind of lethargy came over me, bleeding away my will, and I felt, as if a finger were laid against my chin, a pressure to turn my head toward him.

"Keep your eyes closed!" Fox shouted. "Do not look at him!"

There was no sound from my captor, but I felt the warm vibration of a chuckle trickle over my flesh. I looked, for my mind was sluggish and my strength of purpose draining out of me, and in the vampire's eyes I was pierced by sharp tines of pleasure.

My body grew taut in his embrace, my skin pricked and sensitive. My throat charged with acute awareness, and this dreamy, electric feeling swept downward, through me, into me, igniting an ache to move closer, be closer . . .

"Little moth," I heard, the brush of his foul mind abrading mine. "The flame will kill you but you cannot resist."

I surged forward, a yearning bursting inside of me, a wanting, a desperate, despicable need. Desire crawled in and over my enflamed nerves, asserted itself—a hateful, beautiful desire to be possessed, and though it felt filthy it was also irresistible.

"Emma! For God's sake!"

I barely heard Fox. From the heart of the vortex pulling me into its gravity, I had no care for him. Had Marius ripped open Fox's throat right there in front of me, I doubt I would have so much as blinked. I was euphoric and horrified, the latter, I suppose, a result of that one small, dying breath of myself crushed under the lord vampire's greater will.

I thought, *Mother?* I was going to her. In the eyes of the thing that held me was all fulfillment, all . . . All. Simply all.

Then the voice of the vampire, distant and fine, scrabbled

across my brain, and it said, "You shall not tempt me. It would cost me too much to take you to me." And then . . . then he spoke, or thought, or did the repulsive thing that connected his consciousness to mine, speaking with something of a care, a hint of respect. He said, "There is the touch of the vampire in you."

I hung there, too bewildered to think what this meant. And then it lessened—everything he had invoked, every sensation, every thought, and every part of me he'd summoned forth to swell to my completion . . . it simply ebbed.

The entirety of my self bucked, protested, yearned, and it was too painful to bear. My arms flailed and the sight of the face, hovering as a lover's would just before a kiss, simply faded. There were only my own grasping fingers in front of me, pulling desperately at the empty air as I was left alone.

He moved in the form of a dark mist to Fox. I called out, "No!" but it was not to ward Marius from his prey. I am deeply ashamed that it was in protest at my abandonment. Whatever evil thing he was about to do to Valerian Fox, I craved it for myself. I wanted him to come back to me.

Fox was valiant. He rose to his knees, and though the pain must have been excruciating, it did not stop him. Then he said, "You cannot have me. I reject you in the name of Christ."

A low, chilling laughter spread out under us, like an enchanted carpet that would lift us all up and away into madness and death.

And then I could hear hushed tones, that cryptic voice making some promise. I was unsure, but I thought it told Mr. Fox that it was already too late. And I, I was nearly out of my mind. He would take Fox. But not me. Not me!

I began to weep, in despair and humiliation, coiling my body into a helpless ball. "Mr. Fox," I whispered, trying my voice. It trembled with strain. "You must run . . ."

"Emma, go!" His voice was sharp with command. The small, human part of me was touched. He mistakenly thought I wished rescue. I wanted nothing of the sort. I wanted its opposite with such ferocity—knowing it would be denied me—that I could not breathe the despoiled air around me.

Marius's shadow deepened, and Fox's face changed. The vampire was taking form again, and I instinctively knew this was because he was ready to strike, to bite.

To feed.

Marius reached for Fox and smiled. It was a beautiful, victorious smile, and his jaws opened. Gleaming razors caught the dim light, brilliant white and almost glowing. He nodded to Fox. "You are mine already, are you not? I can take you with me now."

I saw on Mr. Fox's face the defeat of the damned. "Run," I said, a weak, mewling sound. He had not looked into Marius's eyes and thus he could have escaped if he wished. But I knew he would not leave me, even at the price of his own soul.

I wept. I confess, my own person was so thoroughly stripped, I do not know for whom I cried. Was it for Mr. Fox, who was facing a damnation worse than mere death, or for me who was to be denied the same?

"Demon!" a rich, timbered voice thundered, blistering into the exquisite realm of my suffering. My head snapped up, and I saw the form of a large man towering above me. He moved quickly to stand before Mr. Fox and even in this wicked light I recognized the priest, Father Luke.

Tears ran in a pair of steady streams on my cheek. Father Luke did not even glance at me, but forged forward. Latin words spilled out of him with authority, and I could feel Marius hesitate at this new enemy.

The priest held before him a large golden crucifix, the one from the rosary I'd seen him with in the graveyard. He wielded it with absolute confidence and the effect on Marius was instantaneous. The fiend, stone-faced with rage, blinked into mist, which abruptly dissipated.

I could see by the darting glances of both men that they did not know where he had retreated. But I did. He was in the corner. Shrouded in shadow, he gathered his corporeal self behind the priest's back.

I knew what he planned. My head had cleared enough for me to think again. But I was weak; my legs would not support me, and my hands shook in a pitiable palsy. I saw the shadowed Marius, invisible to the others, begin to slide toward Mr. Fox, who mistakenly had gone lax in relief.

Crawling on all fours, I dove to snatch the small reticule I'd brought with me. I dug my hand inside and called, "Father Luke!" I held out the thin switch of the hawthorn I'd brought with me. The priest stared for a moment, and the foul stench that was my reliable harbinger of the fiend's presence grew. It was strong. He was coming.

"Hurry," I said urgently. "He is behind you, in the shadow. He means to take Mr. Fox. Use this."

I shouted this with authority, and threw the stick. The priest caught it, confused for a moment before casting it down. His fist closed tightly on his cross.

"No," Fox shouted. "She is Dhampir. Do as she instructs."

I moved, taking up the fallen hawthorn branch, but my body betrayed me. Marius had formed again, scorchingly handsome—

almost beautiful—and seeming to glow with the red light of evil. Our eyes met for one moment before I remembered to yank my gaze away. But I was still stricken, and the hawthorn fell from my nerveless fingers.

Father Luke fell back, then recollected himself and surged forward, arm outstretched so that the crucified Christ was his weapon. Marius emitted a sound that was the hiss of the snake and the blood-freezing growl of the wolf, combined. He struck out, his arm like a whip, sending the crucifix flying out of Father Luke's hand.

A sob exploded from me, knowing as I did we were doomed. This small, involuntary sound saved us, for Marius whipped about to me, searching for the threat. I saw a flash of fear in his eye, as if some danger might come from my quarter.

Before I could puzzle at that unexpected reaction, Father Luke leapt forward, moving astonishingly fast for a man of his size, falling then rolling across the ground. He came up with the slender stalk of hawthorn. Marius snapped around, surprised and wary of the switch of wood.

Hope flared, then quickly died as Father Luke took the pointed stake by its ends and, in one swift, downward motion, brought it down over a raised knee and broke it in two. He held out the broken pieces of the stick in the formation of a cross. *"Deus, in nómine tuo salvum me fac, det virtúte tua age causam meam,"* Father Luke intoned commandingly. Marius retreated a step, his eyes on the makeshift cross.

I watched as Father Luke advanced, and all of a sudden, I knew. "Pierce him!" I called.

"Do it!" Fox bellowed behind me.

We all froze—all four of us—before the priest broke apart his talisman and, grasping the shorter piece, the one with the hastily filed point I'd fashioned, made the quick, slashing motion of an experienced knife artist.

Marius twisted defensively. The jab caught the lord vampire in the upper arm, yet the wound appeared to cause him great agony. He roared and stamped, his great cloak whirling as he hunched over, grasping the gash. With a great rush of air, he dissolved once again, the foul-smelling mist hanging in the air for a moment before dispersing at lightning speed in all directions, like talc in a gust.

The silent tableau of the three of us remained in place. Then Father Luke flung down the hawthorn stick and turned away, falling on his knees to pray.

I rushed forward, and took up the stick. The tip glistened in the dark with what I could only assume was blood. Marius's blood. I was exceedingly confused. Wadim had released not a drop of fluid or blood when Fox had pierced him. Only bits of dried rust-colored old blood had appeared on the stake. This made sense; Wadim had been dead. But was not Marius equally dead? How was it blood flowed in the veins of a dead being?

I threw the useless thing aside and felt a rush of bone-crushing fatigue as I turned back to the others. The priest still murmured his prayers. Mr. Fox was still kneeling on the floor, in pain as he struggled to rise.

Sickness stole over me, crawling like spiders from the pit of my stomach. I felt as bereft as if I'd endured a rape of the most violent kind. I looked from man to man, searching for something to say, for some normal thing to banish the encroaching horror as what just had transpired began to take root in my awareness. I had been moving on instinct, but now—now I could think again. I could remember, and feel the violation.

And, oh, God, I was sick!

I doubled over and sank down to my knees, a boneless, nerveless heap, desiring only to expire in shame and the deepest humiliation. A moment later, gentle hands lifted me, bore me away from that place. I looked, and it was Mr. Fox who held me.

He touched my face gently, touching the burning spot where Marius's shadow finger had rested. "Emma, I am so sorry."

"What am I?" I cried.

His look was pity and tenderness and it made me weep again. I could not stop, not even when he spoke in short, hushed tones to Father Luke. They did their work with Mr. Hess, and I watched, exhausted and bereft. They staked him, breaking off the tip and closing his coat over the evidence of the deed, and then Father Luke prepared the body using holy water. Mr. Fox did something with salt and muttered prayers in a language that made the priest's eyebrows crawl upward over his forehead.

They laid our friend to rest. And when this was done, Mr. Fox smoothed my hair from my face and said, "I shall get you home now."

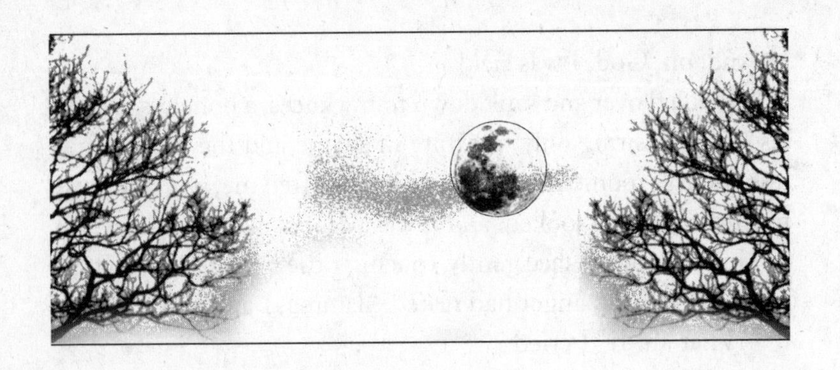

Chapter Eighteen

We did not go back to Dulwich Manor. I was in no condition for that. The men conferred, and it was agreed we would return with Father Luke to the rectory at Saint Michael in the Fields.

Three quarters of an hour later, I found myself sitting in the small, rather claustrophobic confines of a parish drawing room with a Catholic priest and a self-confessed vampire hunter, drinking strong Madeira wine as though it were lemonade. I did not look at anyone. I kept my eyes forward and unfocused as the horror of the last hour rippled through me over and over again. I could still feel the lingering trace, like the smear of slime left in the wake of a bloated slug, of the great vampire's touch.

Neither man tried to comfort me. For this I was grateful. I was allowed exactly what I needed: to be left alone until the wine began to relax me.

"I suppose I should begin by asking who you are," the priest finally said after a protracted and heavy silence. I glanced up from contemplating the deep crimson in my glass. He was talking to Mr. Fox.

I studied the elegant man sitting quietly, encased in the enigmatic stillness he wore so well, the very thing that had driven me to nearly pulling out my hair on so many occasions. *Yes, indeed, Mr. Fox. Let us find out who you are.*

Fox looked at the priest with flat, expressionless eyes. "For many years, I have been hunting the vampire you just confronted," he said.

"I suppose you have a compelling reason for such a dangerous occupation." Father Luke's voice was modulated, wearing the authority of a Roman cleric, but it was not mild. Nothing about the hulking man could ever be so.

Mr. Fox allowed a hint of emotion to pass over his features. And then it was gone. "He took something from me."

My eyebrows beetled as I watched the priest, observing how sanguine he was. All this talk of vampires and he did not so much as touch the crucifix suspended prominently from a chain around his neck. And he had accepted Mr. Fox's answer—which was no answer at all. But then, one doesn't press another too closely when one has secrets of one's own.

"Who are you?" I demanded abruptly, startling both men. I never would have behaved so crassly if not for the floating, free feeling the wine had given me. I uncurled a finger from around my wineglass and leveled it at Father Luke. "You are no ordinary priest."

He smiled quietly as he arranged his hands on his lap. "Let me just say that I am aware of the presence of a vampire in this area, and have been for some time. Which you guessed, Mrs. Andrews. I am afraid my thespian skills are lacking. It did not occur to me to feign surprise until after you were gone. I gave myself away, I fear."

"Yes," I said, and suddenly wanted to weep with relief. Finally, truth. "The tree up on The Sanctuary. I saw him there."

Father Luke shook his head. "That is not where he sleeps. I have already looked." He raised his eyes first to Mr. Fox and then me. "I have not discovered that place yet. Nor have you, obviously. I have thought it likely Silbury Hill, or the Long Barrows. Those are tombs, after all. If he has indeed set up his resting place there, we will never find him even if we had every man and woman in the village searching for a hundred years. It is simply too vast."

"What are these crypts, and the stone circles?" I asked. "What do they represent?"

"Death," he said simply. "Avebury is a necropolis, Mrs. Andrews. A city organized around funereal purposes. A city of the dead, to be precise."

Mr. Fox said, "Which lies along the Saint Michael line, populated by strongholds built by the Church. They are attempting to protect something."

Father Luke spoke as if choosing his words carefully. "The forces concentrated along the meridian line are of interest to the Mother Church. Chapels, churches, and such guard the places along the line where the barrier between worlds might grow, from time to time, alarmingly thin. Saint Michael's is one such outpost."

I was rather stunned at this revelation. According to what he was telling us, under the blessing—indeed, the mandate—of Rome, he manned an outpost along the line where the living and the dead were believed to meet. All of my earlier musings on the Church's involvement, which had seemed outlandish at the time, appeared to have come very close to the truth.

"From before the first missionaries," Father Luke continued, "when this land belonged to pagan worshippers, even back to the earliest settlements in this area, this place has been known to be holy. That is why the stones were brought here, spread out along the hillside to form the monument, the Serpent." He paused, waiting to see if this got a reaction from either Mr. Fox or me. "It is a very . . . particularly important place, one that has played a significant role in the battle between good and evil throughout the centuries."

Fox lowered his chin to rest on his steepled fingers. "Do you know why Marius has come?"

Father Luke paused, then replied carefully, "The modern church does not officially recognize the existence of vampires."

"You are not going to bore me with doctrine," Mr. Fox challenged darkly.

"I merely wish to make the point that I am not speaking with any official standing."

The feeling was returning, that awful invasion, as if maggots had infested my veins. The smell of Marius's breath pricked my nostrils; the memory acutely vivid, and yet even now—and through all of my disgust—desire for what he offered stirred in me. My hand shook as I put my glass to my lips and drained the last of Madeira.

Then I spoke. "The tree, the one up on The Sanctuary. It has the words 'The Blood is the Life' carved on it. And I found a broken plaque on the ground with a fish symbol, exactly like the one on your ring."

"The tree is a holy symbol," Father Luke explained. "Hawthorn, called whitethorn or even Christthorn by some, is what the Roman soldiers used to construct the crown of thorns for Jesus. Also, it is not native to England, but is from the east. The fact that it blooms twice a year, most oddly at around the Christmastide season as well as summer, enhances its mystique."

"It must have real powers," Fox reasoned. "You saw what just scratching the skin with the cutting from the tree did."

The priest frowned as he gave this some thought. "Yes. That was quite clever." Rising, Father Luke consulted a stack of books on a shelf behind his chair. "Let me read to you what Sir John Maundeville wrote: 'Then was Our Lord led into a garden, and there they made him a crown of the branches of the Albiespyne, that is Whitethorn, that grew in the same garden, and set it upon his head. And therefore hath the Whitethorn many virtue. For he that beareth a branch on him thereof, no thunder, nay no manner of tempest may dare him, nay in the house that it is in may not evil ghost enter.'"

But I had already known, somehow, that the hawthorn would hold sway over evil.

Mr. Fox's voice, as dark as velvet, cut in. "Folk wisdom has it a vampire can be imprisoned in a tree."

Father Luke bowed his head and smiled somewhat bitterly. "It does indeed."

"That tree on The Sanctuary. It was sealed with the symbol exactly like the one on the ring you wear. I believe, Father, that you should tell us all you know."

The priest closed his eyes for a moment. "The symbol is the mark of my order. For generations, our priests have been here at this church. There is a power, a being which is bound in some way to The Sanctuary."

"Is it a vampire, an ancient and powerful one?"

"I do not completely understand the nature of it myself. In the siege, when Cromwell laid waste to the Catholic presence in this land, much was lost. We managed to hold on to the church."

"You lost the house," I put in. "Dulwich Manor. It must have been part of this 'outpost' originally. The bishop had Latin sayings carved into the wood. They are about this danger, aren't they?"

He nodded. "When Cromwell's armies came, they took the house and all of the lands. A local man who was influential with the Roundheads impressed upon the invaders to leave the church be. He was persuasive, and ultimately successful. That was why the outpost was not disturbed and left to Rome in the midst of their purge. No doubt copious amounts of money changed hands to accomplish this. More important, during this time, the hawthorn tree survived, thanks to the Lord's blessing."

"Why is it so important?" I implored. "What is it?"

"A prison. Its tenant is something unspeakably evil. As I said, I know little, although I will refer you to the Old Testament story in the book of Tobit, for this is how it was explained to me. In this book, God sends the archangel Raphael to protect Tobit's son from the demon Asmodeus." He smiled wryly. "Raphael used incense made from a gutted fish to entrance the demon and lure him into a tree, where he imprisoned him. So, you recognize this is akin to what has happened here in Avebury. Thus, the apotrope on the seal, which you noticed, Mrs. Andrews. The same one on my ring." He glanced down at the gold band with the engraving of the fish.

"It was shattered," I said. "I found it in pieces."

"Yes. The seal had been broken. That was how I knew that I, of all my predecessors, would be the one called to execute the duty for which generations of priests have been trained. If this being on The Sanctuary is what Marius has come for, he shall be stopped. I have been well trained for this."

"With what, prayer?" Fox became impassioned. "I do not care to merely stop him. I've come here to destroy him." There was a rather desperate quality to his tone. Poor Mr. Fox, I thought drowsily. The vampire Marius—or Emil, or whoever—took something from him. Something he cared for very deeply, it was obvious to see. Perhaps it was a woman. A wife, a love . . . I was startled by the sudden jealousy I felt.

"You must leave it to me," Father Luke said quietly.

"We can help you," Fox urged. "And you must help us."

The priest bowed his head. "You have to understand, sir, that I took a most sacred vow. Do you understand? I am a priest, and I am well equipped to handle the events facing me, despite what you believe."

"People are dying, man!" Fox exploded.

Father Luke nodded. "I am painfully aware of that. And I am not unsympathetic, believe me. I have some items that can aid and protect you in your own struggle with Marius." He cast me a smile without rancor. "You might require more than one crucifix and a small vial of blessed water." He stood. "I have some relics, items of religious significance that have been blessed by truly holy men. They have certain power, for only goodness can fight what you must face."

"Goodness," Fox repeated, rising to meet him. Father Luke was taller, Mr. Fox leaner, and yet the two men looked a pair. Not friends. Not enemies, either.

"Goodness is exactly the issue, sir," Father Luke explained. "What benefit will water blessed by a corrupt priest have you? The blessing must be done by a man right in the eyes of God. Not a perfect man, mind you. We would be ill fated if that were required, for those are in short supply." His smile was meant to be wry. It appeared grim.

"Then you are saying not all holy water is effective?" I asked.

"Nothing done outside of the state of grace is effective. Consider a host consecrated by a priest whose faith is faltering. Or any sacrament performed while the priest is engaged in some sin of deceit, or perverted lust, or greed."

Fox's expression was fierce as he comprehended. "Indeed. So that is why my weapons have sometimes failed me. It has seemed there was no sense in the way two crosses will repel differently, or whether holy water will scorch corrupt flesh."

Father Luke nodded. "Come with me, then, and see what I have for you. You may join us if you like, Mrs. Andrews."

I declined, and after they had left, I bolted out of my chair. Alone, I sought to rid myself of the memory of Marius. It sat like curdled blood in my veins. The wine I had drunk caught my balance in a vortex. I steadied my hand on a table and bent my head, waiting for the wave of sickness to pass. I wanted nothing more than to curl into a tight ball and weep until I was clean again. It would be a relief to seek my sister's side and apply my time to needlepoint and sewing baby clothes, to redeem myself, live at last in the friendship and peace I'd always desired.

Yet I had only to think of Henrietta, and my thoughts changed. Cowardice receded sharply, and I felt like an empty vessel, devoid of all but the determination written into my bones to protect her. It was not bravery or heroism; it was love, simply that, and it did not banish my fear and disgust and dread. It merely made them irrelevant.

I stood and began to pace a tight circle as I gathered my courage back to its sticking place, as it were. On a table by the door, I noticed a carved stone Celtic cross that seemed a bit pagan for this setting. From one arm dangled a black ribbon from which a gold badge hung. Carved on the face was the scene from the church painting, that of a winged angel standing upon a serpent. Saint Michael the Archangel, the patron of this church and the power meridian which it guards.

I peered at the serpent, trying to see if it were a dragon, as in the painting I'd seen in the church. It was difficult to say but I rather thought the heroic figure standing victorious over his foe appeared more Saint George than angelic. Mr. Hess had mentioned the Feast of Saint George as being significant in the seasons of good and evil. It never occurred to me how closely these two were linked—Saint George and Saint Michael. They could have been variants of the same legend.

I cradled the gold disk in my hand. It was heavy. It must be worth a great deal of money. On the back, I found the fish symbol, along with the words "Knights of the Order of Saint Michael of the Wing."

As soon as the men returned—with Mr. Fox's bag held tightly against his side, filled, I assumed, with his boon—I pled the urgent desire to return to the manor. My wish was granted. I fancied Mr. Fox's grip was gentle, almost caressing, as he helped me to my mount. We rode home without any conversation, but as we were bidding our farewells to one another, he took my hands in his.

"I have not forgotten my promise. We shall talk tomorrow, and I will answer any question you might pose."

I was contented to wait. I needed to sleep, for the weariness went deeper than bodily fatigue. I was exhausted to the deepest corner of my soul. The defiling stench of Marius's touch—not so much to my flesh as my brittle, aching will—was still with me, and it remained with me as I plunged hard into troubled sleep.

After an interminable morning and a never-ending game of Pope Joan, in which even purposefully losing to Alyssa won me no favor, I was on pins and needles to speak to Mr. Fox. Mary, however, had a mind to have a word with me. While I was exiting the water closet, she pulled me aside.

She had noted my friendship with Mr. Fox, it seemed. "He is a single man, after all," she observed speculatively.

"We are both sorely disturbed by the death of Mr. Hess," I told her carefully.

"Is that all?" Her eyebrows inched up her forehead in an obvious innuendo.

"Mary! I am just out of mourning. We are friends only."

"Well, I am glad to hear it. He is not completely suitable, you know. I thought at first he might be interesting, but he never seems to warm to the company. And it is not a good time for . . . well, anything more than friendship. Alyssa would be most put out if you were occupied with a romance. You must make a point to spend more time with her."

My stretched nerves snapped. "Sometimes it seems as if my family would be happy if I would think of nothing but Alyssa and her whims and her preferences and her moods. I am sorry if my friendship with Mr. Fox troubles you, but there is no harm in it."

"Emma," she said, seeming contrite, "I am not attempting to play favorites. It is just . . . her condition."

"When you were increasing with Henrietta, did you teeter on the brink of severe illness should a frown crease your brow? This is nothing short of tyranny, Mary."

She took a bracing breath. I saw she sincerely meant to offer help. "I do not wish to intrude on what was surely a private conversation, but Alyssa told me you and she had had something of a confession. Your neglect is particularly hurtful after such a deeply felt discussion. She feels ignored."

"I have not ignored her. I . . ." But I had. With good reason, but who would know this?

Mary took up when I could not finish. "It is not only Alyssa. Yes, as a widow, you are not subject to the same social prescriptions as an unmarried woman. But, Emma, you cannot comport yourself as you have been with Mr. Fox. I do not like the amount of time you are spending in his company. You two seem secretive."

"That is ridiculous," I defended, although I could not quite summon the indignation I needed, for she was quite right.

She frowned at me. "He is so very . . . odd."

"Well, I am odd, too. Or so I've been told often enough."

"Oh, Emma."

We left on poor terms, and I cannot say I was unaffected by this. Despite the larger concerns awaiting my attention, I still cared deeply for the growing rift between myself and my relatives.

It was not until after luncheon that Mr. Fox and I were able to speak. We went to the garden, which was cast under a canopy of gunmetal-gray clouds. Cold rain spit down from these, driving us under the shelter of the folly. We remained in full view of

the house—a measure of convention I took from my conversation with Mary.

"Now you will tell me," I said to him. "What is it you know of my mother?"

I had not spoken harshly, nor pleadingly, but calmly. He regarded me with equal placidness, neither one of us blinking.

"I know nothing of your mother—" he began.

I ignored the dismay that stabbed through me. "Then why did you ask so specifically about her?"

"I suspect . . ." His face collapsed, and I saw he was not being evasive at all. It truly pained him to speak. "Mrs. Andrews, please understand. It gives me no peace to say this to you."

I felt the quickening of panic, but I drove on in spite of it. "You called me 'Dhampir.' That beastly gypsy—he called me that, too. What is it?" At the way he flinched, I exclaimed, "Mr. Fox!"

"It is a term from Romania."

"What does it mean?"

He closed his eyes for a moment, then opened them and stared directly into mine. "It means 'little vampire' when translated literally."

There is something of the vampire in you. I made a small sound, a strangled cry.

Fox pressed on. "It is supposed that a Dhampir is the child of *strigoi vii*. The Dhampir is a legendary hunter of undead and cursed beings. It can see and sense them, and possesses instincts to defeat them."

I absorbed this, frozen, numb. Dhampir. Wadim's voice came to me: *Your mother will weep, Dhampir. You should have stayed asleep.*

"It means," Fox said gently, "that you are a child of *strigoi vii*."

The living vampire. I trembled violently as I backed away

from him, rage and terror coursing through me like a black tide. "No. She was not like Wadim. Shc was not evil. She was ill, that was all. She—"

"Emma," he said, starting forward.

My hand lashed out before I knew it would, landing hard on his cheek. His head snapped back. The sound of that slap was like an explosion.

He hadn't been expecting it. Neither had I, but the violence felt good. It felt clean and natural, purely human, and I was glad I'd done it. I hated him at that moment. I hated everything dirty and hateful that he'd just said.

I fled back to the house. The sensation of being unclean sent me to the chamber pot in my room. I retched until I was weak and shaking, lying on the floor until the maid came in and found me. She went for her mistress before I could stop her.

When Mary came in, she put me to bed. I let her. She called in Roger, and they whispered together. Of course, they were fearful of the wasting disease. The dreaded wasting disease . . .

I lay in my bed, Mr. Fox's words echoing inside my head. The *strigoi vii*, the living vampire, is passed by death into existence as the *strigoi mort*. Undead.

My mother was a vampire.

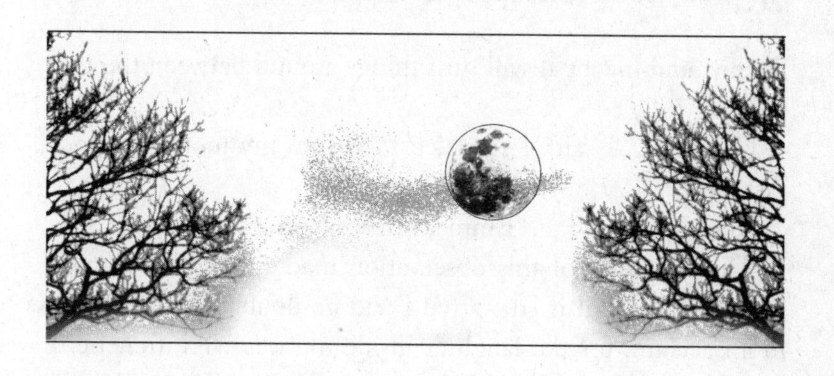

Chapter Nineteen

I opened my eyes the following morning and my first thought came like a falling stone: I am a vampire hunter.

My body moved stiffly, laden with all I'd been through the previous day, but I pushed past it. There was something I had to do. My determination was bitter and resolute, so much so that when Mary saw me at the breakfast table, she misread my mood.

"Are you cross with me about our talk?" she inquired privately.

"No," I said. "I will be going into the village this afternoon. Would it be all right if I used the carriage?"

She gave me a look. "Certainly. But I was hoping you and I could persuade Alyssa to join us for a stroll. Exercise is good for her, and maybe it will turn things around between the two of you."

"I cannot," I said. I shoveled food into my mouth without tasting it.

Mary stared at me. "Emma, you seem strange."

The absurdity of this observation made me smile. I could have laughed, but if I'd started I had no doubt I'd land myself in an asylum, for the laughter inside me was wild, frenetic. I seemed strange, did I? Well, I was strange. I was Dhampir, and if that wasn't the strangest thing imaginable, I did not know what was.

"I am sorry," I managed. "I have something pressing. Please forgive me." I tossed my napkin on my plate and rose. I went directly to the stables to request the carriage be brought out. The wait was short and I was soon on my way.

Uncle Peter did not appear surprised to see me when I entered his rooms. It was as if he'd been expecting . . . no, dreading my arrival. He would have known it was only a matter of time before I would come back and want the rest of Laura's story.

He held his arms out, but in his features, I saw a certain wariness, as if he were prepared for me to reject this offer of affection. I knew I must seem cold. I felt cold, all through me, in the stiffness of my limbs as I moved like a wind-up mechanical doll into his embrace. "I have come about my mother. I want to know the truth. The absolute truth."

Uncle Peter's body drooped, his shoulders rounding under his burden as he trudged ponderously to the chair from which he'd arisen to greet me. Examining his face, I could see deep lines cut into his swarthy skin. He had grown old, I realized. Even in the span of a few days. They had to have been difficult days, and I suspected I knew why.

"It is damp," he said, his voice watery. "Could you fetch me a rug, my dear?"

I did as he asked, laying the wrap over his lap.

"It is troublesome, growing old. The blood thins. You feel a chill all the time." He bowed his head. "I suspected when I left London that the time had come to tell you. Your letter alerted me, although I hoped I was wrong. Then, when I heard of the attack on you in the barn, I knew that, even if I had yet to admit it to myself, the things I'd tried so very hard to forget had come to roost."

"What do you know of the attack in the barn?"

He raised a slender finger and smiled. "Mr. Fox was not as quick as he should have been to destroy the evidence of what you did with those serpents, my dear. A thing like that makes men talk, and if one is listening, one hears evidence others might miss. I have been listening for a long time."

I spoke dully, for I felt betrayed. "Then you know about me. Have you known all along?"

"No, my darling Emma, I have never been sure. That is what I am saying. I feared, yes, but I told myself it could not be. All these years I could never make up my mind if the terrible things I suspected about your mother could be true or if I was, in my unnatural suspicion, an evil and deluded man."

"Then you do know about my mother, about what . . . what happened to her." I could not bring myself to say the word. Vampire.

And, it seemed, neither could he. He lifted a bony shoulder. "I am Romanian. I was raised on the legends and folklore of all manner of ghouls, flesh-eating monsters, baby-stealing crones who fly on broomsticks, werewolves, witches, and blood drinkers. But reality is different than tales told by a hearth on a cold winter's night. There were times, watching Laura at the worst of it, that I easily believed she had been the victim of a cursed demon, and had been transforming into one herself."

His face lightened and he smiled. "But when the breeze blows across your cheek and the sky is bluest blue, such things are absolutely impossible. That is how I have lived since she has been gone—believing while in the darkness and then laughing at my imagination in the light."

I laid my hands palm to palm in my lap, taking my time to gather my thoughts. "Why did you not speak before?"

His face folded into a mask of anguish. "Oh, child, it was always my hope I would never have to."

"But when we spoke last time, still you did not tell me what I needed to know."

"Yes. Darling, forgive me. I was a terrible coward. But you do not know what it is to be old," he said softly. "To feel your vitality fade and your body grow fragile. I simply lost courage. I've kept this nightmare to myself for so long, hoping all the while . . . I was a fool, I know. A weak fool."

I chewed on my lip for a moment, touching two fingers to the pulse beating beneath my earlobe. "And perhaps you did not trust me. You looked at my neck."

Spreading his hands out, he said, "With the powers you possess, it would tempt the greed of these vile creatures. They absorb the strength of those upon whom they feed, did you know? Do not think your gifts protect you, although it would take a being of great magnitude to attempt to take you. I should have warned you. I've been unforgivably mysterious. It was not my intention. I have failed you, and Laura who loved you so."

"It is not useful to blame anyone." I leaned forward. "But it is

time, Uncle Peter. My mother was not mad. It was not a disease that afflicted her, and made her ill."

I saw his throat convulse as he swallowed painfully. "No. This became evident when she recovered."

"She could not have regained her former health."

"No. No, child. She was changed."

I barely whispered. "What was she like?"

He looked away, his eyes focusing on past horrors. "When her strength returned, she commenced frantic attempts to flee her bedchamber, but only at night. She would keen, and I swear I have never heard a more acute sound of suffering. Her hair had turned white"—he pointed to his temple—"in one streak. She would rage, wanting to be set free, saying terrible things."

"What things?" I prompted, pushing the words past the bile rising in my throat. She must have been in agony. Oh, God, she had wanted to hunt, to kill. To drink.

"Of dark things. Emma . . . Very well. Of demons, coming to her in the night. I am afraid she became obsessed with a rather perverted view of religion at this time. She had never been devout, but she was a respectable member of the village congregation. At this time, however, she grew very angry with God. She became enraged when she saw so much as a cross, and refused to attend church. She turned away all treatment, spiritual and medical. She threw the Bible away, ranted against the minister when he came to call on her. All things of religion made her very upset, and Stephen had them removed to keep her calm.

"She managed to escape one night. We never knew how. Out the window, I suppose, although one would have had to fly." His gaze touched mine meaningfully for a second before darting away. "We thought—the mad, they do these things and somehow survive unscathed. It was decided she must have jumped. We did not understand, you see. In any event, your father had no choice after that. He kept her locked up tightly, day and night. She . . . she hated this."

I could feel sweat on my brow, and my stomach clenched with nausea. I knew what my mother was, but the horror of hearing it spoken aloud made it so vivid and real, it was like a physical assault on my emotions. "How was I born if she remained so ill?"

"As I said, she was changed forever from the first onset of the . . . well, the affliction. The madness faded in time. Oh, there remained peculiarities about her. For instance, she could no longer tolerate the outdoors, which she'd once loved, and she liked her room darkened. But she was better, and we were happy to have her restored, even under the conditions that came with it. It was typical for her to languish during the day, then revive in the evening, almost herself, filled with her old vibrancy. Her moods were unpredictable, and a temper that had never before been in evidence became, at times, almost out of control. But, remember, she was still Laura. She was still alive. And they were happy again, Stephen and she. They began to entertain, giving frequent parties."

"But you had to suspect what it was that was happening to her," I observed. "As outrageous as it seems, the signs were very clear—the aversion to light and holy objects."

"I realize, telling you all this now, how absolutely obvious it would seem to you. But there was one thing that stayed my complete belief in what was happening. She had not been bled, you see. There were no marks on her anywhere. And I was glad to surrender those particular suspicions in favor of mere madness."

"Mr. Fox says higher levels of these creatures have charms to seal the wounds so as to conceal the evidence of their presence. I took heart when I heard this. It shows they have fear of us."

His brow furrowed. "Interesting. I have not heard this before. It could be so. But the absence of bite marks was not the only thing that persuaded me I'd been wrong. She discovered she was with child, and she and your father were so happy about it—about you. And for a few years, all seemed well."

I took a moment to mull this intelligence. Was it possible the love of her child, of her family, had given her the strength to resist the calling of vampire blood? My God, what she must have gone through to stay with us, what she must have fought each day to keep from slipping into the world of night and blood. And death.

She had loved me that much, I realized. Joy filled me, sudden and strong. But, of course, this was not the end of the story. "But it did not last," I said.

His face fell. "No. You were three years old, I think, and the madness came again. It was a spring like this, with much rain and the weather cold, like no spring at all. March was as bitter as January, April as bleak as a nightmare. She was found wandering at night again, wet to the bone, and her mind was gone. She grew violent. Except with you." He held up a cautioning finger. "She always loved you, Emma. You can believe this. In the few lucid moments she had left, she begged Stephen to take you away. She was afraid her mind would betray her and you would come to harm. But he could not, for when she was with you, she was calm, almost peaceful."

I squeezed my eyes shut tight and felt the moisture on my lashes. The vampire must have come back for her, bringing storms. A spring very much like this.

"I told Stephen he must lock her away, for this was the cure before," Uncle Peter went on. "But he refused. He could not bear to face the truth, you see. It was worse, so much worse this time, knowing what was to come."

We were quiet for a space, him remembering, me imagining how it must have been. "How did it end?"

His mouth worked. "This is very difficult, Emma." He raised his eyes to me sadly. "One night, she managed to escape the house while the nurse slept, as she'd done many nights before. She simply never returned. Your father thought it best to tell everyone we had found her and buried her in Hampshire, where her people originated. Then we never spoke of her again."

This shock sat like a sickness in my stomach. "You told me she was dead."

"Stephen wished for you to live free of any expectation of her return. He said he knew in his heart she was gone. I respected his wishes."

It did not matter, this small lie. My mother would never be dead. Whether *strigoi vii* or *strigoi mort*, she was still a vampire. The truth hit like a hammer each time I thought of it.

I saw the love and pity in Uncle Peter's eyes. "A part of me has been looking for her all these years. It is unbearable to think of her. Like that." His hand was warm and surprisingly strong as it groped, then secured, mine. I squeezed it back, and held on. "But, Emma, her suffering has given you a great gift. It was transformed by the making of new life—your life. The blood of your mother becomes your blood, and in giving birth to you, Laura gives the world a chance at salvation." He smiled proudly. "You are the child of the vampire. You have the power to battle this evil. You are learning this, are you not?"

I told him briefly of the changes I'd experienced since coming to Avebury. He listened intently, pausing for several moments to ponder. "All the strange things lying beneath this land. The presence of this great vampire lord, too, has awakened you."

I nodded. "But I do not understand all the time what I am to do, nor even what I am able to do. I feel things . . . but I don't understand them."

He reflected for a moment. "There is a monk I met during my travels, someone who knew of these things. I shall contact him. Perhaps he will have some insight."

I nearly wept with a sudden tide of relief. "Then you will help me?"

"Oh, my dear," he sighed comfortingly. He pulled my hand to his lips and kissed my knuckles solemnly. "I will do all I can, for what it is worth. But you must not put too much hope in me. It is upon you, my darling, that we must rely. The power of the Dhampir lies in you."

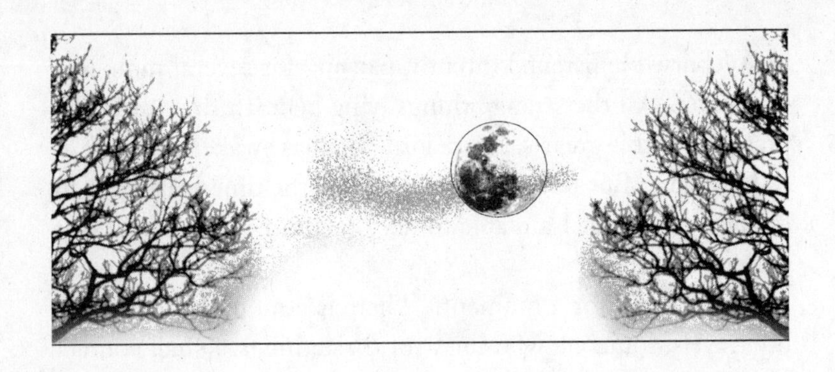

Chapter Twenty

March came to a close, and the rains of April arrived in full force. I moved through the hours woodenly. The toll of those tumultuous revelations of my Uncle Peter left me stunned, grieving. I thought of my mother often, in the quiet hours of night, and I longed to know the answer of Laura's fate. When this nightmare was over, I vowed to myself as I lay awake in my bed, I would find her. And if I had to . . .

I would release her. It was, after all, what I had been born to do.

My numbness wore off with the passing of several miserable days. My anger abated. Mr. Fox was gracious enough to forgive me my violence toward him. He brushed off my attempt at an apology and assumed a casual companionship, for which I was grateful. More than grateful. I would never have admitted it, but I had come to rely on his counsel, his reassuring presence.

The weather broke, and I fled outdoors. The lingering bite in the air did not dissuade me, and I walked boldly, looking out at the row of sarcen stones and taking up the trail to The Sanctuary, and the tree. It was different now, as I approached. I was no longer lost. I knew, at last, who I was.

There is something of the vampire in me. Marius had said these words.

The tree bowed and bobbed in a strong wind. The tangled branches waved back and forth, but a quirk of my own imagination made it seem as if they reached toward me. I read again the words carved in its hide. The Blood is the Life.

I felt the prickle of someone—something?—staring at me. I raised my gaze to the undulating branches. Hidden in the woven thorns, almost invisible, sat the large crow. It rode the wave of the bending wood without perturbation, an intelligent glint in its eye.

"I am Dhampir," I said, my voice riding the wind like a starling. "Through the blood of my mother, I am made to destroy you, you twisted creature."

I imagined contempt in the stare I received back from that horrible bird, but I could not swear to it.

"What did Marius look like to you?" Fox asked.

I let my head fall onto the curved back of my chair. I was tired, having spent this particular afternoon in a game of bowls. In the wake of those drizzly, stubbornly damp days, I achieved a kind of fragile balance among my family, walking the twin worlds of pastoral life and the dark underworld of the epic struggle happening around us.

Each morning, I played with Henrietta, up in the nursery under Miss Harris's watchful eye. Each afternoon, and then each evening before dinner, I checked on her. I was obsessed with her security, and spent much time attending to the various appointments of garlic and holy water to protect her in the night. I also made time for my sister, more to fend off her making complaint to Mary than all else. However, the normalcy of those hours was a balm to me. We sewed together, strolled the garden. Not infrequently we went to the village for a little shopping and a visit with Uncle Peter.

However, my favorite time of day was the time I spent in the library with Mr. Fox, where we engaged in long discussions, even debates at times, on the nature of revenants and other malefactions. Much of the past discomfort between us seemed to have abated, and we were a lot easier in each other's company.

"He appeared beautiful." Gaslight played games of light and shadow over the surfaces of the room. Soft on velvet, sharper on the grainy faces of the wooden furniture. "Elegant. And yet, terrifying power seemed to come from within him."

"That is merely a charm." He reclined on a long divan, looking as if he were at an idyll. He had divested himself of his frock coat, and he had hung his waistcoat on the back of a chair as he often did, so that he lounged in a full-sleeved shirt of unusually fine lawn. It was a shockingly casual appearance, but I did not mind. "The real Marius is monstrous, a creature so terrifying and unsightly, that a glimpse often throws a victim into catatonia. This is what I saw on the midnight street in Montmartre. When a vampire feeds, it rarely bothers with appearances."

I considered this interesting fact. "I glimpsed that at first when he attacked you, but I did not see him clearly. When I did look at him, he was as I described. He must wish to charm me." I reached for another biscuit from the tea tray.

Fox sat up. "I trust you wear the protections the priest gave us. You may be a diversion from his true purpose here, but a worthwhile one, should Marius set his sights on you. You are an opponent of consequence to him. You understand?"

"Yes," I sighed. "I am never without my small crucifix and the vial of blessed water. But . . . I confess, I have not kept up with garlic. I simply cannot abide the smell. And, by the by, I have never understood exactly why is it purported to be effective."

Fox grinned. "An old man I met in a fishing village on the Bosporus once lectured me at length on the healing properties of garlic, as well as its effects in preserving health and prolonging life. It is also thought to purify, as does salt and silver."

My eyes widened as I nibbled the biscuit. "Silver? I was not aware that was of significance. Do you not recall? I threw the silver candlestick when we were at Mr. Hess's house. But my hand first found the larger one, heavier, made of iron. It would have made a better weapon, but I instinctively rejected it."

He cocked his head in disbelief. "I thank God you trusted those unerring instincts, Emma. That thing was about to take me when you intervened."

"But this is so terribly vexing!" I stood suddenly. "Am I not supposed to have singular gift, extraordinary powers? But I do not know what they are, and between you, myself, Uncle Peter, and Father Luke, I know the least of anyone."

"You will learn. The qualities buried within you will reveal themselves. These instincts require you trust in yourself. Be patient, Emma."

I looked at him, realizing he'd spoken knowledgeably. "Have you known another who was Dhampir?"

His eyebrows lifted. "I have."

I shot out of my chair. "I must meet her."

"That would prove impractical. I found her many years ago when I followed Marius to the court of the Ottoman Caliphate."

"But you must tell me of her. Who was she, what was her name?" I resumed my seat, perched on its edge like an eager pupil.

He lowered his gaze, and when he spoke, it was a quiet reverence. "Naimah."

"Nye-ee-mah," I repeated. "It is a beautiful name."

"She was the child of a vampire male, a *strigoi vii* who did not hide his nature from her. Thus she always knew her power. Then, as a young slave girl, she fell in love with her master. When he was attacked by a great vampire lord, she drove it off. She was given her freedom as reward."

"She knew her father—a vampire?"

"The coexistence of the undead in the living world is much different in the Near East. The undead know their place, and the population understands how to control them, for the most part. In my time with her, I learned much of value on the nature of the revenant world."

"Tell me," I urged excitedly.

"The most surprising to me was to understand how the nomadic, solitary life the undead lead leaves the vampire lonely, frustrated. There are blood ties that run through their numbers, and among them are enemies as well as allies. They play out their power games and coups. Assassinations are not uncommon and minions, like armies, are won and lost." He swallowed hard, and I did not understand the bitterness that I

saw come over him. "From time to time, they create companions for themselves."

"Yes, you told me this. But it is rare, is it not? It takes much of their strength to accomplish this."

"We must conclude they do so only when a mortal man or woman captures their attention to such a degree, they cannot resist. It is a kind of falling in love. But, you see, they are so jealous of power, and so viciously competitive and cruel in their nature, they can never coexist for long without rivalry. But the blood will always connect them, as siblings of sorts, or a sire to its offspring."

I shivered. I was disgusted at this idea of twisted families. Then I recollected something that snapped me to attention. "Do you think that is what the dragon symbol means? Could it be a sign, a heraldic arms of sorts, for a certain family?"

"Indeed. A clan, then? Most certainly, it is." His features gathered into a dark look. "I know very little of these things, just enough to recognize that the dragon is a mysterious symbol that strikes terror into the hearts of living and undead alike. More than that, I have not been able to uncover. There are some matters into which the glib lower orders of vampires, among whom I've managed to gather most of my intelligence, will not venture. No one will speak of the Dracula beyond the most furtive mention of his name."

"Could Marius be one of his?"

"I would say it is quite possible, even likely."

A disturbing thought pressed me. I distinctly recalled there had been something seductive, almost cherishing in the way Marius's mind had touched me. He'd seemed to have been intrigued, almost as if he'd discovered an interesting pet, or . . . Or a kinship. If he were related in some way to the Dracula, did that mean that I was as well?

I turned my thoughts firmly away from that direction.

"Naimah knew more than anyone I met in all of my travels," Fox said. There was a trace of a smile on his lips, a hint of memories much more personal. It was clear the woman had meant a great deal to him. Had she been his lover? "She was both revered and feared in her land, but left to live undisturbed. She occupied a small palace, given to her by the sheik whose life she'd saved. It was a veritable zoo. There was a magnificent bird—an uncannily intelligent hawk. She'd had a tiger once, who had given its life to save her when she'd been attacked by a band of revenants. There was also a small, crafty monkey who seemed to read her orders straight from her mind. And she always knew when an animal was evil, for the vampire commands certain creatures, and the Dhampir can sense this."

This was fascinating, but it did not help me. I myself had not felt any affinity with Roger's hunting hounds or the sleek barn cats I'd come across. I sighed with longing. "I wish I understood all that I am capable of."

"It cannot be taught, but rather discovered. Naimah would often preach on that, for while there is wisdom in folklore and tradition, there are ridiculous claims, as well, and they can mislead one into false strategies that will get you killed. You must always beware. For example . . . let me see, ah!" He raised a slender finger and grinned at me. "I have it on good authority that a reliable way to thwart the undead is to scatter millet seeds about the grave, as vampires are obsessed with counting."

"That cannot possibly be true!"

"Yet it is not infrequently employed. I do so myself; it is tradition. Ah, yes, and a tolling bell is reputed to enchant them."

He chuckled, rubbing his long fingers over his bottom lip. "But by far the silliest thing I heard was the technique of removing the vampire's sock, placing a rock in it, and throwing it in running water."

I laughed, and he joined me. I'd never heard his laughter before. Never saw him like this, lightened, unburdened. It changed his entire appearance. The ghostly cast to his eye was gone, the drawn lines and hollows in his cheeks smoothed out. It was like looking at a different man. "I warn you," he said in a teasing tone, "I have not tried it. It could be quite effective."

I smiled at him. "Did you just make a jest, Mr. Fox?"

"I suppose I did. I imagine it is your effect on me, Mrs. Andrews."

This time, the formal address was spoken as something of an endearment. "I cannot see you much affected by anything," I said quietly.

"Then you are not looking very closely. I confess, I marvel at you sometimes. You are unspoiled by the ugliness that has intruded on your life. The things you have seen with your own eyes in the last weeks would have twisted anyone. I know they did me. Learning what you have of your mother is devastating. But you have not abandoned your life nor fallen into melancholy, as one might expect. I admire your resilience."

I flushed, deeply flattered. "I do not see I have much choice."

"There is always a choice." He sobered, and I knew he was thinking of himself. Mr. Fox's world was only the darkness, only the hunt. "There is goodness in you." Speaking with thoughtfulness, he regarded me peculiarly, as if he were seeing me for the first time. "The sort I had not thought existed. Or perhaps I've forgotten what it is to live outside of this war. I have been on my own for too long."

"Why, Mr. Fox," I said when I found my voice, "we are neither one of us alone. Not any longer."

He blinked, and something flashed, caught in his eyes for a glimmer of a moment before he could dispel it. It was merely a fleeting moment of significance, but I knew—perhaps with the instincts of the Dhampir, perhaps simply with that way of knowing by which women are attributed a special intuition—but I knew without a doubt that Mr. Fox *was* ever alone. I could swear to it—he harbored a very deep, very terrible secret.

"But Mr. Ivanescu has left, Mrs. Andrews," the old innkeeper told Alyssa and me the following afternoon. "I am sure he must have informed you of his plans."

Standing in the drafty common room of the Avebury Inn, I was disconcerted by this news. "But he was expecting us! Did he leave a message for me?"

"He did, yes, ma'am." He patted his pockets. "Now, where did I put that letter? I hope I did not set it out with the post."

"And could you build the fire up, please," Alyssa requested, her cloak grasped tightly about her. The innkeeper, familiar with Alyssa's temper, rushed to see to it.

She was in a mood today. "This is the chilliest spring I can remember," she groused, as if someone were to blame. Walking to the hearth, she sank down on a bench. "Perhaps tea would do me good. And a little something to eat. A sandwich, perhaps. Please, Emma, a shaved-ham sandwich! With smoked cheddar cheese, if you would."

I went to request Alyssa's meal. I was not terribly worried by my sister's condition—I knew from experience that something to eat would be immensely restorative. But Uncle Peter's abrupt departure left me shaken. It could not be a portent of good.

I happened to notice a salver sitting on a table and saw it was the tray for the post. I rifled through the letters to see if my note from Uncle Peter had gotten mislaid there. It had not, but I saw another missive in Uncle Peter's hand, written to a Dom Beauclaire in Amiens, France. It might well be this was completely unrelated to Uncle Peter's sudden departure, but I had ceased to believe in coincidences.

The innkeeper reappeared, handing me a page folded and sealed with my uncle's baroque flourish. "Here you go. It was left with my wife."

"Thank you," I said, taking the folded sheet he gave me. But when I read it, the message was impersonal, brief, and frustratingly uninformative. There seemed to be a diplomatic crisis brewing in the Crimea and he had to leave immediately. I was well aware of the tensions in that part of the world. Many people were concerned that if Russia did not abate its aggression, we would be drawn into war. Uncle Peter's note said nothing of his particular mission, merely explained the nature of his absence, and ended with the words: "Do not worry, my dear Emma. I will not desert you."

The door to the inn swung open with a bang and Sebastian lunged inside. "Emma, thank God I've found you!" he shouted upon seeing me. "Henrietta is missing. Fox sent me for you."

I do not recall any of my actions, only that it was with dizzying haste that my sister and I rushed to the trap Sebastian had driven to collect us, leaving the conveyance we had used to come to the village for a servant to fetch. We were underway back to Dulwich Manor within moments.

"She seems to have slipped away sometime this morning," Sebastian explained. "Mary is searching the house with the servants. The men are to ride out and search the forest. Fox said for me to tell you he believes you might be of particular help."

He fears Marius has taken her, I realized. It was what I thought as well.

It seemed to take forever to reach Dulwich Manor. When we arrived, I turned Alyssa over to her husband, and Sebastian dismounted, leaving me the trap. "I will do better on horseback," he explained. "Head for the forest."

I snapped the reins as soon as I was situated in the driver's box. The horse took off like a shot, and I leaned into the speed, veering away from the direction Sebastian had given me. I urged the lively mare to go as fast as she could, and we two raced over the downs, up to the meadow where the thorny branches of Marius's tree scraped against an ugly gray sky.

She was there—of course she was. I spotted her standing alone among the tall grass, her head tilted back as I'd seen her do before when she was conversing with the strange and dark creature that posed as her friend. "Henrietta!"

I yanked hard on the reins, rearing in the horse and bringing the trap to a sudden halt. Flinging down the leads, I leapt to the ground. Henrietta appeared deaf to my cries, standing unnaturally still, facing that horrible tree.

"Henrietta, what are you doing?" I took her by the shoulders as I knelt before her. "Everyone is looking for you. Why did you run off?"

She twisted away from my grasp, refusing to come with me. "Henrietta!" I said, for the first time using an impatient tone with her.

"Marius has come back to me," she said. Her voice was small, frightened.

"No, no he is not here, darling. You need to come home. Come."

She stood stiff as wood. I tried again to tug at her. Her eyes, sad and huge, lifted to mine as she whispered, "He is waiting for you, Cousin Emma."

I bent, ready to sweep her into my arms. I was prepared to bear her away kicking and screaming if I had to, but before I could, I heard something behind me. The fine hair on the back of my neck stood on end and I turned slowly, hearing a low chorus of growls as I did so.

Wolves—three of them. These were not canines, not wild dogs or the howling beasts that sometimes venture too close to a campfire in search of food. These were terribly ugly, slavering, red-eyed, and sporting elongated teeth far more numerous than was natural. They bore down on us with their jaws gaping open hungrily.

"Henrietta, run. Run as fast as you can. Go back to the house. Now!" I was aware of one sprinting behind me, taking the angle that would have been our retreat. "Do as I say!" My voice was sharp, stinging the air with my rising panic.

Henrietta stared dreamily at me.

"Henrietta," I said calmly, fiercely, "go to the trap."

She did not move, entranced again with that horrible expression of agony on her face, as if she knew the battle was already lost. One of the wolves moved into place, cutting me off from her, and my breath caught in my throat, a ragged sob of fear.

But then I noticed that the three were ignoring her. All of their concentration was centered on me. Just me. As they tightened their circle, I saw how they deliberately stalked chillingly close to the child, and yet never so much as flicked a glance her way.

Henrietta began to weep, muttering through her tears. I heard a muffled "no," and then a "please."

I forced myself to turn away from her. She was not in danger. And, I realized with alacrity, I very much was.

I had no weapon. Whatever powers had taken possession of me previously seemed to have abandoned me, for I had not the slightest sense of calmness as I had experienced before. My hands did not itch for a weapon. My eyes did not dart with unnatural speed to track the creatures as they stalked, bony haunches jutting from mange-infested fur. I fixed my eyes on them, tracking first one, then another as they passed, spiraling closer, their leering grins baring rust-colored teeth.

I felt disoriented, and I thought: *He's here. Marius is here, and he means to destroy me.*

Henrietta still stood watching. She sobbed, pleading out loud for the attack to stop. I knew it was Marius whom she beseeched for mercy, because she knew he was here, too.

I thought that if I were torn to bits, she would see it. "Turn away," I commanded her, not willing to risk a glance to see if she obeyed.

I faced the three demon wolves, narrowing my concentration. If I were to die, I would do so fighting. Picking one of the beasts, I watched it warily. It stared back at me, and I recalled suddenly how Mr. Fox had said Naimah had connected with animals. I realized I'd done something of the same thing with the snake attack, sensing their movements, knowing the intention in their primitive brain.

I dug for it, that connection, staring intently at the beast, and suddenly I felt it. Some instinct asserted itself. A glimmer, a trace . . .

The clawed feet—more catlike than canine—slowed. I punched out, and saw a ripple convulse its cadaverous frame. A movement out of the corner of my eye brought my attention to

another wolf just now stepping up with a trace of anxiety in its red eye. It watched me, and I reached for the bond again.

The wolf peeled back its jaw and growled, baring those horrible fangs. But I was not cowed by the display. I understood, somehow, that it was lashing back at me. It had felt me.

I turned slowly, focusing on each of the beasts in turn. My head filled with images. Blood, tearing flesh. These were not mere wolves. These were Marius's minions, animals transformed into flesh-eating monsters. I sliced through their gazes and into their minds, and I saw how to reach into them—as if pushing my hand through a curtain and tightening it into a fist.

I could smell what they did, my brain opening to a universe of scent beyond human capacity. I felt the thirst, the unholy thirst for human blood. My blood. Under their paws, the chalky downs was like dust, and I felt the softness of it as nails bit into ancient limestone for traction, as muscles coiled, readying for attack.

I thought, *I am Dhampir*. I remembered my suffering mother, and squeezed my mental fist until my body shook and I was sweating. I felt them. All of my will centered on their bloodlust, but in my mind, I pictured wolf tearing wolf apart.

Then it happened. Like puppets under a magic hand, they moved. I held on tight to my control as they yelped and reared. The sounds of an animal in great agony is something scarce to be borne, but I did not allow it to shake my concentration as their cries of pain rent the air. I pictured each strike, each tearing of flesh, and made it real.

"Emma! Emma!"

Sebastian's voice came from a great distance. Like time sped up, it flew toward me, growing louder, clearer, suddenly bursting over me, bringing me back.

"Emma!"

I turned, and saw he had Henrietta in his arms. She had her face buried against his neck. She was not weeping any longer.

Dazed, I looked around me, and saw the three bloodied bodies in the grass. And in the tree, the dry, cackling cry of a lone crow scraped across the air.

There was no talking Sebastian out of what he had seen.

"You killed them," he accused. "All three. They tore each other apart. They went mad—and you! You had a look on your face, Emma, such as I've never seen. You did it. Do not deny it!"

After we returned Henrietta to her tearful and grateful parents, I had not even had time to freshen up before Sebastian dragged me into the deserted conservatory.

"You must tell no one what you saw," I said urgently.

"As if I would. I am astonishingly good at keeping secrets." He leaned forward, a rabid look in his eye. "How long have you been able to do . . . that? And what exactly *was* that?"

"I do not wish to speak of it." I attempted to leave but he blocked my way.

"Why not? I will tell you my secret."

I smiled. "It is no secret. You are having an affair with Mr. Farrington."

He was chagrined. "How the bloody . . . ? I've taken such pains!"

"Perhaps it is only I who knows you so well, who sees it," I admitted.

"This preternatural sense of yours is devilish. It must be related to what you did back there with those wolves."

"I did not—"

He sighed and held up a hand to stop my lies. "This is not

the time or place for me to explain, but let us dispense with the denials and the rational. I am not unfamiliar with the realm of unnatural myself." He sighed. "As for Mr. Farrington, it is ill-fated. He is set to marry. He has no stomach for the disapprobation of our kind. It is jail for some, you know. Which is an improvement over earlier ages, when we were burned alive." He peered at me and added more feelingly, "I did not ask to be made this way, you know. I was born to it."

"Then perhaps you will understand my explanation that what happened with the wolves—well, I, too, was born to certain abilities. May we agree to leave it at that?"

He considered this, then shook his head. "Absolutely not."

"Sebastian," I warned quietly, "I cannot speak of this."

He studied me. "I have heard tales of people capable of amazing things in protection of a loved one. Mothers lifting heavy bales to free a trapped child, a father fighting a fire against all odds to rescue his family, that sort of thing. Whatever you did, you did it to save Henrietta." His brows shot down. "Wasn't it strange how they did not go for her? As if they did not even see her."

"Yes." I was carefully neutral in my tone. I myself was only beginning to understand, but I had realized that Henrietta belonged to Marius in some way—he had power over her and some mysterious, dangerous purpose that turned my blood to ice to imagine.

"God help us if anything happened to her." Sebastian blanched at the thought. "Henrietta—I swear, Emma, that child is my heart. Would that it happen to me, or any of us, but nothing must ever hurt her. She is the best of us."

The best of us.

And just like that, I understood at last.

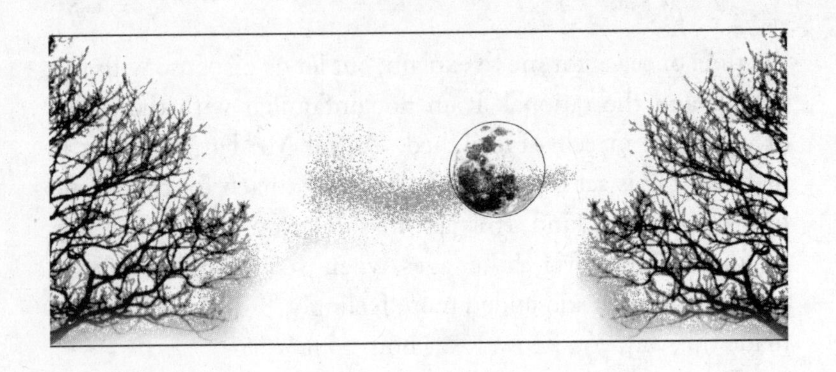

Chapter Twenty-one

Corruptio optimi pessima. The corruption of the best is worst.

It was Henrietta. She, the best of us just as Sebastian said—the most innocent, the most pure of heart and kind of nature—she was in the eye of this. And the power of her goodness was the fuel for Marius's evil.

I stumbled to find Fox, then dragged him into the garden, into the shelter of that ridiculous Grecian folly, so that we would not be overheard.

But he was beside himself with anguish over the morning's events, and spoke first. "I went to The Sanctuary first!" he protested as if I'd accused him. He grasped my shoulders. I guessed it was his own recriminations he answered. "She was not there. I looked all over the area."

"He must have hidden her until I arrived. It was me he wanted. He does not wish to harm her." I told him of my conversation with Sebastian, and my new suspicion about how Henrietta figured prominently somehow into Marius's plan.

He was pale as he absorbed this news. His fingers bit into my flesh. "Does he mean to make her a vampire on May Day, in this place where the power meridian furnishes great energy? Is that what this is about?"

I had thought of this as well. "She has to be willing, you said. If he wants her to live with him, she has to agree to it. And he might succeed. The poor child is confused and afraid." I threw my hands out explosively. "Why does he want such a companion? Is he still human enough to wish for a child of his own?"

"Emma," he said softly, collecting me to him to console me. I allowed myself one moment to lean into his strength.

"But why the attachment to The Sanctuary, the hawthorn tree?" he posed suddenly, his thoughts taking a turn. This logic brought me up short. I stared back at him, no answer at hand.

Speculation furrowed his brow. "What does this child have to do with Father Luke and the knights of his order? The Sanctuary, the hawthorn tree—none of that need figure into a plan to make a vampire child. And note the priest has shown no interest in Henrietta."

This was true. But if Marius did not wish to make Henrietta as himself, then what purpose did he have for her?

Fox said, "There is one certain thing we do know. Marius wishes you dead, for you alone can stop him."

Frustration rose within me. "How? How am I to stop him? How can it be this is left to me when I understand so little?"

But it had to be so. He had sent those vile wolves for me, the snakes before that. He had come for me himself, tried to master me with his mind. It could mean only one thing: a fight for Henrietta—the best of all of us. I did not know how, or even why, but I did know, as clearly as I ever had known anything in my life, that she was in mortal danger.

I had a summons from Father Luke asking me to come to tea. It had begun to rain again, and the roads were awash with mud, but that did not stop me. I set out for Saint Michael in the Fields by myself, and stood in an icy, lashing rain and pounded on the door of the rectory. My summons went unanswered. Overhead, the dull murmur of faraway thunder crept across the downs like footsteps, and I thought—only for a moment—that perhaps this was another of Marius's traps.

I lunged through the deluge to the church. It was open, as I had hoped. As I shook off the water beading on my woolen cloak, I noted the naked nail where my crucifix once hung. I regretted what I had done, but I did not think it was wrong. I would do worse if called upon. I wondered if there was an end to what I was capable of in defense of Henrietta.

I entered the nave. The growling skies shook the magnificent stained-glass windows. I wondered if Marius had whipped fury into the heavens, and then I thought—*I am glad.* The more he was thwarted, did that not bode all the better for me?

To my left, a flickering rack of candles illuminated a mournful Madonna painted in oils. I stared at her, thinking of my own mother. The sadness, as always, cut sharply, fresh as if I'd only moments ago learned of her demise. It might be blasphemous not to revile her, but she was my mother, and despite what she'd become, I loved her.

"You were caught in the storm?"

Father Luke emerged out of the shadows, as solid as the thick oak colonnade behind him. His dark hair caught the moving light, and for a moment he looked like the painting of Saint Michael himself, the warrior with the ability to raise a mighty sword and strike the deadly blow to the enemies of Heaven.

He held out his hand to me in a conciliatory gesture. "Come. Let us go to my office."

We dashed through the pelting rain to the back door to the rectory, and stepped into a cozy kitchen. Mrs. Tigwalt came in from what I supposed was the pantry, her brow furrowing in disapproval when she saw me.

"Tea, please," the priest requested. "And a blanket. That first, I think. Mrs. Andrews is drenched."

In the sitting room where he had fed me wine nearly a fortnight ago, he drew up a thickly cushioned chair by the fire. "Take off your shoes and come and sit."

It took several minutes to arrange my comfort to his satisfaction. Only after Mrs. Tigwalt had come and gone with the tea tray did I meet Father Luke's eye. "You wished to see me. And I am anxious to speak with you. I am hopeful we can come to some understanding to help one another."

I had the sense he was struggling with something as he settled in a well-worn leather armchair. "Mrs. Andrews, humor me if this seems unrelated to what is clearly on your mind, but how well do you know Mr. Fox?"

I was stunned by the question, and immediately wary. "We've only met a few weeks ago, but we have grown close with the extraordinary circumstances we've shared."

"Do you recall when we were at Mr. Hess's house, you gave me a switch from the hawthorn tree to use as a weapon? It was good thinking, by the way, bringing a branch from the tree. I understand you have certain instincts which make you rather adept at these things. For instance, you knew where Marius was before he materialized." He smiled at me. "That saved my life."

"A favor in turn, for your arrival there that night saved mine, and Mr. Fox's." I tilted my head. "But you did not come for us. You never knew we'd be there. You intended to sanctify George Hess's corpse."

He inclined his head.

"I read the Book of Tobit," I said suddenly. "Is it a demon in the tree up on The Sanctuary?"

He inhaled thoughtfully. "You take my lesson too literally. I had merely wished to illustrate to you the proven concept of using live trees to harness and hold wickedness. Corrupt and corrupting energy, if you will. What manner of evil, what dark energy or being—this I was never told. It was not deemed necessary. That I know what to do should it be required, that is what matters. My instructions are very clear.

"The day I saw the seal was broken, I knew I would be the one, out of the hundreds of men who served in this church through the years, to uphold the sanctity of the tree. It is part of my solemn vow to prevent the release onto the earth of that which the tree holds—this task I maintain in the utmost reverence. It is required that I alone see to it, for I have been trained. I cannot help you, Mrs. Andrews. I wish for you to understand why and to know that were it within my power, I would tell you everything."

"It could perhaps be a vampire," I pressed, uninterested in his explanation. "Perhaps one of Marius's ancestors whose loyalty he commands."

He shrugged, showing agreement. "It matters not what this Marius plans with the evil imprisoned in my tree. It *shall not* be released. I have assured you I would see to that, and you must trust me."

"It is a rather large request to make of me, Father Luke. How can I trust anyone to see to my chief concern? I care about Henrietta's safety, first and foremost. I must protect her—that is *my* duty, to be undertaken at any cost."

His face darkened. "The danger to your beloved Henrietta is an unspeakable thing. But there is more at stake here, Mrs. Andrews, than this one life, as precious as it might be."

One life? I reacted silently, considering the implications that he might consider this "one life" not important enough to notice. I was resolved, however, that it was the only thing that mattered and in this—I realized—Father Luke and I were at odds.

He had asked that I trust him. I knew I dared not.

Father Luke cocked his elbow on the armrest and frowned as his large hand scrubbed thoughtfully against his chin. "But let us talk more of the hawthorn switch. You do not have it?"

This was no idle musing, I realized. "You think it is important?" I asked pointedly.

"I do not like loose ends. I returned to Mr. Hess's house for it the following day. His housekeeper admitted me, and I was told no one had been yet that day to visit the body. I searched the room. When I could not find it, I hoped you had it."

"No," I said, meeting his gaze in alarm. "But why do you want it?"

He forced a smile. His features, which were so overpowering, achieved mildness when he relaxed them. He could have been handsome, or at least far less forbidding than he was, had humor or peace ever lightened his features. "I am probably worried for nothing."

I knew he did not believe this, but allowed the comment to pass. I had more urgent matters on my mind, namely Henrietta. "Father, is there anything else you can teach me to help me guard the child? I do what I can to protect her as strongly as possible, but somehow Marius is still influencing her."

"There is no speaking to the parents? It would be best if she could be removed from Avebury altogether."

"No, I am sorry to say. I am viewed with suspicion for reasons too complex to go into at the moment. I would have no sway with any tales of danger to Henrietta. They would ship me to Bedlam before they would listen to such a radical suggestion."

"Of course." He frowned deeply as he thought for a few moments. "I am going to do something quite unorthodox, Mrs. Andrews. Pardon me for a moment while I fetch something that will help you."

He returned quickly with a gold filial the size and approximate shape of a candlestick, fitted with a sunburst at the top. "Do you know what this is?" he asked as he held it for me to see. "It is called a monstrance. It is the most powerful force against evil that exists, for it holds the body and blood of Christ. By church law, no one can touch the consecrated host but an ordained priest."

A glass receptacle in the center of the golden sun showed a slim wafer of bread. I looked at the priest in shock.

"I give this to you for the child, even at the peril of breaking with the rules of the Church, perhaps even at the peril of mortal sin. I want you to understand how deeply I am moved by your lonely burden to protect this precious one."

He handed the monstrance to me, adding, "But you must still see to the other things you have been doing. Most important, seal the doors and windows of her rooms. A thick line

of salt will do. Make very certain no one you do not know is allowed in. The old belief that any agent of evil cannot enter a dwelling uninvited is true."

"But there are so many people in the house." I frowned. "You are right. It is imperative to shield her completely from Marius. I shall sit by her side at night. Mr. Fox and I shall take turns."

At the mention of Valerian Fox, his brows forked into a deep "V." "Have a care there, Mrs. Andrews."

I looked at him sharply. "You do not like Fox."

Father Luke hesitated, then said, "We all have our reasons for being here, one way or another. Mine, I have stated clearly. Yours, I understand the most of all. It is the purest of motives: love. But ask yourself, what does Mr. Fox have to gain?"

"He has hunted the vampire Marius for many years," I replied.

"But why? When I asked him, he said simply that this Marius had taken something from him. What? A child, a wife, a sister, a brother? Why is he so reluctant to explain himself further?"

He had hit a sore spot, for although I knew Mr. Fox's tale of witnessing the awful sight of the vampire feeding on the streets of Montmartre, I only now realized I did not completely understand why this had been so compelling as to change his entire life. Or what the vampire lord taken from him. Father Luke was correct. If I had suspected before that Fox had a secret, I knew now it was true. But I trusted him nonetheless. He had more than proven his loyalty to me on several occasions.

"We all have our secrets, do we not?" I said.

Father Luke peered at me with a mysterious smile. "Even you?"

"I should think all my secrets have been revealed."

"Then you must have been referring to my secrets. I do not

deny them, and I realize it must frustrate you but I assure you, what I choose to keep hidden from you will not help you protect your precious child, Mrs. Andrews. My path in this is set. To involve you and Mr. Fox would complicate things, perhaps fatally."

"You cannot think we would ever betray you."

He struggled for a moment. "Not intentionally. But if it came to a choice, and if my goals and yours ever came into conflict, I would have made a grave error in showing my hand, as it were."

"But our ends are the same. How would we be in disagreement?"

He seemed to wince, and I saw this idea was a matter of great dread. "We might. Remember, my orders are quite clear. My loyalties equally so. I am a man of compassion and conscience, but duty must take priority over everything. You must understand this."

I was quiet for a moment. I had accepted that Father Luke would not help us, as he stubbornly maintained his own solitary path. But how could he and I—both fighting on the side of good against an almost overwhelming evil—ever find ourselves in opposition?

He did not trust Fox—he'd said as much. And me? With what he knew of me, did he think . . . ?

Marius's words echoed in my mind. *There is something of the vampire in you.*

Was it me, more than recalcitrant Mr. Fox, he did not trust?

"Please," Father Luke said softly, reaching for my hand and patting it. "We must agree to go separately about our own means and ends. But I will help you, indeed I will, Mrs. Andrews. In any and all ways I can."

I saw this was true. He was not a selfish or cruel man. Indeed, the sincerity I saw in his face was genuine. But he was a man bound by his own beliefs, and his allegiance to his church. And the distance that yawned between his world and mine would not be breached.

As he was walking me out, there was something else I wanted to know, a question he, as a priest, was in a unique position to answer. "Father, you understand that I . . . what I am, and what it means. My mother was afflicted . . ." Emotion stopped me from continuing. Perhaps, if he had donned his vestments and I were able to slip into the solace of the peculiar rite of penance, I could have spoken further. But I did not need to.

"I am aware," he said calmly. "I know of the Dhampir."

I swallowed. "If I am anointed to my gifts by the power of vampire blood . . ." I closed my eyes momentarily and gathered my courage. "Does it mean I am unclean?"

He changed, then, his guardedness slipping away as a look of true compassion passed over him. I thought for a moment he was going to reach for me, to touch my arm or hand reassuringly.

"I do not have the impulse to do evil," I rushed to reassure him. "Quite the opposite. I am determined that my mother's suffering, and her legacy to me that resulted from it, will have been for some good. But if the blood of the vampire is within me, I wish to know . . . Am I cursed?"

His eyes drifted over me, assessing my words. "I wish to tell you no, Mrs. Andrews, for I like you quite a great deal. And I feel great pity for your situation. But I cannot answer the question you pose, not as a point of dogma. I simply do not know."

Chapter Twenty-two

Fox and I said prayers from the missal I'd taken from the church while anointing Henrietta's bedchamber and the schoolroom with holy water. In the windows, we placed fresh garlic and dribbled a line of salt along the two doorways and the windowsill, so fine it was, hopefully, undetectable to the mortal eye.

When we were done, we looked at each other. "Is this enough?" I asked.

His eyes traveled over the room. He shook his head. "If Marius wants the child, these will not deter him. They may make his fetching of her more unpleasant, but stop him?" The frown lines on his forehead deepened.

"What about the monstrance?" I took the gold filial out of

the bag. I'd wrapped it carefully in felt. It felt heavy, substantial, in my hands.

Fox stared at it in awe and appreciation. "I may have underestimated our priest friend."

"So now he is 'our priest friend,' is he?"

Fox shrugged and surprised me with a charmingly sheepish gesture. "Well, I suppose a gift like this can redeem anyone. Vampires find all things holy to be repellent, but this . . . This is something quite extraordinary, and very hard to come by for hunters."

I looked at the gold sunburst, which housed the Holy Wafer. I was Christian enough to feel a deep sense of reverence. Fox came to stand beside me. He must have been thinking similar thoughts, for he said, "Putting the Eucharist in the hands of anyone not an ordained priest is most arduously forbidden. This is not something I would have ever expected from him."

I thought about this, then said, "Sometimes, people surprise you."

He shook his head. "Your faith in your fellow man touches me, but I cannot agree."

I burst into a chorus of chuckles. "Why are you making complaint, Mr. Fox? I believe in you, do I not?" I paused, recalling that Father Luke was not as sanguine in his trust of Mr. Fox. "By the way, did you retrieve the hawthorn stick from Mr. Hess's house?"

He looked at me strangely. "Why would you ask?"

I sighed in exasperation. "Must you answer all my questions with questions of your own? Father Luke was worried about it."

He crossed his arms. "No. Does that satisfy?" He strode to a tall chest and tapped the top. "Before tonight, after the child is asleep, you must come back and put the monstrance here, facing the door. After the nurse leaves, place it like so. Then Marius cannot approach or come anywhere near it. And take the crucifix from under her pillow. I would like it hanging from the headboard of her bed, directly over her head, just as a secondary precaution."

"Here, then?" I hooked the chain over a post, fiddling with it to get it right.

A new voice cut in with startling volume. "What the devil are you two doing?"

Mr. Fox and I jumped guiltily and whirled to face Sebastian, who was standing in the doorway with arms crossed, his shoulder against the door jamb, a mocking grin on his face.

I spoke, snapping the tense silence with a lie. "Why, we are looking for Henrietta."

"Really? In her bed? At this hour? Well, surely you could tell by now she is not here." He pretended to scowl at us. "I hope this is not some tryst, you naughty pair! And if it is, I say it is a despicable choice of accommodations. A child's room!"

I flushed. "Sebastian!"

He held up his hands, laughing, then paused. "What is that dreadful smell? Is that . . . What are you doing with garlic?"

I looked down at the herb in my hand. "Oh, is this garlic?"

"Uh-hum." Sebastian narrowed his eyes and advanced slowly toward me, his clever mind assessing the situation. "And what the devil do you have in that bag?"

"It is Mr. Fox's bag," I said inanely, as if it would matter.

"Emma," Fox said in a low voice. It was a warning. Maybe even a plea.

"Holy Lord! Quite literally." Sebastian saw the crucifix, which I'd slipped over the bedpost. "Is this yours?" He moved, his quick glance catching sight of the gold filial with the flat

chamber of glass on top. "What the . . ." He picked it up and studied it. "What is this contraption?"

"Careful, Sebastian," I said, but he turned the gold vessel over and upside down. I winced. "According to Catholic belief, you are holding the transubstantiated body and blood of Our Lord."

With impeccable timing, Mr. Fox plucked the sacred object out of Sebastian's hands before they could go nerveless with shock. Sebastian gaped at me. "Does all of this belong to you?"

"Actually, it belongs to Saint Michael in the Fields. But we've borrowed it."

"I see. Of course. Why, it was silly of me to ask."

"I must go," Mr. Fox said abruptly, and made for the door. He glanced at me sharply, his meaning clear. It was my duty to find some plausible excuse to placate Sebastian.

When he had left us alone, however, I made a sudden and very rash decision, and I blurted out the truth. "Sebastian, our Henrietta is in terrible trouble." I told him everything in a sudden rush. I simply could not lie any longer, my nerves would not have it.

He listened to everything, his face frozen in an expression blended with equal parts alarm and fascination. When I was finished, he searched for a reply. "This is . . ."

"It is fantastic, yes. But you can speak with Fox, and to Father Luke as well. I am not mad, Sebastian."

He immediately grasped my arms. "My God, Emma, I did not think that. Merely, you must be mistaken, for this is all so very far-fetched."

"Do you think I do not realize how it sounds? I would not have uttered a word to you if I were not desperate. I need you to help me. For Hen's sake, Sebastian."

He sighed, struggling with disbelief. Then he said, "I told you once, I was not a stranger to things of a supernatural kind. There is evil in the world."

"Have you seen these things?" I asked incredulously. "I never sensed you did."

"Not the sort of phenomenon of which you speak. I see . . . Well, spirits, if you wish to know the truth of it." He gave a short, embarrassed laugh. "I never told anyone that. But I always have been able to see the shades of the dead."

"But the truly dead," I clarified.

"I hinted about it once—do you remember? I teased you about seeing ghosts? I thought perhaps you had seen something as I do. But your ability is different." He smiled at me. "So I promise not to think you mad if you offer the same."

"Perhaps we are mad together," I said softly.

The sound of Henrietta and Miss Harris out in the schoolroom reached us.

Sebastian sprung to the door in a burst of forced cheerfulness. "Hen, darling," he called. "Cousin Emma and I are in here." He glanced at me. "We've . . . we've come looking for you." He laid a finger to his lips. A silent pact.

I had another partner. I blinked away the sting of unshed tears of gratitude and nodded.

Henrietta appeared in the doorway, her face alight with delight at finding us. "I am right here!"

"So you are. Hello, Miss Harris."

Henrietta's nursemaid made no comment, but from her expression I could see she was taken aback to find us here. "Mr. Dulwich. Mrs. Andrews."

"May we speak to Henrietta privately?" Sebastian asked.

Miss Harris gave us both a sharp look but she left us three to ourselves without protest.

Sebastian kneeled before the child. "Darling, I want you to tell me about Marius."

Her happy face changed abruptly. "No. I am not to talk about him to anyone." Her eyes slid to me. I assumed I, especially, was to be kept in the dark.

"You must not speak of him to Emma?" Sebastian prodded, concluding the same thing. Henrietta nodded. "But what of to me?"

She thought about this, then shook her head. "I do not know."

"Just tell me something, darling. Does he come in here at night?"

She hesitated before confessing, "Sometimes."

"What does he do?"

"He sits with me. He talks to me. He taught me chess." She glanced back and forth from Sebastian to me. "He said that you would try to take him away from me."

"Did you let him in, Hen?" I moved so that I stood side by side with Sebastian. "I thought you were afraid of him."

"He got angry when I didn't do what he said. And he got so ugly when he was angry, I was frightened of him. But then, he was nice again. He was sorry."

Sebastian was about to say something else, but I laid a hand on his arm. I could see the struggle in the child and thought it best we not press further right now. There would be time later. "Thank you for trusting us, Henrietta." I knelt down and hugged her, but she felt stiff in my arms.

Sebastian and I left her to her afternoon nap, but he was not done with me. “In the billiard room. It should be empty,” he commanded with uncharacteristic seriousness.

When we shut the door, he blurted out. “I saw him. Marius. I saw him. I did not know it at the time, but it must have been he.”

My head snapped back in shock. “How . . . ? But you said you did not see his shade.”

“Not his shade. Him, in full form. It was very late one night, or, rather, early in the wee hours of the morning, and I was drunk. I did not believe it at first.”

“Where did you see him?”

“In the schoolroom. I was coming back from a rendezvous with James, that is, Mr. Farrington. The empty rooms on the third floor are where we are in the habit of meeting. I was headed to my own room, but I wanted to first check on Hen. I do, you know, from time to time. Then I heard something in the schoolroom. I said I was not at my best, so when I looked in, and I saw him, I thought it was not real.”

“What was he doing?” I asked, astonished.

His lips trembled slightly. “He was dancing with Miss Harris.”

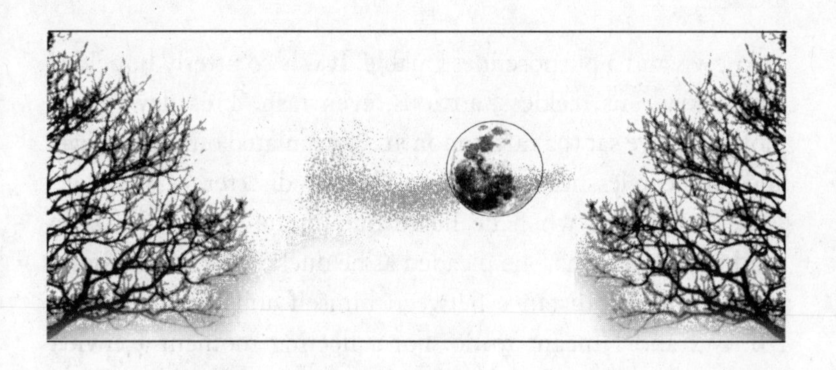

Chapter Twenty-three

The abject hopelessness of realizing how stupidly we'd misjudged the situation was acute. We had been undone. Marius was too clever, too accomplished at this, and I was only new to the world of vampires, to the dark deeds they did and the seemingly legion of powers they commanded.

I cannot think of my reaction without a cringe of shame, for I placed my face in my hands, and I wept. This alarmed Sebastian, who fetched Fox, but he knew no better what to do with a sobbing woman than Sebastian did.

In a clumsy effort to comfort me, Fox took my hands and said, "It is to be expected, setbacks like this. We are at war with a formidable enemy, Emma."

We *were* at war. Against a monstrous enemy, with powers

unknown and a purpose inestimable. It was so utterly hopeless; and it made us reckless, anxious, even rash. This flawed our plotting as we sat that afternoon and formulated our next move, and such carelessness must always lead to disaster.

Sebastian fled when he heard our insane plan. "Please do not hate me, Emma," he pleaded as he ducked out of the room, quickly putting distance between himself and the mad thing Mr. Fox and I meant to do. For a fleeting moment I envied him the cowardly act, for it would have tempted me, had I had any choice in the matter. Pass this cup from my lips and all that, but the moment of wavering dissolved with a glance at my comrade.

Mr. Fox was, as ever, resolute and calm. I took strength from that. We decided together on what must be done, but it was me, only me, who was responsible for what happened.

I went into Henrietta's room that night and placed the monstrance where Fox had directed me. The crucifix went into place over the pillow where her head lay. I turned down my lamp to a mere glow and sat vigil with a slender stake which I had sharpened myself to a wicked point.

I heard Miss Harris stir in her sleep in the next room, and I clutched the weapon at the ready. But eventually her movement subsided, and after many long hours in the dark, I, like Peter, John, and James, whose spirits were willing but flesh too weak, I am ashamed to admit that I fell asleep.

When I did, Marius came.

The feel of him woke me. There was a deep, crypt-like chill along my right side, the scent of evil I was now learning to identify. I came clean out of sleep with an audible gasp that scraped like sand across the air. I shot to my feet, and the stake,

which had been on my lap, fell to the floor. Henrietta's steady breathing signaled she still slept peacefully.

My brain fogged from sleep, my nerves shocked numb, I was momentarily disoriented. This was not what I had expected, this sudden surge of presence, this full-on attack. The stillness around me compressed as Marius gathered a corporeal presence from the dust. I dared not look directly at him—I was not about to repeat my previous error—but I knew where he was. Tall, regal, his black-clad body consumed the shadows, taking the shape of a man.

I acted, quickly, explosively—lunging to my left, reaching to the top of the chest of drawers. My hand groped for the stem of the monstrance. My fingers brushed only air. The monstrance was gone.

I heard his laughter. A man's voice, cultured and smooth, vibrated in the air and I had a moment of pure terror, for the voice slithered into my head. I felt Marius wrap around me, bite into me, into the empty spaces where he had inhabited me before and touch me with his putrid presence.

I was used to the acuity of my senses. I was used to the pulse of that feeling under my skin, the one that drummed with persistence to unleash my powers. Thus, even though I was terrified, I was also somehow confident. Despite the absence of the monstrance, I realized I was not without my abilities. It was time I saw what I could do.

Turning, I faced the monster. His body was serpentlike, an elongated perversion of the human form. His face was the handsome aspect I recollected. As my heartbeat slowed and my panic receded, I thought I might look at him, as long as I did not allow even the slightest glance into his eyes.

He moved in that liquid way of his, his body surging forward, gliding rather than striding. On his face was a victorious leer. Keeping my head, I looked toward the headboard. The crucifix Mr. Fox had bidden me place over Henrietta's head had been removed. I fished out the cross I wore under the high neck of my dress and held it out in front of me. "By the power of Christ—"

But Marius thought this amusing. "You are no priest. And I am no demon."

He might have shaken the confidence of another. But I was Dhampir, and I felt the shudder that went through him. "You will leave this child alone. She is protected by her goodness. She is protected by my love."

He laughed. "You are young, Dhampir. Untested. Vulnerable." Vicious glee infused his voice. "Why, you do not yet know what you are, do you?"

He kept his distance. Despite his taunting words, he was sizing me up, abrading my confidence and watching to see what effect his taunts had on me. But he did not approach, for even the small crucifix kept him at bay.

As if he read my thoughts on this, he scoffed with sly pleasure. "Soon, I will be strong enough even to resist your Christian symbols. Soon, I will tower over all others, even your pathetic broken Christ." When he spoke, I saw the razor edge of his teeth.

"There is time before Beltane to stop you," I said, advancing. I fought my fear, telling myself I was made for this.

"You know of Beltane?" he said. He should have been displeased by my knowledge, but there was a gleam in his eye, a savoring glee I had not anticipated. "What else do you know,

Dhampir? Ah, you are an interesting adversary. Quite remarkable, but you do not know your place. You will see what I become, and before I destroy you, you will weep with awe."

I stepped forward again, and he coiled backward, shying away from the cross with wary stealth. I was emboldened by this reaction. "But you are not strong enough for my cross as yet, are you?"

Confidence seized me. The surge of power and triumph was intoxicating. Only that morning, at Sebastian's revelation, I had thought us outmaneuvered, perhaps even defeated. But now—now I had the great vampire lord Marius cowering by my hand. He was backing out of the room. Behind me lay Henrietta, untouched and peaceful, and I felt—quite stupidly—the exhilaration of having won the battle.

I had not calculated on Miss Harris.

It seems now such an obvious omission, knowing as I did that Marius had compromised her, but I assumed she was asleep, her work to remove the safeguards Fox and I had put in place accomplished. I simply did not expect what happened next.

With my back to the door leading through the sitting room to her bedroom, she was upon me before I even had a hint she was there. Hands curled into claws, Miss Harris screamed in the most bone-chilling manner and launched herself at me.

I was startled and off guard enough that she nearly knocked me off my feet. Mindful not to turn my back on Marius, I fought back, snapping my fist with a force and quickness that surprised me. My blow connected with her cheek, but she did not drop. She was screaming wildly, wordless, guttural noises that raised the fine hair on my arms. I hit her again while she flailed at me, snagging my hair and pulling down ferociously until I heard it tear. I struck her again, stunning her, but again she did not stop. All the while, I was furiously trying to work out how I could get back the stake I had dropped earlier.

The noise woke Henrietta, who commenced screaming as she saw her nurse and me grappling with each other at the foot of her bed.

"The lamp!" I called. "It is Emma, darling. Light the lamp!"

She did so, then stood bewildered and frightened beside her bed, her pink toes curling against the cold wood. Miss Harris immediately flew to her, sobbing.

I spun this way and that, ready to confront Marius. But he had gone.

"Run, Henrietta!" Miss Harris was nearly hysterical. "She's mad. We must get out of here!" The nursemaid, who only moments before had been as wild as a cat on fire, changed suddenly. Clutching Henrietta, she skittered away with her with a cry that was a fair imitation of alarm. I stopped in my tracks, realizing she was making a convincing show of being afraid of me.

Henrietta was clinging to her and staring at me with a guarded edge. "Hen, darling, come to me," I said, making my voice calm. I had not yet guessed the game. I was thinking only of the danger, of Marius returning, or Miss Harris absconding with Henrietta.

Miss Harris pulled Henrietta behind her bravely. "Do not harm us, please," she mewled. Once the child was tucked out of sight, she showed me her teeth. They were small, normal, but the smile was pure triumph, ugly and evil.

I could hear footsteps coming, and it dawned on me how all of this would appear. "Listen to me, Henrietta. Please, for God's sake and for yours, listen. You know I love you. I would never hurt you. Come here, darling. Come away from Miss Harris."

But Henrietta did not so much as peek from behind her nursemaid.

"Marius is not your friend," I said urgently. "He is a vampire, and Miss Harris is in his thrall. She is his servant. Henrietta, please, listen—"

Roger burst into the room, Mary behind him. Miss Harris whirled and flung herself at them. "She attacked me! Oh, Mrs. Dulwich, she was doing something horrid, and I tried to stop her."

"No. It was Miss Harris who attacked me," I shouted, approaching the child now that Miss Harris had moved away. But Henrietta did me in without saying a word. At my step forward, she cringed away. Seeing this, her parents turned hard eyes toward me.

"What is this, Emma?" Mary asked.

I had only one hope, although I knew it was futile. Marius had been very clever. He'd cast out a line and I'd taken the bait like a stupid carp. I said it anyway. "Ask the child."

"Henrietta, are you all right?" Mary held her daughter now, scanning her with feverish eyes. "What happened?"

"Miss Harris and Cousin Emma were fighting."

"And look," Miss Harris said, taking the cross I'd hung from the bed from her night robe pocket. I noted with a detached interest that it did not repel her. She must not be a vampire yet. *I shall have to remember to tell Mr. Fox*, I thought dully.

Roger took the cross in his hand. "It is a Catholic crucifix." He eyed the miniature of the dead Jesus in his hand with distaste. "This should not be near the child, it will give her nightmares."

Miss Harris pointed at me. "Mrs. Andrews put it here. And this." She swept up the sharpened stake I'd let slip from my lap, and handed it to Roger.

He turned to me, horror on his features. "My God, what is going on?"

"She was talking about vampires. She is mad!"

I had been incalculably stupid. I realized that now. I had been completely and utterly fooled. I had underestimated Marius.

Mary went to the bed, ripping down the downy sheets. She found the garlic, picked it up in trembling hands, and showed it to Roger. He stared at it stoically, he who had been my champion all these years. The bleak, hard expression on his mild features; that was the most difficult to bear.

"Miss Harris, take Henrietta down to the kitchens and heat her some milk." Roger's tone was sharp, with an edge that could cut steel.

I refused to cry. It was my own damnable fault. I had been duped, so thoroughly duped.

Mary and Roger stood side by side. Roger spoke. "We want you out of this house tomorrow. Before lunch. We will send servants to help you pack."

Could I have pled to them the truth, explained as best I could? It would never have done any good. In any event, I did not try. There is something that happens to a person when they are subjected, as I was for so many years, to the harsh judgment of others. A wound. And it is a wound that never heals, no matter how one grows, finds confidence, even fulfillment.

They believed my mother's legacy had come to pass. Oh, it did not escape me how sublimely ironic it all was. Yes, it was, in fact, her fate that had made me Dhampir, and so, in a way, they were right. But they did not know this, of course. They simply thought I had finally gone mad.

* * *

Alyssa would not see me. I had tried to go to her and was turned away by Alan, stern-faced and severe, but with a gleam of triumph in his eyes. "Alyssa is beside herself. I tried to tell her she was wrong about you, to think you had changed." It struck me how ugly he could be, despite the even, regular features. Especially when he was haughty, such as now.

"Please give her a message, then," I asked, eating my pride.

"No," he said, his lips trembling with the smile. "She should have known what her mother tried to tell her. Blood will come true."

I gave a small laugh of defeat. "Blood will run true," I corrected softly and swept past him. I thought of the child Alyssa carried. I would never see my nephew or niece.

I would never see Henrietta again.

I went to my room, where my belongings had been already packed by the maids, my things neatly laid into my mother's portmanteau. Sebastian was waiting. He held his hands out for mine. "Emma . . ." The pity in his eyes was too much. I turned away.

"It is up to you now," I said quickly, before my voice could fail me. "You and Mr. Fox. Henrietta's life is in your hands. You must find the truth."

An appalled expression came over his face. "How can I?"

My heart sank. "I do not know, Sebastian. But you must keep her from Marius if you can. And Miss Harris."

"What do you wish me to do—stuff Miss Harris's mouth with garlic? If I do that I shall be banished with you," he said bitterly, then shook his head as he pinched the bridge of his nose delicately. "Never mind. You know I will do all I can."

"I have to find Uncle Peter." My head shot up. "Yes, that is where I will go. He knows more than he told me, I am sure of it."

I kissed Sebastian and he held me tightly for too long. "I love you," he said.

"I love you, too. You've been my greatest friend. I will tell you where you can reach me when I know more precisely where I am going. For now, know that I am heading to France. I will come when I can."

He clung to me a moment too long. "Pray it will be in time."

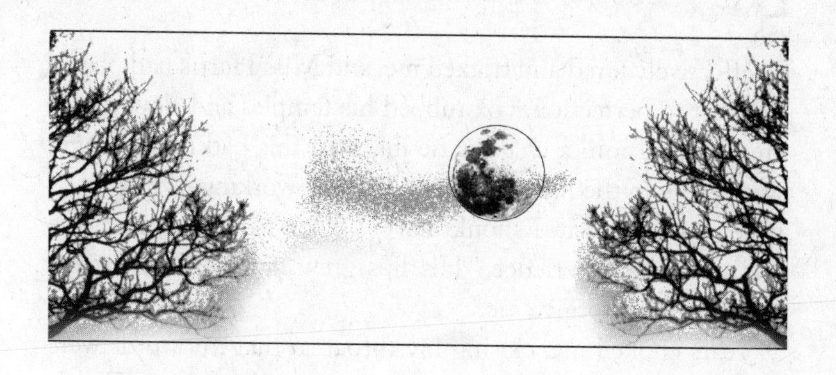

Chapter Twenty-four

I have been thinking," Valerian Fox said as I entered the library. He was ensconced behind several piles of books at a table by the window, completely unaware of what disaster had transpired, and of my banishment. "If Henrietta is somehow a sacrifice for what Marius has planned, it could be the blood of an innocent is needed to release the force in the tree. Blood sacrifice is a common practice among demonic worshippers. We merely . . . Emma, what is it?"

I must have looked like death. I could barely speak. "I have been discovered. I must leave, Mr. Fox. That is what I've come to tell you."

He froze. "Emma, explain yourself. What has happened?"

I related to him the events of last night, of how Marius had so effectively lured and tricked me, and Miss Harris had played her part to perfection. Fox rubbed his temples and slowly lowered himself into a chair as he ingested this bad news. Anger was visible in the flare of his nostrils, the working of his jaw. "I never thought of it. I should have. Of the two of us, I am the one with the experience." His lips grew taut with bitterness. "God, Emma, forgive me."

Tears choked me, closing my throat so that my words were harsh and rasped with emotion. "Please consider going to Father Luke. Resolve your differences. If the two of you would simply trust each other, you could work together. He is a good man, but you must make him see it is important for you both to stand united. Marius must never have Henrietta—for whatever purpose he desires. I am to leave this house and I can do no more. I am depending most fiercely on you, Mr. Fox, to make certain no harm comes to her. Sebastian—he knows everything. He can help you now, in my absence."

"Go to the village, stay there. I will join you and we will continue our work."

To my utter humiliation, tears slipped down my cheeks, hot as firebrands on my skin. "I am going to France to find Uncle Peter."

"You believe he is in France?"

"It is possible he will go there at some time soon. I saw he wrote to a Dom Beauclaire in Amiens. The letter could not have had anything to do with his diplomatic mission, since his current duties lie in the Crimea. I have wondered if he contacted this Beauclaire in regards to my mother, since, with his worst suspicions about her being recently confirmed, I know he is nearly as anxious as I to find out what became of her. I can only hope he will head there upon his return, and I can meet up with him then."

"Curious that he would seek out a monk, don't you think?"

I started at this odd question. "A what?"

"A monk. Well, I assumed this Beauclaire is one. The Benedictines use the name Dominic when they take orders, and it is used as a sort of address, as one would say 'father' to a priest. They are sometimes called black monks, although I don't know why. And the Benedictines are still in France. But maybe I am wrong."

"A monk." I felt a glimmer of hope at the revelation. "Well, as peculiar as that sounds, I suppose that is not too difficult to imagine such a thing as a monk would figure into this mystery. A helpful member of the clergy would be a tremendous asset. We already know the importance of holy items and prayer in combating revenants, so who better than a member of the clergy to advise me?" I was suddenly excited. "I think it likely he could prove knowledgeable—else why would Uncle Peter contact him?"

The appearance of the maid interrupted us. She was looking for me. "Ma'am, your bags are ready to be sealed. Can you come and check them, please?"

"I will be there shortly," I told her. She retreated and I turned to Fox. "This is our goodbye, then."

Mr. Fox grabbed my hands. "Emma . . ." His eyes bore into mine. I could see in his eyes a depth of feeling he had never allowed me to see before. And I felt—I knew—it was for me.

I fled upstairs to oversee the final packing of my mother's portmanteau.

* * *

The note was an impulse, born out of that moment when Valerian and I had parted. I felt perhaps I should have said something in return. Further, I feared I had given him the idea that I had been discomfited by his touch or the way he had spoken my name. Wishing very much to avoid leaving him with this impression, for it would have humiliated me to have him suspect how undone I had felt at his show of emotion, I dashed a note of farewell while my bags were sealed and brought downstairs. In it, I was gracious but cool as I thanked him for the aid he had provided and would continue to provide to Henrietta in my absence. I also made an apology for my abrupt departure from him, dismissing it as a result of pressing concerns and time constraints.

Collecting my gloves and reticule, I then hurried to slip the letter into Mr. Fox's room before proceeding downstairs to make my departure.

I entered his bedchamber, looking to place my missive where the prying eyes of a maid or other servant would not espy it. I thought of the duffel bag. He would certainly never allow anyone else to touch that, so my letter should be safe enough inside.

I found it hidden under the bed and hastily unfastened the clasp. As I stuffed the folded paper inside, my hand brushed something soft and curiously shaped. I drew out a slender object wrapped up with rags.

Maybe it was those instincts of mine, which had served me so well. A sense of unease injected itself into my veins. I peeled back the tattered scrap of cloth. My heart climbed up my throat and pressed painfully to cut off my air. Before me lay the hawthorn switch, with Marius's blood still red on the sharpened tip.

* * *

I must admit my pride was crushed, my heart blistered as I put the plains of southern England behind me and set sail from Lyme Regis across a choppy, inhospitable sea. I proved a not very good sailor. I was ill during the crossing, and disembarked on the French shore desolate and raw but I had no time to get my legs under me, for the spring was fast approaching, and May Day was only a few weeks away. I set off immediately to Amiens to find the monk, Dom Beauclaire, and hopefully my Uncle Peter.

The Benedictine Order, which had been reinstituted some years after the French Terror, occupied a half-crumbled château. I traveled to the site by hired carriage, astonished to find an ancient edifice standing like a blight on the gentle countryside like something out of a forgotten fairy tale.

The structure had once been fanciful, with towers topped with blue coned roofs and crenellated walls. But the roofs had faded to gray. The walls appeared treacherously close to tumbling, thick with lichen and moss. Weeds grew where once maidens in pointy slippers skipped over cobbled paths.

I climbed the numerous stone steps that led to the massive front door, out of which a smaller portal had been cut for ordinary use, and raised a rusted iron knocker fashioned into the shape of a lion's head. A young man wearing a horsehair robe, with a pink scalp above an unkempt tonsure, answered my summons. "I must speak with Dom Beauclaire," I told him in English.

He allowed me inside. "May I inquire your name?" he asked curtly in heavily accented English.

"My name is Emma Andrews. I have come to see one of the friars. Would you tell Dom Beauclaire I am the friend of Peter Ivanescu?"

His lips curled. "It ees Franciscan monks who are referred to as friars. You are not of zee one true church?"

I had been through too much to endure his scathing glare. "Does Dom Beauclaire only speak with Catholics?"

My effrontery surprised him, and like most who enjoy bullying, he backed away at my challenge. "Wait here," he said, curling his lip. "I will inform him."

A thin, reedy voice spoke. "There is no need, Dom Henri. I am here."

The man from whom this pronouncement had emanated moved into the room with the aid of a young monk on one side and a simply wrought cane on the other. The monk at the door stepped aside as I entered the château. The smell of mold assailed me.

Dom Beauclaire's eyes were bright with interest, locked on me as he advanced. In the light, I could see his skin was not so much wrinkled as translucent, finely lined, and mottled lightly with spots suggesting an age far past three score.

I sank into a reverent curtsy. There was something about this man that seemed to dictate such a show of respect. "Thank you for seeing me."

His voice held an abundance of laughter as he bade me rise, and reminded me that he was not a king. "I have been told about you, Mrs. Andrews. Come with me." His words were also tinged with the musical cadence of the Gallic language.

Under the guidance of his young charge, he led me away from the frowning doorman into a small, spartanly furnished room that opened up off the main hall. It contained only a few wooden chairs and a table up against a wall. For decoration there was a lone oil painting of a monk—perhaps Saint Benedict himself—and a crucifix.

When we were seated, Dom Beauclaire said to his escort, "Go and leave us, Alliot. I will have madam call you when I am ready."

His eyes twinkled after the other monk left us with visible reluctance. "I am afraid young Dom Alliot is rather shocked at my insisting on being left alone with a woman." His laugh was conspiratorial, as if he savored this whiff of scandal. I realized that although he was old, and a monk, this man was still French.

"You said you had been told about me?" I began, making it a question.

"Mr. Ivanescu's letter was quite complete," he said. "Oh, he is not here, but he told me of you. I have expected you."

"But how could you? I only thought to come when my family cast me out."

"And why did they do that, my child?" he asked, as if he knew.

"They discovered I was . . ." This was difficult. My fear of being spurned should I speak the truth nearly stopped me. But I had nothing to gain by being dishonest. "I was protecting a child from a vampire." I stared at him, hardly daring to hope he would believe me. I was fully prepared for him to roar for Alliot and have me taken away. When he did not, I added weakly, "They did not believe me."

His eyes were compassionate as he lifted a bony shoulder. "Who would?"

My question was pitched barely above a whisper. "Do you?"

Dom Beauclaire paused, taking my measure. "Do you know what this place is, Mrs. Andrews?" he finally said.

"This abbey? It is unusual, I can see, being an old château."

"And tell me, then, why have you come here?" he asked.

"I do not know. My Uncle Peter wrote to you. I thought . . . I simply had no place else to go."

He smiled comfortingly, nodding as if he approved. "It is as good a place to start as any. It is often after distractions are removed that we find the true path. You have come to the place you belong. You are Dhampir, are you not?"

My shock was numbing. It took me a moment to find my voice. "How did you know?"

"Because your kind find us, sooner or later. Take my hands."

They were dry and cool. I fancied I could feel the bones under the paper-thin skin. But when he gripped me, it was with surprising strength. "Are you a woman of faith?" he asked, peering deeply into my eyes.

I wanted to say yes. Instead I answered truthfully. "I do not know what that means anymore."

He nodded, and seemed pleased, although I could not fathom why. "What one has faith in makes all the difference. For one such as you, born of the blood of the beast, what is required most of all is to have faith in yourself. Do you?"

I hesitated. "I want to. I am learning."

"But you are afraid."

It was not a question, yet I nodded. He released my hands. *"Bon."* Sitting back, he raised his gaze to the ceiling, letting it roam slowly from left to right. "You are mistaken about this place, Madame Andrews. It is not a monastery. It is an archive. I will tell you of its treasures, and some of its secrets. But first"—he layered his hands one over the other on the hilt of his stick—"you must tell me everything."

The tale, as I told it from beginning to end to the black monk, seemed like something far beyond reason, even to me. I could not look at Dom Beauclaire, afraid I would see doubt,

horror, even disgust on his wizened features—or, worse, that wary, veiled look I'd seen in my father's eye. The one Roger had worn, and Mary, only days ago.

When I was finished, he said simply, "The thing imprisoned in your English village must never be allowed to live again."

"Can you help me?"

"In truth, I do not know." His wise eyes watched me closely. "Take heart, Madame Andrews. There is a child involved, you say. Where there is the heart of innocence, there is always hope, for that is where God lives most."

I was hardly reassured by his warm words. Her innocence was precisely why Henrietta was such a powerful draw for the evil gathering on the Wiltshire downs. "When do we begin?" I asked anxiously.

"Right away, I should think, as time is of the essence. You must have unlimited access to the archive, and to me, for no one knows the collection as I do. Therefore, it is best you stay in the château. Do not worry about seeming improper. Many come to this repository to study, and so it is quite regular. Dom Alliot will help you settle into a room."

"Can you help me find a way to destroy Marius? Will that even protect Henrietta, or is it too late?"

"I will see you this evening, madame. We will have many days, and many questions. Some will be answered. Others cannot be."

Alliott sent for my belongings at the village inn and led me through shadow-ridden halls and up a set of stone spiral steps to a barren, chilly tower room. I was brought food. When my portmanteau arrived, I unpacked a few things. That done, I sat by the glow of my lamp against the bare gold-brown stones and took in my surroundings, considering not only the iron bedstead and long table with a chipped, ancient chair, but the remote location, the sturdy lock on the door, and the barred window. I realized this had once been a prison. My imagination twisted. That evening, as I waited for the call from Dom Beauclaire, I thought of long-dead souls who might have occupied this room and the hours they had spent here, waiting for clemency or execution.

I rushed to the door and tried it, half-fearful it would be locked. It opened. I sighed, scolded myself, and shut it. Then I settled down to wait.

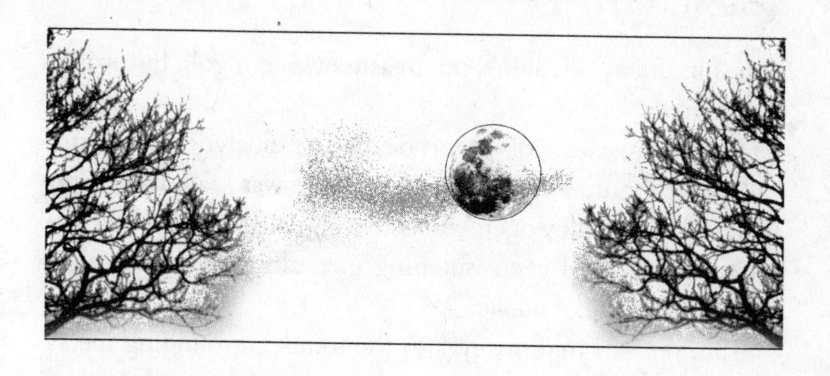

Chapter Twenty-five

It was after midnight when Dom Alliot brought me down to the magnificent archive for the first time. If you are not in the habit of visiting a lending library or if you have not perused—as I have—the towering stacks of books in the great country houses, you perhaps would not realize how beyond imaginable was the amassing of materials stuffed inside the Amiens château.

Room after room, and on into the great hall, I proceeded through stories of shelving, ladders to reach the upper balconies, and free-standing stacks in the open spaces, lined up in militarily precise rows. Glass-encased flambeaus flickered on the walls, illuminating the leather spines. It was a cave of wonders, but unlike Aladdin's, my treasure was not gold but words. Knowledge.

The reedy voice of Dom Beauclaire floated toward me. "Madame Andrews, this way, please." He was seated at a large table, surrounded by open books that revealed cracked and yellowed pages. He'd been watching me, taking in my reaction. "You have a love of books?"

"Oh, yes." I lifted my eyes to the tomes surrounding me. "I have never seen so many."

"This is a very extraordinary collection. From many lands, from sources banned and banished, these are the books not fit to be housed in Rome. But valuable nonetheless." His gaze lifted to roam over the various materials. "Some were rescued from the Alexandrian library before it was burned. Some date back further than Egypt, written in symbols and painstakingly transcribed. We understood the hieroglyphic texts long before the Rosetta Stone." His pursed mouth quirked at the secret. "These are all ancient writings for the most part, for it is an old knowledge we keep here, together with the controversies of our own age. Which is where we start tonight.

"Sit," he said, gesturing. "Madame Andrews, there must be trust between us. You must understand why I can believe you, and all the others who came before you, those who were unfortunate to learn that the Holy Mother Church has known for many, many years of the existence of the *nosferatu*." His gnarled hands slid a large, leather-bound volume to me. One crooked finger tapped the page. "Start here, madame."

I read aloud:

> *For here we are told that dead men, men who have been dead for several months, I say, return from the tomb, are*

heard to speak, walk about, infest hamlets and villages, injure both men and animals.

I looked up. "What is this?"

"Go on," the monk urged.

Whose blood they drain and thereby making them sick and ill, and at length actually causing death. Nor can men deliver themselves from these terrible visitations, nor secure themselves from these horrid attacks, unless they dig the corpses up from the graves, drive a sharp stake through these bodies, cut off the heads, tear out the hearts; or else they burn the bodies to ashes. The name given to these ghosts is Oupires, or Vampires . . .

Dom Beauclaire leaned back, his movements stiff and labored. I was reminded that he was very old, his body fragile, and the hour was very late. "Look to the front piece. Written by Dom Augustine Calmet—a member of my own order—this work, *Dissertations sur les Apparitions des Anges, des Demons et des Esprits, et sur les Revenants et Vampires,* was published in the last century. Not hundreds of years ago, mind you, when superstition ruled our minds."

"I was told the position of the Church is that vampires do not exist."

The hint of a smile on his wrinkled face warmed it. "Indeed, it would seem that is not so, at least unofficially. There are some things Mother Church does not permit to be commonly known, for reasons many do not understand. The fact remains Dom Calmet believed, and wrote of his belief in this, an official church document that has never been declaimed by Rome.

Moreover, he came to his conclusion after a thorough investigation of the evidence."

"Is this related to Father Luke, the priest I told you of?"

"Ah. Father Luke." Dom Beauclaire's sparse eyebrows leapt higher on his wrinkled brow. "And that secret society, with some members of which I am quite familiar. But that can wait." He pushed a stack of scrolls at me. "Alliot has instructions to assist you while I am gone. My old bones get the better of me these days. As Our Lord so aptly put it: the spirit is willing but the flesh is weak."

"Dom Beauclaire, I cannot thank you enough," I said emphatically.

He rose, leaning heavily on the table. "Good luck, Madame Andrews. I will pray for you."

I began my instruction by reading the numerous and varied accounts of the vampire throughout time, and all over the world. Here in France and in much of Europe, these creatures were known by the Roman name *nosferatu*. In Greece, it was *vyrkolakas*. The gypsy name was *mullo*. In India, it was the *bhuta*. The Scots knew the legends of the *boabhan-sithe*, the dead that returned from the grave to drink the living blood and lived their cursed existence forever.

Most legends favored staking, beheading, and purifying fire to kill them. Salt, garlic, and wild rose were frequently named as being aversive to the undead, but not deadly. The ringing of a bell was said to entrance them. Drowning was emphatically stressed by some, while others discounted any effect at all.

"How will I know which of these methods are accurate?" I asked Dom Beauclaire one evening.

"I shall tell you the same as I have told all those like you who have found this place." He lifted his head to peer at me quite intently. "You will feel your way, madame. There is no instruction in the art of the Dhampir. Your gifts will manifest singular to you, both in the type and in the strength. These skills will follow from both your unique nature, as all gifts and talents do, as well as the magnitude of the vampire that made the one who passed its blood to you."

My heart skipped, as it always did at the reference to my mother, and her terrible condition. "But Valerian Fox told me of the woman he'd known," I said, "who had a connection to animals. Then, when the wolves threatened me, I was able to reach into them with my mind. I would not have thought of it had I not known of Naimah's skill."

"It is a coincidence, yes, but not necessarily instructive. There will naturally be some occasions in which you will possess the same ability as another, but these are cheats, *oui?* They are not worth the cost. If you model yourself on someone else, you travel a false path."

"Then how am I to know what I am, and what I should do when faced with Marius?" I protested.

"The best way for you to prepare is within, not without." The old monk reached his hand across the table, grasping mine and smiling bracingly. "You will learn. Do not despair, Madame Andrews."

I was childishly sullen, although I saw the sense of what he told me. I was sick with worry for my Henrietta.

"It is a fearful affliction, as is my impatience. I beg your forgiveness if I seem petulant, sir."

He waved away my apology. "Oh, madame, please. I have had swords drawn against me, as well as other interesting threats made against my life." He chuckled, as if these recollections amused him. "You hunters are an emotional lot. I have known many in my time. Oh, I understand, of course. It is quite natural when one deals with matters of the undead. Trust me, it is your curse that you will never feel up to the task, no matter how many times you have won in battle. You will constantly wrestle with doubts about your abilities and be absolutely convinced at every moment that you do not know or possess nearly enough."

I gaped at him, mostly for the nonchalance with which he spoke of what I most acutely felt. When he saw my expression, he shrugged and smiled at me reassuringly. "Ah, I am not insensitive to how these insecurities torment you. I merely observe they seem to be unavoidable, *oui?*"

"So you are saying I am *normal*?"

He tapped his gnarled finger to his parchment lips. "But after all, Madame Andrews, it falls upon you as Dhampir to face alone unthinkable evil with powers beyond mortal comprehension using means that for unknowable reasons vary in their potency and reliability, and all the time without any training or education other than your own ability to find what you need within yourself." He lifted a bony shoulder in a Gallic shrug. "If one of you loses your temper with me now and then, I do not mind so much. I have not suffered injury yet. So let us not trouble ourselves with apologies. I have information, *oui*, but not everything you need to know will be found here. But it will help."

With that, he came to sit beside me. "What are you researching at the moment?"

I showed him the sources I'd collected. "I am trying to educate myself generally, of course," I explained. "However, I am particularly interested in a reference to a serpent or a dragon. It seems to be a repeated motif in the Avebury area . . ."

My voice trailed off when I saw his reaction. I waited until he cleared his throat. "The dragon?" he asked.

"Yes," I replied excitedly. I grabbed a charcoal and quickly sketched the shape of the winged reptile. "It was in paintings in the church, and the gypsy who attacked me had a tattoo of this on his arm. Have you seen this particular symbol?"

"Oh, yes, many times, many times." His old face crumpled, exaggerating the lines of age. "I am afraid, however, I will be of no help to you. The information on the Dracula is kept elsewhere." He lifted his hand in anticipation of my obvious question. "And no, I do not know where. No one knows where. I suspect it sits in the heart of the Vatican, where only a select few can access it."

This was deeply disappointing. And troubling. "Do you know the reason for all of this extraordinary secrecy?"

His eyes glowed. "I do not *know*, but I can imagine. Whenever I have heard that name . . ." He paused, then spoke in sharp syllables, "Dracula . . . It has meant terrible things. For the hunter does not always win, Madame Andrews. You know this. When the Dragon Prince is involved, it goes poorly for mortals."

A few days into my stay, I received one of my regular notes from Sebastian, giving me an update on Henrietta's status. As usual, he reported she remained stable and seemingly well. This was only partial relief, for how long could I expect her to be safe? This increased my sense of urgency and did my patience, so necessary in the tedious research in which I was engaged, no good.

Sebastian also sent disturbing news, which quickened my pulse when I read it. Miss Harris had gone missing. I could not make up my mind if this was a good or bad omen. I could not help but be pleased she was no longer in proximity to Henrietta, but the question arose: Had Marius simply no longer needed her now that I was out of the picture? The thought soured my mood. Was the lord vampire so confident then?

Sebastian reported Mr. Fox remained at Dulwich Manor, but his mysterious comings and goings were a growing annoyance to his hosts, and Sebastian feared Mary and Roger might soon ask him to leave.

I turned broody after reading this. Going to the great atlas which rested by itself on a podium in one sunlit corner, ready for frequent reference, I opened it and turned its crisp pages until I found a map of England. I traced my finger west from London, under Oxford to the point just north of the Salisbury plain, where Stonehenge was located, to the town of Avebury. I frowned, finding the Saint Michael line along which it lay, beginning with Saint Michael's Mount at Marazion in Cornwall all the way across the south of England to Canterbury in Kent.

On this map, there were curious notations. Northeast of Avebury, near Royston, was a legend indicating something called Wanderbury Stone Ring. To the west was a similar mention for Hurlers Stone Circle. Outposts, Father Luke had said, along the power meridian. It was then I noticed Glastonbury, and my thoughts sputtered to a stop. Glastonbury was on the Saint Michael's lay line. Had I known that?

The proud tones of Mrs. Tigwalt, Father Luke's territorial housekeeper, came into my recollection. She had told me the legend of Joseph of Aramethea, who, upon reaching England, struck his staff to the ground, causing the Holy Hawthorn to grow. That had been, according to the legend, at Glastonbury. And nearby, at what was still known as the Chalice Well, Joseph

was rumored to have secreted the cup of Christ, which was why it ran red with His blood.

Red with blood . . . I had not believed her at the time.

I excitedly searched for everything on Glastonbury I could find, calling on Alliot to aid me. A few hours later, I found in a small pamphlet something that solidified my suspicions.

The design of the emblem denoting the Chalice Well—two circles intersecting, the center part an oval—was remarkably similar to the fish symbol I'd seen on Father Luke's ring and the broken seal under Marius's tree. The pamphlet gave a name for the sign as the *vesica piscis*.

My heart skipped a beat. This *vesica piscis* marked the site of the holy well, which was actually a set of pools fed by a natural spring—hence the twin circles—where the Holy Grail was said to reside. Due to the iron deposits through which the spring flowed underground, the pools of the well were supplied a steady stream of water tinged with red.

The significance of this reached deep into my bones. Who has not put a cut to their mouth and felt that sour tinge on the edge of the tongue? A stream running with ferrous oxide would taste . . .

It would taste like blood. Blood flowing from the very earth.

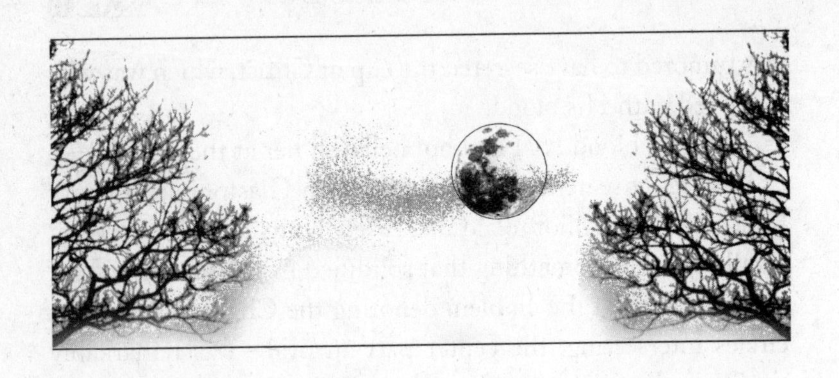

Chapter Twenty-six

When I told this to Dom Beauclaire, I was wary he might think my interpretation wrong, even profane. But his eyes glowed with excitement. "Excellent! Come." He took my arm and leaned heavily on me as he directed me through the old rooms. "Of course, what we need might be housed in one of the other archive locations. I do not recall having much here on the subject."

"Other locations?"

"Oh, many." He waved his hand as if to dismiss the pride in his smile. "An old Bohemian castle outside of Prague, a Venetian palazzo sinking into the Adriatic—I worry constantly about that one. Some are general, as this one is. Others have their own specialty: curses, witchcraft, hauntings, and of course vampires. The main repository of the revenant manuscripts lies in Copenhagen."

I had been stunned by this place, by the vastness of the collection in the hall. The revelation that there was more was almost too much to fathom.

He chuckled at my gaping amazement. "A network of secret locations scattered across many lands is thought to best safeguard against fire or intentional destruction. There are many who would see the archives, and all the wisdom they contain, lost to mankind forever."

We eventually uncovered information in some old journals of an eighteenth-century man obsessed with England's Arthurian legends indicating he had found evidence that Glastonbury was the actual location of the mythical Isle of Avalon, the final resting place of the legendary King Arthur.

"But it is nowhere near the sea," Dom Beauclaire puzzled. "How can it be an island?"

"It is set inland now, but long ago the area all around it was swamp, and the miles of flatland were under water. The tor is elevated. See this drawing, how high it rises? It would have appeared as an island." I read on. "Odd, how the legend of Arthur is tied so closely with this place. Both the quest for the Grail, which is at the Chalice Well right there in Glastonbury, and the burial on Avalon."

Dom Beauclaire held up a finger as a thought caught hold. "Your King Arthur is somewhat of a Christ figure inasmuch as it is believed he will rise again someday to protect his beloved isle, *oui?*" His head came up sharply. "Where is Stukeley's book?"

We kept *Avebury, a Temple of the British Druids*, always on hand, because Dr. Stukeley's research was vital to our theories. He opened the book to the detailed drawing of the Great Stone

Serpent, and bent over it, studying the figure for a long time.

I peered over his shoulder, but I knew by heart the lay of the sarcen stones, how they formed the shape of a great snake, the West Kennet and Beckhampton avenues forming the spines, flowing off into the tail. The Sanctuary lay at the head of the serpent.

"This is indeed remarkable. It is a serpent, there is no doubt. Very significant. The serpent is regarded as a symbol of eternal life," Dom Beauclaire said, raising his head at last.

"I had heard this," I said.

"Now, let us go back to the tale of your King Arthur. Again, renewed life when the king rises again for England, *c'est vrai?*"

I saw his point, and an idea occurred to me. "Yes. And think, too, of how the Holy Grail was sought by Arthur's knights because it was believed—still is believed—that it possessed the gift of eternal life for any who drank from it."

His smile faded into a frown of concentration. "Let us think on this a moment. In this we see the confluence of the profane and the holy. In the vampire, one finds another life after death. It blasphemes eternal life." His lined face went cold. "This place where this great serpent of stone lies, you said you were told it is where the living and the dead both reside."

"It is along the lay line, where the worlds of the living and the dead meet," I clarified. "This is what Mr. Hess told me. He had researched it for all of his life."

Dom Beauclaire appeared suddenly haggard and old, frighteningly fragile. "And there is the sign of the Dracula, which you have reported seeing in abundance."

When I saw the fear in his eyes, the bottom dropped out of my heart.

"My dear Madame Andrews, this suggests something quite alarming. There are evils in the ancient world that warriors of virtue have battled, and vanquished. If there lies in this holy prison something so vile, so destructive and virulent that it requires all the charms we see laid out before us, then this thing is terrible indeed. I am thinking it is an ageless vampire, one so great it could not be killed by the tools those who dealt with it had to work with."

"But what does Marius want with it?" I asked. Then something occurred to me. "Vampires acquire the powers of those they feed upon," I murmured, seeing it all now. "If he were to release it, then kill it, take it into himself—"

Dom Beauclaire raised a shaking hand to his face. "Imagine the power. If the Dracula is involved here, it has to be immense, unimaginable . . . My God, Madame Andrews, think of it; the ability to destroy and dominate would be enormous."

"Perhaps you should rest," I urged, suddenly alarmed by his palsied state.

"The day will come very soon, Madame Andrews, when I will rest." He drew himself upright. "Tonight we must work. There is little time to find a way to arm you against this fight. The spring is nearly upon us, and when the time of evil breaks on these lands, something most terrible, most unimaginably wicked, will be unleashed."

I dreamt of the hawthorn tree coming to life and reaching its deadly arms toward me. A large black crow nestled in its branches, its flat, black eyes like jet beads afire with glee. In the twisting bark, I saw faces flash, ugly, twisted visions of my sister, of Mary and Roger, and Alan. They hated me. Then I saw

Marius's shadow behind them, and the crow cawed in triumph. I tried to cry out to warn them, but they would not listen.

I broke out of my dream, out of sleep, and sat bolt upright as the perfect memory of Marius assembled in my mind, bringing with it a flood of emotions that left me near tears. I still felt him, sometimes. Inside me, in my mind, in my veins.

I quickly rose from bed and dressed, disciplining myself to study my notes. A short while later, someone rapped upon my door. I assumed it was Dom Alliot with my breakfast. "Put it on the table by the bed. Thank you."

But it was Dom Beauclaire who answered me. "Madame Andrews, I have someone here to see you."

I immediately started, looking up to find a tall, lanky figure ducking under the transom. He straightened, stared at me, and said, "Hello, Mrs. Andrews."

Breath seemed quite beyond my capacity. His presence sucked the air from the room, leaving me in a vortex of shock. "Mr. . . . Mr. Fox. What the devil are you doing here?"

I cannot do justice to the unexpectedly violent emotion that came upon me. It was as if up until that moment, I had not fully comprehended how alone and frightened I'd been, and it was only then, as I looked on his composed face with the exotic cheekbones and obsidian eyes, that it all came crashing over me. I was vaguely aware that I was angry with him, that I was not quite certain just how much I could trust him. And yet, it did not diminish the sheer relief of that particular familiar face, appearing here when I was feeling so isolated and far from home.

I tried to stand, but my knees turned to water. My vision blurred—I am ashamed to admit—with the flux of tears and,

as the one side of his mouth pulled upward in wry acknowledgment that my reaction flattered him, I had to hold myself back from foolishly throwing myself into his arms.

Instead, I went rigid—a good Englishwoman's comfort—and said nothing more while I waited for my pounding heart to quiet.

"Forgive my intrusion," was his reply. I bit off my reassurances that indeed, it was no intrusion—no, not at all—then the single blade of panic rushed through my happiness. "Henrietta—?"

He stepped forward, holding out a halting hand. "No, no. All is well. Or rather, as well as can be expected. Perhaps it is better to say nothing has changed."

"Miss Harris, she is still gone?"

He nodded, his brow creasing. "A new nurse has come. But Sebastian is not content to rest his guard of the child. He accompanies them everywhere, and he has set a watch on them at night without their knowing."

"I doubt there is much Marius misses."

His eyes sliced a glance to the monk to my right. I, too, looked to Dom Beauclaire. He was happy to see me pleased, I saw.

Then, like icy water dumped shockingly over sun-heated flesh, my body went cold. I remembered Mr. Fox's deception with the bloodied hawthorn switch. He had lied to me. He had betrayed me.

I drew myself together. "What has brought you here?" I was satisfied at the coldness I'd injected into my tone.

"May we speak privately?"

I did not know at first if Dom Beauclaire would allow this,

for it meant, after all, a man and a woman alone in a bedchamber, but he tactfully withdrew with a measured look in my direction.

I had taken no notice that Mr. Fox had his satchel bag with him. He placed it now on the table and drew it open. From its depths he took an oilcloth, folded over so that it looked like nothing more than rags.

He handed it to me. "This belongs in your possession, not mine."

I unwrapped it with shaking hands, for I already knew what it was. I gazed upon the hawthorn switch, tipped with the vampire lord's blood, in my palm. "I knew you took it," I said. "I found it when I went to leave you a note of farewell."

"Then you already knew I had lied to you," he said quietly. His dignity composed his face, but his eyes blazed with agony, perhaps even humiliation. Would a man such as this commit dishonor without good reason? I asked myself. I wanted so badly to believe in him.

"Why?" I pleaded, uttering the single word softly but with passion.

"Why did I take it, or why did I lie?"

"Both, I suppose."

"You know why I took it." His nostrils flared, pride asserting itself to the fore. "There is vampire blood on that thing, and although I do not know how to harness it, there is no doubt it holds great power. Power I wished to use to defeat Marius."

"You kept it from me. Did you think I would misuse it? Squander it?"

"I lied," he said carefully, "to protect myself." He bowed his head, gesturing to what I held in my hand. "But you must have

it, learn how to use it. You are Dhampir, you will know what to do."

"But I do not."

"Then you will. Or we will together. It is not an easy thing for me, Emma. I have been alone a very, very long time—much longer than you can even imagine. I can only say I have come to understand that you and I, we must allow nothing to come between us. If we are to have any chance in this war, we must stand together."

I gazed at the sharpened point, black with the dried blood. "I did read something in a journal here, kept by a Greek hunter who studied the nature and use of vampire blood. It said something about the power held by a revenant's blood being the result of how the vampire absorbed the life, the essence, and the strengths or weaknesses of those they feed upon."

Fox agreed. "Of course. The blood is the life. Consuming life feeds the vampire, its victims' blood feeds its blood. And life is the essence of magic." He leaned forward eagerly. "What of the possession of vampire blood by another vampire? Would that give the possessor the same power to absorb the energy of its victim?"

"I . . ." I had not read anything to answer that specific question. But something stirred inside, the faint vestiges of knowing. I somehow knew the communion of blood, even through the medium of the stick, would form a bond, though I did not understand how or why. I said, therefore, only: "I do not know."

Mr. Fox pierced me with a look, and I was surprised by the desperation, the gravity I saw there. He had told Father Luke that Marius had taken something from him. He wanted very badly to destroy the vampire lord, and I do not think I had known until that moment how fervently and single-mindedly he was dedicated to that goal.

He pressed my hand, in which lay the tainted switch. "When the time comes," he said to me, "you may know what to do."

He drew up a stool. Folding his hands on the table, he trained his gaze on his grasped fingers. "You must think me craven," he said at last.

I settled on the edge of the bed. "I do not recall it ever mattering to you one way or the other what my opinion was."

"That was never true. If I am reserved . . . it is with reason." He touched a pile of books, his long fingers reverent as they ran lightly over the leather bindings.

"How did you find me?" I asked.

He gave a small chuckle, a hint of the charm that had so captivated me. "I have been tracking vampires for years. Finding one Englishwoman in France was no challenge."

His eyes drifted down to the book open on the table. Idly he thumbed the pages. "You know, Emma, I came here to bring you back."

I did not feel ready to leave. The very thought made me acutely, uncomfortably aware of my lack of knowledge. "I know Beltane is not far off. But I need more time."

"I need you with me." He seemed to catch himself, adding, "If we are to kill Marius and save Henrietta, we must remain together. For now."

How foolish I was to be disappointed.

"I should like to rest and eat," he said, taking his leave. "I would like to join you in the archive later, if I may. Dom Beauclaire suggested it, but it must be agreeable to you."

"Of course," I replied. When he'd gone, I felt different. Better.

I did not know why his presence here made me glad, for he had not brought any news to improve our situation, but I was—for once—not alone.

Fox was already with Dom Beauclaire when I entered the room where we had been working. "Ah, Madame Andrews," Dom Beauclaire said in greeting, "I have asked Mr. Fox what it is he wishes most to learn, and he has told me it is the history, and perhaps insight into the purpose, of this priest of the Order of Saint Michael of the Wing."

I was taken aback. "Father Luke?"

"You may consult the source materials yourself, but I shall summarize it for you in the interests of time. The knighthood does indeed exist. It was formed first as a Royal Brotherhood of the Order of Saint Michael of the Wing in Portugal in the wake of victory in the Holy Land during the crusades."

He held up a cautionary finger at my frown of confusion. "Apocryphal annals tell a different tale. You see, after returning victorious in the wake of their battle with the Saracens, some of the knights fell under a peculiar malaise, one you would find familiar as the indications of the vampire. The Order went into action to cleanse the villages of this plague. However, this meant a purge of military heroes who had fought bravely. It caused a terrible public outcry against the Order. The knighthood fell into disuse after this scandal, and it was generally believed to have been disbanded."

"But it was not," I guessed.

"They have existed as a secret society of extirpators of all manner of beings beyond the realm of mortal justice who would harm men's bodies, and souls. They are not Dhampir, not merely hunters, but guardians and warriors against creatures you or I could never imagine, much less face. Much less fight, for it requires great spiritual strength as well as physical skill." His face was chillingly stony, his eyes flat. I guessed he knew far more particulars than he was sharing. I was grateful for his discretion. I was already too burdened to be curious.

"Then Father Luke was correct," I said to Fox. "He is indeed well equipped to battle Marius."

But Fox was still grim. "He is entrusted with the guardianship of the thing imprisoned on The Sanctuary, not destroying Marius."

Dom Beauclaire agreed. "The Order is strict, specific, and very careful in the priests they select. These are not shepherds. These are warriors prepared to kill for duty." Dom Beauclaire wagged his bent finger and peered at us intently. "Have a care with this priest. His allegiance to his cause will be absolute. And he will be ready to do whatever his duty demands to see the good of the world protected."

"But his goal is ours," I protested. I noticed how weak I sounded, and realized I voiced more of a wish than a certainty.

"Do not be so certain. He has a strong sense of purpose, *oui?* And it is not concerned with Marius, or your little Henrietta. His duty is to the Church, and his sacred mission."

I felt deflated. Much as I would like to believe otherwise, it seemed Father Luke could prove dangerous, if he thought our cause endangered his. I turned to Fox. "His path is likely to cross ours in any event. We have no choice but to include him."

"Agreed. We keep him close. But we dare not trust him."

Our mistake came to me in the quiet of my room. I cannot say what triggered it, or for how long all that figured behind the moment of epiphany had been lying dormant in my brain. I know Father Luke and his secret order of knights were much on my mind. I kept thinking of that painting, the one of Saint Michael, and how the serpent Satan had gnashed his gleaming fangs in frustration at his victorious foe. I had seen fangs like that with my own eyes, snapping maliciously for my blood.

And serpents were signs of eternal life, but they were also symbols of evil. The eternal vampire, foul creature, vanquished by sainted knight or archangel. Michael. George.

And the Great Stone Serpent, made of stone and more ancient than history itself, marking the land where forces raged, bringing life and death together.

And the season of spring. Renewal and Life, with one small festival of evil. Beltane, or May Day . . .

No, I thought. My heart began to pound, heralding the insight before it resolved into clarity. *Not* May Day. Somehow, I suddenly knew.

Mr. Hess had spoken of the importance of the Eve of Saint George, a feast of evil to rival All Hallows' Eve. Both holy days were preceded by an evening of revelry of wickedness that was allowed to reign briefly free and strong.

'Twas the month before the month of May. Coleridge's opening line from the eerie, haunting tale of poor, ill-fated Christabel, who was visited by the evil Geraldine in a midnight garden and destroyed . . .

I gasped as it came to me. My eyes shot wide and stared unseeing. The high unholy day which Marius awaited was the Eve of Saint George. April 22—not even so much as a fortnight away. And I was here, in France! It would take much of that time just to travel all the way back to England.

I flew down the ancient corridors of the château. As fortune would have it, I found Alliot quickly. "Take me to Mr. Fox's chamber," I instructed. "And summon Dom Beauclaire at once."

The room given to Mr. Fox was not far. When I pounded insistently on his door, he readily answered, his shirt unbuttoned and sleeves rolled up to his elbows. His skin was wet and he was holding a damp flannel square which dripped unheedingly upon the floor. The sight of him in such a state of dishabille threw me into a deep flush, but I pushed past into his room and declared, "It is not Beltane, Valerian! Marius shall act on April 22, the Eve of Saint George. A good eight days earlier than we thought!"

He caught my hand, making me stop and face him. His touch was cool and damp, and I was aware how the spicy scent of his soap tingled in my nostrils. We stood uncomfortably close. His dark eyes bored into mine as he assimilated my announcement.

I said quietly, "We've nearly run out of time already."

Dom Beauclaire appeared, supported by Alliot on one side and his battered cane on the other. I repeated what I'd told Fox. "I must return to England," I told him. "We have only twelve days to prepare. I will leave for Calais in the morning with Mr. Fox and look for a ship."

His old eyes glittered and he shook his head. *"Non,"* he barked, the sound abrupt and distinctly French. "You are not ready."

His face was stern, wearing its age with a steely dignity that was hard to refuse. In all of our time together, I had never seen him anything less than agreeable, but his proud temper asserted itself now. "You are the guardian of more than the child you love. All children need you. The world needs you, Madame

Andrews. You must be certain you have done all you can to be ready. Take more time with me."

He was right—had I not said this very thing so many times? I was not ready. But that no longer mattered.

"I have only twelve days," I said, and that, really, was the end of it.

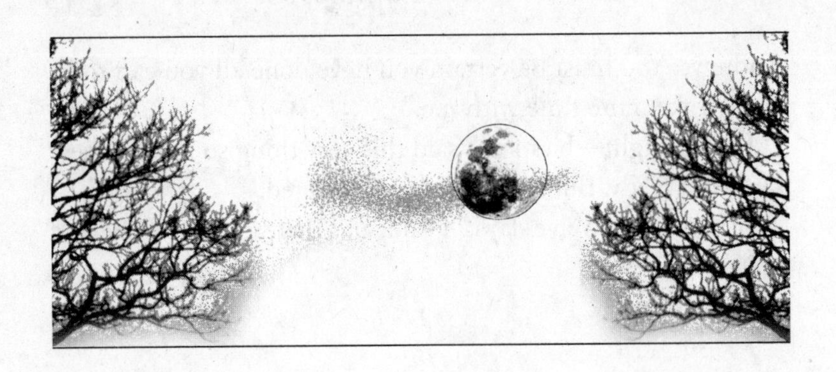

Chapter Twenty-seven

We found a ship leaving from Boulogne-sur-Mer. Fox let a room at an inn, where we could wait out the hour until it would be ready. I sank into a dusty chair, exhausted from our swift flight from Amiens. Fox, however, was restless. He placed his bag on the table and began to unpack it, inspecting the equipment assembled within.

I watched silently as he lifted a bundle of stakes, each honed to a deadly point. He weighed each in his hand as he evaluated its worth. Eight in all. A short-handled ax followed, then a cloth-wrapped item I could see, from the way the folds covered it, was a large cross. A silver vial. Holy water, I assumed.

The muscles of his shoulders flexed as he heaved a large, heavy, flat-headed mallet out onto the table. A dance of nerves

tickled my back as I imagined him swinging it high, then bringing it down to bear on one of the stakes he'd made to drive it through the corpse. I closed my eyes for a moment against the reminder of our grisly purpose.

When I opened them, I found him looking at me. "I am near madness with worry for Henrietta," I said, shaking my head to throw off my dark imaginings. "We must find a way to make certain she is kept safe through all of this. We must find a way to get to her, though I do not know how. Neither Mary nor Roger will allow it."

He was tense, and although he nodded, I felt the stab of doubt. Would he protect the child at all costs, or was it only killing Marius that meant anything to him? Just as Dom Beauclaire warned us not to underestimate Father Luke, I must not make a similar mistake with Fox.

"We should take her away, kidnap her if we must," I pressed.

Mr. Fox shook his head, firmly but with sympathy. "He will find her, Emma. He has bound her to him, though I know he has not defiled her, for he needs her pure. But he will use her when the time comes. She is not safe, not anywhere."

The ship Mr. Fox found for us was old, the mates dodgy, and the captain would have—I had no doubt—tossed us overboard if he thought there was any profit in it. But we had nothing much for either captain or crew to covet, and that was our protection. That and the steely glint in Mr. Fox's eye which brooked no nonsense, and the undercurrent of danger that seemed to emanate from his very pores.

We disembarked swiftly, and hired a hansom to take us to the railway station for the train to Basingstoke, where we might book a car north to Marlborough. I was tired, and slept on the way, curled against the shabby squabs. Hunger wakened me, for I'd had nothing since the sparse breakfast of bread and cheese at the Boulogne-sur-Mer inn.

Valerian was watching me. "It is only a little while longer."

"I must eat something." I sat up and stretched. "I am faint with hunger. I regret I am not one of those whom anxiety deprives of appetite. Rather, I grow ravenous."

"Do not apologize," he said, signaling to the driver to take us into the next village. We found an inn and ate a splendid repast of lamb stew finished with a shiny apple and rich cheese for dessert.

"Do you wish to continue traveling, or should I let rooms?" Fox asked at the conclusion of the meal. "If we ride on through, we will make the train in the morning."

"Let us go on," I said. "I am anxious to be back in Avebury."

We departed with dusk gathering on the western horizon. I was wary of the nighttime these days. But Valerian was beside me, and, lulled by the rocking motion of the conveyance, we grew sanguine and content in each other's presence until his voice rumbled across the sandpaper shadows. "I have not been a good friend to you."

I was a little sleepy. "Not a perfect friend, mind, but saving my life over and over again certainly counts for something, I should think."

"I would have you return the favor."

I rolled my head against the backrest to try to make him out in the dim light. "Pardon me?"

"I wish for you to save my life, Emma."

"Of course I shall, should it ever be in danger. You need not ask."

He waited a moment, then his gaze locked on mine. "You have not asked me why I took the hawthorn stick with the blood of the vampire on it."

"I suppose this is to do with whatever terrible secret you've been keeping."

His shock melted to thoughtfulness. "There was no hiding it from you, was there? But I wonder if you have guessed."

I sighed. "Valerian, do not ask any more patience from me. Whatever it is you are hiding, I pray you speak of it now."

"I will do better than that. I shall show you." He spoke so low I could barely hear him. "But I must extract a promise in exchange. It is a great thing I will ask of you, but if you have any caring in your heart for me, you will do this, Emma." His eyes closed, and his voice went dry. "I have no one else."

Five words. *I have no one else.* Indeed, spoken as they were by this quiet, dignified man, with heat sizzling in every syllable, I could not refuse him, though I suddenly wished I could. "I will do whatever it is. You can depend on me, Valerian."

Still he did not move, except to open his eyes and lock them on my face. "Vow it."

"Yes, then. I vow."

He seemed to relax. The shadows in the carriage were deep, and his eyes were like hollows, the lean cheeks gashed with shadow under the high bones. "My God," he said with a small, humorless laugh. "Look at me. I am afraid."

I was growing afraid as well. He produced a lamp from his bag and gave it to me to hold while he lit a match and set the oiled wick to a low, soft glow. His hands came up to his cravat and pulled at the simple knot. In the silence, the slippery sound of the finely spun linen being unwound snapped crisply. I had no understanding of what he was about until he had completely removed the neck cloth and opened his collar to expose the skin at the base of his throat.

I confess my first reaction was a rush of something very powerful, very carnal. Certainly, I did not comprehend at first what he was doing. The sight of his dusky skin, the smell of him, male and fragrant from soap, caused lust to strike hot and quick as a glowing poker in my stomach. I felt my lips go dry as my gaze took in the cords of muscle and strong bones outlined within the warm flesh. Then he turned his head, and in the fading daylight I saw two wounds, round and red, at the artery where the blood flowed under the ear.

Puncture wounds.

My recoil was instinctive, violent. I threw myself against the squabs with a sharp cry of alarm.

I recovered fairly quickly. I was not afraid for my safety. "How many times?" I asked. He knew what I meant.

"Only once. If I should die now, I will be dead, truly dead. Even if I should get bitten again." He said this last with such tragic pleading, as if begging me to see him no differently than I had before. As if I, whose very blood ran with the taint of my mother's undead master, should rebuke him.

"But should I sustain a second, then a third bite," he said, dropping the words like stones, "I will become a monster."

I cried an involuntary "No!" It was a silly, womanish thing, the cry of horror, but, as when he had first revealed his wounds, I could not control my instinctive reaction.

He would not look at me. "After that night in Montmartre, Marius came for me. I knew nothing about vampires then, and I made a fatal mistake. I looked at him, you see, and that was my end. His eyes swallowed me, and I could do nothing to fight him."

Yes. I remembered how that was. The vampire lord took something from you in that one glance, warping the self inside you so that you were as a fly caught in a web, helpless as the spider scrabbles over filaments toward you.

"You cannot imagine how my very soul seethed with repulsion as he tipped my head back and drank on me. I know I told you I had bought a cross to protect me, but I had no time to use it, entranced as I was. I felt the pain . . . but it was not unpleasant. And I felt the strength bleed out of me, more than blood flowing from my body into his. He absorbed a part of my life, absorbed *me*."

His courage amazed me, his calm, although his voice shook on that last word. He took only a moment to collect himself and continued. "I remember thinking I would die. I sometimes wish I had. But I only fell ill, and when he touched something to my lips, I did not know what he offered. I felt and tasted blood, but I thought it was my own. I was so thirsty, and the blood quenched as a bladder of water would after walking miles through wastelands. It is no excuse, however. Then, afterward, I was so sick. I was ready for death. I *wanted* it."

I remembered that. Remembered wanting the unholy eternity when Marius had wrapped himself into my mind.

"We were not Catholic, but the best care to be had was under a group of Carmelite nuns." His smile was ironic. "Because Father was wealthy and influential, they saw to me around the clock. I was never left alone. In my hazy state, they looked like ghosts—or angels, in some of my fevered dreams—in their white habits and winged wimples. And large crosses around their necks, and rosary beads looped at their side."

"That is what protected you. The crosses."

He nodded. "The place was nearly a cathedral, for all of the religious accoutrements kept about. From the hospital, my father took me directly home to England and there I grew well. But I soon came to understand I had not survived my meeting with the vampire unscathed. I was changed, Emma. But you must believe me, trust me, that I am still a man. I do not crave the blood. I am still human."

His dark eyes searched mine, seeking to reassure me. *And himself,* I thought. *He fears it is not completely true. He fears his own nature.*

"Your remarkable strength," I said. "Is that part of it?"

"Yes. I can also see great distances, and I hear more sharply than ordinary men. You noticed it, when I spied you and Henrietta that day down by The Sanctuary. These things are loathsome to me, Emma; they are constant reminders of what Marius did to me."

"Valerian," I whispered. I wanted to touch him, but I knew he would not have it. "Why has Marius never finished what he began?"

"I wear this," he said, showing me the crucifix that hung under his shirt. "I am constantly on guard. Although he has had plenty of time and several prime opportunities to find me over the years, I have been prepared."

His impassioned words seemed to dart about the small dark space. "Naimah must have shown you how," I said.

"She did, and others who have taught me through my many travels." He paused, and I saw his throat convulse. "It is my greatest dread, worse than death, to imagine myself undead. I will never give Marius the chance to take me. Yet I cannot always be certain I am secure. There are times when even I am

caught unawares. Do you recall the night we went to Hess's house?"

I said I did. His fingers kneaded his temple. "I did a foolish thing that night, Emma. I was afraid if he should wake, and I wore this holy amulet, it would add to his horror and confusion. He was our friend, and you loved him. So I left it off."

I gasped lightly. "My God, I remember! Marius went for you."

"Father Luke saved me from much worse than death that night."

I regarded him with curiosity. "I remember what you told me, about a vampire wanting something from its victim. What did Marius desire from you?"

He lifted one steel-sprung shoulder. Everything about him was tensed. He was waiting for me to show some sign that I reviled him, I knew. I was not certain that I did not. I did not know how I felt.

"I never knew," he answered. "There might have been something in me, some quality he wished to claim, some quirk of my youthful spirit. Recall how heroic and idealistic I had been. Or perhaps I reminded him of someone, perhaps even himself."

He fell into a short silence. I wished to give him words of comfort, but where would I find them? This was a breathtaking horror, something so vile it could scarce be imagined. Except for someone like me, someone who had also had to reconcile with the presence of the vampire living inside herself.

I noticed how he stared at me and knew he was waiting for my response. I opened my mouth to tell him how sorry I was, but it seemed such an inadequate thing to say I closed it again without speaking.

"I am not undead, Emma," he said softly, a little anxiously. "But I will not deny that in some small part, I am as he. Marked, at the very least. See, he did not charm my wounds closed; I am branded, to remind me, to show all that I am his." His voice lowered. "All of my natural life until death finds me, he will be my lord. I will only be released when he is dead, or I am."

This was a horrible thought, that Marius could claim any kinship with his victim. With Valerian. Still, it was true. But I was not disgusted by it even though my Dhampir nature abhorred the vampire in all its forms. The fact remained, I held nothing but compassion for Valerian. I had no impulse in me to hate him.

He was awaiting my reaction, I knew. Waiting to see if I were going to revile him now that he had revealed his secret.

I pressed my fingers to the wounds at his neck. They were dry and neat, though they looked angry as if the pointed teeth had pierced his flesh only hours ago. "That is why you are so driven to destroy him. You wish to set yourself free."

Valerian caught my hand in his, his eyes shining. He was so desperately sad, my heart wrenched. "Do you now see why, when I saw the blood on the hawthorn twig, I thought I might take it, learn how to use it? So that when I met him again I could save myself."

I wanted to assure him that I forgave him, but the words dammed up in my throat. I did not hate him for what he was, nor did I loathe what he had done; no harm had come from it, after all. But he had deceived me and I realized I could not fully forgive—at least not yet. "You have been waiting many years for this," I said evenly, "and I suppose when temptation presented itself, your judgment was not as clear as you would have had it be."

"And they have been long years, Emma. Longer than you know, so much longer than you can guess."

The tension tightened around us. The little flame threw ghastly shadows across his face. I felt myself bracing, although I thought at the time this was silly. What more could he tell me? What could be worse?

He, too, girded himself. Then he spoke. "That far-away night in Montmartre, where I slipped away from my father's rooms to sample the temptations of Paris, that was in the year sixteen fifty-five. It was over two hundred and twenty years ago. I was sixteen years old."

He waited for me, for my mind to comprehend this impossible passage of time. I stared dumbly. I wanted to deny him, to scream at him to stop saying these mad things. But I said nothing, did nothing, I merely sat, buffeted by his terrible revelations, helpless and angry.

"I am not immortal. I have aged, but with unnatural slowness. You see how I am changed. Tainted by the bite." He said the word with a wrenching force. "But I am still a man."

I was only grateful that I did not faint. He was *not* a man—the disgraceful thought sprung to my mind. No, not completely a man, but not evil, either.

"Emma." He spoke my name suddenly, throwing it into the near darkness between us like a spear. My silence was unnerving him. Then he gathered his dignity around himself. His shadowed face shifted with the fleeting passage of each struggle as he mastered his emotions. "Can you guess what it is I will ask of you?"

The dread I felt was like a swaddling blanket, constricting and stifling. Oh, God. Indeed, I could guess.

"I will stand with you against Marius." His tone was flat, inanimate. "But in putting myself before him, I undertake great risk. Unimaginable risk. My protections might not serve if

Marius's potency is increased by the feast of evil, and by the power of the lay line. Should I receive the second bite, Emma, I will have no time. That will be my last chance at death."

"Valerian," I said, a warning, a plea for him to stop.

"Should I be bitten again, you must promise—"

"No!" I shouted loudly. In the small confines of the carriage, the sound hurt my ears.

"You know what I ask is not evil. You would be doing good. If I die now, I would still be entitled to death, and even after the second bite, I will be mortal. But I cannot live on with two, with the possibility that Marius could complete my transformation."

"You think I could do it?" I shrieked. "You think I could kill you?"

"I think you could save me," he said gently. "If you have any care in your heart for me, you would."

I raised my hands, wanting to strike him. I intended to, but he caught both of my wrists, his lightning-quick reflexes like the strike of a snake.

"You dare!" I sobbed. "You dare!"

"I will do it myself if I am able!" he shouted. I twisted in his grasp, but he mastered me like a strapping lad would subdue the struggles of a lamb. "But I do not know what further changes may come. I may lose my will. If I can do it myself, I vow to you that I will. But should I not have the means within me, you must tell me you will not fail me."

His hands were like manacles. "You used me," I wailed. I fell against him, my face pressed against his throat, my lips close to where Marius had sunk his razor-sharp teeth into his flesh. "All the time, you lulled me into friendship—for this reason! How could you? How could you?"

"No," he murmured. His mouth was at my ear; the sound

of his voice, the feel of his breath along the curve of my neck. "No. No." Then his hands released me and caught in my hair, one broad palm cupping the back of my head. Blindly I turned, sought, and found his mouth, and took it against my own. My hands were suddenly free. I grasped him, fingers curling to grip the hard-muscled shoulders pinning me back into the carriage squab.

It was dark now, the two of us only shadows cramped inside the carriage. We could not see each other clearly when we broke apart. "I am so sorry, Emma," he said hoarsely. "If you cannot do this, I will find another way."

I started, thinking of what he meant. Someone else *would* be bound to murderous duty. Father Luke? Whom else would he trust?

"No," I said, gulping back my grief. "No. It should be me. I am Dhampir, am I not? I was born to serve against the vampire, and for the sake of the caring and friendship between us, it should be me."

His face spasmed with emotion. "Emma." He touched my face.

I would not allow him to speak further. "I will be the one," I said.

To kill you. I did not say the words. I could not. If it came to it, I would do as he asked. I'd keep him from Marius, just as I vowed, but I would not speak it, not in the dark like this.

"And I must be shriven. You must secure a priest to perform Extreme Unction. Even if I succeed in keeping enough of my will to see to the task myself, you must dispose of my remains in the manner—"

"Valerian," I said, cutting him off. I could bear it no longer. "You must trust me. Please, speak no more. No more."

He hesitated, but nodded, agreeing, and silently gathered me to him. I rested my head against his shoulder. He pressed light kisses into my hair and along my temple until the lulling motion of the carriage caused him to lean his head back. Within moments, I heard the soft, easy breathing that told me he'd fallen asleep.

Perhaps he had not slept in a very long while, for he fell instantly unconscious. It was a heavy sleep, not releasing him even when the wheel hit a rut and bounced us up off the squabs.

But I did not sleep. I thought. Hours passed, and I went through every moment of this horrid adventure in my mind, analyzing with a clarity I had never before possessed. I thought about it all, from beginning to end.

I began to plan.

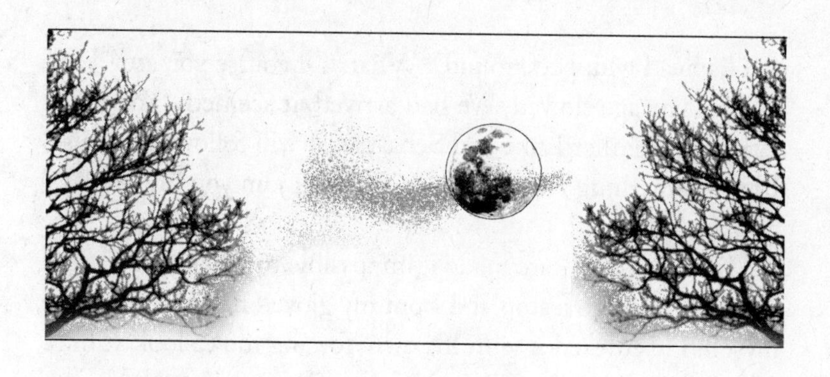

Chapter Twenty-eight

At Bassingstoke, I braced for the storm. I knew Valerian was not going to like what I had decided; I knew he would misinterpret it.

He roused when we'd reached town, the paved streets stirring up a clatter under our wheels to awaken him. "I slept," he said, surprised. He raked his hands through his hair roughly, as if to stimulate a sluggish brain under his scalp.

Pulling back the curtain, he squinted against the light. The day was dreary, a cold mist suffocating the shapes of the houses we passed. I could see people on the street. They did not look at me, busy as they were in their lives, their wonderfully ordinary lives.

"I am not going back to Avebury," I told him.

His head whipped around. "What? Of course you are."

The carriage slowed. We had arrived, it seemed. "You make ready with Father Luke and Sebastian. I will follow, I promise. I have something I wish to do first. I will join you in two days' time."

His speechless stare made it impossible to meet his eye. The carriage jerked to a stop and I put my gloved hand out to catch myself. He covered it with his own, forcing me to look at him. "Cannot explain? Or will not?"

I knew he would take my secrecy to mean that I no longer trusted him, that my view of him had altered. While he'd slept, I had debated how to tell him of my plan knowing that, coming so soon after his great confession, he would view it personally.

And he was correct. But not for the reason he believed.

I thought of the years he had lived. He looked no more than thirty-five. He was strong, his hair untouched by a single strand of gray. The lines on his face were few. The slowed aging had touched him only slightly, taking only a decade's toll for each hundred years. He had been changed by the vampire's bite, and perhaps not even he himself knew exactly how much.

I did not know what he was, living as he did between vampire and human. I would not forsake him because of it, for even knowing what I did, I could not mistrust him. He had given me the hawthorn switch with Marius's blood, he had come for me. I trusted him with my own life. But Henrietta's?

This next thing I would do on my own, in secret. Just to be sure.

"I will explain when I see you," I told him.

"Have it as you must," he said, the bitterness making his voice as brittle and sharp as shattered glass. The driver opened

the door and folded down the steps. Valerian fairly leapt out, then reached up to aid me.

When I was on the ground, I wished to assure him. "I will see you in Avebury. I will not be long delayed."

He narrowed his eyes at me, not releasing my hand for a moment of indecisiveness. Then he gave me a curt nod, his face still troubled, and turned his back on me, striding to the station house toward the platform for the northbound rails. His spine was straight, pulling his height up to its full, and his squared shoulders appeared particularly noble. I said nothing, only watched him go, until I turned to the train that would take me west.

My mission took a day longer than I'd planned, and I arrived in Avebury with my boon only three days before the Eve of Saint George. My entrance into town was stealthy. I booked myself into an inn, a different one from where Uncle Peter had lodged for I did not wish to risk anyone recognizing me. No mention of my appearance must make its way up to Dulwich Manor.

I dispatched a boy to alert Sebastian and Valerian of my arrival and unpacked the notebooks I'd taken with me from the chateau at Amiens. Whereas only a few days ago I'd been in a near panic at the shortness of the time to prepare for the night of Saint George's Eve, now I was calm.

I had made a plan. I had gathered what I needed, and I had trusted no one. The decision to rely only on myself brought a sense of peace, and a deeper determination that locked my insides into a tight knot of resolve. I was used to being alone; it was how I worked best.

* * *

The first to arrive at my rooms was Valerian, looking very correct and cool in a dark coat and trousers, his boots polished and his cravat snowy-white and tied to perfection with not a hint of what was underneath.

"Was your journey fruitful?" he asked, bowing to me as he entered the outer of the two rooms I had reserved for my use, a small sitting room with a table and two cushioned chairs.

The sour atmosphere of our parting lingered between us, heavy with mistrust and suspicion. On my journey, I'd thought of the hurt I'd caused him and had wrestled with regret. However, I was satisfied with my decisions.

Sebastian was close on Valerian's heels, exploding into the room with a declaration of joy. "Thank the stars you are returned! I swear, Emma, you are a sight for sore eyes, sore indeed for lack of sleep. Honestly, when this business is finished I will lay myself down for a monthlong nap."

He snatched me to himself a bit desperately. "Poor Sebastian," I declared, "you have stood up well."

"No I have not! I am wretched. Just look at the circles under my eyes. You do not know what it was like without you, Emma." Then his eyes grew serious. It was not always easy for Sebastian to be sincere. His larking was a mask, a way for him to make a mockery of the world that condemned him, but it was not the same as making merry. Sometimes, when he was at his most biting, I knew he was not merry at all.

He was solemn now, however. "Really, Emma. It is good to have you back."

"We have much to discuss," I said.

We had a tray with coffee and biscuits sent up from the kitchens. Then, I opened my notebooks.

"We must not allow Marius to have Henrietta at any time,

and so that dictates that our confrontation will take place at the house. He will come to her room, and when he does, we will lie in wait and trap him there, after securing Henrietta's safety."

I saw the men exchange a glance at my boldly taking a lead, but neither protested. I went on. "I believe I have improved methods to prevent him from escaping. I will teach you what you need to know, and advise you on what positions we should take in Henrietta's room in order to ensnare Marius when he comes for her."

"Why do we simply not spirit her away?" Sebastian asked anxiously.

"Even if this were possible, given that her parents are not likely to cooperate, Marius will find her," Valerian replied. "He has the power to move like a bat in the night, flying swiftly over leagues without tiring. No amount of distance will ensure her safety."

Sebastian swallowed, his Adam's apple bobbing fitfully. "My God."

"It is best she stay where she is," I concluded with forced calmness. "And in this way, we can control the situation as much as possible."

"It is ironic," Sebastian observed, "that this is what Father Luke has wanted. It always seemed to me his tack was to avoid interference in Marius's plans but learn as much about the situation as possible so as to be best prepared on the appointed night. So, do we inform him of our efforts?"

Fox's eyes flashed. "He has made his choice not to help us. I say no."

"The priest is not working against us on a point of principle," I mused. "We are not in danger of his sabotaging us—I could never believe that of him."

"But our goals are not the same," Valerian reminded me. "We said we would not trust him."

"Agreed. But another man, one knowledgeable in this supernatural fight, is an advantage. We could use him."

Valerian looked cross, but said, "The Chinese general Sun Tsu wrote that it is wise to keep friends close, and enemies closer." He shrugged, acceding the point to me.

We talked about what each of our duties should be. We chose the means we would use to entrap Marius when he entered the manor, and what to do—and who would do it—once he was ensnared.

Valerian insisted on the staking. "I am the strongest. And it will be violent."

I said nothing because I did not agree with this, but would not argue the point. I would simply do what I must when the time came. "You will take care of whoever is Miss Harris's replacement in the nursery before then," I told Sebastian, changing the topic.

"Just how do you imagine I shall do that?" he balked. "The silly creature, a young thing they brought up from the kitchens, is with her all the time."

I did not flinch. "I know violence is not in your nature, but she must be kept from interfering with us through any means necessary."

They were heavy words, and they sat like rocks on our shoulders. We then set about to examine the plan, break it down, and think of every possible avenue through which it could fail, and make adjustments where we were vulnerable. By the time we concluded, I was exhausted. Sebastian, too, looked wilted, although Valerian sat ramrod-straight, as intense as ever.

"We will meet tomorrow," I said, patting Sebastian's shoulder.

"Lord, save me from my addled senses!" Sebastian suddenly declared, and reached into his coat to pull out a packet. "I nearly forgot. This came to the house for you."

"It is a letter from Uncle Peter!" I exclaimed, seeing the handwriting. I moved to the window, wanting some privacy with which to read.

It was not a very long letter. This disappointed me. His usual correspondences were lengthy treatises on his travels, or a thoughtful discussion of an important book he'd read, a stimulating conversation he'd had with some country or other's luminary. This contained only a few paragraphs, which I read quickly.

No doubt the papers are reporting the Treaty of Paris is holding, and the Sultan and the Tsar have kept the peace, but my diplomatic talents are being challenged at their utmost to keep it thus. The damnable French republicans are no longer interested in the Black Sea Clauses now that Napoleon III is out, and Bismark has ignored the Russians, who are assembling a fleet in defiance of the terms of their surrender. I wish you to know how imperative it is that I remain here, for nothing less than a disaster such as this would keep me from your side.

I have, since gaining intelligence from you to confirm my darkest fears concerning your mother, been unable to dismiss her from my mind. I have several thoughts on the subject that may help resolve the troubling question of Laura's fate. I am quite sick with worry over you, darling. Please, take the greatest care and send for me if you need me. Short of impending war here in the Baltic, I will come. I am yours forever and most fondly, Peter Ivanescu.

I folded the letter. "Thank you, Sebastian. Why do you not go back to the house and rest? We will all need to be sharp these next few days."

Sebastian draped his cape over his shoulder with a flourish and kissed me before slipping out.

Valerian headed to the door as well. I had thought he would take dinner with me, and I was disappointed to see he was leaving. But I had put this distance between us, not him. And if he was not exactly angry with me, he was stung. The same distant, aloof air he had once worn to keep me at bay was firmly back in place.

He paused at the threshold, giving me a strange look over a wide, square shoulder. "You did well, Emma. Quite the general today. You . . . seem different."

"Valerian, we must talk. Will you not stay?"

"I think it best if we concentrate on the night of Saint George's Eve. Everything depends on our preparedness, and it is a good idea to keep our minds sharp. Uncluttered."

He paused, then spoke carefully. "But there is one thing I would ask you, and then we can forget all else and concentrate on the task ahead. I knew when I spoke of my past that you would see me differently. It is unavoidable." His jaw tightened. "But I must know if you still intend to keep your vow to do what I asked of you."

I jerked my chin up to meet his gaze straight on. "Indeed," I replied. "I shall honor our bond."

"Tomorrow, I shall bring Father Luke," he said, and left me.

I stared after him, feeling unsettled. I wished there was some way I could explain my actions to him. I knew he mistook my reasons for not confiding where I had gone and why. If there had been time, I would have tried to make him understand. As it was, we would leave much unsaid.

The next morning the rains came, pouring out of the sky like a great bucket drenching the land with biblical vengeance.

"Will spring ever arrive?" Sebastian declared as he pulled off a sodden cape and shook it out at the threshold to my sitting room. "I have never seen a more miserable season."

"I believe that Marius has in mind to put the area under wraps and bog us down in mud," I said, taking his cape and draping it by the fire while he fussed over the soaked cuffs of his trousers. "Did you bring it?"

He nodded, pulling out a package from inside his coat and handing it to me on his way to the mirror. Upon seeing his reflection, he uttered a tormented exclamation, his hands flying frantically to arrange his damp locks.

I'd asked him to meet me here after giving him special instructions. He had agreed to fetch the things I requested, without teasing me. That was when I knew how terrified he was. And despite his complaints about the rain, there was a hardness in his eyes that his foolery could not divert.

"How is Henrietta today? Have you seen her?"

"She is with her maid. Roger, however, is taking up with her. He is fascinated by her knowing chess, and they play in the afternoons."

"Then she is well?"

"She seems well," he said, but something in his tone did not convince me.

"Sebastian," I said with careful consideration, "what are you not telling me?"

He turned his back on the mirror, his gaze touching mine before sliding away. "She is not herself. She smiles, she croons to her doll—not Victoria, mind. I have not seen that doll of late. When Miss Harris disappeared, she hardly reacted at all. You do not know what it does to me to see the child as she is. She has lost her brightness, Emma. Even Roger and Mary have noticed."

I went to him and placed my hand on his arm. "She will be restored soon. It is why I have come back, why we are risking everything. We shall see to it, Sebastian."

He grasped my fingers fiercely, showing his emotions in a rare display. "Yes," he said with heat. "Yes, we shall."

"I have some things I need for you to secret in the nursery. I will not be able to bring them with me, they are too unwieldy."

I placed five long stakes in his arms. They still had the bark on them; only the tips showed the white of newly exposed wood where they'd been hewn to a vicious point. "Put these in her room if you are able. Make certain you tell me where they are. And do not lose them. I have gone far to get them."

"You wish me to keep them secret from Mr. Fox?"

I ignored his penetrating look. "It does not matter once we are in the room, but up until tomorrow night, yes, keep this and the other tasks to yourself."

He nodded. I turned from him and unwrapped the package he'd brought. It was a pouch, the sort of large reticule that no one of fashion would ever be caught dead with but the kind of utilitarian carry bag we used to tote around sketchbooks and charcoal sticks or latest sewing project. "Yes. This is perfect. Where did you find it?"

"That is Mary's. I suppose she's quite forgotten she had it, and so much the better for her. What an atrocity."

"She used to be quite practical. I hope you weren't spied going through her closet."

"Well," he replied drolly, with a wave of his hand, "I was never worried. I am quite good at sneaking about, you know, and quite proud of it. It felt so deliciously naughty, and I do so love that feeling."

I laughed. It felt good to laugh, and I appreciated his mischief. At least, I hoped it was mischief.

He watched as I carefully placed a large vial with rust-colored liquid in the bag. My crucifix, pilfered from Saint Michael in the Fields, followed. Then I drew out an oilcloth containing the hawthorn twig with Marius's blood.

"What is that?" Sebastian asked.

"You best not know."

"A secret weapon, eh? I suppose I should not mention this to anyone either."

I smiled at him, appreciating his easy confidence in me. "I would be most obliged."

He took his leave and I sat with my thoughts for a while before luncheon. Afterward, I had time before Sebastian and Valerian were to assemble again in my rooms. The innkeeper let me use a steady old mare, and I rode out to The Sanctuary. I looked at the tree. I felt no fear, no excitement. I was steady. Then I rode to Dulwich Manor, staying behind the tree line of the park. I wondered what Alyssa was doing, whether she and Mary had sewn anything for the baby. To my surprise, I missed my sister. I wondered what Roger thought of me, if he'd tempered his disgust as time passed.

All I'd ever wanted when I was a child was to be ordinary,

not the daughter of a madwoman. I'd wanted to be accepted, to have a family who loved me. I nearly achieved it, fleetingly. But they were all in there, content, unaware of what would come tonight. And I, once again, remained outside.

How strange that I didn't feel saddened by the thought. There were far more important things on earth than chatting cozily by a fire. I suddenly knew I'd rather be here, preparing to face a nightmare, than in there with them placing tiny stitches in soft cotton and helping Alyssa dream up names. Mine might be a lonely existence, but my blood thrummed and my eyesight was keen and each and every sense alerted me to a scent in the air, the step of a hare in the underbrush, the slight temperature change in the breeze as it flew across the back of my neck. I felt incredibly alive, every nerve dancing in anticipation, and yet calm, too.

I had done everything I could to prepare. Let Marius come.

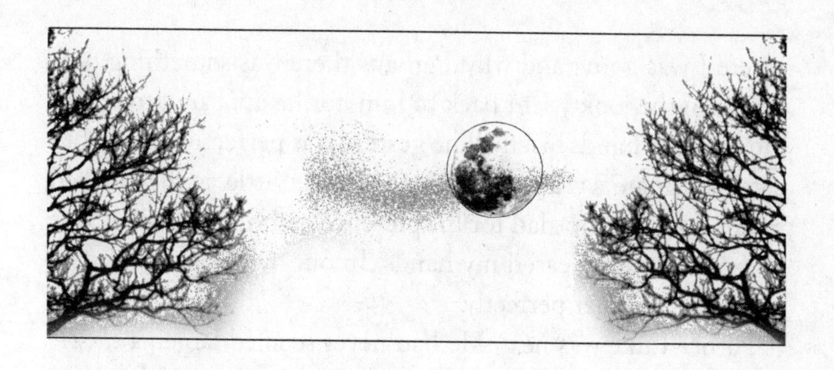

Chapter Twenty-nine

It was the Eve of Saint George and once the sun grew heavy and sank to the horizon, we began our incursion into Dulwich Manor. Sebastian made certain all the necessary doors were left open, and it was nothing to slip inside. Valerian, Father Luke, and I were to go in separately and at different times, moving through the evening shadows of the old house, using the back stairs to the third-floor nursery rooms where Sebastian waited to show us to an empty room situated under the attics.

I was second to arrive. Valerian was already in place, with his shadowed features set in a fierce countenance. He seemed cold at first, making me nervous. I had anticipated he was likely to be still angry at my having left him without an explanation of where I was going and why. Perhaps there was something desperate in the look I sent back to him, for he appeared to relent. He took my hands briefly. The gesture was perfectly proper, but it felt intimate as his eyes softened only a little as they locked mine. I was deeply glad for his presence—and for his silence as he nodded and released my hands. In our own way, we understood one another perfectly.

Father Luke was next. He had never seemed larger, a classical god dressed in black cleric's costume. His massive chest and shoulders strained the cloth of his plain jacket, and his face was pale above the Roman collar. His hair was a bit wild from the elements, and it made him seem less civilized, more the warrior.

"Nasty weather," he murmured as he entered. He said nothing more, but took the loop of beads that hung at his waist and retired to the corner to pray.

In a short while, Sebastian arrived to transfer us to the nursery. "I will bring you, one at a time, into the schoolroom, which is empty. When we've made it in there without being detected, I will stand guard and you may go on into Henrietta's room." He directed Valerian to follow him first. Father Luke remained in prayer. When Sebastian returned, he tapped the priest on his shoulder. "Come," he urged, leaving me alone in the room.

I gripped Mary's pouch which Sebastian had stolen for me, steeling myself against the sudden surge of nerves. Now that the hour was upon me, I found I was afraid. Terribly, terribly afraid. I tried to comfort myself with silent platitudes, but my soul would not quit its quaking at the thought of facing Marius again. I cringed at the recollection of how the foul touch of his mind had left me feeling polluted. Defiled. Nausea rose like a wave, and a terrible thought came to me. Could he have that power over me again?

Panic gripped me as racing thoughts darted in and out of my mind. I was Dhampir, and, after all, the word itself meant "little vampire." I was touched by the same force that had made me. My gifts were sourced from the same place as his. It was in the blood, our blood.

There is something of the vampire in you.

He had tricked me before, caught me completely unawares. He was far too clever for me to know exactly what he was capable of, and what he might do.

My hand closed over the pouch, and I thought of his blood, dried and rusty on the tip of the slender switch of holy hawthorn. He'd left his blood behind. I knew he could never have meant to do so. He'd made a great error then.

Maybe he was not so invincible.

And as I thought of it, I began to think about what Valerian had told me of the magic of vampire blood. Acting quickly on an impulse, I unwrapped it from its oilcloth, a startling idea having seized hold of my cognitions. If a vampire could increase its invincibility by consuming the blood of another being, would not I as a Dhampir have the same power? Could this inoculate me against the intrusion of his will? Could it give me some advantage, some power, to drink of his blood?

I heard Sebastian's step in the hall, and in that moment, I acted. I closed my eyes, opened my mouth, and touched the bloodied tip to my tongue. Immediately, my eyes flew open. I snatched away the stick, violently repulsed by what I'd done. Had I just made a dreadful mistake? Had I only polluted myself, ruined myself?

Sebastian opened the door. I folded the oilcloth over the switch and dropped it in my bag. "We are ready for you," he said.

The oil lamp threw a wild shadow up the wall as he turned, illuminating the lintel over the entrance to the nurseries. I'd noticed the Latin inscription there before, but seeing it again was like a blow.

Aut vincere aut mori. Either to conquer or to die.

It was nearly ten o'clock. We had no idea when Marius might arrive, but it stood to reason that he would wait until deeper into the night. His past sojourns to Henrietta had been in the dead hours when darkness and the sleep of the house's inhabitants aided his stealthy incursions.

We had no light with us, but I could see well enough as we moved quietly into the little room. I was getting good at sneaking about in the dark, I reflected. Father Luke stood by the window, Valerian by the door leading to Miss Harris's old room. I took my post by the schoolroom door.

On the little bed, Henrietta's covers were tousled, as if she slept fitfully. Then my breath caught, and I peered closer. A cold wash of fear rushed through me as I saw Henrietta's bed was empty.

"She's not here!" The sound of my voice in the stillness had the effect of an explosion. For a moment, we all froze, and then Valerian struck a match. Candle glow swelled to an orb of light as he bent to the bed, confirming that Henrietta was not within. The sharp sting of his curse hit the air. "He's taken her. We are too late."

Father Luke fell into step with me as Valerian led us from the room. "Where are you going?" the priest demanded.

"Can you not guess?" Valerian threw behind him, not slowing for an instant.

The priest understood. At once, he spun on his heel and fled through the nursery and into the hall, no longer concerned with stealth or taking care not to be heard. The sound of their footsteps on the wooden stairs thundered, rolling through the house to the far corners. Mary and Roger, Alyssa, Alan—they all would hear the disturbance. But quiet and anonymity were luxuries we could no longer afford.

I was about to set flight after, but I remembered the stakes I'd had Sebastian hide in the room for me. Turning back, I scrabbled under the bed to draw out the five crudely crafted implements of destruction. I had to move fast to catch up with the others and could only manage one stake in each hand. I hated to do it, but I had to leave the other three behind.

In the stables, Father Luke was already astride while Sebastian and Fox were fetching mounts for themselves. Father Luke held the reins masterfully, his mount a large, powerful creature. It skirted sideways under his direction and he held his hand down to me. "There is no time to saddle two horses. Come with me. Mr. Fox will follow."

I lost no time. Transferring the stake in my left hand to my right, I gave him my freed hand. He grasped it and hauled me up as easily as a sack of grain.

I was barely seated when he kicked his horse forward. I clasped him tightly, swallowing my innate terror of horses. We rode hard, the sound of heavy hooves thundering in my ears as we raced madly toward The Sanctuary.

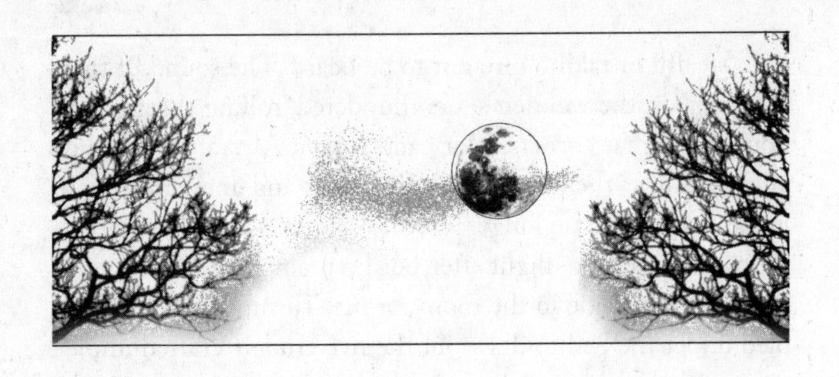

Chapter Thirty

The plain where the head of the Great Stone Serpent had once lain was bathed in a soft moon glow that filtered down through the misty air. It somehow suffused the light, magnified it, so that the eerie effect was sulfurous and thick. Father Luke dismounted, pulling me down as soon as his feet hit solid ground, and we turned together to face the emptiness.

I glanced about anxiously as we walked toward the tree. Henrietta was not in sight. "We must put protections in place," I said as I laid the stakes down and began to rummage in my satchel bag.

Father Luke peered down at me from his great height. "I have already done so. I knew if we failed at the house, Marius

had to come here, for this is where the ritual must take place." His darting eyes scanned the area. The mists were thick, and gathering closer around us. He added in a grim monotone, "The blood is the life."

The impact of that landed like a punch squarely in my stomach. Henrietta's blood, to raise the evil imprisoned in the tree once again to life. I felt the flutter of panic once again, and my confidence wavered.

I straightened and faced him warily. "You never expected Henrietta to be in her bed, did you?"

He looked at me blankly. "Really, Mrs. Andrews. Marius has not survived millennia to reach the power he has by making such predictable moves."

I was becoming angry. "Then why did you not tell us this?"

He remained calm against my snapping accusation. "Did you and Mr. Fox tell me everything? Besides, how could I be sure what the beast would do? You are Dhampir, and at Hess's house, the vampire touched your mind. I expected you would know what he would do." His eyes narrowed. "I see I was in error. Thank God I took precautions."

"You are a knight of the Order of Knights of Saint Michael of the Wing. I was warned I should not trust you."

"Yes," he snapped, and at last I saw a glimpse of his rage unleashed. "I am, and well trained to understand that I must work alone and yet I have betrayed my vows. I knew all along what my mission would be, and exactly what I am meant to do, but I allowed my compassion to alter the course. I was moved by your love for the child. My pity for you, for that little girl, nearly cost us all because it swayed me off the course I made a sacred vow to follow."

My blood grew chill at his hardened expression. "What are

you going to do?" I asked, my voice barely a whisper. I was suddenly fearful that Valerian had been right all along, that we possibly had an enemy in our midst.

The priest seemed to pull his self-control around him. "I will have one and only one unique opportunity to kill the creature when it is first revived. Like a newborn, it will be weak and vulnerable, but only for a short while. That is when Marius himself plans to act, to overcome the fledgling demon and devour it. This is when we strike."

I was nearly breathless with horror. "No. If we allow Marius to advance that far, it will already have been too late. It is Henrietta's blood—the blood of the most innocent—that he must use to resurrect that thing you guard. If you wait until then . . . My God, you cannot mean to allow him to kill her."

His jaw worked. I could see regret warring with determination in his cold, hard gaze. "It is only then that I will be able to destroy the evil that will be unleashed."

I stepped away sharply, reeling from this. "What kind of priest are you?" I accused. But I knew the answer to that, had known the moment I spied his hulking form in the cemetery. Father Luke was a trained warrior, ready to make any sacrifices he deemed necessary.

I held out a finger to him, my voice ringing with resolve. "I am going to save her. Do you hear me, priest?"

I heard Valerian approaching. I spun away from Father Luke and ran to meet them.

Valerian swung off his horse before it was at a full stop. "Any sign of him?" he called as he rushed to join us.

"Nothing yet," I told him. "Where is Sebastian? Is he coming?"

"He is right behind me. He should be here momentarily."

Suddenly, Father Luke shouted behind me. "It is gone! The

crucifix I placed here!" He stalked the empty plain, circling the wicked thorns of the tree, then hunkered down, taking off his leather gloves to touch the ground. "The holy water's been washed away. Someone has undone the seal I laid earlier."

Valerian glanced around. "It could not be Marius. He could not touch any of it."

Father Luke stood, his grim face frozen. "Good God, I did not foresee this."

I dug into my bag and drew out a glass flask. "I have water drawn from the Chalice Well from Glastonbury Tor. And, look, I have brought stakes cut from the Holy Hawthorn of Joseph of Aramithea. I only have the two I could carry from the house."

After a moment of stunned silence, Father Luke was the first to speak. His tone was quiet, full of awe. "Of course. Mrs. Andrews, that was quite brilliant." He held out his hand. "Now, we must not waste time. I am a priest. I made my confession earlier and am in a state of grace. Despite your opinion of me, it should be me to use this holy water to anoint the area. If you will allow it."

Those seconds in which I had to examine my heart to know the right thing to do seemed to take an eternity. Of course I did not trust Father Luke. I very nearly despised him at this moment for his willingness to risk my precious Henrietta. But the instinct in me I was learning to trust bode me to hand the vial into his outstretched palm. My hand shook as I did it. Some of it was rage. Most of it was pure terror that I was making a grave and disastrous mistake.

Valerian and I watched in silence as Father Luke bowed his head and knelt. After a moment of prayer, he began to minister the ablutions that would purify the ground around the tree.

"You could have told me about Glastonbury," Valerian said,

casting me a sideways glance. His voice softened. "Emma, I wish—"

A shriek brought us both up short as a woman flew out of the mists, and in the instant before she flung herself at Father Luke, I recognized Miss Harris. She was screaming the vilest filth. We watched, stunned, as she grabbed the priest, who had been caught unawares. He stumbled, and, to my horror, the vial of holy water fell to the ground.

Valerian dashed to aid Father Luke. I went for the vial, but I was not quick enough. It lay on its side, a rusty puddle under its mouth. I snatched it up, examining it anxiously. The light was not good, but I saw much of it had been wasted.

Whirling, I faced the desperate wraith that had once been a devoted nursemaid, ready to vent my rage. The sight of her turned my blood to ice. Her face was raked with wounds, blood matted in her hair. She bared her teeth, threatening to bite. She was still human, but she was wild. Mad.

"Emma!" Valerian shouted. "She is *strigoi mort*. She must be destroyed. My bag. Give me my bag."

I froze. My God, had my mother been like this? Was this the madness my father had waited to see manifest in me?

"Help me," Valerian shouted as he wrestled her to the ground. "Emma!"

I did not want to approach that thing that had been Miss Harris. I was thinking too much of my own legacy. I could not move. Father Luke was the one who gave Valerian the implements he needed and I watched numbly as he drove his stake into the nursemaid's body, then drew an ax to do what was needed to separate her head from her body. I stood close enough to be spattered by her blood, to feel its heat as it was flung against my flesh.

Father Luke drew me away. In his eyes I saw something that echoed my own fears. I was ashamed of my inability to help Valerian. I had frozen. What had happened?

A soft voice drifted on the mists. "Miss Harris? Where are you? I'm frightened."

"Henrietta!" I cried. I snapped out of my paralysis and spun in a circle, listening. I could not tell from where the voice had come. "Henrietta?" I called again, looking first in one direction, then another.

But she did not answer me. Of course, she would not. She was afraid of me. My mind worked quickly. "Here, darling, here is Miss Harris." I shut my mind against the gruesome corpse that had been the maid she'd so trusted. "She wishes you to come to her."

I saw a shape, a hint in the obscuring fog, just at the edge of the tree line, and was about to go toward it when Valerian shouted, his voice ringing with command, "Emma! Luke!"

I swung around, and found myself confronted by a great wind. Hot air, blazing with an acrid scent that stung the nostrils, blasted into our faces and there before us was Marius in his most magnificent incarnation, a lordly figure, caped and massive and gleaming a great, victorious smile.

My eyes blinked to try and decipher what I saw, for his feet were not on the ground. It was as if he were descending from a great height. Then I saw that he had flown, and was landing smoothly, as graceful as a heron gliding onto the surface of a glassy pond. In his arms he held the limp body of a child.

The dark-headed little girl was remotely familiar. Then I knew it was Margaret Linden, the girl from the village, Mrs. Bedford's friend's child. Another soul, another innocent, caught in this evil. I admonished myself for not realizing Marius might have had other children he had singled out as surety against our work to thwart him.

Things began to happen very quickly. Marius did not speak, nor so much as looked at us, and I, having learned my lesson, did not look at him. He slid with the child to the tree, and I rushed forward, stopped by the sight of something there. A darkness thicker than the night around us began to unfold. A stench began to fill the air, driving the three of us—Valerian, Father Luke, and myself—back with the shock of it.

Marius closed in, his face alight with sickening glee. "Come, general. Our father has sent me. Rise now at long last . . ."

The chant floated in the air, its wheedling, desperate tone raising the hackles along the back of my neck. Marius knelt before the disgusting fog. It seethed impatiently and Marius crooned to it, beckoning the creature to take strength and come forth.

Father Luke tripped to his feet and lunged forward. He had not taken three steps when Marius made a swift movement with his hand, and the priest flew backward, as if a string behind him had been yanked.

Valerian seemed to retreat, then stalked a wide circle around to the tree. He was hoping to sneak up behind the fiend, I realized. His lips were peeled back, a look of naked hatred on his face, so fierce and raw that even I recoiled.

For myself, I was distracted with worry for this new child Marius had brought with him. Would she also be used for the sacrifice, or was it the vampire's plan to feed from her, to give himself strength for what he was about to do? Either way, it was imperative I find a way to get her safely out of his clutches.

Fishing the crucifix out of my bag, I stepped forward and held it out in front of me. Careful not to meet the vampire's eye, I advanced, one step at a time. My legs shook and my voice quavered, but I did not stop.

"By the power of Christ," I said. I saw the flash of bone-white teeth, wetly gleaming and razor-sharp, as the great vampire laughed at me. But he'd paused, and he was watching.

I knew where Father Luke had made the seal with the holy water behind the back of the tree. I positioned myself across from where he had poured the blessed water onto the ground. Armed with my crucifix, I intended to try to back Marius into the trap.

My mind was braced, not only for what Marius would do as I neared, but for the repulsive brush of his mind into mine, the sapping of my will, the loss of my soul, the horror of the vampire's touch so deep and thrilling it would take me to hell without a murmur of complaint. I did my best to ignore this fear, focusing instead on the gleam of the child's dark hair. I fixed my eyes on the pale throat exposed by her lolling head, and I pressed on, sending silent prayers to Heaven to help me. *I must save her,* I prayed fervently. *Help me, help me.*

With the crucifix before me, one step after another, I advanced. But there was nothing I, nor any of us, could do to stop Marius when he bent his head to the child in his arms and whispered something to her. With the index finger of his free hand, he hooked his nail into her flesh and tore open her throat. The life's blood gushed from her like bubbling liquid from a spring.

I screamed, and heard the male cries echo around me. I recognized Sebastian's voice, and dully registered that he'd finally arrived. He, I, Father Luke, and Valerian—all of us watched with horror as the child's blood poured onto the ground and the filthy shape that cowered among the roots of the old tree began to swell.

Marius worked quickly, his finger trailing to the girl's chest. He opened it with no more than a stroke. I fell to my knees, watching helplessly as he drew out the still-beating heart and held it aloft.

A lash of the darkness that seethed in expectation whipped out like a strike of lightning to pluck it from his fingers, and it disappeared into the shadow. I watched sickly as the foul creature thickened, darkened, its stench poisoning the air until tears rolled down my eyes. Or perhaps I was crying.

Marius dropped the child's lifeless body to the ground. Her face rolled toward me, and I glimpsed her pallor, the shadowed eyes, the ashen lips. She'd been a beautiful little girl.

Over her dead form, Marius and I faced one another. Behind him arched the grasping branches of the hawthorn inside which waiting, hovering, thirsty, greedy, hungry for life was that terrible thing.

Marius moved quickly. Like a snake, he rose in one rapid, fluid movement to his full height and surged forward at the same time. His head snapped toward me and his mouth opened, jaws unlocking so that the gaping maw lined with a row of vicious teeth was impossibly wide. It clamped down on the crucifix in my hand, the hard bite clicking down like the closing of a cinch, and the wooden cross with its detailed statue of the suffering Christ snapped in two.

Horror and surprise slapped me. I screamed and leapt back, scrabbling artlessly from under the hawthorn. I had not thought this possible, knowing full well a crucifix was a reliable weapon against the undead, but somehow his fresh kill had made him stronger, nearly invincible.

Marius threw back his head and laughed, then reached his hand to his left. I saw Valerian go down. Marius had known

where he was and what he'd been planning all along. The monster then leveled his gaze toward Father Luke, who was climbing to his feet with visible difficulty, and pointed his finger almost playfully. The mighty priest trembled, clearly in terrible pain. Marius's smile gleamed brighter, the vicious points of his fangs glowing in the murky moonlight, and he jabbed his finger again. Father Luke collapsed back onto the ground.

I looked about anxiously for Sebastian. He must be hiding, or perhaps he'd lost his nerve and run away. I prayed that if that was the case, he'd bring back help.

I waited for Marius to turn to me, to do the same to me as he had done to the men. But he did not. Instead, he pursed his lips and blew. I heard an approaching clatter, something flying through the air, rattling against trees that stood far off in the distance. Sickness washed over me as I realized the stakes—the stakes I'd fashioned from the Holy Hawthorn at Glastonbury—were clattering as they were blown away. They were gone!

I had nearly forgotten Valerian, but he suddenly appeared at the periphery of my vision, stumbling toward Marius from behind. He and Father Luke were severely weakened; whatever Marius had done to them had taken a terrible toll, but they were not in retreat. They would never retreat. This fight was until the death.

Marius seemed unperturbed by our movements. Why should he be otherwise? I thought hopelessly. He had defeated us with powers none of us had suspected. He had been smarter, stronger than we'd thought possible.

Tears streamed down my cheeks as I lay panting on the ground. I did not know what more I could do. I was defenseless, frightened, paralyzed.

The horrible thing next to Marius raised itself, emitting

a noise now. It sounded like a plea, a greedy evil plea urging Marius to hurry.

The vampire lord raised his hand, the wicked tips curling and yellowed. He beckoned, his gaze fixed behind me. His ancient voice, the echo of which I still held in my head, sifted into the air. "Come now, my little one."

I snapped my head and saw Henrietta. Sebastian had his arms around her. He had been guarding her all this time. "Keep her away," I called to him. "For God's sake, take her away!"

He tried. Valiantly, Sebastian tried to pull at Henrietta to draw her away, but the vampire lord had only to whip his hand toward him and Sebastian went down. His screams of pain rent the air as his body twisted on the ground.

"Stop it," I cried helplessly.

Henrietta dashed forward, making straight for Marius. I saw her running, and leapt to intercept her but she skittered out of my grasp. And then from nowhere Valerian sprang forward, coming out of a half-crouch, and snagged the hem of her nightgown. She went sprawling onto the ground, and though she hit at him with her small fists, he held on to her.

Suddenly I heard Roger's voice sound authoritatively. "What the devil is happening here?"

And Mary's, more hysterical: "Henrietta!"

I was not wholly surprised they'd come. Our fast exit from the house had not been stealthy, and our trail would not have been difficult to follow. I suppose I'd been expecting them. I drew myself to my feet and faced them. "Stay where you are," I said. "Do not interfere."

Roger stood with a few house servants, still dressed in his nightclothes. Mary clutched at his arm. He glared at me. "Emma! What the devil are you doing?"

Valerian had Henrietta in his arms. She twisted furiously, rabid to be free. Marius was murmuring, calling to her. Mary screamed and ran toward her daughter.

"Do not come closer!" I shouted, and she stopped, uncertain. She looked back to her husband.

Henrietta began to scream and cry, holding out her arms. But she was not reaching for her mother. She wanted Marius.

"Damnation, I will not!" Roger was furious, his rage directed at me. "Emma, you have—"

"Not now!" I shouted, and my own voice held a new quality, something neither he nor I had ever heard in it before. "Stay where you are, and for God's sake, if you want Henrietta to live, you must trust me and do exactly as I say."

I was somehow not surprised when the ring of command in my voice brought them both up short. They stood gaping at me, but they did comply. I did not expend any time explaining. Turning back to Marius, I squared my shoulders and lifted my chin, banishing all my fears and doubts. The time had come for me to face my natural enemy.

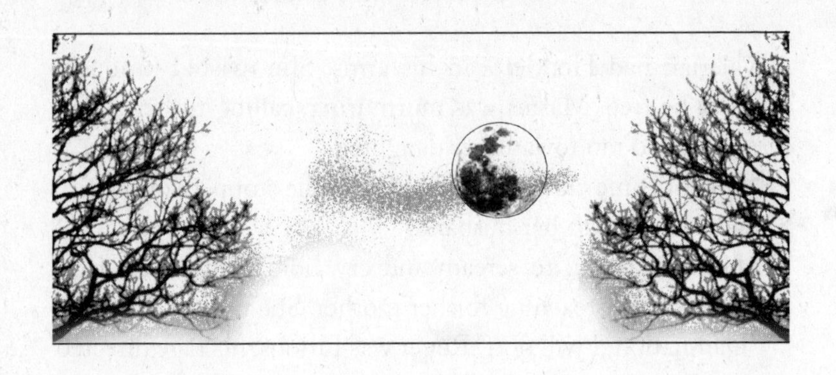

Chapter Thirty-one

"Let her come to me." Marius's voice swelled around us, seeming to rise up from the stones, the ground.

Everyone was still. The thickness of the air seemed to seal us inside a small capsule, trapped together to play out this drama. Only Mary's sobs, soft now, interrupted the blanket of silence.

Then Father Luke moved, but not against Marius. He grabbed Valerian and shook him. "Let him raise the thing! Let him eat it, and then we will take him. It is the only chance, man!"

"No!" Valerian stared at him in horror.

"She is dead anyway!" Father Luke roared. His great fists came down, and although Valerian's strength was not small, he rent the iron-fast grip Valerian had on the child, and set her free. Valerian fell to the ground in pain. Father Luke went down with him, his voice rising in an agonized crescendo. "She is his minion already, do you not see? It is too late, Fox! You cannot save her."

I cried out, horrified to realize this could very well be true. Henrietta wanted Marius, there was no denying that. But the vampire could not have tainted her blood, could he? He wanted her pure. The corruption of the best was what he needed.

But she was enchanted. I could see with my own eyes how she loved him.

When Valerian struck, it was so quick Father Luke did not have any time to react. He brought his foot up, then down to deliver a heavy, sharp jab to the priest's thigh, an exotic motion of measured agility and stunning strength. I heard the crack from where I stood. Father Luke's cry shook us all, even Valerian, who broke free and stood, uncertain and regretful, next to the fallen priest. I could see he was pale, sick with what he'd done, and guilty, too.

Mary's scream ripped through the air in a terrible wail: "Henrietta!"

The child was transfixed, moving woodenly toward the tree, toward Marius, whose face was alight with triumph. I could see the confusion on her features. She feared him, that was plain. What had he done to her? Was it some power, or merely very common intimidation that gave him such sway? She was clearly terrorized by him, and yet she remained obedient.

Marius reached out his arms to receive her and the foul cloud pulsed, knowing its fruition was near. Instinct moved me to stand directly in the path between Marius and Henrietta. Putting out my hand, open-palmed, I reached toward him. The connection he had once used to master me—which I feared more than my own death—now hummed to life. I braced myself against the revulsion, and I stretched.

Marius's head snapped up, and the mad gleam of victory in his eyes dimmed. His jaw convulsed, and I felt his foulness, felt him reaching to possess me again. Dark, raging fear reared up, almost driving me into retreat.

But I held strong. I would possess him. I alone had looked into the eyes of a master vampire and survived, traveled to the great archive at Amiens and delved deep into the wisdom of ages on this creature and others like him. I had my mother's blood in me.

My fear did not ebb. It merely became irrelevant. I thought, *I am Dhampir and I have tasted the blood of my enemy.*

As a vampire gained the strength of those upon whom it fed, so did I gain Marius's strength from the taste of his blood. I had feared my impulse to touch the hawthorn switch to my lips had been a trap, but I now knew it had given me power which I felt now. It pulsed as it rose inside of me, beckoning me to action. I followed the lead of impulse, reaching into his being as he had once reached into mine.

The vampire pushed against my invasion. His strength nearly overwhelmed me, but I slipped behind his fury and touched the writhing will. His name was not Marius. Nor Emil. It was something long, written in symbols on sandstone walls. His cipher stood in the desert, but his body did not lie in the tomb made for him. This knowledge, and more, shot like a shower of burning sparks in my consciousness. And I glimpsed those he'd touched, his minions. A beggar. A Knight Templar. An Arab woman with wide, almond-shaped eyes deep with wisdom and shining with wickedness.

He tried to repel me, whispering inside my head, "I know

you, Dhampir. I know your line, made from the blood of my enemy. But beyond that is the great Dracula. Yes, little vampire, the great prince is also in you, for he is the ancient that binds us all. We need not be enemies. Come with me. Can you feel the promise of eternal life? Time unending, death defeated. It is in you. We are the same; we can be the same. Grant me your blood, and we shall be eternal together."

The temptation of his offering summoned a yearning in me. I still wanted him, like an opium eater both craves and reviles the bliss of the poppy. I did not move, however. He could not reach Henrietta, not with me to block him. I held him; but equally did he hold me. For either one of us to surrender was unthinkable.

Then I felt something at my hand. Sebastian was beside me. "I could only find one," he said as my fingers closed around a slender column. The sharpened pole of the Holy Hawthorn of Joseph of Arimathea fit securely into the palm of my hand.

Exhilaration surged within me as I brought it to bear upon my enemy and saw him step back. He must have keenly felt the singular power of this weapon, wrought from the holiest of places, for he seemed surprised, even cowered for a moment before springing into counter attack.

He flung his hand out in an abrupt gesture and there came an explosion behind me, and a sudden surge of heat. I cut a glance quickly to the side to see that one of the oil lamps had burst, its contents spilling onto the chalky downs. The oil flashed, then caught fire. The flames leapt higher than the fuel warranted, no doubt fed by the evil magic Marius had used to effect the petty trick.

I startled at the sound but quickly realized that the flames were not a danger, merely a distraction. Yet my break in concentration was all Marius needed. Henrietta flew forward and was in his arms before I knew what was happening.

I heard Mary scream, a heart-wrenching sound I forced myself to ignore. Very quickly, the fiend used a talonlike fingernail to slice a clean line in Henrietta's neck just below the ear where the artery lay. Then he bent to allow her precious blood to fall onto the ground, to where the vague shape was unfolding itself into an oily mist beneath the tree. I watched in horror as it pulsed, surging greedily in response to the grisly feeding.

I burst into a run. I had only one stake, one means to kill, and two creatures I had to destroy. But there was no time for anything but desperate action. Henrietta was dying.

Valerian was there, too, suddenly—racing at full speed to hurl himself at his nemesis. The impact of his body jarred Henrietta out of Marius's arms, and I scrabbled toward her, snatching her to me and dragging her away.

Marius grasped Valerian around the neck, lifting him high up off the ground for a moment before flinging him aside, sending him hard to the ground out of his reach. The great vampire lord then turned, hunkering over the pulsing energy he had raised from the soul of the tree.

I heard Mary's piercing cry for her daughter behind me as I raced toward Marius, who was now kneeling in the midst of the shadow. The loathsome thing he had conjured pulsed around him like a mass of scrabbling rats. But it was beginning to assemble itself into shape. A human shape.

It was like watching a corpse reanimate itself. The thing was hideous. Its eyes were black, gleaming, its mouth gaping. There was but a hole where its nose and ears should be. Marius clasped him, his teeth flashing for a moment before he clamped

down on the writhing flesh and began to feed. The horror that lay in Marius's arms flailed, a keening cry of protest ripping across the air as they grappled together in the harsh ballet of predator and prey.

Father Luke's voice tore into the air, filled with rage and frustration. "Now, Emma! Fox! Kill them!"

My hand reached for the vial as I neared the tree, and I unstoppered it, flinging the precious little blessed water onto the two of them. As soon as it came in contact with Marius's skin, he bucked, screaming as if he'd been touched with fire. Releasing the other creature, he stumbled back, whirling upon me in rage. I did not look in his eyes. Instead, I fixed my gaze on his gaping mouth, dripping the putrid black essence of the creature he'd consumed.

The fire he'd made leapt, dancing deliriously as if infused by his rage. It produced roiling coils of smoke on the wet grass as it fought its way toward me. The crisp sound of it crackled in the air and the heat pressed in on my skin.

I steeled my courage and I blocked out the shouts behind me. My concentration deepened as I centered on my target. Marius and I—somehow, I had always known it would be thus. I bore down on him. Now he was *my* prey, and I was relentless. My hand was ready with the wooden stake, and murder was fixed solid and sure in my heart.

"No," Father Luke commanded. "Not Marius. The demon—kill it!"

I hesitated, turning to consider the ancient horror Marius had restored. Its eyes gleamed fiercely as it lay on the ground. It had been temporarily weakened by Mairus's attack, but it was reviving. Marius had not been able to finish feeding from it. It would not be weak for long. If it were left to survive, it would feed off legions of men, and live into eternity to torment humanity for all time.

I had but one stake in my hand.

I raised that blessed weapon over my head. I had no remorse, no hesitation, not even a little. I brought the stake down, impaling the demon vampire into the ground. The foul thing grasped at me, surprised. Perhaps it had never supposed a mere woman could be its destruction. Its talon-like fingers scraped viciously down my arms and the odor coming from him nearly drove me back, but I forced myself onward.

"Emma! No!"

I cannot say that Valerian's cry did not nearly break me. I had made a choice, and in doing so I was fully aware that I had crushed him. Betrayed him even. But I had done what my blood called me to do. Marius would have to be left to him.

Wrenching the stake sideways and out, I ripped open the demon vampire's dry, heaving chest. The wail of the dying creature rent the night. Behind me, I heard screaming, weeping, shouts. A roar tore through, and I knew that was Marius, knowing his prey was lost, sending his rage into the air around us.

Knowing what I was meant to do, I reached in and pulled out the heart of the demon. It was unspeakable. Putrid, oozing a malodorous substance like a festering wound, riddled with glossy white maggots that sprouted from the pulsing muscle onto my fist.

At my feet, the newborn body burst into a million pieces, each of which began to move, swarming around me, climbing up my skirts. They were beetles, I realized. Their hard shells clicked as they clamored over one another to reach me.

I do not know how I stayed calm. I held tight to the steam-

ing heart. There was silence on The Sanctuary now. I did not know what the others were doing. I heard only the insects, only the hissing of the corrupted flesh in my hand as it writhed with the pulsing force of the life Marius had stolen from Henrietta's blood.

I went to the fire Marius had made, and knelt. My emotions rose as a sense of exhilaration filled me. Then I stuck my hand into the flames. The heart shrieked and convulsed. My fingers burned but I held on, my knees bending with the agony of fire roasting my flesh, until the detestable heart withered and died in my hands.

Around me, I heard a hundred, a thousand snaps as the beetles burst, flared, and disappeared into dust, singeing my skirts, my hair, my skin. I smelled the sickening odor of the charred flesh and realized it was my own. Smoke surrounded me. The beetles had been in my hair, on my clothes when they'd ignited, and I did not even realize small flames were still dancing on my person until Valerian threw me down and covered me.

He ran his hands over me, snuffing out the smoldering remnants of the incinerated insects. Then he looked at me, his face filled with pain. I wanted to smile, tell him I was fine, but I seemed to have lost my voice.

Then he surprised me. With gentle fingers, he touched my face. When my gaze met his, I saw he did not hate me for the choice I had made. There was concern in his eyes, and tears. Tears, I think, for me.

"My God, Emma," he whispered. "My God."

The wonder, the pride and admiration in his voice matched my own dazed amazement. I had done it, I realized. I had killed the creature, saved us all . . .

But it was not over, and Valerian knew it, too. As soon as

he had reassured himself that I was all right, he climbed to his feet. I tried to follow, but my world spun and I thought I might faint. My hand hurt so much I felt ill, and my body was weak. I was spent and exhausted. I tried again, dragging myself up to stand behind Valerian as he turned to face his nemesis.

Marius was momentarily distracted, hunkering under the hawthorn over the burnt carcasses of the beetles. His face was twisted in agony as he beheld the destruction I had wrought on the demon he had raised. I could see he was certainly weakened, probably by the energy expended to release the creature and attempt to nurse it back to life. It was in the bend of his back, the limpness in his limbs. I guessed he had thought to be filled with the ancient's power, to snuff us all out like so many ants under his heel, so perhaps he had been reckless.

Now the vampire lord's glittering gaze rose. His black eyes darted nervously among us.

Valerian, beaten but not broken, had his chance. He moved with that preternatural stealth I'd glimpsed before, advancing steadily and with deadly purpose toward the stake I'd left lying on the ground between himself and his enemy.

We were in a tight little circle, caught in the tense struggle for supremacy, our every instinct trained on each other. Marius instantly realized Valerian's intention and went into motion as well. He did not move toward Valerian to head him off as I would have thought. Instead, the vampire circled to the fire. My mind searched rapidly through what I'd read in the Amiens archive, seeking a reason why he would do this. Fire purified; it was the vampire's enemy. What trick could this be? I could think of nothing to explain Marius's direction.

Valerian reached the stake and hefted it into his hand, then turned on his heel and headed toward his prey, so infused with purpose that his strides consumed the space between himself and his enemy with a speed I would have thought impossible. He was without fear, chilling purpose forged into every bone, every sinew.

Marius curled a slow, wicked smile and murmured something low and unintelligible. His body wrenched, indicating he was expending tremendous effort. The heat flared, and the fire he'd made began to move swiftly across the meadow, racing not toward Valerian, bearing down on him, but directly toward me. I tried to flee, but I was weak and dizzy.

Marius laughed, a goading chuckle to taunt Valerian and me. He spoke aloud for the first time, the word coming as from the depth of a crypt: "Choose."

I confess I was not noble enough to want Valerian to go for Marius instead of saving me, but I did not believe for one moment he would allow the vampire to escape. I turned to run, but the battle had drained me. My wounds hindered me as well, and the fire was coming too quickly, driven by the vampire's evil will. I would not make it to safety on my own.

I was not craven at the idea of death. Mark me, I did not want to die, but I had accepted the likelihood that I would not survive the night. It was the pain that terrified me. But in a moment, when the sensation of touch came, it was Valerian's arms I felt, not the scorch of the flames. He lifted me off the ground as easily as if I weighed no more than a doll. I smelled fire and sweat on his skin, and the coppery scent of his blood as he bore me away until the racing flames died, their magic spent.

We collapsed onto the ground. My breathing rasped harshly in and out of my lungs, labored with pain and the dazed fear that had not quite left me. I had not been burned alive. That thought kept coming to me in waves of gratitude.

And Marius was gone. His ploy had been successful, diverting Valerian to me in order to give him the time he needed to disappear. He must have summoned the last of his strength to flee to safety.

The air began to clear, as if the mists, no longer needed by the master who had summoned them, were slipping sulkily away. The moon emerged, a solid and cheerful thing over our heads. And The Sanctuary lay still and quiet, with not so much as a soft spring breeze to ruffle the grass.

I looked around for Mary and found her holding Henrietta, Roger's arms locked tight around them both. Sebastian, too, watched them, smiling as tears streamed down his smooth, pale cheeks, and I felt my own eyes sting. And off a little further, Father Luke still sat on the ground. He looked a broken man; his head was bent, his hands lying limp on his lap. Beside him, as if forgotten, were his rosary beads.

Then the softest, sweetest sound rang like a bell in that terrible silence. A voice—a child's voice—uttered just one word.

"Mama?" Henrietta murmured sleepily. On her neck, a thick line of blood trickled. I cried out softly, weak with relief that she had not been mortally injured after all.

Mary cried out, her anguish raw as she rid herself of it and cradled her daughter in her arms. I smiled, then laughed, joy sweeping through my heart like a mighty hand brushing away the worst of my fears.

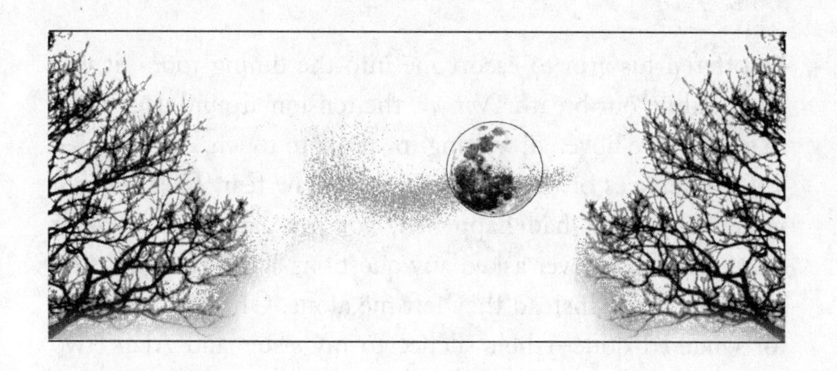

Chapter Thirty-two

In the days that followed, in each hour upon hour of quiet, we, the numbed and the shocked, each made our separate peace with the events of the Eve of Saint George. We were walking wounded, struggling with what we had witnessed, what we'd done, and the terror that had scraped our insides raw.

I moved back into Dulwich Manor at my cousin's insistence. In hushed tones, all of us sipped cups of tea and nibbled delicate sandwiches and sat in the shade of the terrace—all the ordinary things of English life.

But our faces were telling, faces as plain to read as an array of opened books. In Valerian Fox's eyes there was a blankness that wrenched my heart. He moved as a ghost. But when we walked side by side, when he passed me his cup of tea to be filled, when he offered his arm to escort me into the dining room, it was like holding our breath. *Not yet,* the tension around us seemed to say, but we hovered, waiting to speak, to touch.

On the faces of the others, I mostly saw fear. They did not understand what had happened, nor my part in it. Neither Mary nor Roger ever asked any questions about that night on The Sanctuary. Instead they left me alone. Oh, they loved me for what I'd done—their silence to my sister and Alan (two bewildered souls who observed the charged climate with irritation and impatience) was testimony to that. But they did fear me, a fact that made me sad until I consoled myself with thinking it was the sort of fear that bred respect. That was something I'd never had, and I let myself believe that it was better than being understood.

And I? I was drawn into myself, as still and quiet as those around me. Until the day I roused with a sense of mission, and set off to see Father Luke.

The morning air was soaked with that lingering chill that held fast to the early hours of late April mornings. I do not believe I shall ever think of the plains of Avebury without thinking of the mists. They had been foul and choking in recent weeks; the unnatural masks behind which the great fiend had hidden. But this morning, the air felt crisp and clean as I strode briskly along the familiar path, up to The Sanctuary, then beyond it to the small parish of Saint Michael in the Fields.

Mrs. Tigwalt was impeccably polite as she led me into the priest's study. What had Father Luke told her? "He's still doing poorly," she whispered to me before we entered. "He never sleeps. Refuses to eat." The tone of her voice gave testimony of how heavily this weighed on her heart. "Maybe your visit will lift his spirits."

The priest was seated on a chair, an ottoman drawn up so he could rest the leg Valerian had broken. It was heavily plastered and wrapped in a lap rug. He glanced up as we entered, and seemed to go rigid upon seeing me.

Mrs. Tigwalt inquired anxiously if she could bring us anything, speaking pointedly to Father Luke. "Something to eat? An egg, Father? Or a bit of toast?"

He shook his head, and I saw her shoulders slump as she moved out to the hallway, closing the door behind her.

I found myself unable to think of a single thing to say. I was transfixed by the stony expression on the priest's face, a hint of torment underneath that thickened my throat and drove a fist of pressure into the pit of my stomach. And then, I suddenly could not bear it a moment longer. "Father," I said, and rushed to him, going down on my knees beside his chair. He turned away, and I knew that had he had the ability to do so, he would have fled from me, from the comfort I offered.

"I have come . . ." I trailed off. In truth, I didn't fully understand why I had come to see him. I certainly could not put it into words.

He nodded, as if he already knew. Perhaps, I thought rather stupidly, he might tell me what it was that had brought me to the rectory. I was only aware of feeling the need to see him again.

"You must despise me," he said at last.

"No," I assured him. I lay my hand on his forearm but he refused to look at me.

"Then you should. I despise myself." The great depth of his chest gave his words a harsh, terrible rasp.

I drew my hand away, seeing now it was worse for me to try to console him. "Perhaps I should not have come. I do not know why I did." Then a thought occurred to me, and I emitted a strangled laugh. "Perhaps I needed a priest." I cast my eyes down in confusion, for there was some truth in this. But there was a greater truth. "Perhaps, Father, I needed a friend."

He made a strangled sound, as if my words had wounded him. My kindness, clearly, was not wanted. I rose to leave, and in so doing, I noticed flecks of blood on the white kid of my glove, a tiny smear of crimson across my forefinger and a spot on my palm. Not mine. His. "You are hurt!" I exclaimed.

"Please go, Mrs. Andrews."

"What happened? I did not see that you were injured beyond your leg. Who has done this harm to you?" I demanded.

He winced as he pulled away from me, in obvious pain. I stood puzzled for a moment. And then I knew. "You've done this to yourself?"

"It is not your concern."

"But you cannot—"

"This is between me and my God!" His head reared back, and his shame-filled eyes blazed now, inflamed with self-hatred. "Go. Pity me if you must, but leave me be!"

I'd faced a demon vampire, and I would not cower from a priest, even one as physically imposing and intimidating as Father Luke. "It is not what a friend should do."

"Again, you call me friend. We are not friends, Mrs. Andrews!"

I pulled up a chair and sat next to him. "Of course we are." He glared at me. I ignored him. "Why have you submitted yourself to this self-mortification?"

His lips peeled back, revealing a grimace. "Can you ask?" A fist came down on the arm of his chair, shaking the entire room.

"You were the guardian of the being in the tree, and it was destroyed. Your duty was fulfilled. Are you bitter because it was not by your hand? Do you resent that it was a woman, or because it was a layman, that accomplished this?"

His mouth worked, as if he were incredulous that I would think this. I leaned forward. "Tell me, then, if that is not the case."

He squeezed his eyes shut. "Did you see what he did to the girl from the village? Her poor body, broken and cast aside. My God." His voice rose to nearly a shout. "Did you see? I had heard whispers about another child in the village acting strangely. I had even thought, wondered, if Marius had marked her as well . . . But I did nothing. My duty dictated I was never to interfere, that I wait until the moment came. I . . ." His eyes closed tightly, his jaw clenched. "I did nothing."

"What would you have done?"

"Something. Anything. It was wrong, what they asked of me." His eyes flew open and he directed his anguished look at me. "I took vows, believing they were holy. But they were wicked vows. What I did—Oh, God, Emma, what I did *not* do . . . How can the Church of the One True God require such things from its servants?"

"Not the Church, surely—"

"What kind of God asks His people to make such choices?" His large, strong hands covered his face. I saw scrapes on the back of his knuckles, and wondered whether they were from the battle with Marius or as a result of his self-punishment. Sighing, he dropped his hands and looked up toward the crucifix on the wall. "I was called to war, a great war for which I had spent my entire life preparing. And I was trained to accept it might come to be that blood would be shed. The blood of innocents." He shook his head like a lion. "How can one know what those words mean? They sound honorable, but it is not honorable to watch life taken." Grasping my hand, he looked at me with hope I might have an answer for him. "Is it good to do evil in the service of good? Is there such a thing? I would have let your little cousin be killed. I thought it was the only way . . . How can you forgive me?"

I saw suddenly the years of his inculcation, the way he'd trained to take up the guardianship, how the ideals of the secret society had been constructed, link by link, into the armor that had made him the warrior he was. But his mail was falling in pieces around him, his beliefs stripped from him, and in that destruction I felt the powerful heat of his despair.

I drew in a breath, knowing there was no one less qualified than I to provide comfort. Still, I tried.

"I do forgive you. And you must forgive yourself. I am not a priest or a minister, but I have faith in God. He is sometimes not the same as the god men claim for themselves," I said. "His name is taken and used, rather misused, even by His church. It has tricked men before into believing in a false duty."

Father Luke melted back into the chair, his shoulders slumping. "The Order taught me to never be distracted by anything, not even to save a life. I was told mercy was weakness. I was faithful to that! What kind of priest does that make me?"

Mrs. Tigwalt bustled into the room, her lips pursed and her jaw trembling. "This is enough. He is not himself. Come back when he is well."

Father Luke turned sharply away, his outburst cut off. I was not ready to go, but I had no choice. Reluctantly, I backed away, gathering my reticule, dragging my steps. At the door, I hovered.

"We all of us fail," I said. Mrs. Tigwalt stopped her fussing and looked at me. Father Luke cocked his head ever so slightly. "When Peter denied Our Lord, he did not wallow in shame, but made it good. He did not punish himself, for that is God's place. He rose up and grew strong and when the time came for him to suffer, he endured it peaceably."

"Go on with you now," Mrs. Tigwalt told me sharply, her patience at an end. "Come back next week, when he is stronger."

But I never did. Father Luke disappeared before I got the chance.

"Come to London," Sebastian urged. "You can forget all of this, get a new lease on life." He waggled his eyebrows. "Find a proper beau."

I faced him squarely over my belongings spread out on my bed. I was leaving today, much against everyone's wishes. The irony of how different today was from my last departure did not escape me.

"I do not want to forget," I said simply.

His face fell. "No. I suppose we can none of us go back to blissful ignorance. We did not know how good we had it, never knowing such terrors existed in this world. Well." He sniffed, drawing himself up. "So you will not play with me in London? Very well. Never mind I am traumatized beyond all repair."

I rounded the bed and went to him, wrapping my arms about him and pulling him into an embrace. He clasped me gratefully. "Dear me, Mrs. Andrews, what can you be thinking—such improper doings with a gentleman in your boudoir. And one who is besotted with you beyond all proper admiration, at that."

I laughed and pulled back. "You may be the great love of my life, Sebastian."

He smiled. "Your heart is spoken for, you wretched woman. Have you had an opportunity to discuss matters with Mr. Fox?"

I paused. Valerian and I had not spoken as yet. "It is not the time," I stated.

"You are a coward," he chided affectionately.

"Imagine that," I said, smiling ruefully. "After all we've been through, I find I am not intrepid after all."

"Well, he is not the simplest man I've met. You can see that a mile off. There is a mystery there, mark me." He broke away with a deep, nourishing breath. "Well, thank God I am done with all this darkness and suspicion. It is only parties for me from now on, and lovely gossip and fashion and all the refreshing intrigues of society life. I think I will start a rumor to amuse me. I do love a scandal."

I laughed. "You make it sound so sordid."

"Oh, but it is, my dear, it is—deliciously so." He stopped, serious again. Touching my chin, he shook his head at me. "You are a brave, foolish woman. Ah, well, I shall not cry over the fun we could have had."

"Emma!" Alyssa's voice arced into the room. She stood in the doorway, glaring at Sebastian. "May I speak with my sister?" A crackling cloud of tension around her drove Sebastian away at full flight, a parting smirk behind her back his revenge.

I expected a theatrical display, or at the very least a bit of the vapors. But she was stony, direct, and quite a bit more firm than I'd ever known her to be. "I wish you to know I am not a child. No one will tell me what is happening. The house is like a mausoleum and everyone smiles and pats my hand. And now you are leaving."

"Darling, I am sorry—"

She held up a hand to stop me. "I wanted you with me. I

need you, Emma." Her façade wavered. "But I shall be strong. I just do not wish everyone to treat me as if I am a fragile thing. So there it is."

I smiled, suddenly so proud of her. "You are having a child. Your life is your family and that is so wonderful, Alyssa. But my life will take me on a different path. I hope, though, that we shall be better sisters to each other. You have grown up. You are to be a mother."

"And you are different, as well." She regarded me with a calm thoughtfulness. "You were right, Emma—was that it? Whatever awful things you did to Henrietta that made Roger send you away, you were right? You did something and it was brave, I think."

I was touched, because I saw the hope in her face. She wanted me to have been vindicated. She wanted me to be the heroine. I was reminded that she was an orphan like myself. Perhaps, if we had ever been able to know each other deeply, we would have discovered much in common. She was my sister, after all. Inside, beyond what Judith had instilled in her, was a woman I now suspected I might well like.

But it seemed I would not get the chance. Not yet, anyway. "Everything is well now," I told her.

She pouted a bit; she was still Alyssa. Then she pointed to my portmanteau. "When are you going to get something better? That is a disgrace."

"It is my mother's," I said simply, and for the first time in my life, I did not cringe to mention Laura.

Alyssa peered at me, then snapped up a set of lawn chemises. "Really, Emma," she chided, and began to refold them, laying each one neatly in its place.

* * *

My farewell to Valerian Fox took place in the garden later that morning. He sent word for me to meet him there, but he waited for me by the portico doors, and we walked outside together, silent and sad and neither one of us truly knowing what it was we wanted to say.

The sunshine was a shock after so many long, dreary, drizzly days. There's a smell one can only describe as green, the vibrant scent of new life breaking out of its earthly prison, and it tingled in my nose. Birdsong rang out in isolated calls, as if the creatures were tentative and untrusting of the mild clime. In time, they'd grow bold, diving through the air and working furiously to build nests in which to welcome their newly hatched young.

"Will you go with your sister?" he asked at last.

"My life is not by her side, not any longer. I have written to Dom Beauclaire and asked if I might study at one of the secret archives. When I was in France, he kept mentioning the one in Copenhagen as having many of the resources I need, so I may go there."

"It will be a cold winter in Denmark," he commented. We took the path to the right, moving easily with each other. "I have enormous faith in you, you know," he said. "You are a remarkably resourceful lady. The Glastonbury Holy Hawthorn, for example. That . . ." He arched his index finger and smiled, "now, that was genius. I have been wasting my time patiently carving the hard woods of the rowan and ash. What a mind you have for these things."

"But I was born to it."

The words lingered, heavy. I was sure he knew where my thoughts turned.

"You are going to find your mother," he said.

I swallowed. "She needs me, Valerian. She is still . . ." Not alive. I let the sentence hover in the air for an uncertain moment before finishing: "Suffering."

"It will not be easy," he warned. His eyes were full of concern. "I wish I could help." He hesitated. I could feel the tension coil around him, and in his eyes lights of sadness burned like low coals. "Were it possible, I would not leave you."

My heart wrenched. I knew it was not easy for him to say this. He did not strike me as a man who cared to have emotional ties, and perhaps it was not so easy to say good-bye to me as he would like it to be.

I did not betray my reaction, therefore, and replied with an equanimity I did not feel, "But you must find Marius."

His head came up as he inhaled sharply, his eyes going to the horizon as if thinking of the wide world out there into which the great vampire lord had fled. "I have no choice."

We'd come to the row of roses, my cousin's pride. They were ugly and bare just yet. In a month they would be gorgeous, their thorns covered by leaves and petals. "I could not have done a thing without you. I owe you so very much, Valerian. And . . . I should have trusted you. I'm sorry I did not."

He waved his hand. "I do not fault you."

I caught the hand in my two, surprising him. He was still hurt that I had not taken him into my confidence when I'd detoured to Glastonbury. "I am sorry," I said to him, passion in my voice.

"No, Emma. No. You are Dhampir." With great deliberation, his fingers stroked his cravat under which lay the welts on his neck. "You must always trust your instincts. Never question them. Never. I am touched by the vampire. If I cannot trust myself, how can I ask it of you?"

"Valerian," I murmured. "You saved me when you could have had Marius."

He smiled, and for the first time I saw the shadows lift from his face. His hand clasped mine tightly. "Oh, Emma, what good would it have done me to save my soul if you were lost to me?"

His gaze flickered over my face. I felt the tension tighten around us for one excruciating moment and then he broke my gaze, looking off into the distance. "It is not fair, you know," he murmured.

"What?"

"Everything," he said with a sigh.

I swallowed. "Yes," I whispered. "It is most unjust."

His gaze returned to roam my face. "In all of the hardships I have endured through my many . . . *many* years, I have never allowed myself to indulge in self-pity. Not once. But I cannot seem to help myself today." His smile was so sad I felt a lump rise in my own throat. We turned and headed back to the house.

"I have something for you," I said, remembering it as we gained the flagstone porch. I drew a parcel from the pocket of my day dress.

He looked at me in consternation. I could see he recognized the oilcloth in which he'd wrapped the switch of hawthorn that had pierced Marius and still carried precious drops of his blood. His mouth worked for a second or two before he gained his voice. "Why are you giving this to me?"

"I do not need it. And if you find Marius, or Emil, or whatever he is now, you may find a use for it. Should I come to understand the way to tapping its power, I will send word to you." I laughed softly. "So you see, Mr. Fox, I do trust you."

He slipped the oilcloth into the pocket on the inside of his

coat. "I shall endeavor to honor that trust." His eye caught mine. "And you, Emma, you have something you must honor."

I closed my eyes briefly under the stab of that reminder. "It is my hope you will eliminate the need for me to make good on my promise."

"Indeed," he said, taking my hand in his, unfurling my fingers, and touching his lips reverently to the palm. "I shall never wish to disappoint you."

My second departure from Dulwich Manor was much improved from the first.

Mary embraced me with tears in her eyes. "I do not wish you to leave," she finally confessed as we stood on the entrance steps of her great house.

"Darling, it is not forever," I said, and kissed her on the cheek.

"And Alyssa is weeping," she added hopefully, thinking this might sway me.

I smiled. "Alan will console her."

She laughed. "He will not thank you for that."

"But he is her husband. It is his place now."

She studied me for a moment. "Yes. Emma, I want to thank you—"

"Please, Mary," I began but she cut me off.

"I was not kind to you. I did not understand. I still do not, but I know you saved my daughter's life. I confess, I had doubts about you. In the past, we all wondered . . . That is, there were times when we did not know . . . because of your mother, you see . . ."

I waved away her stumbling words. "Things have changed," I said softly. "Let us leave it at that."

She nodded, her eyes glowing. I was glad she spoke no more.

It was enough to forgive each other and to trust the bonds of family held us fast.

"Yes," she said, her voice barely a whisper, "you are indeed quite changed, Emma."

Roger, with Henrietta in his arms, came up to us. "When will you come again?" Henrietta asked.

"I am not even gone yet!"

"But I miss you already." Only Henrietta could speak like this, without petulance or demand. It was merely a statement, spoken solemnly, with her eyes wide and honest.

I searched her face. I could not seem to stop doing so. What was I looking for? Some sign of the vampire, a mark of how he had taken her, almost to a hideous death, laying his hand on something inside her as he had me . . . But her gaze was clear, her features untroubled. I did not feel the mark of the vampire on her. I would never stop worrying about it, though.

"I shall visit you quite soon," I said briskly to ward off my own emotionality.

Her little brow furrowed slightly. Not good enough. And I thought it likely I would, in fact, not see her soon, not for a very long time.

She nearly leapt out of her father's arms to hug me tightly. When she released me, Roger kissed my cheek, an affectation of his I had always loved. But this time, he froze for a moment, with my cheekbone pressed against his lips. I could hear the hitch in his breathing.

Mary, beside him, laid a sympathetic hand on his shoulder. He raised his head and they looked at one another, then down and away. He released me. "Have a care on the roads. The mud will be treacherous after the rains last week."

"Thank you," I said. I found my voice was a bit rusty. I cleared

my throat and turned to descend the steps to my waiting carriage.

Once inside, I pulled back the drape so I could wave to them all as the driver pulled away. Henrietta's small hand extended as if she would summon me back. When the carriage rounded the end of the drive, I let the curtain drop so I did not have to see the house growing smaller on the horizon behind me.

My driver took us across the plains, down the road scored over the pattern of the ancient stones, a path of ages, where death and life came up against each other, and I felt it fitting to leave Avebury by way of this ridgeway. I leaned my head back on the deep cushions, closing my eyes. I should rest, I thought. I must prepare for all that lay ahead. I must be ready. Always ready. *Semper praesum.*

I smiled as my carriage rumbled along the road.

EMMA ANDREWS
LONDON, AUGUST 1926

FROM

JACQUELINE
LEPORE

AND

AVON A

Lindsey Navin

Meet Jacqueline

I am a native Philadelphian, born in South Philly and raised first there, then later in the suburbs. I attended the University of Pennsylvania for both undergraduate and graduate studies, earning a Ph.D. in psychology. I moved with my husband to Maryland immediately after that and have practiced here for more than twenty years as a licensed psychologist. I have three children and a houseful of pets.

Every writer begins as a reader. I cut my teeth on Gothic novels and Nancy Drew mysteries, which I consumed with a voracious appetite, loving every heart-pounding moment of suspense. I began writing when I was in the seventh grade, filling notebooks with unfinished stories of horror, science fiction, and romance. By senior year in high school, I was doing short story collections, but these were never shared—writing was my "dirty little secret."

It was always my dream to write a full-length novel, and I began attempting this in college. I eventually succeeded many years later, and years after that found the courage to "come out" about my peculiar hobby of making up stories. I found a terrific second career as a writer of romantic fiction, but after a while I wanted to challenge myself again to create a new, completely different sort of story. With the Emma Andrews series, I have found my way back to all those Gothic traditions I treasured growing up. So I've come full circle, and just as Emma finds her true self, so have I.

The Origins of Emma Andrews

The Emma Andrews series began as a historical detective series! No vampires in sight, believe it or not.

I was reading historical novels—lots of them—and I felt inspired. As I began to formulate the structure of the series, I couldn't get a handle on the "hook," that is to say the unique quality of my series or lead character that makes it special and different from anything else. Meanwhile, I kept being drawn to the concept of the Gothic novel. I grew up reading the books of Victoria Holt, Daphne du Maurier, Mary Stewart, Phyllis Whitney—and I still love them. My favorite parts were always the spooky elements. So I thought a little touch of the supernatural might be the ticket for my detective—as if she were a medium who is helped by supernatural forces when solving crimes. (Terrible, I know, but at least it was a start.)

Then a stray comment from a friend brought it all together for me (thank you, Donna!). She mentioned how many successful novelists have taken a concept or a character and pushed it way over the top. I had an *ah-hah* moment and the idea for the series veered drastically off course from its original trajectory. Suddenly all the ideas I'd been tossing around combusted into something very hot. I decided the series would have a full-on supernatural theme, and naturally, my mind went to that quintessential evil being, the vampire. I had the idea that my heroine would be a neophyte, an underdog who has to navigate the repressive society of Victorian England and find a way to fulfill her destiny as a vampire hunter.

Now I had not read many vampire novels at this point, save the seminal *Dracula* by Bram Stoker and a few of Anne Rice's early works. I knew there were all kinds of vampire and vampire hunter series out there, not to mention the absolute plethora of vampire romances. (I had not yet read the *Twilight* books, nor Charlaine Harris's Sookie Stackhouse series—both of which I am a rabid fan of now.) What I saw on the shelves looked largely like slick, urban, sexy vampire-type books. My series was going to be different, which might mean it was not sellable. However, I had to write it. If it got published, then great. If not, then that would be great too (although, admittedly, not as great) because I had to tell this story, even if only to myself.

Once I started writing, it became apparent that some of the problems Emma faces in *Descent into Dust* would not be resolved by the end of the book. That surprised me. It also became apparent that her core group—Sebastian, Valerian, and Father Luke—began taking on more prominence as I developed the plot, with exciting stories of their own. I began to look at the series not as simply episodic, though I still intend for each book to still be a separate "mystery," but as an ongoing quest of wider scope. It was unbelievably exciting trolling the Internet and poring over books to get the rich details that would comprise my vampire world. I culled inspiration from established Catholic traditions, world folklore, and Romantic literature, as well as drawing on my own psychology background to map out an exploration of human emotion and the complexities of real relationships. The result is, I hope, something you have found as thrilling to read as I did to write it.

The Cyprian Queen

Read on for a sneak preview of the next Emma Andrews adventure, The Cyprian Queen, *which will be available from Avon A in March 2011. I hope you will enjoy accompanying me further into the dark, mystery-steeped world of vampires and hunters. Don't forget your sharpened stake. And a little holy water never hurt.*

The scrape of the monk's footsteps, like sandpaper on the smooth marble surface of the palace's long central hallway, was startling in the silence. From where I was seated behind the raw wooden table I'd made my desk in what used to be a ladies' sitting parlor, I saw his tonsured head bowed as he advanced toward my doorway, his brown-garbed form dwarfed by the towering windows of the great hall. I think I knew even then that what I'd felt hurtling toward me had finally arrived.

I was going over a Greek translation at the time and was feeling a sense of unease. Nausea rose against the back of my throat. I had come to learn that the undead sometimes posed as scholars to write false documents to mislead and misdirect hunters. I found I had some feeling for detecting this, and I sensed it strongly in this document, a boastful, fraudulent account of the purported powers of the Greek vampire, known as the *Vrykolakas*.

The deceptive author described a breed of revenant that was not subject to the same limitations as the rest of the undead. I marveled at the lies as I read of communities where vampires lived out in the open, sunning themselves in exotic flower-draped grottoes and drinking pomegranate juice, living among their prey like brothers. They were capable, this clever deceiver would have it, of both casting a reflection and a shadow.

My physical revulsion from the blood of its author caused my stomach to flutter precariously, but there was something in the words, some boast, even a lurid triumph, which made me push past discomfort and forge on in the hope of learning something of value.

Upon the arrival of the young cleric, however, I pushed my task aside and struggled to compose myself. Even here, where they knew what I was, I remained guarded, retreating into a reflexive secretiveness. It had always been so; I was used to hiding my . . . oddities. After all, one had to have a care when one had a secret like mine—or one might find oneself situated in the Colney Hatch Lunatic Asylum.

"Mistress," he muttered. Middle-aged, tonsured, rather undignified in his brown robe and shuffling boots. "This arrived for you this morning."

I saw at once by the handwriting on the address that it was from Sebastian Dulwich, and my heart leapt with happiness. This man, my closest, dearest friend, had stood at my side and fought with me during my initiation into the world of undead.

Friendship, and home. I held the letter eagerly but waited until the last of the monk's hollow footsteps faded to silence to break the seal and unfold the heavy paper. When I did, something fell onto the table.

I examined it curiously. I saw it was a packet, folded and sealed with a wax impression I did not recognize. There was no direction or address, and though I assumed this was also meant for me, I set it aside for the moment and addressed the expansive, florid script that was Sebastian's hand.

Dearest Emma, I read:

> *London is dreadfully dull, what with balls and whatnot demanding all of my time. I would not attend,*

as you well know, but for the delicious opportunities to watch the debauches of my peers firsthand. It is so droll to have to wade through the papers to find one's daily dose of gossip, and so I go and find what amusements I can as a spectator of bad behavior.

I am presently engaged in a very interesting intrigue with a groom from the mews whom I like to dress up in gentleman's clothing and present as my cousin from Yorkshire. The accent is dead-on, and the fellow is a crack at impersonating the gentry. It has been a fine diversion, but not enough that I do not miss you sorely. At times, dear Emma, I am positively furious with you for refusing my invitation to join me in Town this season.

I am being a bore, but you must be used to that by now. So, then, how is Denmark? Have you met any ghosts? Any demented princes or waifish chits looking a bit damp? No doubt you are in your glory, up to your neck with books, an endeavor which confounds my brain, though I admit, I did enjoy the recommendation you gave me. Lord Byron is as dry a wit as myself and Don Juan a scoundrel I can adore.

Speaking of the great lover, have you had word from our Mr. Fox?

I paused, a little hitch catching in my chest, as if my heart had missed a beat. I had not, as it happened, had a single word since Valerian Fox and I had said our good-byes last spring. That was five months ago. And I had found the separation much more difficult than I would ever have anticipated.

Recovering, I read on.

No doubt you are anxious for word of our beloved Henrietta. What a dolt I am to delay the good news that she is flourishing.

My heart twisted in my chest, as if it literally leapt for joy. I adored my little cousin, for a sweeter child could not exist, and it was for precisely this reason of her pure spirit that she had been at the center of the evil events that had taken place in Avebury. It was there I had engaged in my first battle with a vampire. I had not even known they existed before that time, let alone suspected the deep ties I myself possessed to that terrible world. I had discovered my powers, the singular ability among mortal men and women to kill vampires. It was Valerian Fox who had shown me this and taught me what I had needed to know. Together, we had fought a powerful lord vampire to save Henrietta, along with the aid of a warrior priest, Father Luke. Sebastian, too, had been an indispensable help to me.

The child appears to have no ill effects. She often asks for you, and in the most admiring of terms informed me when I was out in Wiltshire for a hunt that she intends to be tall and scholarly like you. I doubt my sister-in-law was pleased, despite her love for you. You know how her mother feels about your bluestocking ways.

You are wondering about the letter enclosed. Something of a mystery, but you have not opened it yet, have you? You see how well I know you. You have patiently waded through all my drivel on my latest paramour and whatnot, for you are predictably ordered. It is part of why I love you, my dear Emma, and I am glad of it. But I confess, my delay has been to give me time to warm up my pen, for I hardly know how I am to go about explaining the pages I have enclosed.

I paused, lifting my gaze to the multi-paned window as I drew in the breath I needed to brace myself. My eyes drifted to the glossy blackness of the sea that lay beyond the neglected terraced lawns of the old palace. A sense of inevitability sealed itself in my mind as I thought idly of the terrible coldness of the water, the kind that seizes a body into paralysis. One instant plunge into a rigor not unlike death.

I lowered my head and read on.

The words contained therein are from the journal of a Miss Victoria Markam, an unfortunate young lady whose path crossed mine at a Kensington fete. The night was a bore and my new toy was not with me, so I was rather in my cups and found plain-faced Miss Markam wandering around quite foxed. Naturally this amused me, and we together went on a little adventure to pilfer a fine whiskey from the library. She began to drink like a sailing man, became loquacious, and I learned, much to my supreme lack of interest, that she was a teacher. But then she told me she was formerly employed at a prestigious girls' school in the Lake District. She had fled in the midst of the Michaelmas term and vowed never to return. I assumed she'd committed some indiscretion and been let go, which naturally intrigued me, but as she began to speak of the events which precipitated her abrupt withdrawal from the teaching staff, I began to see her fear. She was truly terrified. I began to pay attention.

With some prompting, I elicited some rather bland accounts of shadows and noises about the place, subtle changes in the students, and a veil of conspiracy. Mere schoolgirl mischief aimed at a despised teacher, I thought, and was inclined to dismiss my flash of interest until she mentioned the deaths in the village. That will get my attention, be it proven to be nothing more dastardly than common influenza, until the day I die. This past spring left a deep mark on me.

I shamelessly plied her with more of the single malt whiskey and pried at her defenses until she told me her dark secret.

The story is this: She had become aware of a group of students sneaking outdoors in the middle of the night. They had grown brazen and secretive, challenging her authority. She believed they were meeting local boys in the woods at night, and so she secretly followed them. However, she somehow lost her way, and according to Miss Markam—who by rights should have been intoxicated into oblivion by now but somehow was as calm and sober as I unfortunately am now—she came upon what she described as a cache of corpses: "human bodies cast about like discarded husks." I quote her, for I remember it exactly. That is not the sort of utterance one is likely to forget. When she spoke of how pale they were, I could not keep my mind from remembering the unnatural pallor of the poor victims we saw this spring. And that word: husks. *It seemed so very apt. She mentioned bruising and cuts, and quite specifically told me that this damage was done about the neck, just under the ear. She believed they had been murdered, and all in the same manner.*

I was pondering this shock when she delivered another. She had previously mentioned the name of the school, but I had not taken note of it. It struck me belatedly. Emma, I can tell you I felt a sick feeling come over me. This could not be coincidence. The Blackbriar School for Girls, Emma, darling—that was where she was employed, and I know you know the name well. Do you recall lamenting to me that your mother had attended this very school when she was a girl, and it had been your dearest wish to follow in your footsteps but your stepmother had forbidden it?

The mention of my mother landed in the center of my chest like the thump of a fist. I gasped out loud, my jaw jerking open. I had not been prepared for that. My beautiful tragic mother was something of an obsession with me. She had haunted me all of my life, even more so now that I had learned the truth about her. It was a terrible truth.

My hands began to tremble, making it necessary to lay Sebastian's letter flat on the table, with my fingers splayed over it to hold it steady.

So there I was, quite overset to realize I was distressingly sober, and I am afraid I made a dreadful decision, one for which I pray you not to despise me. I said, and I quote myself precisely, "I may know of someone whose knowledge in these things may be helpful." She grasped my hands so piteously, and I was glad I had made the offer of aid.

Soon after, we were discovered. Miss Markam, being the sister of my hostess, was quickly borne away to her bedchamber to sleep off her indisposition. I, being a man, was looked upon with disapproval and left alone with the rest of the whiskey. Not long after, a maid found me and handed me the enclosed papers, which she informed me Miss Markam had torn from her journal and sent to me, with the intention of my making good on my mention of seeing the information into your hands in the event you could be of any service.

I have neither seen nor heard from her since that night, and for all I know she is mad and I am a fool. But I cannot help thinking that this is what anyone would have said of each of us just a few months ago when we were chasing monsters about the Wiltshire downs. My mind no longer has the luxury of dismissing the insane.

So I give you these pages. I will tell you I did not read them, and not because of any sense of honor or integrity. My Lord, you know me better than that. Quite simply, I am a coward. I want no part of it. I will stay here in Town until Christmastide, when I will feast and be jolly with my new man. I will think no more of this matter, for I have delivered this intelligence into your hands and my duty is done.

I smiled softly despite my troubled mind. Sebastian had a very amusing flourish, and I could imagine if he were here to speak these words, he would do so with gesticulating hands and a moue of disdain worthy of a king. He meant none of it, of course, as the proceeding lines bore out.

But should you need me, and you have exhausted every other aid and imaginable resource, then I shall be of what little service my humble self can provide. You have but to call.

The reference to himself as humble won a dry chuckle from me, as Sebastian had intended it would. He signed the letter "With Affection" and then his loopy, bold signature.

So it was Sebastian who called me home.